Acclaim for Jonathan

The House *of* Sleep

"An exceedingly clever novel . . . reminiscent of Proust in its characters' ambiguous sexuality, its central, frustrated romance, and most of all its attempt to recover lost time . . . an ingeniously constructed novel." —*Boston Book Review*

"Coe pieces this complex puzzle together with surgical skill and pungent wit, while imbuing the most mundane situations with a touch of the sinister. He proves himself a writer of considerable talent with this meditation on the hold that the past has over us and how small moments can alter our future." —*The Atlanta Journal-Constitution*

"*The House of Sleep* plunges us from romance to tragedy, from *film noir* to farce. . . . There are sublimely silly scenes, but there are also moments of exquisite pathos and beauty. This is a fiercely clever, witty novel, but it is also wise, generous, and hopeful." —*London Times Literary Supplement*

"Balancing self-knowing references to semiotics and psychoanalysis with elegant plot symmetries, Coe proves himself as adept an architect of sparkling, highly caffeinated fictional conceits as he is a satirist of the ambiguities of identity and the afflictions of the sleep-deprived." —*Publishers Weekly*

"Clever and ambitious . . . wittily and wonderfully worked out."   —*The Boston Globe*

"A serpentine novel of ideas. . . . Packed with brilliant comic set-pieces, trenchant satire on the self-serving 'business' of helping people and dexterous plotting which lovingly exploits the thin line between accident and design."   —*Time Out* (London)

"A swooningly romantic and rather serious tale . . . a wonderfully poignant creation. . . . *The House of Sleep* is vastly entertaining."
                    —*Phoenix Literary Supplement*

"Shows energy, tenderness, social commitment, all in a style that comes like breath. The writer is one of the very best contemporary British novelists, thrillingly original as well as accessible."
                    —*The Independent on Sunday*

"One of the strangest, and most moving, encounters in recent fiction. In all: a droll ingenious novel, its satire nicely leavened by true romance."
                    —*Kirkus Reviews*

Jonathan Coe

The
House
of
Sleep

Born in 1961, Jonathan Coe took degrees
from Cambridge and Warwick universities.
He was the recipient of France's Prix du
Meilleur Livre Étranger and Great Britain's
John Llewellyn Rhys Prize for his first novel,
The Winshaw Legacy. He also received the
British Writers' Guild Best Fiction Award for
The House of Sleep. He lives in London.

ALSO BY JONATHAN COE

The Winshaw Legacy

The

House

of

Sleep

The House *of* Sleep

Jonathan Coe

VINTAGE CONTEMPORARIES / VINTAGE BOOKS
A DIVISION OF RANDOM HOUSE, INC. / NEW YORK

FIRST VINTAGE CONTEMPORARIES EDITION,
MAY 1999

Grateful acknowledgment is made to Sony/ATV Music
Publishing and the Songwriters Guild of America for
permission to reprint an excerpt from "Good Morning
Heartache" by Fred Fisher, Irene Higginbotham, and
Ervin Drake, copyright 1945 by Sony/ATV Tunes LLC and
Lindabet Music (ASCAP), copyright renewed. All rights
on behalf of Sony/ATV Tunes LLC administered by
Sony/ATV Music Publishing, 8 Music Square West,
Nashville, TN 37203. All rights on behalf of Lindabet
Music are care of The Songwriters Guild of America. All
rights reserved. Used by permission.

The Library of Congress has cataloged the Knopf edition
as follows:
Coe, Jonathan
The house of sleep / Jonathan Coe.—1st American ed.
p. cm.
ISBN 0-375-40093-1 (alk.paper)
I.Title
PR6053.026H68 1998
825'. 914—dc21 97-34372 CIP

Vintage ISBN: 0-375-70088-9

Author photograph © Paddy Cook
Book design by Misha Beletsky

www.randomhouse.com/vintage

Printed in the United States of America
10 9 8 7 6 5 4 3 2 1

CONTENTS

'I do get confused about time.
If one loses one's emotional
focus' — she stopped, struggled,
went on huskily — 'that's
what happens. Aeons — split
seconds — they interchange.
One gets outside the usual way
of counting.'

Rosamond Lehmann,
The Echoing Grove

AUTHOR'S NOTE

The odd-numbered chapters of this novel are set mainly in the years 1983–1984. The even-numbered chapters are set in the last two weeks of June 1996.

Awake

It was their final quarrel, that much was clear. But although he had been anticipating it for days, perhaps even for weeks, nothing could quell the tide of anger and resentment which now rose up inside him. She had been in the wrong, and had refused to admit it. Every argument he had attempted to put forward, every attempt to be conciliatory and sensible, had been distorted, twisted around and turned back against him. How dare she bring up that perfectly innocent evening he had spent in The Half Moon with Jennifer? How dare she call his gift 'pathetic', and claim that he was looking 'shifty' when he gave it to her? And how *dare* she bring up his mother — his *mother*, of all people — and accuse him of seeing her too often? As if that were some sort of comment on his maturity; on his *masculinity*, even . . .

He stared blindly ahead, unconscious of his surroundings or of his fellow pedestrians. 'Bitch,' he thought to himself, as her words came back to him. And then out loud, through clenched teeth, he shouted, 'BITCH!'

After that, he felt slightly better.

Huge, grey and imposing, Ashdown stood on a headland, some twenty yards from the sheer face of the cliff, where it had stood for more than a hundred years. All day, the gulls wheeled around its spires and tourelles, keening themselves hoarse. All day and all night, the waves threw themselves dementedly against their rocky barricade, sending an endless roar like heavy traffic through the glacial rooms and mazy, echoing corridors of the old house. Even the emptiest parts of Ashdown — and most of it was now empty — were never silent. The most

habitable rooms huddled together on the first and second
floors, overlooking the sea, and during the day were flooded
with chill sunlight. The kitchen, on the ground floor, was long
and L-shaped, with a low ceiling; it had only three tiny windows, and was swathed in permanent shadow. Ashdown's
bleak, element-defying beauty masked the fact that it was, essentially, unfit for human occupation. Its oldest and nearest
neighbours could remember, but scarcely believe, that it had
once been a private residence, home to a family of only eight or
nine. But two decades ago it had been acquired by the new university, and it now housed about two dozen students: a shifting
population, as changeful as the ocean which lay at its feet,
stretched towards the horizon, sickly green and heaving with
endless disquiet.

The group of four strangers sitting at her table may or may not
have asked permission to join her. Sarah couldn't remember.
Now, an argument seemed to be developing, but she did not
hear what was being said, although she was conscious of their
voices, rising and falling in angry counterpoint. What she heard
and saw inside her head was, at that moment, more real. A single, venomous word. Eyes blazing with casual hatred. A sense
that she had not so much been spoken to, as spat upon. An encounter which had lasted — two seconds? — less? — but which
she had now been replaying, involuntarily, in her memory for
more than half an hour. Those eyes; that word; there would be
no getting rid of them, not for a while. Even now, as the voices
around her grew louder and more animated, she could feel another wave of panic swell inside her. She closed her eyes, suddenly weak with nausea.

Would he have attacked her, she wondered, if the High Street
had not been so busy? Dragged her into a doorway? Torn at her
clothes?

She raised her mug of coffee, held it a few inches from her
mouth, looked down at it. She stared at its oily surface, which

was shimmering perceptibly. She clasped the mug tighter. The liquid steadied. Her hands were no longer shaking. The moment passed.

Another possibility: had it all been a dream?

'Pinter!' was the first word of the argument to catch her attention. She willed herself to look across at the speaker and concentrate.

The name had been pronounced in a tone of tired incredulity, by a woman who was holding a glass of apple juice in one hand, and a half-smoked cigarette in the other. She had short, jet-black hair, a prominent jaw and lively dark eyes. Sarah recognized her, vaguely, from previous visits to the Café Valladon, but did not know her name. She was later to find out that it was Veronica.

'That's just so typical,' the woman added: then closed her eyes as she puffed on her cigarette. She was smiling, perhaps taking the argument less seriously than the thin, pasty, earnest-looking student sitting opposite her.

'People who don't know anything about theatre,' Veronica continued, '*always* talk about Pinter as if he's one of the greats.'

'OK,' said the student. 'I agree that he's overrated. I agree with that. That's exactly what proves my point.'

'It *proves* your point?'

'The British postwar theatrical tradition,' said the student, 'is so . . . etiolated, that —'

'Excuse me?' said an Australian voice next to him. 'What was that word?'

'Etiolated,' said the student. 'So etiolated, that there's only one figure who —'

'Etiolated?' said the Australian.

'Don't worry about it,' said Veronica, her smile broadening. 'He's just trying to impress us.'

'What does it mean?'

'Look it up in the dictionary,' snapped the student. 'My point is, that there's only one figure in postwar British theatre with a claim to any kind of stature, and even *he* is overrated. Massively overrated. *Ergo*, the theatre is finished.'

'*Ergo*?' said the Australian.

'It's over. It has nothing to offer. It has no part to play in contemporary culture, in this country, or in any other country.'

'So what — you're saying that I'm wasting my time?' Veronica asked. 'That I'm out of tune with the whole . . . Zeitgeist?'

'Absolutely. You should change courses at once: to film studies.'

'Like you.'

'Like me.'

'Well, that's interesting,' said Veronica. 'I mean, just look at the assumptions you're making. For one thing, you assume that just because I'm interested in the theatre, I must be studying it. Wrong: I'm doing economics. And then, this whole conviction of yours that you're in possession of some kind of absolute truth: I . . . well, I find that a very *male* quality, is all I can say.'

'I am male,' the student pointed out.

'It's also significant that Pinter is your favourite playwright.'

'Why's that significant?'

'Because he writes plays for boys. Clever boys.'

'But art is universal: all real writers are hermaphrodite.'

'Ha!' Veronica laughed with delighted contempt. She stubbed out her cigarette. 'OK, do you want to talk about gender?'

'I thought we were talking about culture.'

'You can't have one without the other. Gender's everywhere.'

Now the student laughed. 'That's one of the most meaningless remarks I've ever heard. The only reason you want to talk about gender is because you're scared to talk about value.'

'Pinter only appeals to men,' said Veronica. 'And why does he appeal to men? Because his plays are misogynist. They appeal to the misogyny deep within the male psyche.'

'I'm not a misogynist.'

'Oh yes you are. All men hate women.'

'You don't believe that.'

'Oh yes I do.'

'I suppose you think that all men are potential rapists?'

'Yes.'

'Well, that's another meaningless statement.'

'Its meaning is very clear. All men have the potential to become rapists.'

'All men have the *means* to become rapists. That's hardly the same thing.'

'I'm not talking about whether all men have the necessary . . . equipment. I'm saying that there isn't a man alive who doesn't feel, in some murky little corner of his soul, a deep resentment — and jealousy — of our strengths, and that this resentment sometimes shades into hatred and could also, therefore, shade into violence.'

A short pause followed this speech. The student tried to say something, but faltered. Then he started to say something else, but changed his mind. In the end, the best he could manage was: 'Yes, but you've no evidence for that.'

'The evidence is all around us.'

'Yes, but you've no objective proof.'

'Objectivity,' said Veronica, lighting up a new cigarette, 'is male subjectivity.'

The silence to which this magisterial remark gave rise, longer than the first and somewhat awestruck, was broken by Sarah herself.

'I think she's right,' she said.

Everyone at the table turned to look at her.

'Not about objectivity, I mean — at least, I've never thought about it like that before — but about all men being basically hostile, and how you never know when it's going to . . . flare up.'

Veronica met her eyes. 'Thank you,' she said, before turning back to the student. 'You see? Support on all sides.'

He shrugged. 'Female solidarity, that's all.'

'No, but it's happened to me, you see.' The faltering urgency of Sarah's voice caught their attention. 'Exactly what you're talking about.' She lowered her gaze and saw her eyes reflected, darkly, on the black surface of her coffee. 'I'm sorry, I don't know any of your names, or anything. I don't even know why I said that. I think I'd better go.'

She stood up to find herself boxed into a corner, the edge of the table pressed into her thighs; squeezing hastily past the Australian and the earnest student proved a clumsy business. Her face was on fire. She was sure that they were all watching her as if she were a madwoman. Nobody said anything as she made her way to the till, but as she counted out her change (Slattery, the Café's owner, sitting bookish and indifferent in the corner) she felt the touch of a hand on her shoulder, and turned to see Veronica smiling at her. The smile was diffident, appealing — very different from the combative smiles she had been turning on her opponents at the table.

'Look,' she said, 'I don't know who you are, or what happened to you, but . . . any time you want to talk about it.'

'Thank you,' said Sarah.

'What year are you in?'

'Fourth, now.'

'Oh — you're a postgrad, right?'

Sarah nodded.

'And are you living on campus?'

'No. I live up at Ashdown.'

'Oh well. Maybe we'll bump into each other anyway.'

'I expect we will.'

Sarah rushed out of the Café before this friendly, frightening woman could say anything more to her. After that dark and smoke-heavy interior the sunlight was suddenly blinding, the air fresh with salt. Shoppers trickled through the streets. It would have been the perfect day, normally, for walking home along the cliffs: a long walk, and most of it uphill, but worth it for the sweet ache in your limbs when you arrived, the feel of your lungs distended with clean, thin air. But today was not normal, and she didn't like the thought of those many lonely stretches of pathway, the solitary men she might glimpse approaching in the distance, or who might be sitting on one of the benches, watching her brazenly as she hurried past.

Writing off the cost of a week's suppers, she took a taxi, was home in no time at all, and then lay in bed all afternoon, the numbness refusing to abate.

ANALYST: *What was it about the game you found so disturbing?*

ANALYSAND: *I don't know whether 'game' is exactly the right word.*

ANALYST: *It was the word you chose yourself, just a moment ago.*

ANALYSAND: *Yes. I just don't know if it's the right one. I suppose what I meant . . . [chat] . . .*

ANALYST: *Never mind that now. Did he ever cause you physical pain?*

ANALYSAND: *No. No, he never really hurt me.*

ANALYST: *But you thought that he might hurt you?*

ANALYSAND: *I suppose it could have been . . . at the back of my mind.*

ANALYST: *And did he know that? Did he know that you thought he might hurt you, one day? Was that in fact the whole point of the game?*

ANALYSAND: *Yes, I suppose it could have been.*

ANALYST: *For him? Or for both of you?*

Sarah was in bed again by the time Gregory got back from his drink. She had been up, briefly, in the early evening, to put on her dressing-gown and pad downstairs to the kitchen, but even there she had remained nervous, and oddly susceptible to shocks. The kitchen itself was empty, and she could hear the sounds of an American soap — *Dallas*, or *Knots Landing* — coming from the TV room down the corridor. Thinking that she

, Sarah opened a can of mushroom soup and poured the contents into a saucepan. Then she lit the cooker, which stood in an area of its own, around the corner, hidden from the rest of the L-shaped room. She stirred the soup with a heavy wooden spoon, finding this activity unexpectedly restful. She stirred three times clockwise, then three times anti-clockwise, over and over, watching the patterns form and slowly fade into the sludgy mass of the soup. Absorbed in her task, she was startled to hear a male voice saying, 'So where do they keep the coffee around here?' and she let out a short, high scream as she wheeled around.

The man came round the corner, saw her and took a step back.

'I'm sorry. I thought you knew I was here.'

She said: 'No, I didn't.'

'I didn't mean to scare you.'

He had a kind face: that was the first thing that she noticed. And the second thing she noticed was that he appeared to have been crying — quite recently, in fact. He sat down at the kitchen table to drink his coffee, and she sat down opposite him to drink her soup, and as she was pulling up a chair she glanced across at him and could have sworn that she saw a tear inching down his cheek.

'Are you all right?' she asked. They didn't get many first-years at Ashdown, but she wondered if he had just arrived at the university, and was already starting to feel homesick.

It turned out that this was not the case. He was in his third year, studying modern languages, and had moved into Ashdown only yesterday. What had distressed him was a phone call from his mother, who had rung from home a few hours ago to tell him that Muriel, the family cat, had been killed that same morning — run over by a milk float at the bottom of the front drive. He was clearly ashamed to be showing so much emotion about this, but Sarah liked him for it. To save him further embarrassment, all the same, she changed the subject as quickly

as possible, and told him that he was not the only one to have
had an upsetting day.

'Why, what happened to you?' he asked.

It did not occur to Sarah until later that it was surprising to
have found herself talking so frankly to such a new acquaintance, someone whose name she had not even, at this stage,
troubled to find out. None the less, she told him all about her
bizarre encounter on the street with a complete stranger who
had glared at her and called her a bitch for no apparent reason.
The new resident listened attentively as he sipped his coffee:
striking, Sarah thought, just the right balance between concern
(for he seemed to understand how traumatic the incident must
have been for her) and a more lighthearted note of reassurance
(for he encouraged her, at the same time, to laugh it off as the
outburst of some pitiable eccentric). She told him about the
conversation she had overheard at the Café Valladon, how it
had turned to the subject of misogyny, and how she had felt
compelled to join in.

'It's a very live subject at the moment,' he agreed. 'There's a
big anti-feminist backlash going on here.' He told her how the
university's new Women's Studies Department had been vandalized recently: someone had broken in and spray-painted the
words 'Death to the Sisters' in foot-high letters all over the
walls.

Sarah was enjoying talking to this man very much, but had
started to feel tired. Sometimes she was subject to a sort of
tiredness which was extreme, by most people's standards, and
once or twice had even found herself falling asleep in the middle of conversations. She didn't want anything like that to happen here: she was too anxious to leave a good impression.

'I think I'd better get back to bed,' she said, getting up and
rinsing her soup-mug under the cold tap. 'It's nice to have met
you, though. I'm glad you're moving in. I think we're going to
be friends.'

'I hope so.'

'My name's Sarah, by the way.'

'I'm Robert.'

They smiled at each other. Sarah ran a hand through her hair, taking hold of a clump and tugging at it lightly. Robert noticed this gesture, and remembered it.

She went up to her room and slept for an hour or two, until Gregory woke her by coming in and turning on the overhead light. Blinking, she looked at the alarm clock. It was earlier than she had thought: only ten-fifteen.

'Home already?' she said.

He had his back towards her, putting something away in a drawer, and grunted: 'Looks like it.'

'I thought since this was the last night you were all going to be together, you'd stay out late. Make an occasion of it.'

It was the beginning of the autumn term, and Gregory had come down from his parents' house in Dundee merely to collect some belongings, to see some old friends, and to spend a few final days with Sarah. They had both finished their undergraduate degree courses in July. Later that week he was due to start at medical school in London, where he would specialize in psychiatry. She was staying on at the university for another year, to train as a primary school teacher.

'Busy day tomorrow,' he said, sitting at the end of the bed, tugging off a shoe. 'Got to make an early start.' His eyes flicked towards her for the first time. 'You look done in.'

Sarah told him the story of the man who had abused her in the street, to which his initial response was: 'But that doesn't make sense. Why would anyone do that?'

'I suppose I was a woman,' said Sarah, 'and that was enough.'

'Are you sure he was talking to you?'

'There was nobody else around.' Gregory was preoccupied with a knotted shoelace, so she prompted: 'It was quite upsetting.'

'Well, you don't want to let these things get to you.' The shoelace untied, he felt for her ankle and squeezed it through the bedclothes. 'I thought we'd gone beyond this. You're a big girl now.' He frowned at her. 'Did it really happen?'

'I think so.'

'Hmm . . . but you're not sure. Perhaps I should write it down anyway.'

Gregory sat at the dressing-table and took an exercise book out of the top drawer. He scribbled a few words, then sat back and thumbed through the pages. His face, reflected in the mirror, betrayed a pleased smile.

'You know, I was so lucky to meet you,' he said. 'Look at all the material it's given me. I mean, I know that's not the only reason, but . . . think of the lead it's going to give me over all the other guys.'

'Isn't it a bit early to be thinking in those terms?' said Sarah.

'Nonsense. If you really want to get to the top, you can never get started too soon.'

'It's not a race, though, is it?'

'There are winners and losers in the human race, just like any other,' said Gregory. He had put the exercise book away and was taking off his shirt. 'How many times have I told you that?'

Rather to her own surprise, Sarah took this question seriously. 'My guess would be between about fifteen and twenty.'

'There you are, then,' said Gregory, apparently quite satisfied with this statistic. 'It applies to everything, as well — even accommodation. I mean, you'd scarcely credit it, but Frank's going up to London in a week's time, and he hasn't even found himself somewhere to live yet.' He laughed incredulously. 'How do you *account* for that kind of behaviour?'

'Well,' said Sarah, 'perhaps he just isn't lucky enough to have a father who's in a position to buy him a flat in Victoria.'

'It's Pimlico. Not Victoria.'

'What's the difference?'

'About twenty thousand pounds, for one thing. We chose that location very carefully. Convenient for the hospital. Excellent

neighbourhood.' Appearing to sense an unvoiced contempt on
Sarah's part, he added: 'For God's sake, I would have thought
you'd appreciate it as much as anybody. You're going to be staying there every weekend, aren't you?'

'Am I?'

'Well I assume so.'

'You know I'm going to have to prepare lessons and things.
I'm doing lots of teaching practice this term. I might be busy.'

'I can't see that preparing a few lessons is going to take up
much of your time.'

'Some people don't have to work hard. I do. I'm a plodder.'

Gregory sat down on the bed beside her. 'You know, you have
a serious self-esteem problem,' he said. 'Has it never occurred
to you that it's largely because of your low self-esteem that you
never achieve anything?'

Sarah took a moment to digest this, but couldn't find it in
herself to get angry. Instead her mind went back to the scene in
the kitchen. 'I met one of the new people today,' she said. 'His
name was Robert. He seemed really nice. Have you met him
yet?'

'No.' Gregory had undressed to his underpants by now, and
he slid a hand absently down the front of Sarah's nightdress,
resting it on her breast.

'You haven't spoken to him or anything?'

He sighed. 'Sarah, I'm leaving tomorrow. I'm going to live in
London. Why would I waste my time getting to know people
I'm never going to see again?'

He removed his underpants, climbed on top of her, and then
pulled down her nightdress so that her breasts were fully exposed. He took hold of her nipples and began to tweak them simultaneously. Sarah examined his expression as he did this,
trying to remember where she had seen something like it before: his brow was furrowed with both impatience and concentration, much as it had been the other evening while she had
watched him twiddling the contrast and vertical-hold knobs on

the television downstairs, trying to get a good picture for *News at Ten*. That, she recalled, had taken him about two minutes, but less than half that time was up before he took her tiny wrists in his hands, pinned her arms to the pillow behind her head, and entered her swiftly. She was dry and tight, and found the sensation uncomfortable.

'Look, Gregory,' she said, 'I'm not really in the mood. In fact, I'm not in the mood at all.'

'It's all right, I won't be long.'

'No.' She took a firm hold of his hips and stilled their rocking motion. 'I don't want to do this.'

'But we've had the foreplay and everything.' His eyes were wounded, incredulous.

'Get out,' said Sarah.

'What — of you, the bed, or the room?' His confusion seemed genuine.

'Of me, initially.'

He stared at her for a second or two, then tutted to himself and withdrew gracelessly, saying: 'You can be *so* inconsiderate sometimes.' But he remained on top of her, and she knew what was coming next. 'Close your eyes a minute.'

She stared back at him, defiant but powerless.

'I spy? With my little eye?'

'Gregory, *no*. Not now.'

'Go on. I know you like it really.'

'I do *not* like it really. I've never liked it. How many times do I have to tell you that I've never liked it?'

'It's just a game, Sarah. It's about trust. You do trust me, don't you?'

'Let go,' she said. Both her hands were enclosed in one of his, and were still pinned to the pillow. His other hand was now hovering above her face, the first and second fingers extended, getting closer to her eyes.

'Come on,' he said. 'Show that you trust me. Close your eyes.'

The tips of his fingers were now so near that she had no

option: she closed her eyes as a reflex action, and then screwed them tight. Soon she felt the pressure of his two fingers against her shielded eyeballs — gentle at first — and she stiffened, a familiar terror stirring inside her. She had developed a method of dealing with this sensation, which involved emptying her mind of all ideas relating to the present moment. Time, for Sarah, was halted as Gregory crouched over her, and if her thoughts turned towards anything at all, it was towards what seemed (for now) the distant past: the very beginnings of their relationship, when she had so enjoyed his company, before they had become locked into this pattern of self-perpetuating quarrels and weird bedroom rituals.

How had they managed to get from there to here?

She had a vivid recollection, still, of the first time she had met him, during the interval of a concert, at the Arts Centre bar. She had not intended to go to this concert, but ticket sales had been extremely low, and the box office staff were reduced to the expedient of handing out free tickets to passers-by shortly before it started, in order to make up the numbers and spare the visiting performer from embarrassment. The programme consisted of J. S. Bach's *The Art of Fugue,* a work of which she had no previous knowledge, performed on the harpsichord in its entirety. The only other person in Sarah's row was a tall, gangly student, his dark hair cut into a severe short-back-and-sides, sitting bolt upright in his chair, wearing a tweed jacket, an old school tie and a yellow waistcoat with a fob watch, who listened to the music with rigid concentration and once or twice sighed loudly or clicked his tongue in exasperation for no apparent reason. Since he seemed to be taking no notice of Sarah, it was a great surprise when he came to sit at her table during the interval, and an even greater surprise when, after a strained silence of perhaps two or three minutes, he suddenly addressed her in a clipped Scottish accent with the words: 'Preposterous tempi in the eleventh *contrapunctus,* didn't you think?'

They were the most peculiar, least comprehensible words that had ever been spoken to her: but they did lead to a conversation, of sorts, and that in turn led to a relationship, of sorts. In all her five terms at the university Sarah had never had a boyfriend, and her social life, such as it was, tended to consist of the occasional rowdy evening out with large groups of friends who had never (she felt) invited her wholeheartedly into their circle. To be asked out to dinner by Gregory, to accompany him to the cinema or theatre, was for a while a new and blissful experience. Most often they went to concerts, and if she noticed that Gregory's tastes in music showed a marked tendency towards pieces that were dry, academic and emotionless, she did not allow it to bother her. Not, at any rate, until she discovered that these same qualities characterized his lovemaking.

Sarah lost her virginity to Gregory, about six weeks after he had started taking her out. It was a difficult and painful experience, much as she had been expecting; what she had not been expecting, however, was that all their subsequent encounters would be equally lacking in pleasure. Gregory made love with the same cool, intelligent efficiency he found so admirable in the most rigorous of Bach's keyboard exercises. Tenderness, flexibility, expressiveness and variations in tempo were not among the items in his repertoire. The best that Sarah could expect — the best she had to look forward to, after several months of these couplings — was the moment of post-coital fatigue, when Gregory, his performance executed and his energies spent, would sometimes speak to her in a cajoling, intimate way she found untypical and delightful. It was on one such occasion that he had asked her an unexpected question.

They were lying in bed together, deep in the middle of a still, airless night, hotly entwined, her head on his shoulder. And Gregory had asked her, seemingly from nowhere, what she thought was the most beautiful part of his body. Sarah had looked up at him in surprise, and told him that she wasn't sure, she would have to think about it, and then he, much to her relief (because she couldn't, to be honest, think of any part of his body that was especially beautiful), had said, 'Shall I tell you what is the most beautiful part of your body?' and she had said, 'Yes, tell me,' but for a little while he had made her guess, and they ran, giggling, through the obvious possibilities, but it was none of those, and finally she gave up, and then Gregory had smiled at her and said, quietly, 'Your eyelids.' She hadn't believed him at first, but he had said, 'That's because you've never seen your own eyelids; and never will see them, unless I take a photograph' (but he never did take a photograph), and so she asked him, 'Well, when have you become so intimately acquainted with my eyelids?' and he answered, 'While you were asleep. I like watching you when you're asleep.' And this was the first intimation she had had, the first hint, of his liking for standing over people in their beds, looking down on them as they slept, something she had regarded as interesting at first, the sign of an enquiring intelligence, until she began to wonder, in the end, whether there wasn't something sinister about it, fetishistic almost, this desire to look down on people as they lay helpless, unconscious, while he, the watching subject, retained full control over his waking mind.

It was harder to get to sleep after that, knowing that at any point in the night he might climb out of bed and stand over her, watching her sleeping face by moonlight. (And that was before she had further aroused his interest by telling him about her dreams, her dreams so real that she could sometimes not distinguish them from the events of her waking life.) But she got used to the idea, as she supposed one gets used to most ideas, and her awareness of Gregory's watchful presence did not unduly disturb her sleeping patterns for several more months (or was it weeks?) until she awoke screaming, in the early hours of one December morning, from one of her recurring nightmares about frogs. This one concerned a man-sized frog which had been squatting by the side of the campus ring road as she tried to hurry by: it had croaked horribly at her and then fastened on to her eyelids with the twin ends of its forked tongue, one on each eye. Sarah had struggled to wake from the nightmare but then began to cry out in even greater panic as she realized that, even though the dream was over, the sensation of pressure against her eyelids wasn't going away: there really was someone, or something, fastening on to them. She tried to open her eyes but found that she couldn't. Something was obstructing the movement of her eyelids. Then the obstruction was removed swiftly and she opened her eyes to find Gregory sitting close beside her, his face bent intently towards hers, his hand — with first and second fingers outstretched — suspended in the air only an inch or two from her eyes.

'What the *hell* were you doing?' she asked, about ten minutes later, when she was fully awake, her breathing and heart rate had returned to normal, and she was convinced, finally, that there were no giant frogs in the room with them. 'What were you doing back then?'

'Nothing,' said Gregory. 'I was just watching you.'

'You were touching me,' said Sarah.

'I didn't mean to wake you.'

'Well then, you shouldn't have put your bloody fingers in my eyes.'

After a pause Gregory murmured, 'I'm sorry,' very softly — meltingly — and squeezed her hand. Then he leaned forward and kissed her. 'I didn't mean to wake you,' he repeated. 'I had to touch them. It's incredible . . .' in the half-dark of the bedroom she could sense his smile '. . . there's so much *life* going on behind your eyes when you're asleep: I could see it. And I wanted to touch it: I could feel it, in my fingertips.' He added: 'I've done it before, you know.'

'Yes, but . . . it frightened me. It felt so real.' Meekly accusing, she said: 'You were pressing quite hard.'

He smiled again. 'Yes, but you do trust me, don't you? Not to hurt you.'

She felt her hand squeezed, her wrist stroked. 'I suppose so.'

'I suppose so?'

The weight of his wounded silence was too much to bear. 'Yes, of course I do. But that's not really the point, is it?'

'I think it's very much the point. What did you think I was going to do to you?'

As he said this, he brought his hand close to her face again. Her eyelids closed of their own accord, and he pressed against them with his fingertips.

'I spy,' he whispered, 'with my little eye. You're not scared now, are you?'

'No,' said Sarah, doubtfully.

Then he pressed harder.

'And now?'

And that was how it had begun, the thing they came to refer to as 'the game', and which became more and more closely associated with their lovemaking; until they began to play it (or rather Gregory began to play it, for Sarah was never anything more than his passive accomplice) not just post-coitally, but even during the act itself; so that it was not uncommon for him actually to reach his climax while lying on top of her, poised above her face, his first and second fingers pressed ever more firmly, ever more testingly, against her closed eyelids.

All of which Sarah remembered now, in the few instants she lay beneath Gregory tonight, as he adopted this position for one more time. For the last time, as it turned out: because all at once, possessed by a spirit of rebellion and a physical strength which surprised them both, she then let out a thin, final shriek of 'No!' and heaved Gregory away from her, so that he rolled off the bed and crashed naked to the floor.

'Jesus Christ, woman!'

Sarah got out of bed and pulled her nightdress back on.

'What the fuck was that for?'

Now she took her dressing-gown from its hook on the back of the door and struggled into it, wriggling to find the sleeves.

Gregory knelt beside the bed, winded, cradling his forehead and struggling for breath.

'Are you going to answer me or what?'

Sarah opened the door wordlessly and ran down the corridor towards the bathroom. She locked the door and sat on the toilet and wept. She rocked back and forth for several minutes. Slowly the crying and the rocking came to an end, and then she washed her face in cold water and looked at herself in the mirror. Her eyes were red-rimmed, and her mouth was set in an unfamiliar, resolute line. She began to rehearse the appropriate phrases.

Gregory, I'm sorry but I've had enough.

I think it would be better if we didn't see each other any more.

This just isn't working, is it?

I think we should just try to be friends from now on.

Strangely, once she had composed the speech in her mind, she found herself looking forward to delivering it: or rather anticipating, with a faint, timorous glow, her sense of satisfaction at having upset at least one of Gregory's most firmly rooted assumptions. In five minutes' time, she told herself, it would all be over: and it seemed suddenly incredible that a relationship which had dragged on, now, for more than a year, bringing in its wake most of what she had learned about happiness but also — and more and more, in recent months — a good deal of frustration, could be brought to an end in a few moments, with a handful of well-chosen sentences: consigning her to — what? — freedom, presumably, the freedom to pursue other, more successful friendships (the names and faces of Robert and — to her passing, unexamined surprise — Veronica presented themselves for a moment). But that was all speculation: in the short term she could foresee nothing beyond simple emotional obliteration: a vacuum of feeling: blackness. And yet even this prospect had started to look inviting.

Blackness enfolded her as she eased open the bedroom door and stepped inside. Blackness and silence: not even the sound of him breathing. She felt for the light switch but thought better of it. Instead she cleared her throat and said, faintly:

'Gregory?'

The bedside light came on immediately and he was sitting up and staring at her, his arms folded, his pyjama jacket buttoned up — as usual — to the neck. Before she could say a word, he had already embarked upon a short, articulate, expressionless monologue.

'I have only one thing to say to you, Sarah, and I am going to say it now, as quickly and as kindly as possible, in order to spare you pain. Your behaviour tonight has confirmed a suspicion which has been growing in my mind for some time: a suspicion that you are — not to put too fine a point on it — far from suitable as a partner with whom I would feel comfortable sharing the rest of my life. Consequently I feel obliged to inform you that our relationship is at an end, as of this precise moment. Since it is now too late for me reasonably to expect you to make alternative arrangements, I will permit you to share a bed with me for this night and this night only. My position on this issue is not open to negotiation and now that I have made it clear, I would only like to remind you that I have a long car journey ahead of me tomorrow, and I expect that you will allow me, on that account if no other, an uninterrupted night's —'

— and here he turned off the light —

'— sleep.'

2

Here, just for a few hundred yards, the town suddenly attempted to make something of its seaside location, and to take on, at last, some of the character of a holiday resort. Twenty bathing huts, shabbily painted in pale shades of yellow, green and blue, stood between the esplanade and the beach. A kiosk sold ice-cream and candy floss. Deck-chairs were available for hire. But there was, about all of this, an air of the perfunctory, the half-hearted. It fizzled away before it had really begun. Few holidaymakers came to this place; few of the rooms available in the various seafront boarding houses were occupied, even at what passed for the height of summer. And today, on this warm, windswept Sunday afternoon in late June, as discarded crisp packets flapped disconsolately against the pebbledashed walls of the public toilet, and seagulls bobbed with the queasy rise and fall of the incoming ocean, there were only two figures visible on the beach. One of them, a young woman of about twenty, her bare arms folded, her hair long, thin and jet-black, stood only a few feet from the water, looking out to sea. The other, who was perhaps fifteen or twenty years older, sat on a bench near the bathing huts, her overcoat folded neatly beside her, a small suitcase at her feet, her eyes closed, her face tilted towards the occasional sun.

The younger woman turned and started walking back across the pebbly beach. She stopped, bent down, picked up a curiously shaped stone, but then discarded it. She kicked a Pepsi can, accidentally, and the sound made her realize what a quiet afternoon it was.

The older woman, hearing the sound, opened her eyes and looked around her.

There were three benches: but one of them had been vandalized, almost dismantled, and was no longer usable; and another was entirely occupied by the supine, dormant form of a middle-aged man, his face purple and shaggily bearded, his clothes giving off a stale odour, his right hand clutching a can of strong cider.

The younger woman, however, still wanted to sit down.

'Do you mind if I sit here?' she was forced to ask, in the end.

The older woman smiled, shook her head and moved her overcoat.

The two women sat in silence.

The older woman was tired. She had walked all the way to the beach from the railway station, carrying her suitcase. She was sweating copiously, and was beginning to suspect that her shoes, which she had bought only two weeks ago, were half a size too small. She had taken them off when she sat down on the bench, and found her bare feet marked with angry red lines which were only now beginning to fade. She continued to curl and uncurl her toes, relishing the freedom, until she realized that the younger woman was staring at her feet; staring at them with a kind of awed fascination. Immediately she crossed her legs and tucked them away under the bench, out of the younger woman's sight. She hated her clumsy, mannish feet and thick ankles, and the way that people stared at them — women especially, and especially (as, already, in this case) women to whom she was herself attracted.

Embarrassed, the younger woman caught her eye and smiled, shyly, apologetically. Now it was clear: they were going to have to talk to one another.

'If you're looking for somewhere to stay,' the younger woman ventured, 'I might be able to help you. I can recommend somewhere.'

'Oh?'

She gave the name of a nearby boarding house.

'And what does it have, to make it different from all the others?'

The younger woman laughed. 'Nothing, really. Only my mother runs it.'

The other woman smiled. 'Well, thank you, but I'm not looking for anywhere to stay.'

'Oh. Only I thought, with your suitcase . . .'

'I've been away,' said the older woman. 'I've just come off the train.'

There was something about the way she said this — something about the phrase 'I've been away' — which made the younger woman think that she was referring to more than just a holiday. It sounded more like a period of exile.

'Oh,' she said. 'A long trip?'

'Two weeks in Italy. San Remo. Very nice.'

So she was wrong.

'You live here, then?'

The older woman was beginning to find this line of questioning rather direct. A wild thought crossed her mind: was it possible — was it just possible — that she was being chatted up?

She decided to test this hypothesis by being completely open, parting with whatever information was required and seeing where this would lead them.

'About three miles along the coast,' she said. 'At the Dudden Clinic. I work there.'

'Really? You're a doctor?'

'A psychologist.' She rummaged in her bag for a Kleenex, mopped her brow. 'Do you know the place I mean?'

'I think so. It's not been there long, has it?'

'Two years. A little more.'

'What sort of . . . hospital is it?'

'We treat people with sleep disorders. Or try to.'

'You mean — people who talk in their sleep, and so on?'

'People who talk in their sleep, people who walk in their

sleep, people who sleep too much, people who don't sleep enough, people who forget to breathe in their sleep, people who have terrible dreams . . . all of these things.'

'I used to talk in my sleep.'

'A lot of children do.' The older woman looked at her watch: there was a bus due at the seafront stop in four minutes. She leaned forward and squeezed the shoes on to her complaining feet. Then, reaching into her handbag: 'Here — have one of my cards. You never know, you might want to visit us one day. You'll be very welcome, if you mention my name.'

The younger woman didn't know what to say to this. She had never been offered anybody's card before.

'Thank you very much,' she managed, taking it.

She thought, as the older woman said goodbye to her, that she could read disappointment in her eyes: not just the passing disappointment of a small expectation raised and not fulfilled, but, behind that, something deeper and more habitual. Her back, as she walked away with her suitcase, was stooped. The younger woman looked at the card in her hand and read the words, 'Dr C. J. Madison, Psychologist, the Dudden Clinic'. Beneath it were some fax and telephone numbers.

The older woman had forgotten to ask for her name. But she wouldn't have revealed it, in any case.

She half-walked, half-ran back to her mother's boarding house, her mind buzzing.

Huge, grey and imposing, Ashdown stood on a headland, some twenty yards from the sheer face of the cliff, where it had stood for more than a hundred years. All day, the gulls wheeled around its spires and tourelles, keening themselves hoarse. All day and all night, the waves threw themselves dementedly against their rocky barricade, sending an endless roar like heavy traffic through the glacial rooms and mazy, echoing corridors of the old house. Even the emptiest parts of Ashdown — and most of it was now empty — were never silent. The most habitable rooms huddled together on the first and second floors, overlooking the sea, and during the day were flooded with chill sunlight. The kitchen, on the ground floor, was long and L-shaped, with a low ceiling; it had only three tiny windows, and was swathed in permanent shadow. Ashdown's bleak, element-defying beauty masked the fact that it was, essentially, unfit for human occupation. Its oldest and nearest neighbours could remember, but scarcely believe, that it had once been a private residence, home to a family of only eight or nine. But three decades ago it had been acquired by the new university, and used for a while as student accommodation; then the students were moved out, and it was given over to Dr Dudden, to house his private clinic and sleep laboratory. There was room at the clinic for thirteen patients: a shifting population, as changeful as the ocean which lay at its feet, stretched towards the horizon, sickly green and heaving with endless disquiet.

The next morning, Dr Dudden stood outside the room where his colleague was conducting a seminar with three of her patients, and listened to their voices through the closed door. His body tensed with disapproval: the atmosphere sounded nothing short of raucous. A medley of voices babbled almost continuously, to be interrupted every so often by blustery gales of laughter in the midst of which he could clearly make out Dr Madison's distinctive low chuckle. Then he heard her launch into a monologue which lasted for perhaps half a minute: followed, this time, by wave upon wave of screaming laughter, accompanied by the thumping of tables and all the other sounds of helpless mirth. Dr Dudden stepped back from the door and shuddered with fury. A rumour had been circulating for some time that Dr Madison's patients had been enjoying their seminars, and here was the concrete proof. It was outrageous; and, what's more, it was unscientific. It was not to be tolerated.

He called Dr Madison into his office at midday. It was a gloomy room towards the back of the house, looking out over an unkept patch of garden. An elaborate calendar and timetable took up half of the largest wall, and alongside it was a floor-plan of the house, showing the day rooms and bedrooms, and the names of the patients to whom they were currently assigned. There were four shelves filled with textbooks and bound journals, while the other walls were covered — brightened is hardly the word — by posters obtained from drug companies and American software manufacturers. Baroque keyboard music played quietly on a cassette player in the background.

His first question was: 'Have you brought the SAQs with you?'

The Sleep Awareness Questionnaire was a document of his own devising, on which patients were required, every morning, to rate various aspects of their previous night's sleep on a scale of one to five. They were asked if they had experienced racing thoughts at bedtime, had needed to urinate during the night, had suffered palpitations or leg movements, nightmares or long periods of wakefulness, and more than eighty other questions. The questionnaire was supposed to be completed at the beginning of every morning seminar, and to form the basis of any subsequent discussion.

'No,' said Dr Madison.

'I find that rather extraordinary.'

'We didn't have time to fill them all in.'

'I find that even more extraordinary,' said Dr Dudden, 'because from what I could hear, you seemed to have plenty of time for telling jokes, and giggling, and gossiping away like a bunch of washerwomen.'

Washerwomen? thought Dr Madison, but let it pass.

'Since you weren't in the room with us,' she said, 'I assume that you were eavesdropping on the other side of the door. And since you were eavesdropping on the other side of the door, I assume that you couldn't hear what we were talking about. If you had been able to hear, you would have found it perfectly germane to the business of the clinic.'

She placed a small, icy emphasis on the word 'business', which Dr Dudden either failed or affected not to notice.

'That,' he said, 'is not in dispute. I'm prepared to believe that you confine yourself, during these . . . *chats*, to the subject in hand. But might I remind you that you are employed here — by me — to approach this subject from the point of view of the clinical psychologist rather than the stand-up comedian.'

'I don't quite understand,' said Dr Madison, smoothing down her skirt in an abstracted way.

'A few minutes ago I was speaking to Miss Granger, one of the patients at your seminar this morning. I asked her what had been causing such amusement, and with some reluctance she told me. She quoted a remark of yours, in fact.' He leaned forward and read from the notepad on his desk. ' "Every Tuesday, Dr Dudden invites the patients at this clinic to attend one of his lectures at the university. This week, it was so boring that even the narcoleptics stayed awake all the way through." ' He looked up. 'Do you deny making that remark?'

'No.'

'You probably think that I am personally offended by it. And indeed I am: but that is not my point.'

'It was only a joke.'

'Oh, I can see that. Believe me, Dr Madison, I can recognize a joke when I see one. Might I ask you, then, whether you regard narcolepsy itself as — to use your own word — a joke, or whether you regard it — as I confess I do — as a serious and debilitating psychophysiological condition which causes much trauma and distress to its sufferers?'

'I specialize in narcolepsy, doctor, and have done for many years. You know that full well. So I don't see how my commitment to treating it — the seriousness of my commitment — can be called into question.' She sighed. 'Besides which, I assume you're aware that cataplexy brought on by laughter is one of the syndrome's more disturbing and socially embarrassing symptoms. These workshops are designed to help the patients deal with that: to try to make them comfortable with their laughter again. I would have thought it obvious that humour was an absolutely essential therapeutic tool in this process.'

'An ingenious explanation,' said Dr Dudden, after a pause. 'But not a satisfying one.' He folded his arms and swivelled his chair slightly, so that he was no longer addressing her directly. 'This morning, you will recall that I led a discussion group with four chronic insomniacs. Do you know what you would have heard, if you'd stood outside *my* door, on this occasion?'

'Snoring, probably,' said Dr Madison, before she could stop herself.

The corners of Dr Dudden's mouth twitched for a moment; otherwise he betrayed no emotion.

'I see that sleep apnoea is also on your list of suitable topics for levity. I must make a note of that.' He even pretended to scribble something down on his notepad, while Dr Madison looked on with growing incredulity. Then he said: 'In point of fact, what you would have heard, if you had strained hard enough, is the sound of pencils scraping upon paper, as four Sleep Awareness Questionnaires were properly completed, and then the sound of voices talking, one at a time, in reasoned and measured tones, as the results of these questionnaires were collated and analysed.'

Dr Madison decided she couldn't take any more of this, and rose to her feet, hoping to escape.

'I take your point, doctor. And if that will be all . . .'

'It won't be all, I'm afraid. Please sit down.' He waited, pointedly, for her to settle again. 'I'd like to remind you that you're expected to assist Dr Goldsmith this afternoon, in conducting the preliminary interview with Mr Worth. Is that clear?'

'It may be clear, but I'm afraid that it's quite impossible. I have several appointments scheduled already, and a considerable backlog —'

'I see.' He picked up a pencil and began tapping it on his desk, as his cheeks pinkened with vexation. 'So you persist in your objections, do you?'

'Objections, doctor?'

'You've already made your attitude towards this admission quite clear. Or have you forgotten the conversation we had just before you left?'

Dr Madison had not forgotten it at all, even though it had merely been the latest in their long series of increasingly heated confrontations. Dr Dudden had shown her a column from a recent weekday edition of the *Independent*, written by a freelance journalist called Terry Worth who worked, apparently, for a number of national newspapers: usually writing about film but sometimes branching out into more general subjects. In this column he had announced his intention of entering a competition which was to be held at a repertory cinema in London, where they were staging a ten-day 'Cinethon'. There would be continuous screenings throughout the event, twenty-four hours a day, and a prize was being offered to the audience member who could clock up the longest uninterrupted period of film-watching. Revealing that he was already a long-term insomniac, Worth had claimed that he would be able to stay awake through all 134 films, and Dr Dudden, upon reading this announcement, had immediately contacted the newspaper and asked to be put in touch with him.

'Just think of the research possibilities, apart from anything else,' he had enthused to Dr Madison. 'We'll have him driven down here the minute the event is over. Get him put straight into a bedroom and then — a seven-electrode montage to assess sleep disturbance and architecture . . . sixteen channels to record EEG . . . manual scoring of the sleep record from optical disk . . . full sleep questionnaire, of course. It's an *unmatched* opportunity to see what sort of effect continuous exposure to media images might have on dream content.'

'And is that the only reason?' Dr Madison had asked.

'It's reason enough, isn't it? What are you implying?'

'I just wondered if the newsworthiness of this story might have occurred to you at any point. Will Mr Worth be paying for his own treatment?'

'That is neither here nor there.'

'And will he be writing about us for the newspaper? Is that part of the deal?'

'There is no *deal*, Dr Madison. I find that insinuation highly objectionable. And even if there were, I would ask you to bear in mind that this clinic operates largely as a private concern, that we are dependent on income from the patients themselves, and that there is nothing intrinsically evil about the idea of try-ing to generate a little modest publicity every now and again.' He had opened his desk diary at a page already marked with blue ribbon. 'Mr Worth will arrive here a fortnight on Monday, late in the morning. I see that you will have returned from your holiday the day before, so I suggest that you and Dr Goldsmith conduct your first interview with him in the afternoon. I'll pen-cil that in, shall I?'

'Whatever,' she had said, with a dismissive shrug; and the in-solence of that remark, and that gesture, came back to Dr Dud-den now as he stared at her across the desk, almost trembling with rage.

'Don't think,' he said quietly, 'don't assume for one *minute* that my good nature is inexhaustible.'

'The thought had never occurred to me,' said Dr Madison.

After a few seconds' silence she realized that their conversa-tion was at an end. She left, closing the door softly behind her.

Shortly after midnight, wakeful, her casement window open to the warm breeze and her room sheened with moonlight, Dr Madison heard footsteps on the front terrace. She put on her dressing-gown and peered through the window. There was a man outside, leaning against the balustrade, smoking a cigarette. Its golden glow, a tiny pinprick of light, came and went as he drew upon it. He did not look frightening. He did not look like an intruder. She decided to go down and investigate.

On her way she was stopped by Lorna, one of the technicians, rushing along the corridor with an anxious look on her face.

'I was just going to wake Dr Dudden,' she said. 'Something peculiar's happened. I set up the patient in Bedroom Nine and put him to bed about an hour ago. I watched him for a while and there was still no sign of him going to sleep, but he seemed OK. He was lying quite still. Then I went to make myself a cup of tea, and when I got back he was gone.'

'Gone? You mean he'd taken off all the electrodes himself?'

'I suppose so.'

'Bedroom Nine — that was Mr Worth, tonight, wasn't it?'

Dr Madison hurried down towards the bedroom in question and found a scene much as Lorna had described: the bed empty, the sheets tousled, the network of wires and electrodes tangled up at the head of the bed and leaving smears of glue over the pillows. This was highly unusual: although the insomniac patients often wanted to get up in the middle of the night, it was rare for one to elude the vigilance of the technicians and take the matter into his own hands.

'Don't worry,' said Dr Madison. 'I think I know where he is. I'll go and talk to him.'

'What about Dr Dudden?'

'Don't wake him up. I don't think he needs to know about this.'

She made her way towards the common room at the front of the house, where a pair of French windows allowed access to the terrace. She could see the man outside, pacing in the darkness. The windows were frequently used, but their hinges were rusty and they gave out a grating squeal. The man turned with a start and looked at Dr Madison as she approached, advancing swiftly into the shadows. His face, even in this blackness, shone paler than the moon.

There was an electric light above the terrace, but Dr Madison had not switched it on.

'Mr Worth, I presume?' she said.

'That's correct.' Like her, he was wearing pyjamas and a dressing-gown.

'I'm Dr Madison. Dr Dudden's Girl Friday, as it were.' She paused to see how he responded to this phrase, whether he registered its slightly mocking undertone. The moonlight, and the cigarette glow, illuminated just enough of his face to reveal the hint of a smile. 'You seem to have deserted your post.'

'Yes. I couldn't sleep.'

'We didn't expect you to.'

'No. I don't, you see.'

'All the same, I assume you know that you were supposed to ask permission before getting up.'

'I was told that, yes, but I didn't think it was serious.'

'Well, the equipment you were handling is very delicate, and very expensive. Besides which, you've now got glue in your hair, which can't be very comfortable for you.'

The man touched his hair tentatively, wincing with distaste. 'So I have. Well, I'm sorry about this. I hope I didn't damage anything.'

'Not this time. But there is another thing — we don't really like our patients wandering around after dark. I thought somebody might have explained that to you as well.'

The ocean rumbled angrily in the distance. Waves were breaking upon the rocks with weary irregularity. He listened to them for a while before explaining: 'I've got to relax somehow.'

'Yes, I understand that. Don't worry. I'm not going to put you in detention, or set you a hundred lines.'

Now he laughed, and said: 'Why don't you call me Terry?'

'Thank you. I will,' said Dr Madison; but instead of offering her own first name, as Terry had expected, she said: 'Did you manage it?'

'Pardon?'

'Your film marathon. Ten days. A hundred and thirty-four films. How did you get on?'

'Oh, that. Yes, I managed that all right. No problem. I think I'm going into the *Guinness Book of Records*.'

'Congratulations.' It seemed to Terry that Dr Madison wanted to go inside again, but something was holding her back; some semi-reluctant urge to prolong the conversation. She said: 'Dr Dudden will be delighted. You're already his favourite.'

'Oh?'

'That's his area, you see. Sleep deprivation.' Then, after a pause: 'Rats.'

Terry misinterpreted this, and asked: 'Have you dropped something?'

'No: that's what he uses. Rats. He deprives them of sleep, to see what happens.'

'What a delightful hobby. And what does happen?'

'They die, usually. But their lives are never in vain, because he gets to add another paper or two to his bibliography.'

'I'm beginning to sense,' said Terry, 'that Dr Dudden's Girl Friday is not the most devoted of servants.'

'Everything I tell you is off the record, by the way.'

'Of course.'

In spite of this reassurance, she seemed to recede further from him, almost imperceptibly, cloaking herself in even thicker darkness. He could not make out her face at all. 'It's not about curing people, you know,' she said. 'All he's interested in is knowledge. He won't cure you.'

'Maybe not,' said Terry. 'But this place might.'

For a moment they were both conscious, again, of the waves'

murmurous onslaught; clouds scudding through the moonlight; the immensity of the ocean. Stubbing out his cigarette,
Terry licked his lips and savoured the taste of salt.

'Yes, there is a certain . . . atmosphere about this house,'
said Dr Madison. 'You'll find it very restful. How long are you
staying?'

'I'm booked in for two weeks,' said Terry. 'But that's not what
I meant. There's another reason why I thought it might — well,
not *cure* me, exactly . . .'

He tailed off. Dr Madison waited.

'I used to live here, you see.'

'Live here?'

'Not for long. When I was a student. Twelve years ago. I
haven't been here since. That's partly — mainly, I suppose —
why I decided to come. Curiosity.'

Dr Madison said, laconically: 'Well, that's something you
have in common with Dr Dudden, then.'

'How do you mean?'

'He was a student here as well.'

'Really? When?'

'I don't think you would have overlapped.'

'You never know, though. What's his first name?'

'Gregory.'

'Gregory Dudden . . . Doesn't ring any bells . . .' His mind, in
any case, had latched on to a different memory. 'I had a friend
at the time — it's funny, I've hardly given her a thought since
then, but seeing Ashdown again, it . . . brings things back . . .
Anyway . . . *She* should be the one coming back here, because
she had the *weirdest* . . . syndrome, I suppose you'd call it.'

'In what way?'

'She had dreams — incredibly vivid dreams — dreams so
vivid that she couldn't tell the difference between the things
she dreamed and the things that really happened to her.'

'Hypnagogic hallucinations,' said Dr Madison. 'Also known as
pre-sleep dreaming.'

'There's a name for it? You mean it's quite common?'

'No, it's not common at all. It can be one of the symptoms of narcolepsy. Was she narcoleptic?'

'I'm not sure.'

'Did you know her well?'

'I suppose I did, yes. We lived together for a bit — just a few weeks — the year we graduated.'

'When you say lived together . . .'

'No, I mean, we just shared this flat. We never . . .' The words faded into ambiguous silence — half-careless, half-regretful. Only when he added, 'She was called Sarah,' was there something newly soft and reflective in his voice. Then it turned brisk again. 'I'm sorry, I'm probably keeping you up. You must be tired.'

'Not really. Are you?'

Terry barked with laughter. 'I'm always tired,' he said, 'and never tired. That's my curse, I'm afraid. I certainly don't feel like sleeping now. We've got all night, as far as I'm concerned.'

'All right, then,' coaxed Dr Madison. 'Tell me about Sarah, and her dreams.'

3

'Tell me about your dreams,' Gregory had once said to Sarah, sitting on that same terrace, one bright November morning many years earlier. 'Tell me how long this has been going on.'

Sarah had warmed her hands on the mug, shivered slightly in the ocean breeze, and looked at him fondly. This was during the early months of their relationship, long before they grew apart. She still found, in those days, that he could be very kind. She still regarded him as a wise and understanding man. Sitting on that terrace, leaning instinctively towards him so that their knees touched, she felt her anxieties begin to dissolve. She forgot that they had been arguing more often, recently, and over pettier things. As for the sex, she told herself that it would improve over time. She tried to ignore the fact that as she spoke to Gregory, he was writing her words down in a notebook, marked 'SARAH'S PSYCHOLOGICAL PROBLEMS'.

In any case she was excited, there was no denying it: for they had just made an important discovery. They had stumbled upon an explanation for something which had been baffling Sarah for the last five years or more. They had discovered, that very morning, that she could not tell the difference between her dreams and her memories of real life.

'Tell me about these dreams,' Gregory was saying. 'Tell me how long this has been happening.'

And so Sarah took a deep breath, and told him.

It had started, she said, when she was fourteen or fifteen years old. She was unhappy at school, had frequent problems finishing her homework, and lived in particular fear of her History teacher, one Mr Mountjoy. At the end of one difficult evening, having found herself completely incapable of writing an essay on the causes of the Franco-Prussian War — an essay which she was supposed to read out in class the next day — she had gone to bed in tears, resolved in her desperation either to bunk off school the next morning or to feign illness of some sort. But instead she awoke to an immediate sensation of light-heartedness, with a pristine memory of having written the essay, and having written it, she knew, to a high standard: she could visualize it in her exercise book, four and a half sides long, several crossings-out on page three but otherwise neat and presentable, the title double-underlined in red ink and with even a few footnotes thrown in at the end to give it a scholarly sheen. And it was not until almost half past eleven that same day, the first period after break, when she opened her exercise book just before being called up to address the class, that she discovered that this essay, incredibly, did not exist. That was the conclusion she finally came to, at any rate: at first she thought she must have made some foolish mistake and written it in another book, and she searched frantically through her briefcase, looking at her English, Geography and French books, her panic mounting so visibly and audibly that Mr Mountjoy had to interrupt the current reader in mid-flow and ask what was the matter. She explained that she must have left the essay in her locker and asked permission to go and fetch it: which was granted; but a search of her Maths, German, Physics and Biology books in the unaccustomed silence of the deserted locker-room still failed to produce the vital essay; and then, seized by a bewilderment bordering on hysteria, she had fled the school building altogether and run to the municipal park where, head in hands, she had tried in vain to make sense of this sequence of events and began to wonder seriously, for the first time, whether she was going mad. The essay never turned up and she was put in detention that week (Mr Mountjoy not believing a word of her story): and while everybody else forgot the incident, Sarah did not forget it, and never spoke about it to anyone, even though she went on to experience other, similar misadventures at irregular intervals over the next few years. Once, a few terms later, she had bitterly reproved her best friend Angela for failing to meet her at a prearranged time outside the swimming baths: Angela denied that such a rendezvous had ever been suggested, and the argument led to a rift between them which was never quite healed. There was another occasion, too, when Sarah baffled her family by stopping off at the chemist's on her way home from school, and bringing back — in response, she insisted, to a specific request from her mother — six tubes of smoker's toothpaste, ten sachets of pot-pourri and at least a year's supply of suppositories.

Although too ashamed to admit it even to her closest friends or family, Sarah became convinced that she was the victim of delusions: vivid, uncontrollable flights of the imagination which at first she had no reason to connect with her dreams (since the dreams she could remember usually had little to do with reality, but tended, like everyone else's, towards the grotesque and fantastic: she often had nightmares about snakes, for instance, and even worse ones about frogs). It was only that morning on the terrace, with Gregory's help, that the truth had suddenly come to light. And although Sarah had been upset by their argument the night before, in another sense she was grateful for it: because it was this argument, and its strange consequences, that had finally unlocked the door of the mystery.

The trouble had begun the previous afternoon, when Gregory told Sarah that they were both invited out to a birthday dinner being given at a local restaurant (yet to be decided upon) by a fellow medical student: someone called Ralph, whom Gregory himself did not, it seemed, know particularly well. Sarah asked if she had been included in this invitation by name, and Gregory was forced to admit that she hadn't: as far as he was aware, Ralph didn't know that they were lovers, and had merely told Gregory that he could bring along a friend, if he wished. That figures, said Sarah. Gregory asked her to explain this remark: and she told him that she used to be friendly with Ralph until an embarrassing episode that had taken place a few months ago, following which they hadn't spoken.

'You know that fish restaurant down by the harbour?' she said. 'The Planetarium?' (It was called that because of the domed ceiling over the main dining-room, on to which a local artist had recently painted a large nocturnal skyscape.) 'Well, he invited me there once. Just me and his parents, who were down for the weekend. God knows why I was singled out for this honour: I think he may have had a bit of a crush on me. Anyway, it was a Saturday night, and it was very crowded, and towards the end of the meal, just as we were having coffee, I started to feel really ill. I mean *really* ill. I think it must have been the mussels. I went to the loo and thought I was going to be sick but nothing happened: so then I went back upstairs and everyone was getting ready to leave, and I was still feeling really terrible, but still, we got our coats and then we all stood on the restaurant steps saying goodbye. His parents were going back to their hotel in town, you see. Anyway, there we all were, chatting and saying goodbye, and then suddenly I *knew* I was going to be sick. Any second. And sure enough, right in the middle of the conversation, without any warning, I just buckled over and threw up all over the steps and the pavement. There it was, my entire meal, splashed all over the steps of the restaurant for everyone to see. And the amazing thing was, Ralph and his parents *never stopped talking*. I mean, that's real breeding for you, isn't it? They just carried on as if nothing had happened. The only thing Ralph's mother did was to pass me a Kleenex, so I could wipe my mouth. And then they just chatted on for a couple more minutes, arranging what they were going to do the next day, and then they kissed him goodnight, and then his father leaned over to kiss *me* goodnight, and just as he did that it happened again, I suddenly felt sick and before I knew what was happening I was throwing up all over the steps again, only this time half of it went over his father's trousers and shoes as well. And still, you know, they never batted an eyelid. Never said a word. And then his parents thanked him for a lovely evening, or something, and off they went in one direction, and we went off in another, and all he said to me was, "Are you OK now?" in this really cold tone of voice. So then we got into a taxi and went back on to campus, and we didn't even kiss goodnight or anything. I got the impression he thought the whole thing was quite funny, in a nasty sort of way, because his parents were posh, and I wasn't, and he thought I'd given an amusing demonstration of how the lower orders behaved in front of their betters.'

'No, you're doing him an injustice,' said Gregory. 'I don't know Ralph very well, but I'm sure he'd never take that kind of attitude.'

'Then why has he never spoken to me since?'

Gregory had no answer for this, but spent most of the next few hours reassuring Sarah that it was safe for her to come out to the dinner. At a quarter to eight, all the same, when they arrived outside Ralph's hall of residence on campus, she was still expressing doubts.

'What if he's taking everyone to the same restaurant?'

'What if he is?'

'Well, that would just be so embarrassing, wouldn't it?'

'I can't help thinking you're making a bit much of this, Sarah.' They were climbing the staircase by now.

'That's easy for you to say. The point is that I know, I just *know*, that this whole thing has become a big joke with his friends. I can just imagine him telling them all that story and having a big laugh about it. It'll be a standing joke with them.'

'That is nonsense,' said Gregory emphatically. They had arrived in Ralph's corridor. 'I am training to be a psychiatrist, Sarah. A specialist in the workings of the human mind. And if I know anything at all about human nature, I can guarantee that he won't have mentioned the matter to another soul. All this is just another example of your paranoia and persecution complex.' Stopping outside Ralph's room, he snatched down a note that had been pinned to the door, and read it aloud. 'Ralph's friends,' he read. 'Meet eight-thirty, at The Vomitarium.'

And it was at this point that Gregory's and Sarah's versions of events started to diverge; although it only became apparent the next morning, when Sarah awoke, quite early, to find that Gregory was no longer lying in bed beside her. She got up and drew back the curtains. Looking down, she saw him sitting on the terrace, staring out to sea, wearing his thick blue greatcoat which he had buttoned up tightly.

Sarah pulled on some clothes and went down to the kitchen, where she made two mugs of coffee. She carried them outside, gaining access to the terrace through the French windows in the television room.

'Here you are,' she said, putting his mug down on the table next to the notebook in which he had been writing. 'You look freezing. Is anything the matter?'

'I couldn't sleep,' he said, sipping the coffee gratefully. 'In fact, I had a terrible night's sleep last night.'

'Oh?'

'Yes. You kept waking me up.'

'How do you mean?' said Sarah.

'You kept me awake. You were somniloquizing.'

'I was what?'

'Somniloquizing. Talking in your sleep.'

'I don't do that.'

'Well, last night you did.'

'Really? What was I saying?'

'Oh, I don't know.' He gave a massive, elongated yawn, and frowned. 'Something about a cottage by a river, I think.'

'How peculiar.'

'Very.' Slowly, the coffee began to revive him, and he asked: 'So, how did you enjoy yourself yesterday, in the end?'

'It was all right,' said Sarah, after a rather surprised pause.

'I liked Harriet, I must say,' Gregory prompted.

'Harriet?'

'Yes. Amusing girl, I thought. Made the evening go with a bit of a swing.'

'Who is she?'

Gregory glanced at her; an impatient look. 'Harriet. Ralph's new girlfriend. You were sitting next to her all evening.'

'Sitting next to her? Where?'

'At the restaurant.'

Sarah blew along the surface of her coffee. She decided that he was playing some boring game. 'I don't know what you're talking about.'

'Look,' said Gregory, exasperated. 'It was just a remark. I don't have to be punished for it, do I — just for saying something complimentary about another woman?'

'Well, since I've never met the woman in question, I'm scarcely in a position to comment.'

Gregory turned on her. 'I'm talking about *last night*, Sarah. I'm talking about the woman you sat next to, and had a conversation with, *all evening*.'

Without another word Sarah stood up, turned, and disappeared from the terrace, leaving Gregory to glower and sip his coffee, sulkily assuming that he had breached some unspoken piece of boyfriend-girlfriend protocol. When she came back about ten minutes later, she looked worried and apologetic. She slid carefully into the seat beside him and said:

'This is going to sound very strange, I know, but I have no memory at all of going to the restaurant with you last night. I have my own memory of what happened, and it's completely different.'

Gregory watched her intently.

'For the last few years, ever since I was a teenager, every now and again I've had these peculiar experiences. I remember things differently from how they happened. I imagine things. I make things up. I don't know how it happens. I've never told

anybody about it. You're the first person. I'm telling you now' —
she looked at him, and her voice began to quiver — 'because I
trust you. Because I love you.'

Gregory pursed his lips: for a moment she thought he was
going to kiss her. Instead he picked up his pen, then opened his
notebook again and flicked eagerly to the first blank page.

'But this is *fascinating*,' he said. 'You mean you have no recollection of coming to the restaurant? Sitting next to Harriet?
Singing "Happy Birthday"? Ordering monkfish?'

Sarah's brow began to furrow. 'I don't know . . . It's familiar
. . . Faintly familiar . . . But there's another memory — a much
stronger one.'

'A kind of alternative memory?'

'Yes. Yes, I suppose so.'

'This,' said Gregory, scribbling furiously, 'is *fucking* brilliant.
Something like this doesn't fall into your lap every day of the
week. So what do *you* think happened last night?'

Sarah's recollection coincided with Gregory's only as far as
the moment when they discovered the note pinned to Ralph's
door. After that, she claimed, they had had a violent argument,
at the end of which she had refused to come with him to the
birthday meal: Gregory had gone alone, while Sarah had made
her way to Jonah's, which was a popular self-service restaurant
on campus.

'When did you get there?' asked Gregory, still writing everything down.

'I don't know — about eight?'

'And how long did you stay?'

'Quite a while. There was nothing else to do. About an hour.'

'And what did you eat?'

'Is any of this really necessary? Does it have any relevance?'

'Everything is relevant. It's vital that we establish just how
specific this . . . hallucination was. Now, what did you eat?'

'Soup. Just soup.'

'Just soup? Weren't you hungry?'

'They didn't have much food left. I didn't fancy either of the main courses.'

'What were they?'

'Well, it was either cottage pie, or liver.'

Gregory started to write this down, but paused in mid-word. He looked up, his eyes gleaming. 'But that's what you said last night — while you were asleep.'

'What?'

'It wasn't "cottage by a river" — it was "cottage pie or liver".' He threw down his pen and laughed, more in triumph than amusement. 'Sarah, this whole thing was a dream. You *dreamed* it.'

It took just a few minutes to convince her that this was the most rational, the most plausible, in fact the only conceivable explanation; and that was how Sarah came to learn that she was not the victim of delusions at all, but that every so often she was liable to have a dream so real that she could not distinguish it from the events of her waking life; so real, furthermore, that it was capable of wiping these events from memory, so that they had to be remembered through the dream, recovered from beneath the dream, peered at through its cloudy, erasing surface like the original words of a palimpsest.

'But that explains everything,' she said. 'All the weird things that have happened to me. All those misunderstandings . . .'

'Because it's happened before?' said Gregory. 'You've had this sort of dream before?'

'Yes. Lots of times.'

He turned to a new page in the notebook, and wrote a heading in his characteristically neat, minuscule capitals. 'Come on then, Sarah,' he said, smiling excitedly. 'Tell me about your dreams.'

Sarah's relationship with Gregory came to an end eleven months later, in the first days of her postgraduate year. Her sleeping patterns, never very regular at the best of times, had grown more and more erratic during that period, and her dreams had continued to prove unreliable.

Often it was at moments of the most intense emotional disturbance that her dreams became most lifelike and deceptive, and the night she split up with Gregory was a case in point. She had no way of knowing it, but she started to dream very early that night, only a few minutes after she had slipped reluctantly into bed: for she had then fallen, with unnatural rapidity, into a deep sleep which was immediately accompanied by a dream as treacherous as any she had ever experienced. When she awoke the next morning, the substance of this dream was lodged in her mind like a vivid, bitter-sweet memory. She was convinced that the event she had dreamed had really happened.

In spite of Gregory's pompous, hurtful speech, in spite of the fact that it was Gregory who lay next to her, wheezing heavily in his sleep, it was not Gregory that she dreamed about. She dreamed about Robert, the new friend she had met in the L-shaped kitchen at Ashdown. She dreamed that he was in great distress, and that she was the only person who knew why. She dreamed that Robert's sister had died.

The next morning, she expected to see him at breakfast in the kitchen; but he wasn't there. Gregory left for London at about ten o'clock, without saying goodbye, and after that Sarah went on to campus to sit in the library, where she failed spectacularly to get any work done for several hours. She thought about Gregory a little, but more often she thought about Robert, and wondered how he was coping with his terrible news. Probably he would already have gone home: there would be parents to comfort, funeral arrangements to make.

She sat in the library until four o'clock in the afternoon, brooding over this unhappy turn of events. Even now, Sarah had not quite learned the habit of monitoring her dreams, of keeping a constant watch over the boundaries between her dream world and her real life, and it still did not occur to her that she might have dreamed Robert's sister's death. It did not occur to her that Robert's display of grief over the loss of his family cat, combined with the malicious slogan he had repeated to her — 'Death to the Sisters' — might have inspired this misleading fantasy. In any case, she had no accurate recollection of their encounter in the kitchen the night before: it had been entirely displaced by her dream. And while Robert himself would no doubt have been touched to know that she was sitting in the library thinking about him, worrying that his whole future life might be blighted by the premature death of his sister, there was really no need: for he was, at that moment, lying in the bath at Ashdown, with nothing more serious on his mind than a vague uncertainty about where he was going to eat that evening.

Finally, it was a sharp thud on the desk beside her that startled Sarah out of her reverie. Someone had banged three books down and was now standing over her, smiling in an excited, rather self-satisfied way. It was Veronica, the strange, friendly woman from the Café Valladon.

'I thought I'd find you here,' she said. 'I brought you something to think about.'

The books' titles were *The Second Sex* by Simone de Beauvoir, *Sexual Politics* by Kate Millett and *The Sadeian Woman* by Angela Carter. Two of these Sarah had read already.

'Give them a try,' said Veronica, 'and then come and talk to me. You'll find me in the Café most days, especially in the afternoons.'

'Thanks,' said Sarah. She was too surprised to add anything else.

'You're welcome,' said Veronica. As she vanished into the darkness between two stacks of books, Sarah was left with an impression of her long, supple back.

The bath-water was getting cold as Robert completed the task of shaving. As usual, he had left his least favourite part — the throat, and in particular the Adam's apple — until last. The water, cloudy with soap and the grime from his body, was now also prickled with little black hairs. He rinsed his razor under the tap, attempting to dislodge the final recalcitrant shavings. Wind howled around the walls of Ashdown as he sank further into the cooling water: at least it protected him from the fiercer chill of the bathroom, which was, absurdly, by far the largest and loftiest room on this floor of the house. He ran the razor over his cheeks again, dreamily: then he lifted a leg out of the water and examined its thin, pipe-cleaner whiteness with distaste. The hairs lay lank and flat against his shin and thigh. After a thoughtful moment he placed the blade of the razor just above the knee, and began to scrape. Soon he had cleared a little bare patch, about two inches square.

He found shaving his legs absorbing at first, then merely mechanical. He stopped concentrating on the soft abrasive motion of the razor, and let his mind begin to wander in random patterns. First of all he thought about Muriel. Robert's family had kept three cats during his lifetime, but she had been his favourite: the sweetest-natured, and the most affectionate. Even so, he was shocked — and somewhat ashamed of himself — to think how visibly affected he had been by the news of her death yesterday. He was sure that Sarah had noticed him crying when he talked to her in the kitchen. She probably despised him already. That was always what his father used to tell him, whenever he cried: 'If a woman ever sees you like that, she'll despise you. No woman likes a man to be weak. You want respect. Nobody respects a cry-baby.' He could hear these words now, spoken in the only tone he could remember his father ever using towards him: scornful, unforgiving.

Sarah had not seemed to despise him, though. Perhaps she hadn't noticed, after all: she might have been too wrapped up in her own problems. That had been a peculiar story, about the man insulting her in the street. He hoped she wasn't still worrying about it. She had nice eyes: metallic, pale blue, bordering on grey. Ambiguous eyes, warmly inviting and coolly intelligent at the same time.

He was not using a safety razor, and now a sudden shaft of pain from somewhere in the region of his calf made him flinch. He had nicked himself quite badly: a trickle of blood flowed into the bath-water. Shaving his legs wasn't the relaxing, pleasantly mindless business he had assumed it would be, then: a modicum of concentration was required. Even so, there was something deeply satisfying about it, some fundamental quality of rightness. He had never seen the point of hairy legs. He had always asked his previous girlfriends for their opinions on this subject, and had been astonished to find that they considered them attractive. Just as well, really: but he couldn't help regarding it as an inexplicable lapse of taste.

He had nearly finished, now: just the ankles to do, and they would be a stretch. He would give himself a little rest first. He lay back in the grey water, now thick with dark hair, and stared for a while unfocusingly at the cracked and begrimed wall tiles. They reminded him of the showers at school, and that was another nasty memory: communal showers, all that teasing, and furtive comparison . . .

Robert had been in the bath for more than an hour: enough time for Sarah to have left the library, caught a bus from campus and arrived back at Ashdown, anxious to wash her hair. There was no lock on the bathroom door. The trick was to put the towel-rail up against it, but Robert, being a new resident, had not discovered this yet. That was how she came to burst in upon him unexpectedly, without even knocking.

It all happened in a rush. Sarah screamed in shock and mortification but Robert screamed in agony, for he was in the middle of shaving his left ankle, with his leg raised high in the air. When the door crashed open his hand had slipped and the twin blades of his razor gouged deeply into the leg, twice, at right angles, leaving a double scar that would stay with him for the rest of his life, like French quotation marks. And this time the blood came in more than a trickle: it jetted out and flooded the bath-water, turning it strawberry-pink in what seemed to be no time at all. Sarah stared at him, appalled, transfixed, and for a moment he thought that she was even going to rush to his help; but he managed to forestall this by shouting: 'It's all right! It's all right! I was shaving, that's all.'

'I'm sorry, I — I'll come back when you've finished.'

She made for the doorway but paused when she got there. She was shielding her eyes and looking away. 'Are you OK? I mean, do you need any help? There's a First Aid box in the cabinet.'

'Thanks. I'll be fine. Just — just leave me to it, will you?'

She stepped out of the room, but paused again in the corridor. 'I thought you would have gone home,' she said, quickly, enigmatically, and then disappeared.

Robert did not waste any time pondering the meaning of this remark. He climbed out of the bath and staunched the flow of blood from his ankle with toilet paper, then bandaged it tightly. He was dripping wet and very cold. He dried himself with his small, threadbare towel, and limped back to his bedroom.

Sarah came to find him a few minutes later, just as he had finished dressing. She had washed her hair and combed it out, but not dried it, and it looked darker than he remembered from the night before, mousey even. For some reason he was touched by this: or perhaps he was already approaching that vulnerable condition of the heart where even the smallest and most mundane details take on a luminous, transfiguring quality. Whatever the cause, he felt his chest tighten as she sat down on the bed opposite his desk, and found himself, for a moment, completely incapable of speech. Even breathing was difficult at first.

'Is it still hurting?' she asked.

'Oh . . . just a bit. It'll be fine.' He hoped she wasn't going to ask him why he had been shaving his legs in the first place.

'I didn't mean to . . . well, I'm sorry if I disturbed you. People usually put the towel-rail up against the door, you see.'

'Oh. Right. Well, that's what I'll do, then: next time.'

Sarah nodded. This was not proceeding at all as she had hoped. She wondered how they were possibly going to re-establish the easy, trusting atmosphere of last night's conversation.

'Anyway,' she said, 'I just came to see that you were OK, really. You know, you looked pretty . . . upset last night, and I wanted to know that you were coping.'

'Coping?'

'Well, yes: it must be very hard for you.'

He summoned the courage to look at her now, pricked by curiosity at the note of genuine, tremulous concern in her voice. What was going on here, exactly? Did she really think he was the kind of man to be laid flat out with grief for days over the death of a cat? Did he appear that pathetic? Unable to tell, from her question, whether she was patronizing him or simply making fun, he said guardedly:

'Oh, you know, it's not such a big deal, really. I'll get over it.'

How very male, Sarah thought, to be putting on this bluff display of resilience. Did men really believe that they weren't allowed to show their feelings, even when discussing the death of someone close to them — almost as close, in this case, as it was possible to be? She saw how tense and anxious he was in her presence, how uncomfortable at the thought of having this husk of insensibility peeled back, revealing the softer, truer nature underneath. But she knew that it was in both their interests to persist.

'When I said that I thought you'd gone away,' she went on, 'I meant that, you know, the funeral must be soon.'

'Funeral?' said Robert.

'For — I'm sorry, I've forgotten her name . . .'

'For Muriel, you mean?'

'Yes. For Muriel.'

He shrugged, laughing uneasily. 'Oh, I don't think we'll be making that much of a fuss over it,' he said. 'That would be a bit over the top, don't you think?'

Taken aback for a moment, she mumbled: 'Well, whatever you all think is . . . appropriate.'

'I mean, when this has happened before,' said Robert, 'we haven't bothered with a funeral or anything.'

'This has happened before?' she asked, horrified.

'Twice, yes.'

'Oh God, Robert, I just . . . don't know what to say. That's awful. To think that lives can be so . . . blighted, and yet — you carry on, somehow.'

'Well, I must say, Muriel's is the hardest to take.' He sat forward, nearer to her, and rubbed his hands, warming them at the flame of her sympathy. 'I was closest to her, I suppose.'

'Yes, I can imagine.'

He allowed himself a nostalgic smile. 'Every evening, you know, she used to come into my room, and she'd curl up on the bed next to me. I'd stroke her little head and . . . just talk to her. Talk to her for hours sometimes.'

'That's so sweet.'

'In a way —' he laughed now '— in a silly way, she knew me even better than my parents did. Certainly my father.'

'They weren't so fond of her, as you were?'

'Well, *he* never took to Muriel, there's no denying it.' He sighed. 'They rubbed each other up the wrong way. You know, silly little habits of hers used to annoy him.'

'What sort of things?'

'Well, he didn't like the way she used to pee on the sitting-room carpet, for instance.'

Sarah took this information in slowly. A new picture was beginning to emerge: a child, dysfunctional in some way, and a family who had perhaps never learned to cope with her; per-

haps never even learned to regard her as fully human. The
situation was more painful, more tragic than she had first
imagined. And now the real meaning of Robert's earlier, puzzling remarks began to suggest itself.

'Look, Robert,' she said carefully. 'What you said before,
about a funeral being over the top — I do think it's very important, you know, that your family . . . marks this death in
some way.'

'Well, I did talk with Dad last night on the phone, about —'
he grimaced '— disposing of her. I wanted to know if some sort
of cremation was possible.'

'And?'

'He just laughed. Told me I was being pathetic. He said he
was just going to dig a hole at the bottom of the garden and put
her in a bin-liner. Like he did with the others.'

Sarah looked at Robert earnestly for a long time, and then
said, with great care and emphasis: 'But you think that's wrong,
don't you? You *know* that it's wrong.'

Robert nodded. 'Yes. Yes, I do.'

'Good.' Sarah rose from the bed, now, and stood by the door.
'OK, Robert, I'm finding this conversation . . . a little hard to
cope with, and I'm going to go downstairs for a while. But I
want you to think about what I said, and remember that, you
know, however bad things have been, in your family, you can
always talk to me about it. I'm always here.'

Just as she was leaving, they looked directly into each other's
eyes for the first time; and something happened then, some
connection was made, just for a moment, before Sarah turned
away and left the room, relieved to have gained the sanctuary
of the corridor and to be heading safely out towards the
clifftops and the autumn breeze. As he listened to her reced-
ing footsteps, Robert began to breathe again in long, uneven
breaths.

He did not see her again for several days after that; or at
least, while he may have glimpsed her from his window, on

her way to or from the house, or been offered a fugitive vision of her disappearing into her bedroom or passing through the L-shaped kitchen, he never had the opportunity of speaking to her, and became convinced that she was purposely avoiding him. One evening towards the end of the week, he challenged her about this, and she admitted that she was shocked by his behaviour — by his failure, specifically, to return home in the aftermath of his sister's death. Once this mistake had been brought to light, of course, it was easily dealt with. Robert burst into laughter as soon as he realized what had happened, but she was too embarrassed to see the funny side, and was disturbed, besides, by this further evidence of the perfidy of her dreams. She apologized rather coldly, and made no effort to prolong the conversation.

That night, however, long after most of the other students had gone to bed, Robert looked out of his window and saw Sarah standing alone on the moonlit terrace. She was looking out into the darkness and leaning against the balustrade, upon which she had balanced what appeared to be a tumblerful of white wine. He went downstairs to join her, gaining access to the terrace through the French windows in the television room, where the rusty hinges gave out a grating squeal. She turned when she heard him approach, and smiled an encouraging smile.

They began talking on the terrace, and continued in the kitchen, and it was after four o'clock in the morning when they finally said goodnight and went upstairs to their separate rooms. It was probably, at that point, the longest conversation Robert had ever had in his life. The melancholy silence which had always enveloped him at home — his mother timid and deferential, his father morosely taciturn — had never prepared him for this kind of fluid, impulsive exchanging of confidences. By the time they had finished, he felt drunk with talk; high on confession. They had discussed everything, it seemed, and had held nothing back from each other. It had begun with the

collapse of Sarah's relationship with Gregory, and after that
they had ranged freely over romance, friendship, families and
gender, the shared intimacies and the self-revelations coming
ever thicker and faster as the subjects themselves grew larger
and more complex, until Robert realized that he had trusted
Sarah with secrets about himself, about his parents, about his
home life, that he had never thought

Stage One

thought there was something strange about the rooms at the Dudden Clinic, and now realized what it was: that although they contained wardrobes, and washbasins, and dressers, and desks, and easy-chairs, and all the other appurtenances of residential accommodation, they contained no beds. Of course, this made perfect sense. Punctually at 10.30 p.m., washed and wearing their nightclothes, the thirteen patients would make their way from the day rooms and settle down to sleep under laboratory conditions in the thirteen small, simple bedchambers — each flanked by an adjacent observation room — which took up much of the ground floor. There was no need for beds anywhere else. But it still seemed odd that there should be no bed against the far wall of this room, which he now found that he remembered well as the room Robert had occupied in his last year at the university, and which seemed in every other way to be unchanged. Even the furniture was the same; and it was all in exactly the same position.

It surprised Terry that he should remember Robert's room better than he could remember his face. He tried to recall the last time he had seen him, and had a sudden, badly focused flashback to a grey Saturday morning, during their last summer, with Robert sitting near the edge of the cliff and talking to Sarah, both looking tired and haggard. That was twelve years ago. After that he had disappeared: done a comprehensive and unequivocal vanishing trick which now, in retrospect, struck Terry as being rather impressive. He had thought little of it at the time, being heavily preoccupied that summer with the launch of his own glorious career. Sarah, he seemed to remember, had made sporadic efforts to track him down. Un-successfully, though.

Terry sat at the desk overlooking the sea and flipped open his PowerBook. He didn't know what he was going to write, but the machine's compact solidity, its laminated textures and neat, sexy contours never ceased to arouse and console him. He fetched the power cord from his suitcase and looked around for somewhere to plug it in. The only suitable mains outlet turned out to be just behind the wardrobe; but while there was enough space between the socket and the back of the wardrobe to accommodate a regular three-pin plug, Terry's chunky AC adaptor was not going to fit. The wardrobe would have to be moved. It was made of teak, and very heavy. Terry put his whole weight against one side and shoved it about six inches along the wall, so that the mains socket was now fully exposed; and then he noticed something else. Something had been written on the wall, but the wardrobe had been hiding it. There was some writing, about three feet above the skirting board, and a smudge of some unidentifiable brown substance. There were two words.

'Charming,' said Terry to himself, aloud, and resolved to re-port it to Dr Dudden. It might earn him some credit.

He booted up and skimmed through the files, his finger sweaty and jittery on the trackball. There were more than a thousand documents, in more than thirty folders, but nothing seemed to inspire him on this occasion. Next, he took a slim personal organizer from his jacket pocket, switched it on and began searching through the diary section. He hadn't looked at this since the beginning of the Cinethon, and this time some-thing immediately caught his attention. He reached again into the pocket of his jacket, which was slung over the armchair, fetched out a mobile phone and punched a couple of keys to call up a number from memory. The ringing tone was answered almost immediately.

'Hello, Stuart? It's Terry.'

'Not too bad. No ill-effects so far.

'Listen — why haven't you asked me to write about the new Kingsley film? It's out on Friday.

'Armstrong? What are you, out of your mind? He knows nothing about him. Nothing. He knows nothing about anything.

'Of course I'm not on bloody holiday. I'm sitting down here in Arsehole-on-Sea with nothing to do all day, bored witless. I could be writing your whole fucking paper for you.

'Who's releasing it? Fox? Well, they could send me down a tape, couldn't they?

'Of course I could. When would you need it for?

'That's no problem.

'No, I'll phone them myself. I'll do it now.

'He's had enough breaks. He doesn't need any more breaks. More fucking talent is what he needs, not breaks.

'No, *I'll* phone them. I'll get it all sorted. No problem. Tomorrow afternoon.

'No, there's no need for that.

'It's simple: if you haven't heard from me in half an hour, then they're sending me down a tape, and I'm doing it for you. Give it half an hour, then phone Armstrong, and tell him to fuck off.

'Yep. Simple.

'*Ciao.*'

Galvanized now, Terry snapped the mobile shut and hurried downstairs. What used to be the television room in his student days was now the patients' common room. There was still a television in the corner — a large colour set, with the volume turned down, on which a punkish-looking man in a chef's hat was chopping vegetables and gabbling away silently to the empty room — but this wasn't what Terry had been hoping to find. He clicked his tongue impatiently and went looking for a member of staff.

In one of the observation rooms he found Lorna, the technician. She was sitting down, a clipboard on her lap and a mug of tea between her hands, watching a television screen which was mounted on a shelf above the polysomnographic equipment. She noticed Terry appearing in the doorway, glanced at him, but did not otherwise allow him to deflect her attention. Together, they watched the screen in silence for a few seconds. It showed the blurry, black and white image of a woman wearing a nightgown, asleep in bed, her head festooned with electrodes. The woman remained perfectly still, as did the camera. Once or twice the screen flickered. Terry looked at Lorna, who was watching intently, then contemplated the screen again for another minute or more, while the image remained unchanged.

'Bloody hell,' he said at last. 'I hate these European art movies, don't you?'

Lorna smiled, picked up a remote control unit, and paused the tape.

'You shouldn't be watching this at all,' she said. 'What do you want?'

'Is this the one they're remaking in Hollywood with Ted Danson and Goldie Hawn?'

'Dr Dudden was looking for you,' said Lorna. 'Just a few minutes ago.'

'Yes, I know. I was supposed to be seeing him at eleven. Seriously, though — what were you watching that for? Can't you tell me?'

'Not without breaching confidentiality.' In spite of which she pointed, after a moment's hesitation, at a wad of computer paper on her desk, covered with pen-tracings from the polysomnograph. 'According to that,' she said, 'there was a burst of activity at four thirty-seven this morning. So I thought I'd be able to see something on the tape: catch her moving her legs or something. But I can't find anything.'

'Why's it in black and white? Can't this machine play in colour?' Terry was bending down to inspect the video recorder.

'It can if you want it to.'

'What about sound? Where's the sound?'

'There's a volume control on the side of the monitor.'

'So it's just like a regular video, is it? I mean, it can play regular tapes?'

'I dare say.'

'And is there one of these attached to every bedroom?'

'Yes.'

'Would I be able to use one of them tomorrow morning?'

'Well, we do have a vacancy in Bedroom Three at the moment, because one of the patients has cancelled. So *technically* speaking, that machine won't be in use. But I *very* much doubt whether Dr Dudden —'

'What time does the post get here?' Terry asked.

'About nine-thirty.'

'Brilliant. That's all I need to know.' He switched on the mobile again and was already hitting a number on his way out. 'Thanks,' he said, turning in the doorway. And, with a final glance at the screen: 'Give me a shout when the nude scene starts, will you?'

After he had phoned the relevant publicity department and persuaded them to send down a VHS copy of the film by registered post, Terry found that he was already twenty minutes late for his interview with Dr Dudden: who, upon seeing his apologetic face appear round the door, merely returned to the perusal of a typescript spread out on his desk, and murmured: 'Come in, Mr Worth, come in.'

Once Terry had sat down, he added (still seemingly absorbed in his papers): 'Perhaps my watch is fast, but I make the time to be eleven twenty-three.'

'Yes, you're right. I'm late.'

Dr Dudden looked up at last. 'I see.'

'I must have overslept.'

This remark met with an unwavering stare. Terry crumbled in the face of it, and started back-pedalling furiously. 'You probably get these jokes all the time,' he said, weakly.

'Occasionally,' said Dr Dudden. 'My colleague, Dr Madison, is a great believer in humour as a therapeutic aid. Perhaps we should organize a group discussion on this subject.'

Momentarily numbed into silence, Terry could only nod.

'Now.' Dr Dudden gathered the sheets of his typescript together and stacked them into a neat pile, then picked up a file with Terry's name on it. 'On arrival yesterday you received a complete medical examination from Dr Goldsmith. No irregularities were found: in fact he seems to have concluded that you are in excellent shape.'

'Good.'

'I notice one or two striking features of his report, however. For instance, you claim an average coffee consumption of between thirty to forty cups per day.'

'That's right.'

'Have you drunk any coffee since arriving here?'

'No. There doesn't seem to be any on the premises.'

'We only allow our patients to drink coffee as part of a controlled experiment, to see how it affects their sleep patterns. You went looking for some, then?'

'Yes.'

'And how do you feel, not having drunk any in the last . . . nineteen hours?'

'Uncomfortable.'

'Thirty to forty cups a day seems rather excessive to me. Why do you drink so much?'

'It helps me to stay awake.'

'I see. That,' said Dr Dudden, 'is a singular remark. Most insomniacs in my experience are looking for ways to help them to sleep, not to stay awake. I see from this report that you've been taking no medication for your complaint.'

'That's correct.'

'And that you have never, in fact, sought out a medical opinion at all.'

'No.'

'Most people find insomnia a depressing and in some cases devastating condition. That hasn't been your experience?'

'I often find that I get tired and sleepy during the day. That's why I drink coffee. But it's not a major problem.'

'Has it occurred to you that you may not really be insomniac?'

'I don't understand.'

'One of the most important and fundamental distinctions to be made at this stage in a diagnosis,' said Dr Dudden, 'is between psychophysiological and subjective insomnia.'

'Subjective?'

'Yes.'

'You mean . . . I might be imagining it. Or putting it on. Malingering.'

'That, with all due respect, is an unhelpful word. To imagine that you are going without sleep can be just as distressing as really going without it. And it's by no means uncommon. A great many of my patients come here, spend the night in the lab and claim not to have slept a wink. I'm then able to confound them by presenting them with scientific evidence that they have slept soundly — sometimes for up to six or seven hours.'

'That must give you great satisfaction,' said Terry.

'It always gives me satisfaction to help people,' Dr Dudden answered, drily, as he reached for the telephone. He dialled an extension number. 'Lorna? Could you bring me last night's EEG on Mr Worth, please?' He replaced the receiver abruptly and said to Terry: 'You are under the impression, I take it, that you didn't sleep at all last night. When my assistant supplies us with this data, we should be able to establish the facts of the case. Meanwhile . . .' He reached for Terry's report again. 'I wonder if you can clarify another point for me. From what you said to Dr Goldsmith yesterday, there seems to have been an extraordinary change in your sleeping habits some . . . twelve years ago.'

'In nineteen eighty-four, yes.'

'Prior to which, you claim to have frequently slept for up to fourteen hours a day.'

'Yes.'

'This was when you were a student.'

'Yes.'

'A student . . . at this university, I notice.'

'That's right. Like yourself.'

Something awoke, briefly, in Dr Dudden's eyes: a sudden wariness, which made it clear that he didn't like his patients to spring surprises on him.

'I suppose that's something your researchers dug up,' he said.

'No,' said Terry. 'Dr Madison told me, last night.'

'I see. You've become acquainted with my colleague, then?'

'Superficially.' Terry and Dr Dudden looked at each other, and tried to read each other's smiles. 'I lived in this very house, as a matter of fact. For a few months.'

'So did I,' said Dr Dudden. 'I lived here for two years.'

'That's quite a coincidence. But we never overlapped.'

'I think not. Otherwise . . .'

'Otherwise I'm sure we would have remembered each other.'

'Precisely.'

'I did,' said Terry, 'have a friend called Sarah. Sarah Tudor. And she once went out with someone called Gregory. Gregory: that is your first name, isn't it?'

'Yes, it is.'

'Yes. Dr Madison told me, you see, last . . .'

'. . . last night. Of course. While you were getting superficially acquainted.'

'Yes.'

'Now, just let me think . . .' Dr Dudden sat back in his chair, and rolled his eyes towards the ceiling, rather obviously feigning an attempt at recollection. 'There *was* a girl here called Sarah, now that you mention it. I suppose we did see each other from time to time. It was hardly what you'd call . . . *going out.*'

'Dr Madison thinks she may have been narcoleptic.'

'Dr *Madison* knew her as well?' Now the wariness was turning into something like panic.

'No, of course not. It's just that I mentioned to her, last night, how this girl called Sarah used to have very vivid —'

They were interrupted by a knock on the door, and the arrival of Lorna, with her piles of computer paper. Dr Dudden seemed glad of the diversion.

'Ah, wonderful, wonderful. That's what I like to see. Quiet efficiency. Everything running like clockwork. What a treasure you are, Lorna. Have you met Lorna, Mr Worth? Have you been introduced to our chief technician and polysomnographer?'

'No, I haven't.' Terry rose to his feet and shook her hand. 'Nice to meet you.'

Lorna stared at him in bewilderment. 'But you spoke to me just a few minutes ago. About the video machine.' Seeing that recognition was still slow to dawn, she added: 'I put you to bed last night. I wired you up.'

Terry laughed. 'Yes. Of course.'

Breaking the difficult silence, Dr Dudden took the paper out of Lorna's arms and invited her to leave. When she had gone, he asked Terry whether he was usually so bad at remembering new faces.

'I don't know. I've never really thought about it.'

'You mean you've never really noticed it before?'

'I suppose I don't tend to meet that many new people.'

'I would have thought that in your line of work you were meeting new people all the time.'

'Well, yes, I suppose I am: but then I hardly ever see them again. So the problem doesn't arise.'

'But there is a problem?'

'No, I don't think so.' It was the first time Dr Dudden had seen

Terry looking rattled. 'I'm very tired, you know. I haven't had any coffee for nineteen hours. It's no wonder I don't recognize everybody.'

'You'd rather have coffee than sleep?'

'I've told you already: I don't sleep. I never sleep. I haven't slept for years.'

'Well, let's see about that.' Dr Dudden looked at the note Lorna had left on top of the paper, summarizing her findings, then flicked brusquely but attentively through the sheets themselves. They were covered with jagged lines in different coloured inks, and judging from his occasional grunts, he seemed to be finding them quite surprising. 'There's a long interval here with no recordings at all,' he said at one point.

'Yes. I was getting bored, so I took the equipment off and left the room.'

'Not unassisted, I hope,' said Dr Dudden, but fortunately did not wait for the answer. 'Well —' as he laid down the paper, and scribbled a quick memo to himself '— it would seem, last night at least, that your subjective perception was correct. You didn't sleep at all. No sleep-onset REM, as we might have expected. Not even Stage One. Not even drowsiness, for that matter. Which, given the experience you've recently been through at the cinema, is quite remarkable, I must say.'

'I told you,' said Terry. 'I don't sleep.'

'Everybody sleeps, Mr Worth. I hope you're not going to try to persuade me, now or at any other time, that you have had no sleep at all for the last twelve years.'

'I've had very little,' said Terry. 'Although, as you say, perhaps I've been imagining it. Or dreaming it, or something. Do people dream that they've had no sleep?'

'Certainly. That happens all the time. However, it seems to be unlikely, in your case. Let's just check off some of the things you discussed with Dr Goldsmith. Are you an alcoholic?'

'Not to my knowledge.'

'Your daily alcohol intake is certainly excessive, according to these figures. But I dare say that's not the underlying cause of your difficulties. The caffeine addiction we've already mentioned . . . No allergies, I see . . . You don't suffer any discomfort in your legs at night? Any urge to keep moving them?'

'No.'

'And you don't snore?'

'How would I know?'

'Your sleeping partner might complain.'

'I don't have a sleeping partner.'

'Mm. And what about depression? You wouldn't describe yourself as depressed?'

'Not really. I think that if I was ever depressed, it was before this started: back when I was a student, and all I wanted to do was sleep.'

'Do you have any theories about why you wanted to sleep so much?'

'I suppose I was happier when I was asleep than when I was awake. I used to have very nice dreams.'

'Ah.' Dr Dudden wrote this down. 'That's very interesting. What were these dreams about?'

'I don't know. I could never remember them.'

'Then how did you know they were nice?'

'It was just . . . a sense I had. When I woke up.'

'Mm. And then this stopped, did it? In nineteen eighty-four?'

'Yes.'

'Perhaps you could tell me something about that period in your life.'

'Well . . .' Terry shifted in his seat, as if he found this subject uncomfortable. At the same time, a tiny, nostalgic smirk appeared around his lips. 'When I left university — a few weeks after I left — I got this job, and quite soon afterwards, I precipitated this — well, crisis is the word, I suppose.'

'What sort of crisis?'

'I closed down a magazine. Single-handedly.'

'And how did you manage to do that?'

'It was a film magazine, and they published this article which I was supposed to have checked. Unfortunately, I allowed certain . . . errors to appear in this article, and these errors turned out to be libellous. It attracted seven libel suits.'

'Seven.'

'Yes. I can't remember all the people involved, but there was certainly Denis Thatcher, Norman Wisdom, Vera Lynn . . .'

'I see.'

'. . . Cliff Richard, Kingsley Amis, Edward Heath . . .'

'The author managed to libel all of these people, in the course of one article?'

'Yes, owing to an oversight on my part. Or rather . . .' The smirk became at once wider and more private. 'Well, it was just bad luck, I suppose. Luck, pure and simple. That was the beauty of it.'

When it became clear that he wasn't going to elaborate on this, Dr Dudden said: 'And you then found yourself out of a job, presumably.'

'That was when I started working freelance. I'd been going to write a book. It was going to be about a director — quite an obscure director, someone not much written about — and about . . . other things, as well. Theoretical things. About loss, in a way. The idea of loss.'

'But you never finished it?'

'I never started it. I was having to do so much work, just to support myself . . . I was working till midnight, most nights, and then I was starting to find — oddly — that I wasn't all that tired at the end of it. So instead of going to bed, I'd stay up all night. Watching videos. And that was really how it began.'

'Would you agree, then,' said Dr Dudden, 'that you were using these videos as a substitute for the dreams which had once —'

As he spoke, a small alarm clock on his desk began to bleep. He put down his pencil and closed Terry's file with a brief sigh of frustration.

'That's it, I'm afraid,' he said.

'What?'

'Time's up. It's eleven forty-two, and I have another appointment to keep at a quarter to twelve.'

'But that was just getting interesting.'

'We run a tight ship here, Mr Worth. If you had not been twenty-three minutes late, we could have made a good deal more progress. Now it will have to wait until tomorrow.'

'Surely we've got another three minutes, at least.'

'No. During the first interview, that time is set aside for me to ask you certain practical questions. For instance . . .' He paused, and a blankness crossed his face. After sitting there for a second or two, vacant-eyed, he fumbled inside one of his desk drawers and eventually produced a sheet of paper with some typed questions on it. 'Ah, yes. Funny how I can never seem to remember these.' He proceeded to read out the first question. ' "How are you settling in at the clinic?" '

'Very well, thank you,' said Terry; regarding him now with some astonishment.

' "Have the staff been courteous and helpful?" '

'Perfectly,' said Terry; deciding not to voice the thought that Dr Dudden himself had so far proved neither.

' "Is your day room clean and comfortable?" '

Only now did Terry hesitate. 'Comfortable, yes,' he said. He allowed himself a moment to enjoy Dr Dudden's look of incipient horror; and then he told him about the writing on the wall.

'Psst!' said a voice.

Dr Madison paused in the corridor and looked around. It was not obvious where the noise was coming from.

'Psst!' it said again. A finger emerged from one of the doorways, beckoned her, then disappeared. Dr Madison followed it into Day Room Nine, where she found Dr Dudden waiting for her, his face pale with fury (not an uncommon sight), his posture betraying every sign of shamed agitation.

'Come here,' he hissed.

She joined him by the wardrobe.

'Look at that,' he said. 'Just look at it.'

He pointed at the words 'STUPID FUCK', which had been scrawled on the wall in ink. Next to them was a large brown stain.

'Mr Worth discovered that,' he went on. 'A bloody *journalist* discovered that, God damn it. Isn't that typical? Isn't that just typical of our luck?'

'Why had no one noticed it before?'

'It was hidden behind the wardrobe.'

'And what was Mr Worth doing moving the wardrobe?'

Dr Dudden ignored this question. He said: 'I realize you won't want to hear it, doctor, but this exactly proves my point. This is precisely why we have to be careful what . . . sort of person we allow in here. This is the sort of thing that happens when you open your doors to riff-raff.'

'Are you by any chance referring,' said Dr Madison, 'to the NHS patients?'

'I don't think I need to spell it out,' said Dr Dudden. 'That woman in your group, for instance. The Brixton woman. I don't mean to be snobbish, but . . . what can you expect from someone like that? No class, no character . . .'

'This is not Maria Granger's room.'

'I don't mean her specifically: it's the general principle.' He peered closer at the stain on the wall, and wrinkled his nose. 'What kind of person,' he said, 'what kind of *scum* would smear the walls of a room with their own excrement?'

'A disturbed person, presumably. The sort of person we're supposed to be here to help.' She gave the stain a cursory glance, then stepped back. 'Anyway, I think it's probably blood.'

'I'm going to find Mr Worth,' he said. 'On no account must he mention this in his article. *Somehow* we've got to keep him quiet.'

'I'm sure Mr Worth doesn't have the slightest intention —'

'Have a word with the cleaning staff: immediately. Get them to wipe it off.'

When he had gone, Dr Madison remained for a few minutes in Day Room Nine, staring at the words on the wall, and at the stain: and whether it was rage at her colleague's insensitivity, or compassion for whatever wretched creature had felt some inarticulate need to desecrate the room in this way, her eyes were soon cloudy with tears, and she found herself rubbing at the wall with her sleeve in a spasm of sudden, violent irritation: a kind of frenzy.

A few weeks ago, Terry wrote, *I found myself overhearing one of those recurrent dinner-party conversations about who is the 'greatest' film director at work today. The two participants were both critics: one of them, a member of the old school, argued for the veteran Portuguese director Manoel de Oliveira, while the other, who seemed to think of himself as some sort of Young Turk, carried the inevitable banner for Quentin Tarantino.*

It was like . . . well, what was it like? It was like watching two teams of blind men trying to play football on a derelict pitch, when no one had had the decency to tell them that the goalposts had been taken down years ago.

It was the Taranteeny I felt really sorry for. At least his opponent's position had some sort of antiquated coherence. But as for the Turk (perhaps, remembering the Young Fogeys, we should coin a neologism for this specimen: the Old Turk), he didn't seem to realize the sheer crappiness of his argument — which was that by 'revitalizing' B-movie clichés, Tarantino was actually achieving some sort of (and yes, he really did use this word) 'originality'. I think, God help him, he may even have mentioned postmodernism at some particularly desperate moment.

Reader, I couldn't find it in me to put either of these saddies out of their misery. Silent sympathy seemed to be the only appropriate response to the spectacle of two exhausted Don Quixotes still chasing after the spectre of originality in modern cinema. My one piece of advice to them, if they should happen to be reading, would be that they check out Joe Kingsley's Chalk and Cheese 4 *(PG) as soon as possible, and learn what they can from it.*

Terry performed a quick word-count on his computer, and found that he had already used up almost a third of his review space. Not that it really mattered: he always enjoyed laying out his theoretical wares in this way. Still, it was probably a good thing that he had brought himself round to the film at last.

Kingsley, it goes without saying, is the master of cliché. He makes Tarantino look like a bungling amateur in this area, because he has never fallen for the neo-humanist fiction that old conventions can be given a new twist. And the Chalk and Cheese *series is cliché itself — mismatched cops assigned to the same case — stripped down to its purest and most satisfying essentials. Number 3, directed by ex-pat Englishman Kevin Wilmut, made the fundamental mistake of trying to freshen things up with a romantic undercurrent and a political sub-plot: the dead hand of Wilmut's literary, B B C background was all over it. Clearly, though, someone at Fox has come to his senses and put Kingsley back at the helm of the series which kick-started his career and which he has since made brilliantly, paradoxically, his own.*

Four hundred and eighteen words. What next, he wondered. Summarize the plot? (But of course there was no plot.) Discuss the performances? (But the actors in this film didn't perform, they went through motions.) Mention the dialogue? (But the dialogue was exactly the same as in the earlier films.) In truth, the film itself had barely skimmed the surface of Terry's consciousness. As soon as it had arrived in the morning post, he had taken the Jiffy bag up to the Observation Room attached to Bedroom Three, where Lorna had shown him how to get the video working. The tape supposedly lasted for ninety-seven minutes, but it had not taken him that long to watch it. He sat in total absorption through the opening credits, enjoyed the first scene (a protracted gunfight which brought several of the other patients crowding into the room to find out what all the noise was about), then fast-forwarded through the first expository scene and any other subsequent dialogue scenes which lasted for more than thirty seconds; congratulating himself, into the bargain, on watching the film in just the way that its makers — with their eyes fixed firmly on the video market — would have intended.

It would be stretching a point, Terry now wrote, shifting his chair back into the shade of the building (for the sun, reflected by the glittering ocean, was starting to blank out the screen of his PowerBook), *to claim that* Chalk and Cheese 4 *is flawless. Kingsley's detractors — whose uncomprehending criticisms mean, I trust, less than nothing to him — like to claim that his films resemble ninety-minute pop videos. This is in fact a sublime compliment to which he hasn't (yet) quite earned the right. There's the occasional falling-off, here, a sporadic tendency to flag: timing some of the shots at random, I was surprised to find that many of them were more than six seconds long. But fifteen minutes after finishing the movie, this critic isn't complaining: I'm still high on its irreverence, its joyous contempt for the audience, its contagious hatred for political or any other kinds of correctness, its hooligan energy. An energy which, incidentally (to go back to our dinner-party duellists) is the only kind available to the film-maker nowadays. This is the crazed, manic energy of the bull at the end of the fight, fatally wounded but ploughing ahead, driven only by pain and anger and the mindless will to go on living. This is the condition — terminal but frantic, 'gasping but somehow still alive' — of the American cinema in these dying days of the twentieth century. And Kingsley is its master.*

A shadow crossed the computer screen, causing Terry to look up. Dr Dudden, having emerged silently on to the terrace, was waiting to address him.

'A brief word, Mr Worth. The briefest of words. Far be it from me to interrupt your labours.'

'That's all right,' said Terry, squinting into the sunlight.

'Dare I hope — dare *we* hope, dare all of us hope — that this is an early draft — the first tentative steps towards your article?'

'My article?'

'About the work that we do here.'

'Oh.' Terry hadn't given this a moment's thought. He wasn't even sure, at this point, that the clinic was interesting enough to merit a piece for the Features page. 'No, I'm still thinking about that one.'

'Ah. Still in the planning stage.' Dr Dudden forced a smile, which mingled practised insincerity with a desperate need to ingratiate. 'When you do come to write it — and far be it from *me*, of course, to dictate, or even to attempt *any* sort of influence or . . . input, in any way — but when you do come to write it, I do hope that the small . . . irregularity in your day room won't mitigate, or in any way —'

'Irregularity?' said Terry.

'I'm referring, of course, to the unfortunate — erm — *graffito* to which you so kindly, so thoughtfully —'

'Oh, that.' Terry smiled blandly. 'Well, you know, I can only record what I see: take things as they come, so to speak . . .'

'Hmm.' Dr Dudden's answering smile was weak, uncertain. 'I can take it that we understand each other, then.' When this was neither confirmed nor denied by Terry, he turned, wavered, paused, turned back again, hesitated and finally managed to say: 'We have some good news, by the way.'

'Oh?'

'A small breakthrough last night, according to your E E G.'

'In what way?'

'You entered Stage One sleep. For twelve minutes: at about three o'clock in the morning.'

'And this is the first time it's happened?'

'While you've been under my observation, yes. As I say: a small breakthrough. Naturally, I can't take any credit for it. I've done nothing to treat you, as yet.' He waited (in vain) for Terry to manifest some enthusiasm, then added: 'Anyway, I assumed you'd want to know about it.'

When Dr Dudden had disappeared back inside the house, Terry read through the last few lines of his review and suddenly wanted nothing more than to finish the thing off as quickly as possible. For some reason, this talk of a breakthrough disturbed him, and he found it hard to concentrate, hard to regain the level of engagement which had powered him through that final paragraph. In a fit of impatience and boredom, he decided to do something lazy — to end with an obvious cliché, and assume that readers would take it as a self-referential joke in keeping with the argument of the review as a whole.

I can't recommend this film highly enough, he wrote. *It's a laugh, it's a riot, it's a refreshing blast of stale air. In short: fun for all the family.*

Next, he inserted a page break and typed out his invoice.

TO: Writing review of *Chalk and Cheese 4*
654 words @ £ 1 per word = £654.00
Plus V A T @ 17.5% = £114.45
Total = £768.45.

Halfway through making this calculation, Terry was distracted by the noise of a window opening high up in the house. He turned, craned his neck and found that the window in question was one he recognized. It belonged, in fact, to a room which he was intending to explore again, as soon as the opportunity presented itself: the room he had once lived in, up on the third floor, a long, low garret which (he now remembered) gave access directly on to the roof. Someone had pushed the window open, but he couldn't see who it was. Then, a moment later, something flew — or was thrown — out of the window itself. At first Terry thought it was a seagull, then a racing pigeon: a blur and a flutter of white against the sky's perfect, midday blue. But if it was a bird, it had forgotten how to fly, for after riding the currents of air for a few seconds it began swooping down to earth in slow, decreasing spirals. As it came closer, Terry recognized it as a large paper dart, which now hovered briefly above his head, took a sudden turn and shot out towards the sea, then described a perfect curve of 180 degrees, came straight towards him at chest level, then dipped, lost momentum, and finally, using his computer keyboard as a landing strip, came to graceful rest on his lap.

Terry heard the window being pushed shut again. He stood up with the dart in his hand, shielded his eyes and looked to see if any figure could be made out behind the distant, reflecting glass. But it was too late.

Then he smoothed open the paper and read the scrawled message: ASK HIM ABOUT STEPHEN WEBB.

5

Robert's long, nocturnal conversation with Sarah had a profound effect. Treasuring the memory of her kindness as she had listened to him, the soft burr of her voice as she had offered her own confidences, he quickly sank into a romantic coma from which there seemed to be no awakening. He loitered in the kitchen, waiting for her to appear; lurked in the corridor outside her bedroom; haunted the television room in the evenings; went for superfluous walks along the cliff path at the hour when he guessed her lectures would be over, rehearsing phrases of surprised greeting. He bought presents for her and threw them away almost at once, finding them unsuitable, inadequate; he combed his hair hourly and shaved twice a day (including his legs, although this was not for her benefit). But for most of the day he merely sat in his room, while his work lay neglected, and stared sightlessly at the walls, his mind acting as a private cinema screen upon which ever more tantalizing scenes would be projected: scenes in which he would be stroking her hair, reaching out for the first tentative clasp of her hand, brushing his lips against the immaculate curve of her ear, kissing the fine down on her neck. For days he sat in his room and dreamed like this. For days he convinced himself that the next time they met, their love for each other would reveal itself abruptly, spontaneously, in some sweet and irresistible outpouring.

But there was one problem. Sarah seemed to have disappeared. Nobody in the house could remember seeing her lately, and her bed, according to Mrs Sharp, the caretaker's wife, had not been slept in all week.

When more than eight days had passed in this manner, Robert found that he could stand it no longer: he would have to leave the house and look for her on campus. An hour and a half's exhausted trawling of the Library, the Arts Centre and the Union building yielded nothing, however, and finally he took a bus into town and made for the only other place where a student might conceivably be found on a wet Saturday morning: the Café Valladon. Here he discovered no customers at all apart from his old friend Terry, sitting in the corner with a chaotic spread of essay notes laid out on the table in front of him.

First-time visitors to the Café tended to expect something quintessentially Gallic and sophisticated, all *café noir* and *pain au chocolat*. Instead they found heavy pine tables and benches, old milk bottles thick with candle wax, and walls covered with antique nautical instruments and row upon row of hardback and paperback books purchased from jumble sales. They found almost inedibly chunky oatmeal cakes, slices of granary bread with cheddar cheese and honeyglazed ham, and huge mugs of black coffee and sweet aromatic tea. They found a perpetually dim, cavernous interior, with Slattery sitting behind the counter and never rising to his feet to serve the next customer until he had finished the latest sentence of whichever philosophical volume he was then immersed in. And they usually found, it has to be said, something more vibrant in the way of social and intellectual life than this thin, pasty, earnest-looking film student, who glanced up when Robert entered and signalled his greeting by pushing out his three-quarters-empty mug, grunting, 'Same again, will you?' and returning to the contemplation of his papers.

Robert had not seen much of Terry this term, and noticed, when he came back to his table with the refilled mug, that he looked if anything even more unhealthy and bloodless than usual. His eyes were puffy, and as he scribbled away manically on his notepaper he would have to pause every twenty or thirty seconds in order to let out an enormous yawn which would momentarily suspend the operation of all his other faculties. Terry — as Robert had come to know during their two years' friendship — abhorred sunlight and could only really be happy in one of three locations: the inside of a cinema, the Café Valladon itself (where the habitual gloom suited him down to the ground) and, best of all, within the darkened interior of his own bedroom, which is where he would, by choice, spend most of the day: for it was Terry's claim, during this period of his life, that he needed an absolute minimum of fourteen hours' sleep, without which he was good for nothing. Not that he found sleep in any way a relaxing experience, or even that rest was his primary object whenever he sought it out. The business of sleeping was, in his case, tantamount to setting out on a nightly quest, and it was this, presumably, that accounted for the hungry and careworn look which haunted his endlessly tired eyes. For Terry was plagued by dreams: dreams, he insisted, of near-paradisal loveliness; dreams of sun-dappled gardens, heavenly vistas, ambrosial picnics and perfect sexual encounters which somehow combined physical ecstasy with prelapsarian innocence. Dreams which took on the quality of the most pristine and idealized childhood memories, which were beyond the inventive powers of the most fertile, accomplished and assiduous fantasist. Every night he was visited by these dreams. Every night they seduced and tormented him: this much, at least, he knew. But at the same time he was never able to supply any specific details, because it was their peculiar characteristic, every morning, to slip from the reach of his grasping memory in the few fatal seconds it took him to regain consciousness. Terry was addicted to his dreams: they constituted the purest, most vital, most precious part of his life, and for this reason he spent at least fourteen hours a day pursuing them through his sleeping mind. But it maddened him that he was able to remember only the most teasing fragments, so that he could never describe them to anybody else, or take comfort from their memory when he was awake. Every so often, it was true, tiny shreds and scraps of a dream would suddenly bob to the surface, and he would write them down as quickly as possible, on anything that came to hand: so that it was not uncommon for his lecture notes on (for instance) constructions of femininity in *film noir* to be punctuated by cryptic phrases such as 'the smell of roses; the warm breath of a lion', or 'a valley; a woman; thistledown', or 'naked, between the branches of a pear tree'. But this was small recompense; not nearly enough, he felt, to compensate for the terrible knowledge that he was being offered nightly visions of a better world which was fated to dangle forever out of reach.

'You look dreadful,' said Robert as he sat down.

'I feel it. You look pretty dreadful yourself, if it comes to that. What are you doing here, anyway?'

'Looking for someone. And you?'

'Waiting for Lynne.'

Lynne was Terry's latest girlfriend. He had a habit of drifting in and out of relationships, none of them lasting more than a month or two: women who initially found him interesting were soon, it seemed, put off by his eccentric sleeping habits and his single-minded obsession with cinema. (On a bad day he was quite incapable of conversing on any other subject.) Terry himself rarely noticed when any of these relationships had gone into decline, and always professed himself surprised and baffled when finally confronted by the irrefutable evidence that they had been terminated: the sudden disappearance from his wardrobe, say, of all his girlfriend's clothes, or his dawning realization, emerging into the mid-afternoon sunshine from the blackness of some screening room in the university's Film Department, that it was more than a week since he had last seen the woman who was supposed to be sharing a room with him. Whether something like this was about to happen with Lynne, Robert had no idea. He merely asked a non-committal question:

'How is she?'

'Fine,' said Terry, taking a cautious sip of his scalding hot chocolate. (He never drank coffee, because it kept him awake.) Then he scowled. 'We're meant to be going for a drive this afternoon. A day out, sort of thing.'

'Sounds nice.'

Terry shook his head. 'Waste of time. There's a Douglas Sirk film on BBC 2, as well.' He looked up at Robert hopefully. 'You wouldn't like to come with us, would you? There's plenty of room for three. It might liven things up.'

Robert had been on excursions with Terry and his girlfriends before. The prospect of listening to several hours' worth of mutual sniping held little appeal.

'No, thanks,' he said. 'You know how it is, when you're with a couple . . . I'd only be in the way.'

'No, but it's different with me and Lynne,' Terry insisted. 'We're getting on really well together at the moment. No arguing, just lots of . . . companionable silences. You wouldn't feel uncomfortable at all.' He stood up and searched through his pockets. 'I wouldn't mind something to eat. You haven't got any money, have you?'

Their collective resources came to little more than three pounds, as it turned out, and Terry thought that he would need most of that for petrol. However, with a conspiratorial look around the Café, he said, 'Don't panic,' and from a bookshelf above the adjacent table he fetched an old hardback copy of *Great Expectations*. Opening it carefully, he said, 'Look at that — page two hundred and twenty.' Inside was a ten pound note.

Robert was impressed. 'When did you put it there?'

'About six months ago,' said Terry. 'When I was a little more flush. I had a hunch it might come in handy: go and get a couple of sandwiches, will you?'

Shortly afterwards Lynne arrived, while Terry was downstairs in the toilet.

'He asked me to come with you today,' Robert told her, 'but I don't think I will. I don't like to intrude.'

'Oh, *please* come,' she insisted. 'Honestly, we could do with having someone else around: we're getting on so badly at the moment. We don't seem to have anything to say to each other.'

'Where are you going, anyway?'

'Just up the coast. I know it's a bit damp now, but the forecast said it was going to be bright and sunny later.'

After they had been driving through wet mist for some two hours, the rain turned torrential at about three o'clock; and that was when Terry discovered that his windscreen wipers didn't work. They pulled off the road and stopped in a layby. Lynne offered round a packet of Polos which was all that they had in the way of provisions.

'This is great,' said Terry. 'This is so much better than sitting in my room watching *Written on the Wind*.'

Robert wiped away the condensation from his back window and peered out at a bleak stretch of coastline, murkily visible through the thick rain. He said: 'I think I've seen that, anyway. Over-the-top melodrama with Rock Hudson as an oil tycoon. Sort of tacky 'fifties version of *Dallas*.'

'Well, yes, that is how someone like *you* would describe it,' said Terry dismissively.

'And what does that mean, exactly?'

'The true *cinéaste*,' said Terry, 'knows that Sirk is one of the most important directors ever to have worked in Hollywood. Even a basic psychoanalytic reading of his films makes it clear that he had a profound understanding of the sexual neuroses underpinning the American dream.'

'Blimey,' said Robert, turning back to the window.

'Does it never occur to you,' said Lynne, addressing but not looking at her boyfriend, 'that you're looking for something in these films that isn't really there?' There was a bitter, jaded edge to her voice.

'I'm not saying that his films are perfect,' said Terry. He thought about this statement, and began to elaborate, in his best trainee-lecturer style: 'It's possible to conceive of a perfect film, of course. That's not to say that it would be pleasant or uplifting. It might be the most depressing film ever made. The important thing is that its vision would be consistent, and flawless. I'm convinced that such a film exists. What I'm doing at the moment is acquiring the skills with which to search for it.'

'Like trying to remember the perfect dream,' Robert prompted.

'Oh, don't get him started on his dreams, for God's sake,' said Lynne. 'I've had it up to here with his dreams. You'd think he was the only person who ever had dreams at all.'

'I hardly ever dream, these days,' said Robert.

'I do, all the time.'

'What about?'

'Well, for one thing, I dream of having a ten-minute conversation with Terry where he doesn't mention Ingmar Bergman. But that's just my little fantasy.' She pondered. 'Oh, I don't know . . . silly, trivial dreams . . . A couple of nights ago, for instance, I dreamed I was lying in a hospital bed next to Winston Churchill. He was eating a bowl of peas and every so often kept flicking one at me. Then the hospital turned into my grandmother's bungalow and all these firemen appeared, singing the theme song from *Hello, Dolly*.' She could see that Terry was not impressed. 'Don't look at me like that. We can't all have the most profound dreams in the world.'

'I'm not saying anything.'

'Well, why don't you go out and try to get those wipers working, anyway? Do something useful for a change.'

Muttering angrily, and pulling his jacket tightly around himself as if this might somehow ward off the rain and the cold, Terry climbed out of the car and spent several ineffectual minutes pulling and prodding at the windscreen wipers in a half-hearted fashion. Car maintenance was not one of his strong points.

'I had a dream about a hospital once,' Robert said, in the meantime. 'In fact it's about the only dream I can remember. I must have been about nine or ten . . . I'm in this very arid landscape, very hilly and dusty. And there's this woman, a middle-aged woman, in a nurse's uniform, and she's standing by the side of the road, pointing: pointing off into the distance. There's a big building somewhere ahead of us on the road — that's what she's pointing at. I can see it faintly, and I know it's a hospital. Some sort of military hospital, actually. And just behind her there's a notice. She's standing in front of it so I can't read it all.'

'Do you know what it says?' Lynne asked.

'No. There's just one word, but I can't see what it is. That's the maddening thing. All I know is that it's in a foreign language.'

'Does anything else happen in the dream?'

'No. That's it.'

Lynne pondered these details. 'Is the nurse telling you to go to the hospital, do you think?'

'I don't know. I suppose so.'

'Well, I think you should have that dream analysed. If you can still remember it after all these years, it must be trying to tell you something.'

Terry opened the door and flopped wetly into the driver's seat.

'Well, that was a waste of time,' he said; after which they all fell silent, listening to the intermittent drone of passing traffic, the hiss of tyres against wet asphalt. Robert thought it was the most depressing sound in the world: it reminded him of family holidays in Devon, his mother and father bickering in the front seats, drinking flasks of coffee in a fogged-up car in some seafront car park, the weather dismal even in July. In the evening they would eat at a cheap local restaurant, his father would get drunk on wine and spirits and his mother would have to drive them all back to the cottage or boarding house. He had a sudden, vivid recollection of his father urinating against the wall of some bed and breakfast place late one evening, the landlady thrusting open a sash window on the second floor and shouting down at him. 'I'll call the police!' she had threatened finally, but his father merely guffawed. 'I am the police!' he had called back; and the next morning they were leaving anyway.

Terry tried switching on the radio, but the only things he could find were some opera and a football commentary. Soon he switched off and yawned; then turned to Robert, asking: 'Who did you say you were looking for in the Café this morning?'

'I didn't. It was someone from the house.'

'Oh.' Something about the way he said it must have aroused Terry's interest. 'Male or female?'

'Female. No one's seen her for about a week. I'm a bit worried about her.'

Lynne had been gazing out of the window, rigid with boredom, taking no part in this conversation. But now she roused herself and said: 'Her name wouldn't be Sarah, by any chance, would it? Sarah Tudor?'

Robert sat up sharply in the back seat. 'How did you know that?'

She smiled with satisfaction. 'Just a hunch.'

'You don't know her, do you?' Robert asked.

'Oh yes, I know her all right. She lived just down the corridor from me in my first year. We all got to know Sarah.'

Robert wasn't sure exactly what she meant by this, but he didn't like the sound of it.

Terry asked: 'What does she look like?'

'Quite small,' said Lynne. 'Quite skinny. Pale blue eyes. Always wears a denim jacket. Blonde hair, medium length, quite short: a bit like straw.'

'It's nothing like straw,' Robert protested.

'It's exactly like straw: that's why they call her Worzel.'

'Who calls her Worzel?'

'Everybody does: after Worzel Gummidge, the scarecrow. Of course,' she added, 'that's only one of her nicknames.'

Already dreading the answer, but unable to stop himself, Robert asked: 'What are the others?'

'Well, some people call her Sarah Spew, after a famous incident where she went to a restaurant and threw up all over the other guests. Some people call her Gregory's Girl, because she used to go out with this obnoxious guy called Gregory. And some people call her Rip van Winkle, because she has this charming habit of falling asleep when you're talking to her, if she doesn't find you particularly interesting.'

Robert frowned. 'That might not be her fault,' he said. 'There is this condition, I think —'

'But *most* people,' said Lynne, who hadn't yet finished with the litany of nicknames, 'most people just call her Mad Sarah.'

His heart sank even further. 'Why's that, then?' he asked, unnecessarily.

'Because she's completely mad. She comes up to people and claims to have had conversations with them, and done things with them, and all the time she's just inventing it all. She's completely barking.'

This had gone far enough, Robert decided. 'I don't believe that, actually.'

'It's true,' said Lynne. 'That's why I thought it might be Sarah you were looking for: because I saw her just a couple of days ago, and she was talking about you. She was saying all sorts of things, and I bet she was making half of them up.'

In spite of himself, he was excited to hear that Sarah had not forgotten him in the last week, that she even considered him interesting enough to discuss with her friends. 'Why, what did she say?'

'Well, she said that your cat had died recently and you were really upset about it.'

'Yes, that's right.'

'And then that you sat up half the night with her on the terrace in the freezing cold, talking about the meaning of life.'

'We did, as a matter of fact.'

'*And* she's been going round telling everyone that you've got a twin sister.'

There was an expectant silence. Terry turned and looked at him, facetious, challenging. 'Well?'

'Well what?'

'You're not going to try and tell us that *that's* true, are you?'

Robert returned his stare. He was conscious, too, of Lynne's eyes upon him. 'As a matter of fact it is,' he said.

Terry was briefly — very briefly — dumbstruck. He looked from Robert to Lynne, from Lynne to Robert, trying to decide if this was part of some elaborate joke. 'I've been to your house,' he said. 'I've met your family. You don't have any brothers or sisters.'

'What else did she say about her?' Robert asked, ignoring Terry for the time being.

Lynne said: 'Well, according to Sarah, you had a twin sister called Cleo, but your parents couldn't afford to bring up both of you, so they gave her away for adoption when you were just a few days old and you've never seen her since.'

Robert said nothing, although his expression suggested that he was occupied with some reluctant, intensely private train of thought. Terry registered this and was determined to prise the truth out of him.

'Well — is she lying? Is she making it up?'

'Of course not. How could anyone invent something like that?'

'You've got a twin sister called Cleo, and you've never told me about it?'

'Why should I? It's not as if I've ever met her.'

'You've known me for two years — we've been friends for *two years* — and you've never told me that you had a twin sister. And yet you meet some weird woman, and you get talking, and five minutes later you've poured out the whole story to her?'

'She's not a weird woman. There's nothing weird about her.'

Lynne snorted at this, and said: 'Anyway, Terry, you *do* know Sarah Tudor. *She's* the one who's started that . . . you know, started that — thing, with Ronnie.'

And Robert would later remember the moment he first heard this name: how an immediate premonition had visited him: the awareness, at once, that he was in freefall, plummeting towards a limitless chasm. He knew for certain that all the hopes he had been building up over the last week — he had thought them so vague and insubstantial, but suddenly recognized them, now, as concrete monstrosities — would come to nothing. Panic engulfed him.

'Oh, you mean it's *her*?' Terry was saying. '*That's* who we're talking about? Of course I've met her. She was sitting at our table the other day when Ronnie and I were having an argument.'

'Quite small . . .' Lynne prompted.

'Quite thin, pale blue eyes, denim jacket, blonde hair a bit like straw. And *completely* off her trolley.'

'That's right,' said Lynne. 'You noticed that as well, did you?'

'Mad as a hatter, we all thought. Ronnie had been coming out with all the usual stuff about men being rapists and wife-beaters, and then this girl — who none of us had been talking to, or anything — suddenly broke into the conversation and said she agreed. Then she got up and left, practically knocking the table over in the process.'

'I'm in love with her,' said Robert.

Terry and Lynne turned in their seats, as one, and regarded him mutely. Neither of them queried his statement, but making it had given Robert such quick, unexpected pleasure, such a sense of release, that he decided to repeat it anyway.

'I'm in love with her,' he said. 'I think she's wonderful. I think she's the most lovely and beautiful person I've ever met.'

Terry was stunned into silence: he had never heard Robert say anything like this before. Lynne just shook her head disbelievingly and looked out through the windscreen again. 'Well, *that's* a novel point of view,' she conceded.

'When you say that she's been with this man called Ronnie,' Robert continued flatly, 'I assume you mean that they're having an affair?'

'I didn't say that she'd been with a man called Ronnie. That's not what I said.'

For a fatuous instant Robert clutched at these words, thinking that perhaps he'd heard wrongly the first time, that perhaps everything was still going to be all right.

'I thought —'

'You really have picked a good one here, Robert. You've really excelled yourself.' Then Lynne explained, patiently and not unkindly: 'She's having an affair, but not with a man. Ronnie is female. It's short for Veronica.'

The chasm opened again: twice as wide, and blacker than he would have thought possible.

'But you told me that she'd been going out with a guy called Gregory,' he said, tumbling.

'Well, now she's going out with a girl called Veronica.'

It was Terry, at last, who took it upon himself to spell the thing out: 'She's a dyke, Bob.'

Robert looked to Lynne for confirmation; as if hoping, even now, that this was some cruel male fantasy his friend was spinning for him. But Lynne simply nodded. 'As of Monday,' she said.

The rain had almost stopped, by now. Terry turned on the ignition. 'And I still cannot *believe*,' he added, 'that we've been friends for two years, and you've never told me about your twin sister.'

He checked his mirror and flicked on the indicator, easing the car out into the road in the direction of the breaking clouds, the pale faltering sunshine.

The day after her long conversation with Robert, on a warm but blustery Friday afternoon, Sarah had wandered into the Café Valladon and noticed Veronica sitting with three other women; had halted in the doorway, uncertain how to proceed; had seen Veronica detach herself from the group and approach her, a smile of recognition and welcome lighting up her face; had felt the touch of a hand on her forearm, and found herself guided towards a separate table, where it appeared they were to have a tête-à-tête. She had taken the books out of her canvas rucksack and explained that she had not managed to look at them all; Veronica had apologized for dumping them on her in that way, with the implication that her reading in certain areas was somehow deficient; it had been a crass thing to do, little more than a ploy, really, to make sure of seeing her again. Veronica had gone behind the counter and fetched some coffee (Slattery being in the thick of one of those protracted and mysterious absences which seemed to interfere so little with the smooth running of the Café). And then they had begun to talk.

Sarah had called on Veronica again the next day. They went for a meal together, and then went to see a late film in town, and Sarah missed the last bus home: she woke up, the next morning, in a sleeping-bag on the floor of Veronica's room on campus. The morning after that, she woke up in her bed.

It was a click that woke her: somebody switching on a portable cassette player. She snoozed through the first few minutes of the tape, then surfaced and began to take note of her surroundings during a Billie Holiday song:

I've got those Monday blues
Straight through Sunday blues

'Well — have you?' Veronica asked, sitting on the edge of the bed.

'Have I what?'

'Got those Monday blues.'

'Is it Monday?' Sarah sat up anxiously and looked at the bedside clock. It was ten-fifteen. 'Oh, fuck — I had a nine-thirty lecture.'

'You've got sleep in your eyes.' Veronica tried to touch it with her forefinger, but Sarah flinched and sank back under the duvet. 'I bet you'd like some coffee.'

'Mm, I would, quite.'

'So would I,' said Veronica, 'but unfortunately we drank it all yesterday.' She stood up and stretched, her body strong and wiry beneath a T-shirt so long that it reached below her knee. 'I think we should have something in Jonah's, anyway. Coffee, breakfast, the full works. What do you say?'

Breakfast was not served after ten-thirty, so they dressed quickly, arrived just in time and were rewarded with bacon, mushrooms and large portions of solidifying scrambled egg. Veronica dispatched her portion hungrily, then started dipping her fork into the rubbery hillock of egg which Sarah — sitting stiffly opposite her, and looking somehow distracted — had left untouched. Neither of them spoke much: at least, not until they were joined for a few minutes by a History student called Lynne, and even then it was Veronica who did all the talking. Sarah sat playing with her sachet of sugar, tipping all the sugar to the bottom half and then folding it in two, then inverting it and repeating the process, until the sachet itself came apart and sugar spilled out all over the remains of her breakfast.

'I could see that was going to happen,' said Veronica. Lynne had left by now.

'I'm sorry.' Sarah laughed. 'It's a bad habit of mine.' She ran a hand through her hair, taking hold of a clump and tugging at it lightly. Another habit: a gesture Robert had already been captivated by. And now Veronica, too, noticed it for the first time.

'What d'you want to do today?' she asked.

'I don't know,' said Sarah. Her voice was toneless. 'I'm feeling a little bit strange, to be honest.'

'I'd noticed.'

'It's just that . . . what it is . . .' Sarah looked across at the table next to them. Although the restaurant was almost empty, three young male students had chosen to seat themselves there, and were starting up a fitful and desultory conversation. 'This is really embarrassing, but . . . you know what I was telling you yesterday, about my dreams?' (Could she really have told Veronica this already, after knowing her only a couple of days?) 'About how vivid they are, sometimes?'

Veronica nodded.

'Well, I had one about *you* last night.'

'About me?'

'About us.' She glanced across at the three students. They were munching Kit-Kats wordlessly. 'We were . . .'

'Yes?' said Veronica.

'. . . in bed together.'

Veronica shrugged. 'Sounds fairly harmless. Is that the only reason you're looking so tortured?'

'You know how it is,' said Sarah, 'after you've dreamed about someone. The next day, you don't see them the same way.'

'That's true,' said Veronica. 'Especially if it's an erotic dream, I find.'

'Well, exactly,' said Sarah, almost in a whisper.

'What do you mean, "exactly"?'

'I mean . . . "exactly".'

'This was an erotic dream: is that what you're telling me?'

Sarah nodded; and then she said (her voice lower than a whisper now): 'I wish those creeps would go away.'

'What makes you think it was a dream?' asked Veronica.

'I'm sure they're listening.'

'Well, *you're* obviously not.'

Sarah looked at her, her eyes widening. Veronica's question had finally broken in upon her, and its implications became suddenly, shockingly clear even as she heard it repeated.

'What makes you think it was a dream?'

Sarah's next words were faint: 'I know it was.' Then fainter still: 'I'm sure it was.'

Veronica smiled and shook her head. She said: 'I think I'm going to fall in love with you, Sarah.'

6

At two o'clock that afternoon, Terry went into Dr Dudden's empty office and — quite without his permission, or indeed knowledge — efficiently disconnected the telephone. He plugged his PowerBook into the phone socket and pressed the send button, thereby setting in motion a rapid but complex chain of events. Converted from binary data into analog signals, his film review was propelled down the telephone lines by electric current and just a few seconds later arrived in the Arts and Features Department of the newspaper, where a fax machine reconverted it into digital information and fed it to a thermal print head for reconstruction on paper. Passed in this form to the Arts Editor, it was briefly scrutinized, chuckled over and approved for publication, so that the following morning it could be glanced at by perhaps one in twenty of the newspaper's 400,000 readers: one of them, on this occasion, being Sarah, who fell asleep while attempting to read Terry's review in her staff room during morning break.

When the sleepiness started she could feel it, but not fight against it.

The words zoomed in and out of focus before her eyes.

She willed herself to concentrate, but it was no good. Her eyelids were getting heavy: heavier . . .

Catherine woke her, ten minutes later, by shaking her shoulder gently and saying: 'Sarah, wake up. Break's almost over.'

'Was I asleep? Oh, hell.' Sarah sat up in her chair and blinked around the room. Her colleagues were all beginning to leave: even the bell had not roused her this time. Just as he was going through the door, she called after Norman (a tall, rather anxious-looking student teacher in his early twenties): 'I'll be along in a little while, OK?'

'Yes, that's fine.'

'Twenty minutes or so.'

He must find me very peculiar, she thought, opening her bottle of mazindol and popping a couple of pills in her mouth.

Too polite or too scared to say anything, though.

When the room was empty, she refilled her coffee cup and gradually, effortfully, managed to remember what she had been reading in the newspaper. It was a film review by Terry. Strange to think that she still received these weekly updates on his critical opinions, even though she had not actually seen him for more than ten years. From her passing acquaintance with his journalism she could draw a surprisingly complete picture: she was familiar with his tastes in music and films, she knew that he still lived in London, she could imagine what his social life was like, she could even hazard a reasonable guess at his income (three times more than hers? Four?). And yet to him, she must have become completely invisible. Did he ever think about her? she wondered. Ever remember the time they had shared a flat together, after graduating; ever ask himself what had become of her?

Not that it really mattered. Not that it made any difference.

She looked at the review again and couldn't remember how much of it she had read. Skimming through it now, she found it more comprehensible than most of Terry's outpourings. The general tenor, at least, appeared to be enthusiastic. 'Fun for all the family' was his (hardly very groundbreaking) conclusion, and on reading this phrase Sarah indulged herself in a bitter little smile. Well, she thought, that was just fine, for people with families. What about the rest of us?

This was an area into which her thoughts seemed to be leading her more and more often, these days, and she resolved to escape it immediately. Throwing the newspaper aside, she reached for a tall, unstable pile of folders and took out a handful of Key Stage 2 assessment forms — one of the many new administrative by-products of the National Curriculum — and these distracted her, after a fashion, until it was time to go and check on Norman and the progress of his English class.

She did so with certain feelings of foreboding, for Norman aroused in her a complicated mixture of amusement and sympathy. In his favour, he was enthusiastic and good-natured, and seemed to take a genuine interest in the children (which did not translate itself, unfortunately, into anything resembling a rapport). But he was dangerously naive, and for someone so young his teaching methods seemed curiously old-fashioned. Sarah knew, all the same, that this was an easy criticism to make: the classroom atmosphere had changed so much during her eleven years in the profession that she shuddered to think how *she* would have fared if she was starting out now. She admired anyone who was prepared to try it, really.

Yesterday's lesson, of which she had attended only the last ten minutes, had been largely shambolic. In accordance with a government ruling that pupils should be made to familiarize themselves with 'classic poetry', Norman had attempted to steer the class through John Donne's 'Go, and catch a falling star', which Sarah had thought far too ambitious for a group of nine- and ten-year-olds. Their initial response of stunned boredom had transformed itself, by the time she arrived, into a chaos of facetiousness and hilarity. The chief troublemaker, as usual, was a boy called Andy Ellis, who when asked to respond to the line 'Teach me to hear the mermaids singing' said that it reminded him of the name of a film which he and a friend had recently rented from the video library because they'd heard it was about lesbians. Ignoring Norman's attempts to change the subject, he went on to explain that this had been a deeply disappointing experience, owing to the film's paucity of what he disarmingly referred to as 'girl-on-girl action'. This had led to an animated discussion among the male members of the class, not about Donne's use of marine imagery, but about whether it was possible to get a glimpse of Sharon Stone's pubic hair on the video of *Basic Instinct* by skilful use of the freeze frame. At the end of the lesson, very unwisely in Sarah's view, Norman had asked everyone to write their own poems about stars and to bring them into class the next day.

The lesson was already in some disarray when she arrived, although things calmed down a little when she appeared and made her way to a vacant desk in the back row. Sarah got the sense, however, that each successive poem was meeting with greater waves of derision, and one girl — Melanie Harris — was clearly struggling to fight back tears. Following Sarah's arrival, a couple of unexceptional efforts were read against a steady but containable backdrop of murmurs and giggles; and then it was Andy Ellis's turn.

It was the very first line of Andy's poem — *Listen up now, you dirty motherfucker* — which, for Sarah at least, set off the initial alarm bells. If it had been up to her, she probably would have intervened at that point, but Norman was locked into a horrified silence and allowed the whole performance to proceed uninterrupted.

> *Listen up now, you dirty motherfucker*
> *If you messin with my bitch I'm gonna git you sucker*
> *Gonna go down on the street, gonna get me a hit*
> *Then I come round to your house and I beat you to shit*
> *You gonna see stars, motherfucker, see stars*
> *You gonna see stars, motherfucker, see stars*
> *Gonna kill the little bitch if I find you in my bed*
> *Gonna take out my Uzi, pump her pussy full of lead*
> *Then you're the next one, you know the score*
> *Ain't no one allowed to go fuckin with my whore*
> *You see stars, motherfucker, see stars*
> *You see stars, motherfucker, see stars.*

While about half the class looked on open-mouthed with either awe or amazement, Andy was rewarded with a noisy ovation from most of the boys and even one or two of the girls. Sarah could not help being professionally interested, in spite of her mounting unease, to see that responses to the poem seemed to divide up along gender rather than racial lines. Andy himself was from a (rather well-off) white family, which made his attempt at gangsta rap quite creditable, she thought; and she also liked the characteristically inventive way he had managed to incorporate the star motif. She wouldn't have said any of this, of course: a simple request to see him afterwards and a hasty transition to the next reader would have been her way of handling the situation. Norman, on the other hand, seemed determined — once he had recovered his powers of speech — to wade on into ever deeper waters.

'That was very interesting, Andy,' he said, when the hubbub had partly died down, 'but I wonder if you yourself have really *understood* what you've written.'

'Of course I understand it.'

'Yes, we understand it, sir,' said another boy.

'We understand every word, sir,' said another.

(Sarah resisted the temptation to cover her face in her hands. She knew that they never called the teachers 'sir' unless the mood was particularly evil.)

'Are there any words you don't understand, sir?'

'Don't you know what a pussy is, sir?'

'Of course he doesn't. He hasn't even seen *Basic Instinct*.'

'That's enough!' Norman shouted, above the laughter. 'This "poem" of yours, Andy, is nothing but a farrago of obscenities.'

'Please, sir,' said someone, putting up his hand, 'I don't know what a farrago is.'

Norman ignored him. 'It's just a lot of filthy nonsense, isn't it, without rhyme or reason.'

'It does rhyme, actually,' said Andy. '*And* it's got a story, just like the poem you made us read yesterday.'

'A story, eh? Well I didn't notice any story.'

'Well, sir,' said the boy sitting next to Andy. 'This black man is very angry with his friend, so he's going to kill him.'

'Yes, sir. And his woman.'

'Because she's been a bitchin' whore, sir.'

'Shut up! The lot of you.' He homed in on Andy. 'Is this your own work?'

'Yes.'

'Nonsense. How could you have possibly made up something like that?'

'Well, I listen to a lot of rap music, and that sort of gave me the idea. People like Onyx, and M. C. Ren, and The Notorious B.I.G. Miss Tudor says it's very good for us to open ourselves up to influences from other cultures and traditions.'

Norman glanced at Sarah with a look that was half accusation, half desperate appeal. She smiled back sweetly.

'Anyway,' Andy continued, 'yesterday you told us that Pulp and Oasis wrote poetry.'

'Well, yes, but —'

'So what's the difference here, sir? It isn't because Onyx are black, is it?'

'You're not a racist, are you, sir?'

God, these boys are good, Sarah thought. For a moment she was almost proud of them.

'Right. That's it.' Norman's lips were quivering, and his face had turned chalk-white. 'Andy, see me afterwards. You're in *deep* trouble, now. You don't know how deep. Now the rest of you, just shut the f — . . . Just shut up' — as the class erupted into laughter again — 'just shut up and listen to the next poem. I don't want to hear another word out of you lot until the bell goes. Is that understood?'

The restoration of order was only superficial, and Sarah was doubly apprehensive when he chose Alison Hill as the next reader. She was by some way the youngest member of class, and was withdrawn and quiet at the best of times. Now, after

Andy's brazen theatrics, her voice sounded weaker and more timidly monotonous than ever.

'My poem is called "Holes in the Sky",' she declaimed at great speed. 'When stars die they turn into black holes. An astrologer was looking at three stars in the sky. Through his telescope. There was a little star and two big ones. One of the big stars died and turned into a black hole. The other two stars were very lonely. There were no other stars for millions and millions of miles. Just black air and empty sky. I feel sorry for those two lonely stars, said the astrologer. But he was too far away to do anything about it. So they just stayed there in the sky, looking sad, and although they twinkled sometimes, all the darkness and emptiness made them very scared.'

A semi-respectful silence ensued. One of the boys clapped sarcastically.

'That was very good, Alison,' said Norman. 'Really very good. I did however notice one tiny mistake. Did anyone else spot it?' There were no takers. 'Well, you said that the man looking through his telescope was an astrologer, when I think you meant that he was an astronomer.'

'What's the difference?' someone asked.

'Well, it's a very important difference.' Norman wrote the two words on the blackboard, and turned back towards the class looking pleased with himself. 'You see, there are only two letters changed between the words, and yet they mean completely different things. An astronomer is a serious scientist, who spends his time looking through telescopes and other scientific instruments to find things out about the stars, and an astrologer is a frivolous and superstitious person who only pretends to study the stars, and makes up horoscopes and other bits of nonsense.'

Sarah could sense another imminent change of mood. Alison seemed to be paying little attention to any of this: the expression on her face was listless, distracted, and for a passing moment Sarah felt that she could see within it the faded reflection of some other face, some nameless face from the past. (Perhaps it was the way that she held her mouth slightly askew, and chewed carelessly on her lower lip.) Meanwhile, the rest of the class were recovering their appetite for mischief.

'Are you saying that horoscopes aren't serious, sir?'

'Yes, I am.'

'But they're in the newspapers.'

'You shouldn't believe everything you read in the newspapers.'

'I think you can learn a lot about people from their star sign,' said one of the girls.

'Yes, you can. What sign are you, sir?'

'I bet you're Leo, aren't you, sir? Leos are supposed to be very strong and masterful.'

'Is Scorpio rising in Uranus, sir — or is it just the way your trousers hang?'

After the lesson was over, Sarah and Norman walked across the playground together on their way to the dining hall. She didn't talk to him about the lesson much, except to make vaguely reassuring noises and to hint gently that his choice of the Donne poem yesterday hadn't been very appropriate. He was badly shaken by the experience: the accusation of racism, in particular, had shocked him quite deeply.

'They were just trying to wind you up,' said Sarah.

Norman stopped walking and looked at her. The sun was bright on the playground, and his eyes narrowed involuntarily as he said: 'Do you think so?'

Sarah nodded. She ran a hand through her hair — the thick, almost shoulder-length grey hair by which Norman was already fascinated — and ended, without noticing it (for she had never noticed it) by taking hold of a clump and tugging at it lightly. 'You're doing fine. Really.' She laughed. 'You know, we've all been through it. When I think about my first teaching practice . . .'

They walked on a little further.

'I've got a letter for you, by the way,' said Norman. 'It's in my briefcase in the staff room.'

Sarah's immediate assumption was that this was a letter he had written himself: that there was something he wanted to say to her, some declaration too momentous to make in person. It was a great relief when he added: 'It's from a girl at college who says she knows you. I was talking about you with some friends, and this girl — I don't know her very well or anything — says that she knew you years ago, when you were a student.'

The relief gave way to puzzlement. 'Doesn't sound very likely. All my student friends are in their thirties now. How old is she?'

'Oh, about twenty, I think. Her name's Ruby. Ruby Sharp.'

And now it was Sarah who stopped walking. They had almost reached the doors to the dining hall, and children trickled past them in groups and in pairs, slouching moodily.

'Yes, I did know a girl called Ruby,' she said. 'Not very well, but . . . I know the girl you mean. That's extraordinary.' She broke into a smile, and for a moment what she saw, as she gazed ahead, was not the redbrick façade of the science block but something altogether less tangible: a pale, childish face; a shock of red hair; a beach . . . A pang of recollection shot through her, and her throat was suddenly dry as she said to Norman: 'And she's living in London now, is she? Training to be a teacher too?'

'I think she's doing biology, in fact.' He opened the door for her, and they were at once assaulted by the dining hall's clamorous humidity. 'But she lives in the same hall as a friend of mine, and that's how I came to . . . Well, you came up in the conversation, somehow . . .'

Sarah found it hard work talking to Norman over lunch. The mention of Ruby's name after all these years had revived a complex of emotions, not all of them pleasant. And yet there was really no need for it to disturb her: there could be no harm, if she was sensible about it, in being reminded of Mr and Mrs Sharp, the caretakers at Ashdown, and the little red-headed daughter they had sometimes asked her to look after in the daytime while her mother was out at work. Those afternoons spent upstairs with Ruby and Veronica, playing cards or Scrabble: the day at the beach with Robert . . .

Yes, it always came back to Robert, and this was always where Sarah began to get angry with herself. Twelve years had gone by, twelve years since she had seen him (she could not count their last farcical encounter at Ashdown, even though that in its way had been the most bruising of all), and yet still she only had to be reminded of him — the tiniest, most incidental detail — for all the old pain to come rushing to the surface. A pain which neither the passage of time itself nor those gruelling months in analysis (and yes, what a waste of money *they* had turned out to be) had ever succeeded in dulling.

She was thirty-five, she told herself. She was childless. She was divorced. Wasn't it time to put that distant, shortlived, not-so-very-significant friendship behind her?

Her train of thought was broken as Norman asked her to pass the tomato sauce. She watched with unconscious fascination as he mashed it vigorously into his pile of thin, watery potato.

Ruby had done her best to keep the letter brief and polite. She was not sure how Sarah would react, being approached by someone she had known so fleetingly, so young, such a long time ago. It was almost like writing to a stranger. She carefully stressed that it was only the memory of Sarah's former kindness towards her, and the odd coincidence of hearing her name spoken by Norman, that had prompted her to get in touch. She had no other specific reason for writing; no agenda. Even so, she half-expected never to receive a reply.

But Sarah was charmed by the letter, and that very afternoon she sent back a note via Norman, enclosing her telephone number and suggesting that they should meet, perhaps go out for a meal. Which is how Ruby came to find herself travelling to

North London only a few days later, one Monday evening, and making her way towards Sarah's house through the unfamiliar streets with a pencilled address clutched in her hand.

It was easy enough to find: the first house in the street when you turned in from the tube station. It was a small, neat end-terrace: two storeys and a basement, with boxes of ivy and salvia outside the front bay window. Ruby was ten minutes early, so she walked past the house and carried on up the hill for a few hundred yards, savouring the evening sunshine and the hint of modest adventure attendant on visiting this new part of London, so different from the busy but featureless area where her own hall of residence was located. She liked the steepness and narrowness of the streets, the tall houses, the tree-lined pavements, the sense of traffic being held at bay. There were few private cars on the road, and no buses or taxis. It was almost silent.

Silence pervaded, too, the first few seconds of Ruby's and Sarah's reunion. Neither woman seemed able to speak.

'My God, it *is* you,' said Sarah finally; then explained her initial uncertainty by adding, 'Your hair . . .'

'Oh.' Ruby laughed, and touched it, as if she had momentarily forgotten that it was there. 'Yes, of course. A slight image change.'

Ruby's hair used to be flame-red. Now it reached to her shoulders in fine black strands.

'I did this a year ago,' she said. 'People don't warm to redheads, for some reason. It was just something I noticed.' Then, eagerly: 'Yours looks great. I love grey hair, when it's worn like that. When it's worn young.'

Sarah smiled, and said, 'Well, come in.' Then they both broke into delighted laughter, and hugged.

Sarah had been watching the news on Channel 4. Now she turned the volume down and went to fetch a bottle of Frascati from the fridge. Ruby sat on the sofa in front of the television, but found that she couldn't settle. She began to look around the sitting-room, which ran the length of the house and was decorated neutrally, in creams and whites. There wasn't quite enough furniture to fill the available space. The front and back gardens were small, plain, well kept, and the house itself seemed clean and attractive, but Ruby found it heartless. It was not what she had been expecting.

'I was so surprised when I got your letter,' Sarah began. She sat opposite Ruby and leaned forward in her armchair, shivering slightly, feeling absurdly ill at ease. 'I'm amazed you remembered me at all, let alone my name.'

'I never forget things,' said Ruby. 'I'm very retentive that way.'

Sarah could see that Ruby was distracted by the television, so she flicked it off with the remote control, and put on a CD of piano music instead: Bill Evans, a third anniversary present from Anthony (and one of the few she had ever liked). She doubted if it was to Ruby's taste, but thought it might help to lighten the atmosphere.

'I went up to Ashdown again the other day,' Ruby now said, abruptly.

'Oh?'

'Not to go in, you understand. I just went up and looked at it from the outside. There are no students there any more. It's been turned into a clinic, where they look after people with —'

'— with sleep disorders, yes, I know.'

'Oh. Who told you that?'

'My GP, actually.' Sarah sipped her wine. She knew she was drinking it much too fast. 'He offered to refer me there.'

'Why's that?' asked Ruby, and realized this sounded too forward. 'I mean, if you don't mind me asking . . .'

'Well, if I start answering *that* question,' Sarah said, 'we'll have got on to the story of my life very quickly. I think we'd better eat first, don't you?'

'The story of your life's exactly what I want to hear,' said Ruby, following her to the front door. 'I haven't seen you for twelve years, after all.'

'But *why*, Ruby? Why should it matter to you?'

'Because you gave me some of my best memories,' she answered, simply.

Sarah was very touched by this. 'Yes,' she said. 'They were good times, I think.' As they set off down the main road, she asked: 'How are your parents, by the way?'

'Dad died a few years ago . . .'

'Oh no . . .'

'. . . but Mum's fine, absolutely fine. She runs a boarding house now.'

It was only a short walk to the restaurant, which, being new, seemed to be experiencing a certain number of teething troubles. They decided it was warm enough to sit outside on the terrace, and were immediately besieged by waiters, who competed among themselves to take their order, and then delivered the first course with alarming haste.

'What were we saying?'

'You were going to tell me how you knew about Ashdown,' Ruby prompted. 'And this was going to involve telling the story of your life.'

Sarah ground some pepper on to her soup, and asked: 'Well — do you know what narcolepsy is?'

'Yes, roughly,' said Ruby, surprised. 'It's when people fall asleep all the time during the day, isn't it?'

'That's it, more or less. Well, I've got it.'

'Oh.' Ruby had no idea what this meant, in practice. 'I'm sorry. Is that serious?'

'It's certainly a nuisance.'

'And the clinic would have . . . helped you with it, would they?'

'Possibly.' Forestalling further questioning, Sarah said: 'There were two reasons why I didn't want to go. One is that I couldn't afford the fees, and the waiting list for NHS patients is nearly two years. And the other —' smiling, a little severely '— the other is that it happens to be run by this guy called Gregory Dudden, who was at university with me.'

'I see,' said Ruby, hesitantly.

'Gregory and I . . . have a history,' said Sarah. 'He was my boyfriend for a while. My first boyfriend, in fact. You know, it was one of those student things that seems to make sense at the time, and then a few months later you look back and ask yourself . . . what was I *thinking* of?'

Ruby continued to nod, although this explanation seemed to lie outside the realm of her experience. 'So . . . so what does it mean, then, that you're narcoleptic? How does it affect you?'

'It's changed a bit, over the years. The main thing is that I sleep very badly at night, and can't help falling asleep during the day. That's been happening for almost twenty years now. There are other symptoms as well, but they've been getting slightly better recently: the cataplexy, for instance.'

'Which is . . .?'

'That means that if I laugh a lot, or get too excited about something, I lose muscle tone. I'm conscious, but I go into a kind of faint. I can feel it coming on, but there's nothing I can do about it. All sorts of things can make it happen: anger, joy, frustration . . .'

'It sounds like more than a nuisance,' said Ruby. 'I had no idea.'

'Well,' Sarah shrugged, and tried to sound offhand, 'it's cost me a job or two over the years. Falling asleep in class is supposed to be something the kids do, not the teacher.' She refilled their wine glasses: hers was empty, Ruby's almost full. 'The thing is, they only managed to diagnose it about three years ago. A lot of GPs are only just learning about it. The first doctor I saw didn't have a clue. He made me go and see a shrink.'

'What sort of shrink?'

'A Lacanian psychotherapist.'

Ruby was out of her depth again. 'They didn't lock you up or anything, did they?'

'No, nothing like that,' said Sarah, apparently quite amused by this idea. 'I suppose it wasn't a complete waste of time. At least he made me realize why I don't like people touching my eyes.'

'Your eyes?'

'Yes. I'm very sensitive about them.' Sarah gently pushed aside her soup bowl, only half-finished. 'I'm sorry, I'm probably shattering all your childhood illusions about me. I must seem like a mass of neuroses.'

'No, not at all, I . . .' The waiter, who had been hovering by their table, now cleared their dishes away. Ruby waited for him to leave. 'So, what else should I know about you? Did you get married?'

'Oh, yes. Been there, done that. His name was Anthony. An academic.'

'And?'

'He left; a while ago. Found someone else.'

'Oh.' Again, Ruby found herself saying: 'I'm sorry.'

Again, Sarah shrugged. 'These things happen.'

'You know, it was probably just a fantasy of mine — one of those childhood illusion things — but I always hoped you were going to marry your boyfriend from college.'

'Who do you mean?'

'You know: Robert.'

Sarah's laugh was short and forced. 'Robert? *He* was never my boyfriend.'

'No? But that time on the beach . . .'

'I was seeing someone else then. A woman, actually. Her name was Veronica. Robert . . . just happened to be with us that day. I can't even remember what he was doing there.' Noticing Ruby's look of bewilderment, she added: 'It gets more and more complicated, doesn't it?'

'I'm not shocked or anything,' said Ruby. 'One of my friends from school's bisexual. Or says she is.'

'I'm not sure I believe in that word,' said Sarah. 'Or any word which takes something complicated and tries to reduce it to a formula. Besides —' wiping lipstick from the rim of her glass

'— it's not really about sex. Not for me, anyway: that's not what I'm looking for. It's funny, you know, everyone seems to think it gives you twice the choice: but it doesn't work out like that, somehow.'

'Has there been anyone since Anthony?'

'Not really. I think Norman may be nurturing one or two fantasies in that direction, so that's a little bridge that may have to be crossed soon.'

'You say he was just a friend,' said Ruby; quietly now, and slowly, choosing her words with caution, 'but I think Robert really cared for you. There are things he said to me on the beach that day — and I know I was only young — but I can still remember them . . .'

'I don't know why you're dragging up something that happened twelve years ago,' said Sarah, her voice suddenly tight. 'I told you: Robert was a friend, nothing more, nothing less. And if he *cared* for me so much, why did he drop me like a stone as soon as we left university?' There were other things she could have said, on this subject, but Ruby looked downhearted enough already. 'Anyway,' she finished, more gently, 'how could you possibly remember anything he said to you, all these years on? You were only eight or nine.'

'I'll never forget that day,' said Ruby. 'That amazing sandcastle we built together — I dreamed about it for weeks afterwards.'

'That's right . . .' Sarah began to smile again, faintly, as this memory returned to her. 'You called him the Sandman, didn't you? We both did, for a while: it was our name for him.'

'It was so sunny. So still. Just the loveliest day . . .' Ruby looked Sarah full in the face now; earnestly, brimmingly. 'I've always wanted to pay you back for it, you know: both of you.'

'Don't be silly.'

Ruby sensed that she had said too much: so she joked, 'Apart from anything else, I got a bicycle out of it.'

'You did?'

'Don't you even remember *that*? That was one of the best pieces of advice anyone ever gave me. You told me how I could persuade my parents to give me a bicycle.'

'I don't remember.'

'Well then, I'm not going to remind you,' said Ruby, affecting a pout.

They were hungry again, by now. After the speedy arrival of their first courses, the waiters seemed to have disappeared *en masse*, and Sarah had the distant intimation of some unknowable crisis brewing in the kitchens.

'You make me feel old, Ruby,' she said, with a sigh.

'Me? But you're surrounded by kids every day — why should I?'

'I don't know . . . Because it's so long since I last saw you, and you've changed so much in the meantime.'

'You're not old, anyway. Mid-thirties isn't old.'

'My life's half over.'

'So the better half's still to come.'

'I hope so.'

'Are you going to carry on teaching?'

'Oh, I suppose,' said Sarah, without much enthusiasm, as a harassed-looking waiter finally brought them a mushroom risotto and a chicken tagliatelle, which he deposited with perfunctory apologies. 'I can't say that it's much fun at the moment, to be honest. Half my colleagues are either taking early retirement or seeing stress counsellors twice a week. Just when we've nearly killed ourselves implementing one new set of guidelines, the government springs something different on us. We spend so much time preparing for inspectors, and writing reports on the kids, and writing reports on each other, and setting budgets and balancing books, I've almost forgotten why I wanted to teach in the first place.' Ruby was staring at her across the risotto. It occurred to Sarah that she was probably giving her the most depressing evening of her young life. Pricked by this thought, she added: 'And then every so often, you know, something happens — some new challenge comes up, and you think to yourself, Yes, I *do* want to be doing this, this *is* worthwhile. Like — well, at the moment for instance, there's this girl in my class . . . very quiet and shy — it's often the quiet ones — and there's some . . . *sadness* about her, some secret she's holding in. And to know that I'm the only person who might be able to reach her . . .' Hearing herself worry aloud about this, she was ashamed to think how much of the evening she had already spent dwelling upon her own problems. 'Anyway, Ruby, isn't it time I found out something about *you*?'

But Ruby was determined, and artful, and although she was happy to make conversation at first about her friends at college and her mother's little seafront hotel, she kept steering her way back to Sarah, and to Ashdown, and the day at the beach. As for the meal, they gave up all hope of dessert after a while, forced some money upon one of the elusive waiters, and finally managed to take their leave. When they walked to the underground station together and said goodbye amid many expressions of gratitude and promises to keep in touch, Ruby still had one more question to ask.

'This narcolepsy of yours,' she said. 'They can cure it, can't they?'

Sarah shook her head. 'Unfortunately, no. Once you've got it, you've got it for life. There are drugs to help with the symptoms, and it does seem to be getting better with age. As I said, the cataplexy isn't so bad any more; and there was another thing — pre-sleep dreaming, they called it — that seems to have gone altogether.'

'What was that like?'

Sarah folded her arms and felt a chill run through her. It was getting late, and the evening had turned cold. It had been nice seeing Ruby, but she didn't want to think about the past any more: she wanted to be home, alone; to be playing that CD again, and finishing the wine, and getting those reports done.

'It's hard to explain,' she said, 'but I used to have dreams . . . so real . . .'

And was she becoming nostalgic even for that, she asked herself, as she walked quickly home? Even for the fact that she had once been unable to tell the difference between her dreams and her memories? It was time, surely, to forget those days: time to concentrate on today's challenges. She thought about Alison Hill, and how she could best begin to excavate the buried sadness she had glimpsed, once or twice, behind that serious expression. She thought about her face as she had sat in the classroom, not listening to Norman's comical diatribe about astrologers and astronomers: the way she had chewed carelessly on her lower lip . . . But still the images which Ruby had now brought back to disconcerting life persisted in tugging at her, and within an instant she had moved on inexplicably from Alison to Veronica: yes, Veronica, of all the ghosts who might have risen up, unbidden, to her reminiscent eye that evening: Veronica sitting

Stage Two

sitting in the Café Val-
ladon, reading a book and chuckling quietly to herself between
sips of her black coffee and drags on her cigarette. It was early
December, getting on for the end of term, and Veronica was
well wrapped up, wearing the colourful lambswool sweater
they had chosen together on a shopping expedition a few
weeks earlier. The Café itself was warm and steamy: the thick
amber windows, opaque at the best of times, were today further fogged up with layers of condensation. Cigarette smoke
swirled so thickly in the air that Sarah could barely see her way
forward. When she reached the table she stood over it, expectant, waiting for the look upwards, the smile, the closing of the
book, the kiss. (In public, they kissed on the cheek: it was all
they allowed themselves.) Finally, seeing that Veronica was so
absorbed in the novel that she had not even noticed her arrival,
Sarah broke in upon her silence by saying:

'So — has The Owl appeared yet?'

She stooped over and leaned across the table for the kiss. Her
face against Veronica's was cold and tingling.

'God, you're freezing,' Veronica said. 'Is it snowing out there
or something?'

'Almost.' Sarah sat down and took a sip from Veronica's mug.
'Well, has he?'

'Not so far. It's getting really gruesome, though.'

Sarah picked up the cigarette packet. 'Can I have a gasper?'

'Of course. Go ahead.'

'Gasper' was their secret word for a cigarette. Like many of
their codewords, it had been borrowed from the book Veronica
was reading: *The House of Sleep*, by an author neither of them

had ever encountered before, whose name was Frank King. This was one of the hundreds of books Slattery had acquired from jumble sales in order to decorate the walls of the Café Valladon, and it happened to stand in the centre of the shelf above their favourite table. Sarah had started reading it once while waiting for Veronica to arrive, and had immediately been entranced by its dated 1930s jargon and the incredibly convoluted plot, which ostensibly revolved around a cache of stolen documents and a notorious criminal called The Owl, but seemed, in reality, to be little more than the pretext for a baffling sequence of midnight kidnappings and grisly assassinations. That day — only a week or two after they had started going out — Sarah had read some of the choicest passages aloud to Veronica, and over the following two months the book had become a shared, intensely personal joke between them: one of the many hidden bonds that held them so firmly together and made their relationship so impenetrable to outsiders.

'Go on, then, what's happened?' asked Sarah, lighting the cigarette.

'Well, this guy Smith —'

'Who's he? Is he The Owl?'

'We don't know yet. Anyway, he's got Henry Downes *and* Robert Porter *and* Aileen all tied up in their chairs, and he's threatening to torture them if they don't tell him where the bonds are. Well, just Aileen, actually. With a red-hot poker.'

'Aileen? You're kidding.'

'No, I'm not. Listen to this: "Slow minutes dragged past remorselessly. Smith drew out the poker again. It glowed redly now, and the kitchen was filled with the suggestive smell of hot metal." '

'Brilliant,' said Sarah, laughing delightedly.

' " 'Now, Porter,' he said, advancing to Aileen. 'Where are they?' 'I don't know,' muttered Porter. His lips were quivering. 'I shan't ask you again. First a slight burn on the face as an earnest. It will be painful, of course, and leave a scar. If this does not move you, I shall take the eyes — one by one. And may I remind you that — I keep my word.' Aileen tried to shrink back as the hot metal approached her face. Her eyes closed, and her cheeks grew paler still. But she did not speak or cry out. Henry struggled desperately with his —" '

Veronica stopped, looking up and realizing that the pallor of Aileen's cheeks was suddenly matched by Sarah's. Her smile had become pained and frozen.

'Oh.' Veronica closed the book. 'I'm sorry. That was tactless of me.'

Sarah shook her head and tried to look cheerful. 'No, it's all right. Carry on, that was funny.' But this pretence didn't last for long. She sat back in her chair and closed her eyes. 'Actually I feel a bit sick.'

Veronica leaned forward and made as if to lay her fingers on Sarah's eyelids. She flinched and drew away. 'Don't.'

'I'm sorry.' Veronica drank some coffee and decided to change the subject. 'How did it go today, anyway? I haven't even asked you.'

Today was Sarah's first day of teaching practice at the local primary school. She had been nervous about it all week, and had frantically over-prepared herself, arriving with enough material for about six hours rather than the forty-minute lesson she had been required to teach.

'It was fine,' she said. 'It was good, in fact.'

'Did you get my card?'

'Yes, I did,' said Sarah; and for a moment her eyes shone intimately, with pure, unconditional love. 'Thank you.' Tapping ash from her cigarette, she added: 'It wasn't the only good luck card I got, as it happens.'

'Let me guess: Robert?'

'I'm afraid so. A plaintive little missive slipped under my door at some point in the night.'

'Poor lamb. He's besotted with you.' Veronica said this with a certain malicious edge, which Sarah noticed and could not help quietly relishing.

'Don't be hard on him,' she said.

'So what happened? What were they like? What did you do with them?'

'Well, I thought I was going to play safe, and give them something like Stevie Smith to begin with, but at the last minute I thought, No, let's try a bit harder here, let's go in at the deep end, so I made them read that Maya Angelou poem — you know, "Song for the Old Ones"?'

'That's all about slavery, though. They wouldn't have known what you were talking about.'

'But they *did*, that's just the point. There were a few difficult things in it that I had to talk them through, but you'd be *amazed* what kids can understand, and talk about, if the — you know, if the writing's good enough . . . We had this great discussion about it, and — you can't imagine what it feels like, Ronnie, to know that there are these thirty children and today, because of me, there's something in their heads that wasn't there before. It's just the best feeling . . .'

Veronica grinned and said: 'I knew you'd be good at it.' Then she asked, more softly: 'You're not going to do that much preparation every time, are you?'

'I shouldn't think so. Why?'

'Because I'll hardly get to see you. You haven't been round for days.'

'Well . . .' Sarah drew breath, and her voice took on an excited tremor. 'I've been meaning to talk to you about that. I wanted to ask you something.'

Veronica waited. 'Yes?'

'There's this guy who lives at Ashdown, and he's just moved out of his room, back on to campus. And the thing is . . .' (she met Veronica's eyes, which were hungry, expectant) '. . . well, technically it's a double room. There are two beds in it, and it's absolutely massive. It's on the second floor. So I was wondering . . . well, I was wondering if you wanted to move into it.'

'By myself?' she asked, teasingly.

'Actually . . . no. I meant the two of us.'

'Two *lovers*?' said Veronica, giving the word a mischievous emphasis which had Sarah glancing around the Café in alarm. 'Two lovers sharing the same room? What would the university authorities say?'

'Well, nothing, of course. How would they know . . . about us?'

Veronica was enjoying the joke too much to let it go. 'Think of the scandal, though.'

'If you think it's too . . . I mean, if you have a problem with that . . .'

'Sarah,' said Veronica, taking hold of her hand and first squeezing, then stroking it, 'I would *love* to move in with you. I'd love it.'

'Really?'

'Really.' The smile began to flicker at the edges of her mouth again. 'Poor old Robert, though. He's going to go *crazy*.'

'And talk of the devil . . .' said Sarah, looking towards the door.

Robert hesitated before joining them, but only briefly. He could never deny himself the pleasure of sitting with Sarah, even when it was tempered by the agony of seeing how happy she was in Veronica's company. It was Veronica he chose to sit beside, in any case: either to avoid the impression that he was staking any sort of claim, or simply because he had more excuses for looking at Sarah if he was sitting directly opposite her. 'Hi,' he said, spilling a few drops of coffee from his overfilled mug as Veronica moved up to create a space for him. 'How did it go today?'

'It was great,' said Sarah. 'It was absolutely fine.'

'Really? I knew it would be.'

'The kids were great, the staff are really nice . . .'

'And you were a success? They liked you?'

'Yes, they seemed to. The whole place just had this really nice atmosphere. I mean, I know it's probably too early to be thinking this, but . . . if they could take me on at the end of the year . . . you know, it would be just perfect.'

'Really? You'll be looking for a job round here, will you?' Already his mind was at work, and he was tailoring his plans to meet hers. He could find work in the area too, if necessary; or he could stay on at the university, do a postgraduate course.

'Well, yes, we both will,' said Sarah. 'You know, I told you — Ronnie wants to start this theatre group.'

'Oh yes.' His spirits took a familiar nosedive; but he was determined to play the game, so he turned to Veronica and asked, 'How's that panning out?'

'Oh, it's coming along.' She had opened *The House of Sleep* again, and was only half-listening to the conversation. 'I'm sussing out potential sponsors at the moment.'

'Sponsors?'

'You know, businesses and things. That's the way things are going these days: private enterprise.'

'Ronnie's got a real head-start,' Sarah enthused. 'Knowing so much about economics.'

Veronica laughed; not derisively, at this summation of her financial skills, but at something in the book that seemed to have amused her.

'*Bring 'Em Back Alive*,' she said. '*The Paths of the Prudent. Clad in Purple Mist.*'

'Pardon?' said Sarah.

'These are the other books advertised at the back. *The Case of the Painted Girl. Connie Morgan in the Lumber Camp*: wow, that one sounds like a real dyke classic. Listen to these . . . *Wife in Name Only, At War With Herself, The Gay Triangle* . . . This is amazing: I think I've got material for a thesis here.' Then she burst out laughing: 'Oh, look, here's one for you, Robert. *You and Your Hand*. Something for you to read while you're thinking about me and Sarah, perhaps?'

'Ronnie!' Scandalized, Sarah kicked her playfully under the table. But when Robert looked into her eyes he saw that they were directed not at him, but at her lover; and they were laughing, laughing joyfully and with a lightness that was for her alone: utterly private, utterly exclusive. He bit back sudden tears and abruptly, for an instant, he lost consciousness: when it returned, it brought in its wake a vivid but unexpected phrase:

. . . *In your eyes tonight I saw a sightlessness* . . .

Veronica was getting up to leave. She was saying something.

. . . *A disregard that made me feel* . . .

Made him feel what? How did he feel?

'What shall we do, then?'

He heard Veronica's words now.

'When are we going to move in?'

'I'll come and find you later,' Sarah was saying. 'We'll talk about it then.'

Veronica said goodbye to them both, and left. They didn't kiss in front of Robert.

Silence imposed itself. Sarah offered him an apologetic smile, and he did his best to return it.

'What was that about?' he said at last. 'You're moving in together?'

Sarah nodded. 'She's coming to live at Ashdown. We're taking over Geoff's old room.'

'Right.' Something else for him to absorb, to live with. 'That'll be nice.'

'Yes. Yes, I think it will. I think it'll work.'

'Good.' He opened the copy of *The House of Sleep*, skimming through it, seeing nothing. 'That means your room will be free now, does it?'

'I suppose so.' *Now* what was he going to ask? Surely he didn't nurse some fetishistic desire to move in there himself? 'What about it?'

'My friend Terry's looking for a room, that's all. Would it be OK if I mentioned it to him?'

'Yes, of course,' said Sarah, hugely relieved. 'That would be fine.'

Another silence: longer, even more oppressive. Sarah was groping for smalltalk. A dozen bland, pointless remarks died on her lips.

'Is this one of Slattery's?' Robert asked, still affecting to read the novel.

'Yes. It goes up there.' She pointed at the empty space on the shelf.

'This friend of mine — Terry,' he said. 'He keeps a ten pound note in one of these books.'

'Really? What for?'

'You know — a fall-back. Just in case he ever gets caught short.'

'That's a good idea.'

'Clever, isn't it? It must be a million to one chance that anyone would ever find it.' Sarah could not see where any of this was leading, and Robert's next fumbling, uncertain words made it little clearer. 'Sarah, if ever I want to . . . leave anything for you, I'll put it here. In this book.'

'What do you mean?'

'Page . . .' (he flicked through the pages at random) '. . . page hundred and seventy-three. Then you'll always know where to find it.'

'What sort of thing? You mean money?'

'Possibly money: or . . . well, anything, really. I don't know.' This was true: he barely knew why he was telling her this. It seemed important, somehow. 'You'll remember, won't you?'

'Robert . . .' she began; but couldn't bring herself to tell him that in choosing his vehicle for this mysterious communication, he had managed to hit upon the very book which symbolized everything that she and Veronica felt for one another: the signifier of their love. How could she taunt him, now, with that particular irony? It was far too cruel. 'I've got to go,' was all she said. 'I'm . . . Look, I'm sorry if we teased you.'

Robert ran his finger along the green spine of the book, and said nothing.

'I'll see you back at the house: yes?'

'OK,' he said. And when Sarah had gone, he stared dumbly opposite him at the space where she had been sitting: struggling to reconcile himself, for the thousandth time, to her absence.

Terry came into the Café about ten minutes later, and found Robert bent over an exercise book, his tongue protruding abstractedly from between his teeth, his hunched shoulders suggesting gloom and concentration in equal measure.

'You look like someone agonizing over the first draft of his suicide note,' he said.

Robert gave a short, mirthless laugh, and snapped the exercise book shut with surprising alacrity. He didn't want Terry — or anybody else — to know that he had started writing a poem about Sarah.

'Mind if we interrupt your labours?' Terry asked.

'We?'

'Yes, I'm supposed to be meeting some people.'

'No, that's all right. Sit down. I've got some news for you, anyway. I think I may have solved your accommodation problem.' Then he told him about Sarah's newly vacant room.

Terry had recently decided to leave his campus hall of residence, because of a noisy next-door neighbour who was preventing him from getting the necessary fourteen hours' sleep a day. He liked the idea of coming to live at Ashdown, and the arrangement was already settled by the time his friends joined them at the table. They were both film students, one called Luke, the other Cheryl; they wore the traditional film department uniform of black Oxfam cast-offs, and, like Terry, looked sorely in need of a few square meals and a long holiday in the sun.

'What's this book, then?' asked Luke, picking up *The House of Sleep*.

Robert winced to see him handling it. He felt as though a holy relic were being defiled.

'It's just something I found on the shelf,' he said. He tried to take the book back, but Luke was hanging on to it.

'So who's Frank King, then?' He looked at one of the front pages, and ran his eye down the list of other novels by the same author. 'It says here that one of his books was made into a film.'

'That's right,' said Terry. '*The Ghoul*, it was called. Filmed in 1932, with Boris Karloff and Cedric Hardwicke.'

'*The Ghoul*? I never heard of it.'

'Ah!' Terry beamed with triumph. 'That's because all the prints have gone missing. In England and America, anyway.'

Robert discreetly replaced the book on the shelf.

'So how do you know about it?' asked Luke.

'Well, I've been reading this piece about lost films. And in fact —' Terry paused, looking pleased with himself '— I've developed a theory about them. Do you want to hear it?'

'Great,' said Cheryl. 'Another of your theories.' She was smiling, though.

It seemed that Terry's latest theory had been conceived that very morning, after a particularly tantalizing and elusive dream, something to do with apple blossom, and a blonde-haired woman, a sunlit hillside and a broad-brimmed hat. It concerned lost films and lost dreams, and Robert, for one, was quite happy to listen and let it wash over him, if only to purge himself of the memory of his latest encounter with Sarah and Veronica.

'I know it's a cliché to say that films are like dreams — like a collective unconscious,' Terry began, 'but I was thinking that nobody's ever really followed the idea through. There are different sorts of dreams, aren't there? And so obviously there are horror movies, which are like nightmares, and then there are dirty movies like *Deep Throat* and *Emmanuelle*, which are like wet dreams.' He sipped from his mug of treacly hot chocolate, warming to his subject. 'Then there are remakes, and stories which keep getting told again and again, and those are like recurring dreams. And there are consoling, visionary dreams, like *Lost Horizon* or *The Wizard of Oz*. But when a film gets lost, and it's never been shown, and the print goes missing and nobody's ever seen it, that's the most beautiful kind of dream of all. Because that's the kind of dream that might just have been the best one you've ever had in your life, only it slips from your mind just as you're waking up, and a few seconds later you can't remember a thing about it.'

'Does that ever happen, though?' Robert asked. 'I mean, surely if someone's gone to all the trouble and expense of making a film, then they're not just going to lock it away in a vault and never show it to anyone.'

For the benefit of this *naïf*, the movie experts ran through an inventory of all the lost movies they could think of: the eight-hour version of *Greed*, Jerry Lewis's *The Day the Clown Cried*, about a clown who works in the Nazi concentration camps, the missing reels of *The Magnificent Ambersons*, Orson Welles's legendary *The Other Side of the Wind*, *The Blockhouse* — a Second World War drama starring Peter Sellers, shot entirely in a warren of underground bunkers beneath the island of Guernsey — the missing gas chamber scene from *Double Indemnity*, the four deleted sequences from *The Private Life of Sherlock Holmes* . . .

'But Wilder's such a middlebrow talent, anyway,' said Terry. 'Who would ever go to the trouble of restoring one of his films?'

'He's my favourite director, actually,' said Luke. 'Who's yours?'

This, of course, was a favourite game. Terry puckered his lips. 'I don't think I have one,' he said. 'Or at least, I'm sure that he's out there, somewhere, but I just haven't found him yet.'

'Him?' said Cheryl.

'It would have to be someone of . . . uncompromising integrity. Someone who writes as well as directs. Film for me is fundamentally the expression of one artist's personal vision.'

If the others thought that he was being pretentious, they held their tongues.

'I want to write myself, eventually. And direct. I'm writing a script at the moment, in fact.'

Robert sipped his stone-cold coffee, Cheryl started unwrapping a sugar cube and Luke examined his nails.

'I'll tell you about it, shall I? It's the life story of this man, you see, and he's going to be played by the same actor all the way through and it's going to be shot over a period of fifty years. You'll see him age from a young boy to an old man in the space of one and a half hours. Brutal jump cuts from his face at the age of twenty, full of youthful enthusiasm, to his face at the age of seventy, lined with bitterness and disillusionment. A vertiginous, fast-forward chronicle of hope withering into despair.'

There was a short pause. Then Luke said: 'Rather difficult to insure, I would have thought,' and got up to pay the bill.

Christmas came and went, the spring term began, and within a few weeks Terry decided that he had at last discovered his favourite director. In the small hours of one Saturday morning, BBC2 screened a subtitled print of *Il Costo della Pesca* (*Dearly Have We Paid for the Mullet*), Salvatore Ortese's 1947 neo-realist drama of two rival families in the small fishing village of Trapani. Although he was distantly familiar with the name of this little-known Italian film-maker, Terry had never seen any of his work before; and its impact was immediate, revelatory, like a thunderclap. He watched it alone, in the darkness of Ashdown's television room, after drinking half a bottle of red wine: before the film started his senses were muddled and he felt ready for bed, but within five minutes he was wide awake again, and rushed upstairs to his bedroom in order to retrieve a notebook in which to record his responses. He was transfixed by the extreme close-ups of the ancient, weathered old fishermen's faces ('face as landscape', he wrote in the book), by the stark black and white photography of the austere Sicilian coastline ('landscape as character', he added) and by the primal simplicity of the drama and its rigorous concentration on the painful economics of the characters' lives ('vigorous concatenation painful ergonomics', he wrote, having finished off the rest of the bottle). It seemed to Terry that here at last was a director who, by combining an unaffected sympathy for the lives of ordinary people with a plain but finely-judged cinematic vocabulary, represented everything he thought the medium should aspire towards.

Later in the afternoon that same Saturday, he arrived at the university library just before it was about to close and photocopied the entry for Ortese from the *Cambridge Companion to Film*:

ORTESE, SALVATORE (1913–75). Italian director, worked in editing and dubbing from the mid-thirties and was rumoured to have assisted ROSSELLINI (qv) on the screenplay of *Luciano Serra, Pilota* (1938). He directed numerous short documentaries during the war, and made his feature film début with *Il Costo della Pesca* (*Dearly Have We Paid for the Mullet*, 1947) which along with Rossellini's *Roma, Città Aperta* and De Sica's *Sciusciá* (both qv) marked the first flowerings of neo-realism. His films of the 1950s, including *Paese Senza Pietá* (*Land Without Pity*, 1951) and the more upbeat *Morte da Fame* (*Death from Starvation*, 1955), show his continuing commitment to the movement which he felt had been betrayed by his fellow directors, particularly De Sica, the sentimentality of whose *Umberto D* (1952) he publicly reviled. As the Italian cinema of the 1960s fell under the sway of fashionable sex comedies and the gaudy excesses of Federico FELLINI (qv), the bleakness of Ortese's view of economic and human relations merely intensified, and his one colour film for a major studio from this period, *Ê la Vita!* (*Life's Like That*, 1964), had to be re-shot because its ending was considered unduly pessimistic. (The film concerns a loving mother who turns prostitute in order to pay for her schizophrenic son's medical treatment. Finally she becomes housemaid to a wealthy Florentine couple, but in Ortese's original version, just as she has almost raised enough money for her family to move out of their cramped and unsanitary apartment, she loses both her legs in a freak vacuum-cleaning accident.) Ortese's last film has never been publicly shown. A reputedly horrific, remorseless indictment of the military establishment, and — in its director's words — 'a hymn to the degradation of the human spirit', *Sergente Cesso* (*Latrine Duty* [US: *The Army Stinks*], 1972) failed to find a distributor and indeed has only ever been seen by a handful of people, including one Italian critic who is said to have left a screening after only ten minutes and told reporters that Ortese 'should be put to sleep like a sick animal'. Unable to raise any more money for film projects, Ortese spent the last three years of his life as a virtual recluse in the Tuscan mountains, where he died of pneumonia in the winter of 1975.

And so there was a 'lost' Ortese film! Terry felt a sudden thrill as he read these last sentences. He knew at once that it would become his obsession to trace both the known and the unknown work of this director. On Monday morning he called in at his supervisor's office and received her permission to make Ortese's life and career the subject of his third-year dissertation.

Obsessions, of course, can never be shared. Over the next few weeks, whenever he tried to explain his feelings about these films, or arranged screenings for his friends in the projection rooms on campus, he came up against a solid barrier of boredom and incomprehension. It was on one such occasion, late in the spring term, that he had a minor quarrel with Robert over aesthetics.

'Why don't you ever like cheerful films?' Robert asked him, as they left the film department and walked through the campus car park. 'Why do you only like films that are miserable and depressing? Why aren't your favourite films the same as everyone else's — like *Casablanca*, or that one with James Stewart at Christmas?'

'Because they're not the work of real artists,' said Terry. 'And there's no mystery about them, no enigma.'

'Oh, but that's so élitist. In fact you're the ultimate élitist, aren't you? Because you're convinced that the only film worth seeing is one that nobody can ever see.'

It was true that although he had sent out more than twenty letters about Ortese to archives and resource centres all over the world, Terry had so far been unable to locate a single viewing print of his most elusive film. None the less, this had not stopped him working on a 5000-word essay entitled 'Screening the Unscreenable: A Case Study of Audience Responses to Salvatore Ortese's *Latrine Duty*', which his supervisor had adored, and which he was now preparing to submit — with her encouragement — to a prestigious national film magazine called *Frame*.

'And that's another thing,' said Robert. 'I think it's ridiculous that you've written an article about a film you haven't even seen.'

'But has anybody seen it? That's exactly the point. Does it even exist?'

'I think you're going mad. I worry about you, you know. I worry for your mental health and your physical well-being.'

'*You* should talk,' said Terry. They had reached his car, and he searched his pockets for the keys. 'You're the one with the weird fixation.' He realized this sounded harsh, and asked more kindly: 'Robert, when are you going to get over her?'

'Why should I want to do that?'

Terry sighed, and eased himself into the driver's seat. 'Are you not coming with me, then?'

'No. She said she might be eating at Jonah's. I think I'll go and look for her there.'

'It'll end in tears,' said Terry, starting the engine. 'I'm warning you.'

Robert remembered something. 'There was a guy looking for you this morning. A strange little guy. American accent.'

Terry grimaced. 'Not Joe Kingsley?'

'That's the one. Said he had something important to ask you.'

'I'm sure it can wait,' said Terry, and drove off along the campus ring road at irresponsible speed, glancing into his mirror only once to see the figure of Robert, still standing in the car park, rooted, forlorn.

8

For many years now, Terry had not given a moment's thought to Salvatore Ortese or his mythical 'lost' film. But when he left the clinic on Tuesday morning and took the bus on to campus, he was astonished by the speed with which those memories came rushing back; astonished by the sharpness and immediacy with which he experienced, once again, those ancient pangs of hunger for forbidden knowledge. They began to steal over him as soon as he entered the library. Its doors slid open automatically with a noise like a seductive exhalation of breath (another instant reminder of his student days), and soon he found himself standing by the old familiar shelves: the rows upon rows of green-backed volumes he had once pored over so fanatically that he had almost learned them by heart: *Positif*, *Film Comment*, *Sight and Sound*, *Cahiers du Cinéma*. It was here, he remembered, that the search had begun, when he had trawled through every yearly index to these publications and followed up even the tiniest reference to Ortese and his films. How passionate he had been, in those days; how driven. In his interview with Dr Dudden, Terry had described it as a period of depression: but he realized now that this was wrong. Maybe he had been sleeping for almost fourteen hours a day, but at least he had had an objective then, a goal. When did all that energy become dissipated; when did he allow it to be swept away by randomness?

Terry brooded over this question as he succumbed to an illicit cup of coffee in the empty restaurant attached to the campus Arts Centre. He had been hoping for a nostalgic visit to Jonah's, the old self-service cafeteria, but it seemed to have disappeared. There had been many changes to the university in the last twelve years: this restaurant itself was new, brand-new, shiny with mirrored surfaces and chrome furniture and the reflecting glass of a dozen colourful abstracts. The cinema next to it was new as well, and there was a new concert hall and theatre, called the Stephen Webb Centre: a detail which might have given Terry pause for thought, had he actually noticed it. But he was far too busy contemplating the mystery of his lost ideals; too busy trying to remember, among other things, the last piece of research he had done on Ortese. It must have been during his trip to Italy in November 1984. Terry had been to Milan, to write about the making of a film — although *Frame* had never used the article — and had then travelled down to Rome for a few days, where he talked his way into the *Cinecittà* archives by diligently courting the sweet and sexy brown-eyed receptionist whose job it was to keep the likes of Terry at bay. Finally she had granted him access to the stills library, and there, after spending more than a dozen hours knee-deep in transparencies and eight-by-ten black-and-whites, he had found (and yet he had forgotten this; how could he have forgotten it?) almost what he was looking for. He had found, at any rate, proof that the film existed; proof that it was more than the product of mere rumour and journalistic speculation. He had found a photograph.

One photograph. A poor memento, perhaps, of the film which to Terry's fevered imagination had become the artistic equivalent of the Holy Grail: but all the more precious for precisely that reason. And what had become of it? This was the incredible part: Terry could scarcely remember. He had brought it back from Italy with him, certainly, and must have stashed it away somewhere, but he had changed addresses at least six times since then, and had no idea whether the photograph would have survived all of these moves. The idea that it might be lost suddenly horrified him.

How could his attitude towards this priceless relic have become so cavalier? If *Latrine Duty* had run for two hours, at twenty-four frames per second, this meant that out of the 172,800 images which made up the film, he had obtained (stolen would be the more correct term) what was quite possibly the only surviving remnant. Today, for the first time in twelve years, the hugeness of this realization returned to him. He began to doubt whether he could wait until the end of his stay at the clinic before rushing back to London and searching for it, amongst the boxes and files full of junk that nowadays passed for furniture in his flat.

Terry ordered another cup of coffee, then found to his surprise that he couldn't finish it. He thought that perhaps it was too bitter, and added some sugar, but this didn't help. He noticed that his hands were starting to shake. He felt wide awake, but with a strange, nervy, artificial excitement that interfered with the more deep-seated restfulness he had felt settling upon him during the last few days. He decided, most unusually for him, that it was time for a walk.

He walked for most of the afternoon: into town, at first, in search of old haunts which he was not surprised to find long vanished. The Café Valladon was gone, replaced by a Christian bookshop. The Planetarium was gone, replaced by a Tourist Information Centre and a scrawny museum offering interactive local history. The library was still there, though, and so was The Half Moon, and so was The Crown Hotel where his parents had sometimes stayed, and so was the cinema which was currently showing, he noticed with a micro-flicker of professional interest, *Toy Story*, *The Birdcage* and *Chalk and Cheese 4*. There was still a faded air about the place, a mustiness like the faint odour of sad memories you find when opening a long-disused drawer. Very soon he began to feel thoroughly depressed. And so he set off along the cliff path, the route back towards Ashdown which he had always indolently disdained as a student, but which now beckoned irresistibly with its promise of vigorous exercise

and a cleansing sea breeze. Terry calculated that if he made
good time, he would arrive ten minutes early for his five o'clock
appointment with Dr Dudden.

As Terry strode purposefully along the cliffs in the direction of
Ashdown, Sarah was making slower, more meditative progress
through the park on her way home from school. It was the day
after her encounter with Ruby, and she was still preoccupied
with the memories it had stirred.

Summer was yet to assert itself, this last week in June. A few
isolated, freakishly sunny days had been enough to persuade
most Londoners that a heatwave had arrived, so that singlets,
shorts and T-shirts were much in evidence today, even though
the sky was cloudy and a skittish northerly breeze threatened
to scatter thin raindrops. Sarah was beginning to shiver, even
in her work clothes; and her first thought, when she saw Alison
Hill sitting alone on a bench, was that she looked not just bored
and lonely, but cold.

It was sports day at school, so there were no lessons that afternoon. Sarah had watched the first few events and then decided
that her presence was no longer required; and those pupils who
were not taking part had been given the option either of staying
to watch or going home for the rest of the day. It was a slightly
alarming surprise to discover that Alison had done neither.

'Hello,' she said, standing over the small, frail figure on the
bench. 'What are you doing here, all by yourself?'

'Just sitting,' said Alison placidly.

'Well — do you mind if I sit with you for a minute?'

Alison — not having much choice — shook her head.

'Not watching the sports, then?' said Sarah, as she settled
beside her.

'No.'

'Bit boring, you think?'

'Mm.'

'So . . .' Sarah wondered how best to approach this. 'Do you live near here, then? We must be nearly neighbours.'

'Quite near here,' said Alison. She pointed towards one of the park gates. 'We live over there. Not *on* the main road, but quite close by.'

'The Seven Sisters Road, you mean?'

'Yes.'

'Well, that's not far from my house,' said Sarah. Technically a lie, but justified in the circumstances, she thought. 'Would you like to walk home together? Only, it's not always a good place to be by yourself, this park.'

'I can't go home, yet,' said Alison. 'Mum'll be at work.'

'Don't you have a key or something?'

Alison shook her head. 'I thought I did, but I can't find it. It's supposed to be in my satchel. I think I might have left it at home.'

'But — what time will your mother be back?'

'Seven o'clock, she said.'

This was not for another four hours. Having established, quickly, that there were no neighbours or relatives for Alison to call upon, Sarah came to an inevitable if reluctant decision. Abandoning her half-formed plans for a shower, a nap, a few chapters of her Lorrie Moore novel followed by a serious assault on the assessment forms, she said to Alison: 'Well, how would you like to come home with me for the afternoon? You could come back and have some tea and watch some telly.'

Not seeming too excited by this offer, Alison bowed her head and nodded. 'OK.'

'Come on then.'

They got up and walked towards the park gates in silence. Sarah was wondering why Alison had not made any reference to her father, and tried to recall the few details of her family background she had picked up from a dimly remembered conversation in the staff room a few months ago. In fact there *was*

no father, she was fairly certain. There had been some speculation — inconclusive, as far as she could remember — over
whether there had ever been a father on the scene, or whether
he had left only recently. At which point, the oddness of Alison's
poem came back to her, and a suspicion began to form.

'That was a lovely poem you read out in class the other day,'
Sarah said. 'What gave you the idea? Have you got your own
telescope? Do you like looking at stars?'

Alison shook her head shyly. 'No, I just . . . started to write it,
and the words came out . . .'

'It was very sad,' said Sarah. 'I felt sorry for the two stars by
themselves, after the big one had died. Did you mean to write
such a sad poem?'

'Well . . .' Alison began, but went no further.

Sarah realized that this line of enquiry was not going to lead
anywhere, and realized too that she could not cope with the
idea of Alison being in her house all afternoon, perched on the
edge of the sofa, subdued and fearful, nibbling biscuits or sitting glassy-eyed with boredom in front of children's TV. And so,
as an interim measure, they detoured via the nearest McDonald's, where Sarah had coffee — or something like it — and Alison had Fillet-o-Fish and a chocolate shake. It seemed to cheer
her up slightly, although she became no more talkative; after
fifteen minutes their conversation dried up altogether.

'We'd better go now,' Sarah said, looking at her watch. 'But
first of all, I want you to have one last look for this key. Are you
sure it isn't in your satchel?'

As Alison opened the bag and rummaged through it with
a resigned, dutiful air, Sarah saw something that instantly
chilled her.

'What's that?' she asked gently, craning forward.

Alison's eyes were wide and guilty, eloquently pleading with
Sarah not to take the matter any further. But she was not to
be deterred. She pulled aside the exercise books and the
scrunched-up grey sweater, peered into the satchel and found,

to her dismay, that her passing glimpse had not been deceptive: there was a dead animal lying at the bottom. For a ghastly moment she thought that it was a rat; but it turned out to be a small, tawny field mouse. Alison had also found a scrap of green velvet from somewhere, and had partly wrapped the animal up in it. It did not seem to have been dead for long: probably less than a day.

'Alison,' said Sarah, looking gravely into her eyes, 'you must never, ever keep dead things in your bag like that. They carry all sorts of diseases. You could make yourself very ill indeed. Do you keep food in this bag?'

'Sometimes,' said Alison. 'When Mum makes me sandwiches.'

'Well, when you get home, you're going to have to ask her to disinfect it. In fact, we'll disinfect it together, when we get back to my house. And what we're going to do now, we're not going to take him out here, in the restaurant, because that might cause trouble; but we're going to go out into the street, and then I'm going to wrap him in tissue paper and throw him in the nearest rubbish bin.'

'But he's *not* rubbish,' Alison protested, tearful now.

'Where did you find him?'

'At school. By the football pitch.'

'And what were you going to do with him?'

'Take him home, and bury him.'

Suddenly, from across the years, a rogue memory emerged and pierced Sarah's consciousness, eliciting (most inappropriately at this point) a private smile. She remembered the absurd conversation she had had with Robert, that day — only their second conversation, really — when he had been talking about his dead cat, and she thought he had been talking about his sister, and she had been horrified to learn that his father planned to take her out into the back garden and bury her in a bin liner. All at once the misunderstanding seemed so delicious that she wanted to giggle; she even wondered if it was worth sharing with Alison, to see if it would defuse the tension; but one look at her unspoilt, unquestioning face, the lower lip beginning to tremble, the eyes swollen from the tears that had flowed (Sarah was beginning to suspect) during many recent nights, was enough to stifle that idea. Instead, she merely stood up and led Alison towards the door, thinking to herself, almost with panic now: *This child is haunted by death. Obsessed with it.*

Three more hours to go until seven o'clock. The mouse safely disposed of, Sarah began to look around for other excuses to delay their return to her noiseless, unwelcoming house: and after a few minutes' walking, a kind of salvation presented itself in the form of a multiplex cinema. Sarah took Alison into the foyer and they stood looking at the posters and starting times.

'Do you go to the cinema much?' Sarah asked.

'Not really. In the holidays sometimes. At home we rent videos.'

Most of the films were completely unsuitable, and in any case carried '15' or '18' certificates. There was one, however, which looked more promising: a comedy called *Chalk and Cheese 4*. The poster didn't inspire much confidence, showing as it did two uniformed policemen pointing gigantic guns in each other's faces, beneath the tagline, 'THEY'RE BACK — THEY'RE ON THE CASE — AND THEY'RE CRANKIER THAN EVER!' But this was the film, Sarah now realized, that Terry had been eulogizing at such length in the paper last week. 'Fun for all the family': hadn't that been his conclusion? Well, for the rest of this afternoon she and Alison were a family, of sorts, and they were certainly both in need of a little fun. Sarah bought two tickets and they went inside.

Once the film had started, it only took a few minutes for her to realize that she had made a terrible mistake. It was offensive on so many different levels that she would have hesitated to take anyone to see it, let alone a sensitive and immature nine-year-old. It wasn't so much the humour, although Alison sat unmoved and apparently baffled through those scenes which were intended to be funny (a sequence, for example, where the two policemen were assigned the task of escorting the President's wife to a speaking engagement, but found, after consuming a heavy meal of baked beans at police headquarters, that they kept breaking wind in the confines of her limousine); nor was it the film's awesome brutalization of women, one of its recurring motifs (there was a sub-plot involving a wrongfully arrested shopkeeper, whose shy, respectable wife was made to perform a striptease for the two policemen in order to secure her husband's release from the cells; naturally she found herself aroused by the experience and later took up stripping as a career). What really alarmed Sarah, what made her hotly ashamed to have brought Alison into the cinema that afternoon, was the film's love affair with death: the way it revelled in death as sideshow, carnival, joke-fodder and comic panacea. Characters would be killed off, blown away, taken out, blasted open with shotguns, all for the sake of a plot twist or even a wisecrack. Casual genocide was committed on passers-by with the random explosion of cars and buildings. The film's one sympathetic black character, a lovable Uncle Tom who served as sidekick to the eponymous heroes, was cheerfully assassinated to supply a few seconds' worth of pathos. This film, which never aspired to anything other than insolent hilarity, was permeated with death; saturated and clotted with it.

To make matters worse, it was not long before the coffee Sarah had drunk at McDonald's began pressurizing her bladder.

'I'll be right back,' she whispered to Alison, with a squeeze of her arm; and then, as she splashed cold water on to her face in the ladies' toilet she decided that, come what may, they might as well walk out of the film now. There was no point in prolonging the ordeal.

Sarah dried her face with paper towels and returned to her seat. But Alison had gone.

'Punctuality, Mr Worth,' said Dr Dudden, looking approvingly at his watch as Terry sat down opposite him. 'Punctuality is the key to organization. Organization is the key to success. I'm pleased to see that you're with me on this one.'

He turned off his portable cassette player (upon which some characterless, even-handed piece of harpsichord music had been playing) and added — presumably to himself — 'That man ignores the metronome markings. Simply ignores them.' Having got that off his chest, he settled himself at the desk and beamed at his patient, who smiled back wanly. In point of fact, Terry was not feeling at all well. His walk along the cliffs, far from refreshing him, had proved physically exhausting: he had not realized that he was so thoroughly out of condition. The one-and-a-half cups of coffee he had drunk that morning were continuing to take powerful effect, and his brain was spinning with an energy that was disconcertingly at odds with the weariness in his limbs: in particular, he could not stop worrying about the precious photograph which might or might not be hidden away somewhere in his London flat. And finally, to make matters worse, two alarming thoughts regarding Dr Dudden had started to take root in his mind. One was that, judging from the heaviness of the bags under his eyes, the doctor did not seem to be getting nearly enough sleep. And the other was even more worrying: because after that compliment about punctuality, delivered in tones far more affable and welcoming than usual, Terry had a terrible suspicion that Dr Dudden was beginning to like him.

This suspicion was promptly confirmed by his next speech.

'You've been here for slightly more than a week, now, Mr Worth, and this seems to me an appropriate time to undertake a small review of our *modus operandi*.

'I say this because, before you arrived, I assumed that the primary benefit of your visit — for me as a researcher — would lie in the opportunity to assess how your dream content was affected by the experience of seeing so many films in such a short space of time. However, since you haven't been dreaming at all, this has obviously not been feasible.'

'I may not have been dreaming,' said Terry, 'but I have been feeling different. More rested.'

'That doesn't surprise me. You *are* beginning to sleep more. Last night, for instance, you spent eighteen minutes in Stage Two.'

Terry nodded, not really understanding.

'Is it a pleasant sensation, would you say — this sense of feeling rested?'

'Well — yes,' said Terry, rather surprised.

'I see.' This did not seem to be the response that Dr Dudden had been anticipating, or hoping for. He leaned forward now, and spoke with some enthusiasm. 'I don't mind telling you, Mr Worth, that you have confounded my expectations, and turned out to be a far more extraordinary specimen than I had imagined. I'm beginning to wonder, in fact, whether your case might not be unique in the annals of sleep research. And what I would like to suggest to you — the *invitation* that I would like to extend to you — is that you stay at this clinic for as long as you like. As our guest. And that these "interviews", as I have rather formally called them, should become . . . well, less formal.'

'Less formal?'

'Friendlier. More in the nature of . . . chats. That way —'

'That way you hope to ingratiate yourself with me, so that I decide to stay around. And then you, as a researcher, have plenty of access to me, as a specimen.'

'That is a *very* cynical way of looking at it.'

'Maybe.' Perhaps it was simply because he felt so weak and breathless, but Terry was beginning to soften towards Dr Dudden in spite of himself. 'These chats, then: can we envisage a two-way exchange of information here? I am supposed to be writing about this place, after all.'

'By all means. By all means. I'm only too delighted to hear that you think our work might be of some interest to the wider world. And I can allow you reasonably free access to our materials — while respecting the patients' confidentiality, of course . . .'

'Of course.'

'So: is there anything you want to ask, to get the ball rolling?'

'Yes, there is,' said Terry. 'There are lots of things.'

'Ask away, then.'

'Right.' Terry sat up in his chair, trying to assume an attitude of concentration. 'Well . . . you said that my case may well be unique, for instance. What exactly were you comparing it to?'

'Only two comparisons come to mind, one of them professionally documented, the other one not. A seventy-year-old retired district nurse from London, known only as Miss M., spent some nights in a reputable sleep laboratory and was found to subsist on only one hour's sleep a night. Her attitude towards people who slept longer than this was quite scathing: she thought that they were idlers and time-wasters. Perhaps she had a point.' He tailed off for a moment, here, and then regained his thread. 'Even more remarkable was the widely publicized case of the director of a London orphanage, who claimed in 1974 to have slept for only fifteen minutes a day since the war. This claim was never verified, however, because he adamantly refused to visit a laboratory. The record for the longest uninterrupted period of sleeplessness is held by a Mr Randy Gardner from San Diego: in 1965, at the age of seventeen, he went without sleep for two hundred and sixty-four hours. His motor and physical functions did not appear to have been impaired at all, and at three a.m. on the last night of his attempt he played a game of basketball, which he won. But I suspect that you, Mr Worth, could break this record quite easily, if you haven't already done so without realizing it. I know for a fact that you have been at this clinic for more than two hundred hours without progressing any further than Stage Two sleep.'

'Perhaps you should explain to me how these stages work: I'm not quite clear about that.'

'It's very simple. Stage One is the transition from wakefulness to drowsiness, during which your blood pressure drops and your heart rate slows down and your muscles relax. The brain at this point is emitting alpha waves at a frequency of seven to fourteen cycles per second. This stage usually lasts for five or ten minutes at the most. Stage Two begins with the appearance of theta waves of three-and-a-half to seven-and-a-half cycles per second, along with sleep spindles and K-complexes. Early in the night this stage also lasts for just a few minutes, and then we see slow delta wave activity beginning, which marks the start of unconsciousness proper. Stage Three is an interim stage, when the delta waves still account for less than half the recording on the EEG. Stage Four is when the delta waves predominate, there's very little bodily movement and the sleeper is hard to awake. Stage Four is the deepest and most restful part of sleep: some researchers call it "core sleep". After maybe half an hour or three-quarters of an hour of this, there will be noticeable body movements and changes of position. Stage Four has been interrupted, the sleeper returns very briefly to Stage Two or Three, and then quickly enters what we call REM sleep, or paradoxical sleep. This actually resembles wakefulness more than sleep: muscle tone disappears, but there is frantic brain activity and the eyes roll from side to side beneath the closed lids. This whole cycle, from Stage One to REM, has taken about ninety minutes and will repeat itself, with some variations, about four or five times during the night.'

'What sort of variations?'

'First of all, Stage Four sleep predominates. Then, as the night goes on, the REM periods get longer and longer. This makes some researchers think that Stage Four is what the brain really needs to refresh itself, and the dreams generated during REM sleep — especially early in the morning — are just something devised by the brain to keep itself amused while the body carries on resting.'

'But so far I've got no further than Stage Two — is that right?'

'Remarkably, yes.'

'And when can I expect to start dreaming again?'

'When you enter REM sleep, probably: if that ever happens.' Allowing Terry a moment or two to absorb this information, Dr Dudden went on: 'I made one other assumption about you, Mr Worth — a very naïve one — before you arrived. I assumed that, like my other patients, you were coming here in the hope that I would cure you of your insomnia: prescribe sedatives, cyclopirolones, something like that. I hadn't realized —' and now he looked at him differently: testingly '— that you and I felt the same way about sleep. That we were . . . allies, if you like.'

Terry squirmed a little. 'I'm not sure that I follow.'

'Let me put it this way,' said Dr Dudden, rubbing his eyes in an absent-minded way. 'Do you think you would have achieved nearly so much, in your career as a journalist, if you'd been sleeping eight hours a night for the last twelve years?'

'No, I don't suppose I would. As a freelance, it gives me a big advantage — I can be twice as productive as everyone else.'

'Exactly. Exactly! Whereas here, Mr Worth, *here*, you must be going out of your mind with boredom, tied down to the bed all night with those electrodes.'

'It's a bit dull, yes.'

'So what do you think about? How do you keep yourself amused?'

'The worst thing is not having a television in the room. If I had a television, it wouldn't be a problem. I listen to my Walkman, I write things on my laptop. Sometimes I read.'

'What do you read?'

'Reference books, if I can find them. I like books of lists. Books that give you little bits of information.'

'You don't read novels, or biographies?'

'No. I don't like continuous narratives, I can't concentrate on them.'

'But you like films?'

'Yes.'

'On the subject of which . . .' Dr Dudden reached up and fetched a box-file from the shelf behind him. 'I was very struck, the other day, by your failure to recognize Lorna, our technician, after being introduced to her twice. I've devised a little experiment, with the help of my colleagues in the University Film Department. Do you mind if we try it?'

'Not at all.'

Dr Dudden opened the file and took out a sheaf of photographs.

'I want to see how many of these you can identify,' he said, and held up the first. 'Any ideas?'

Terry stared at the picture and frowned. There was something distantly recognizable about the face, and a name hovered just out of his mind's reach; but both finally eluded him.

'No. I'm sorry.'

'It's Dr Goldsmith, our neurologist. How about this?'

The second photograph presented no problems.

'Steve Buscemi. He was Mr Pink in *Reservoir Dogs*, and he plays one of the kidnappers in *Fargo*.'

'Very good. What about this one?'

Terry failed to identify the next picture, which was a photograph of Lorna.

'And this?'

'Ray Liotta, from *Unlawful Entry* and *Something Wild*.'

'Just a couple more. Who's this, would you say?'

Terry could see which way the exercise was heading now, and made a concentrated effort with the next picture. The face was certainly familiar, this time; he felt for some reason that it ought to be embedded in his consciousness more deeply than the other two. But still he had to admit defeat.

'It was Dr Madison. One more, to finish off with. I'm told that you might find this one rather more difficult.'

Terry did not find it difficult at all. 'Shelley Hack,' he said. 'She was one of *Charlie's Angels*, for a while, and she played Jerry Langford's assistant in *The King of Comedy*.'

'Excellent, Mr Worth. Excellent. I'm relieved, to tell you the truth. It had occurred to me that you might be suffering from serious memory loss: but the problem is clearly localized. Twelve years!' He put the photographs back in their file, and looked at Terry with a noticeable gleam in his eye: triumphant, proprietorial. 'Twelve years, with only selective damage to your powers of recall. I hope you realize how special this makes you. I hope you realize how *important* you are.'

'I'm not sure that I do.'

Dr Dudden continued to shake his head in wonder. For a nasty moment, Terry thought that he was going to reach across the desk and embrace him.

'I'm going to learn so much from you, Mr Worth. So very, very much.' Smartly, now, he rose to his feet. 'Come with me, in the meantime. There's something I'd like to show you; something that I know will interest you.'

Terry had no idea where Dr Dudden was leading him as they left the office and crossed the stone-flagged entrance hall. To his surprise, the doctor opened a door beneath the main stair-case, and they descended into the basement, which Terry remembered as damp, neglected and unsavoury, and rarely visited by the students. Now, however, its whitewashed walls and strip lighting made it seem bright and clean, even antiseptic, and it was loud with the rumble of washing-machines and driers.

'We decided to put the laundry room down here,' Dr Dudden explained. 'Even in a temple of science, you see, the practicalities must be attended to. However, this is not what I wanted to show you.'

He ushered Terry down towards the very end of the corridor, where their path was uncompromisingly barred by a heavy metal door, bearing the legend: 'RESTRICTED AREA. STRICTLY

AUTHORIZED PERSONNEL ONLY TO PROCEED BEYOND THIS POINT'. It was secured by an electronic combination lock. Dr Dudden entered six digits on to the keypad, then paused.

'Now: you wouldn't describe yourself as a sentimental man, would you?' he asked Terry. 'Or squeamish, in any way?'

'Not at all.'

Dr Dudden smiled. 'I thought not,' he said; then pressed the two remaining numbers, waited for the responding click, and pushed the door open.

9

The beach was little used, and could only be reached by a steep, narrow path cut roughly into the sheerness of the cliff.

From the beach you could see Ashdown, perched on its clifftop, grey and formless in the sunlight.

From the windows of Ashdown you could make out figures on the beach; but it would be hard to identify them.

Robert walked down the path first, carrying the Sainsbury's bag full of food, drink, books and magazines. Sarah came last, carrying a spade in one hand and, slung over her shoulder, a rucksack containing towels and swimming costumes. Ruby was in the middle: she carried a bucket.

The task of escorting a child along this route made Robert realize that it was more dangerous and uneven than he had remembered. Every so often he turned and took Ruby's hand, helping her to negotiate some sudden declivity, some breach in the pathway where the dry, sandy soil had crumbled away. At one point she lost her footing, slipped, and might almost have fallen over the edge had he not stayed her in time; and although Ruby herself seemed not in the least put out by the accident, it made Robert wonder again whether they hadn't exceeded their authority by bringing her to the beach; if they hadn't taken on more than they could really manage. It was an entirely new experience for him, to have accepted responsibility (even a shared and temporary responsibility) for the welfare of this small and vulnerable human being. Consciousness of her absolute, unthinking trust in him coursed through his body like electricity; shocking and wonderful.

Equally wonderful was the circumstance, quite unexpected, which had brought this miraculous day into being: Veronica's absence. It was half-term at the local schools, and for most of the week she and Sarah had been doing some voluntary child-minding for the caretakers at Ashdown, Mr and Mrs Sharp. They needed someone to look after their eight-year-old daughter Ruby, since Mrs Sharp had recently taken on an afternoon cleaning job in the neighbouring village. The two students would take Ruby up to the room they now shared together, and while one of them worked at the old pine desk, crouched over a mound of file paper or a broken-backed library book, the other would help the child with a jigsaw, or read aloud to her, or squat cross-legged on the floor with her over a game of Snap or Pelmanism, or sit with her in the bay window overlooking the ocean, playing noughts and crosses on the steamed-up glass.

In the process, however, Veronica was neglecting her duties as stage manager on that term's production of *Arturo Ui*, and today she decided that she could not absent herself any longer. It was a Thursday in May, and the weather had just turned: suddenly it was warm, as warm as it was ever likely to get during the summer, without a breath of wind and with a cloudless sky as blue as the deep blue at the base of a flame. (Late in the afternoon, breaking a long silence, Sarah would look up and quote six words from the novel she was reading — 'as still, as carved, as death' — and for many years afterwards Robert would remember these words, which never failed, for him, to reawaken the exact substance and texture of that day.) Through the window of his own room, Robert had been staring thought-lessly into this blueness for some time when he heard Sarah's knock at the door (he always knew when it was Sarah's knock), and she had appeared in his doorway with Ruby clutching on to her hand. She wanted to know whether he could keep an eye on her for a while: just for an hour, while she finished writing up some notes. But this one hour was all it had taken for Robert and Ruby to hatch their scheme of walking down to the beach, so that they were able to present Sarah with a *fait accompli*, right down to the preparation of the sandwiches which they undertook together in the kitchen while she sat unwittingly upstairs, putting the finishing touches to her work. Sarah had refused the suggestion at first; then softened towards it; and finally embraced it wholeheartedly. Mrs Sharp had left her with the keys to her cottage, one of a puzzling, isolated row of terraces about half a mile down the road from Ashdown, and it was from there that they fetched Ruby's bucket, spade and swimsuit before heading off to the clifftop and their hazardous descent. By the time they reached the bottom it was two-thirty and, as they might have expected on a weekday afternoon, out of season, the beach was quite deserted.

The first thing they did was to undress.

Ruby, as it turned out, was the least inhibited of the three. She stood placid and uncomplaining as Sarah unbuttoned her dress and helped her briskly into her little blue-and-white bathing suit. Sarah's own bathing suit was a navy-blue one-piece, cut low at the back to reveal (as Robert had always groaningly imagined to himself) perfect shoulder-blades and a musky, even, overall tan. She was wearing a long, pale and gauzy summer skirt, and this she did not take off. Robert's swimming trunks were old and slightly too small: he had removed his trousers but not his T-shirt, and soon realized that this was a mistake, because even the sight of these unveiled portions of Sarah's body was enough to provoke an immediate and maddening erection, which he was obliged to conceal by rolling awkwardly to one side and draping an absurd towel over his upper thighs. Prompting Sarah to enquire, laughingly:

'Are you all right?'

'Yes. Yes, fine.'

'You don't look very comfortable, that's all.'

Sarah took Ruby's hand and began to lead her down towards the sea. As soon as they were at a safe distance, Robert removed the towel and glared with unmitigated hatred at the lump in his swimming trunks, until it went away. How he loathed and de-spised this preposterous organ, with its infinitely predictable patterns of behaviour, its changeless, robotic responses to an over-familiar range of visual stimuli. Sarah must have noticed: there could be no doubt about it. His scalp tingled and the blood rushed to his face.

The tide was far out this afternoon. The voices of Ruby and Sarah could barely be heard, like distant music. There was no breeze to waft them towards him.

Robert looked at the books Sarah had brought to the beach with her. There was a novel by Rosamond Lehmann, whose name he had recently learned to recognize (Veronica being a fan, even to the extent of collecting her books in first editions); and there was a strange-looking volume which seemed to con-sist mainly of short paragraphs divided up into sections under headings like 'Detachment', 'The Self' and 'To Accept the Void'. He read a few lines and found himself confronted by a dense, abstract, difficult language in which there appeared to be couched a series of spiritual and theological epigrams. He looked at the title-page. The book was *Gravity and Grace* by Si-mone Weil, and beneath the title these words had been written in blue ink:

'*For Sarah. Sorry to have bombarded you with all the obvious icons. Here's a less obvious one. All my love — Ronnie.*'

Robert flicked forward through the pages hastily.

Sarah and Ruby seemed to be paddling. Sarah had hitched up her skirt and waded into the shallows. She was kicking wa-ter at Ruby, who was screaming and giggling. Then there was a bigger splash as Ruby half fell, half threw herself into the water. More giggling. Could she swim? He had never thought to ask. Sarah would have found out about that, before taking her down to the sea. He was sure they were both safe.

Robert thought to himself: this must be what it is like, to have a family. A wife and a child. This ceaseless admixture of anxiety and trust.

He found a section of the book called 'Love' and started to read it. Most of it was very obscure, but still the words seemed to carry an awkward, hypnotic conviction, and every so often he was struck by a passage of sudden lucidity:

   . . . The day, if it ever comes, when you are given true affection there will be no opposition between interior solitude and friendship, quite the reverse. It is even by this infallible sign that you will recognize it . . .

The water must have been cold: Sarah and Ruby had already left the sea and were on their way back towards him. Ruby was running in manic zigzags, crossing and criss-crossing Sarah's path.

   . . . if it ever comes . . .

Robert watched as Sarah approached, and felt no stirring between his legs this time. He realized that he had never really watched her walking before. Her limbs were delicate, well formed, and there seemed to be an incredible lightness and elegance in her movements. She was ignoring Ruby's attempts to distract her and smiling at Robert as she came nearer: a somehow serious, pensive smile. This combination of ease and melancholy, lightness and weight, pierced him deeply and he found it difficult to smile back.

'Gravity and grace,' she said, sitting down beside him.

It was exactly what he had been thinking. Shocked to find the workings of his own mind being echoed so closely, he merely said: 'What?'

'You're reading my book: *Gravity and Grace*.'

'Oh. Yes. Yes, that's right. Trying to, anyway.'

'I haven't read it yet. It was a present from Ronnie.'

'Yes, I saw.'

'Are you going to read it to me?' Ruby asked, standing over them and looking askance at the cover, as if she didn't expect much from it.

'Not this one, I don't think,' said Sarah.

'Good. I don't want to listen to a book anyway.'

'What would you like to do, darling?'

'Actually I'm quite happy just —' Robert began, and then stopped, realizing that the question had not been directed at him. Under Sarah's amused glance, he swore at himself silently. What was he thinking of, to imagine that she might have addressed him with such a term of endearment? He was letting his fantasies run away with him. He was out of control.

'I'd like to make sandcastles,' said Ruby.

'All right,' Robert agreed, to cover his embarrassment, as much as anything else. 'I'll come and help if you like.'

They walked down together to the point where dry sand, never reached by the incoming tide, began to shade into the damper variety more useful as a building material. Robert watched while Ruby did a bit of energetic digging, filling her bucket twice with sand and upending it to produce two little mounds, which she stood back to admire breathlessly.

'There,' she said.

Robert nodded. 'Very good.' He held out his hand and took the spade off her. 'Now we're going to make a real castle. Come on.'

Ruby watched while he measured an area in the sand about six feet square, and then dug it out to a depth of four or five inches. Next, he shovelled some sand back into this basin, in order to make a central island some three feet square.

'What are you doing?' she asked.

'All this is going to be the moat. We're going to fill it with water right at the end.'

He sent Ruby off to collect as many shells as she could find, to provide decorations for the walls and ramparts. Meanwhile he piled up a new mound of sand on to the island, and began to fashion the main body of the castle from it. He decided to build six towers: four round drum towers, one at each corner, and two rectangular towers springing up from the middle of the eastern and western walls. The main gatehouse would face south, towards the sea, and would be approached by a causeway, interrupted at mid-point by an octagonal barbican. There would be two drawbridges, one protecting the barbican and one connecting to the gatehouse itself.

He had completed most of this work by the time Ruby returned with her trawl of shells; at which point they took a collective decision to abandon architectural logic and continue by piling tower upon tower, so that the castle began to rise impudently up towards the sky like some impossible neo-Gothic wedding cake. Robert stood with one foot in the moat, one on the castle walls, and busied himself with the upper storeys while Ruby began to stud the lower walls with a profligate coating of limpets and topshells, acteons and periwinkles.

'What happened there?' she asked, stopping for a moment, her attention caught by the sight of Robert's bare foot lodged precariously above the postern door. She touched the foot lightly, tracing the still livid double scar — like French quotation marks — where he had months ago nicked the ankle with his razor.

'Oh, that,' he said, looking down. 'That's nothing. I cut myself shaving, that's all.'

'I thought men only shaved their faces,' said Ruby.

'That's true,' he said, 'mostly. But I was actually shaving my legs at the time.'

'Why?'

'I don't know, really. It was an experiment.'

Ruby was very accepting about all of this. She looked briefly up at Robert with wide, serious eyes, and then returned to her handiwork.

Among her more exciting discoveries was a trio of blue-rayed limpets, a pair of saddle oysters and a magnificent Pelican's Foot. She had handfuls of tellin shells, their elastic ligaments still intact so that the paired valves could be opened out to resemble butterfly wings. Colour was provided by the quahog, of which she had found ten or twelve: she cracked them open and positioned them with their colourful interiors facing outwards, adding a touch of royal purple. More subtly, she arranged row upon row of cowries, offsetting their pasta-shell-like plainness with the occasional well-placed ormer, whose tinted iridescent lining would catch the rays of the sun and reflect them back, making the whole edifice twinkle and shimmer in the sunlight like a fantastic mirage. She reserved her augers and screw-shells for the castle towers, where they served as delicate flag-poles, twirling and spiralling up towards the heavens in festive brilliance, making Ruby think irresistibly of fun-fairs, helter-skelters and ice-cream cornets.

The castle was, they both agreed, a masterpiece.

'It'll still be here tomorrow, won't it?' Ruby said. 'As long as it doesn't rain. Then I can bring my friends to come and see it. Susie Briggs and Jill Drew and David.'

'I don't think it will,' said Robert. He straightened one of the razor-shells they had used as a drawbridge, and stirred up the clear salt water in the moat, setting it into rippling motion. 'You see, the tide's going to come all the way in soon, and when that happens, it'll be washed away. Most of it, anyway.'

'Oh.' Ruby was very disheartened. 'Well, why didn't you think of that before?'

'I did. Only we had to build it here, because the sand's nice and damp.' He picked up the bucket and spade and held out his other hand for her to grasp. 'Come on. Let's go and tell Sarah about it.'

Ruby continued to make disgruntled remarks about his choice of location as they passed over a barrier of crisp seaweed and began to trudge their way back across dry sand. But in Robert's ears her voice faded to nothingness, became one with the windless silence of the beach, the deadly stillness of the late afternoon air, as he approached Sarah and dared a smile at her when she raised her eyes from her book. She had draped a cardigan over her shoulders and buried her feet in the sand, and as he looked at her this time he knew, he knew with an ab-solute and thrilling certainty, that a terrible change had taken place in his life; that it had happened months ago, in his room, the day she had come in with her hair still wet, intending to comfort him; but only today had its true meaning and extent become clear as he realized in this one stretched instant that there was nothing in the world he would not do for this woman; no quest he would not undertake, no sacrifice he would not willingly perform . . .

Your gravity, your grace have turned a tide in me . . .

'That took a long time.'

The words vanished from his mind as quickly and as inexplicably as they had formed. He assumed a tone of flippant outrage.

'What are you talking about? Have you seen the size of that sandcastle? That's a work of art, that is.'

'It looks very impressive. What do you think, Ruby? Do you like it?'

Ruby nodded and nestled up beside her, insisting: 'I did the shells.'

'I didn't know either of you had such a creative bent.'

'Neither did I,' said Robert. 'I think sand must be my natural medium.'

'Are you the Sandman, then?' Ruby asked.

'Perhaps I am. Perhaps I'll be coming to visit you tonight when you're asleep.'

Sarah looked down fondly at Ruby's tired face and drooping eyelids. 'I don't think you'll have to wait until tonight, somehow.'

'I must have worn her out,' said Robert.

It took Ruby very little time to fall fast asleep, and during her sweet, easy descent into unconsciousness, a silence established itself between Sarah and Robert, warm and companionable. Sitting beside her on that empty beach, not so much separated as conjoined by the body of the sleeping child, he felt that he had never been so intimate with her. Beneath the heat of the sun his thoughts blurred, pleasantly, into a thick haze, and he had no desire to read: he was happy just to sit there, savouring this moment of closeness, staring at the ocean until his retina ached with the brightness thrown off by the sparkling water. After a while he became aware that Sarah had laid down her novel and that she, too, was looking seawards, her blue-grey eyes filmy with contentment; sun-drunk.

'What are you thinking?' he asked.

Sarah paused, drew in her breath. 'You know, I hate it when Ronnie asks me that.'

'I'm sorry,' said Robert. 'I didn't mean to be intrusive.'

'No: I said I hate it when *Ronnie* asks me that.'

Something inside Robert rejoiced to hear these words. He was immediately hungry for more. 'But not when I do?'

'When I'm alone with her,' said Sarah, slowly, 'I feel she's constantly trying to . . . read me. Whereas you give me — I don't know — space, somehow. Room to breathe.'

Conscious of his own daring, Robert told her: 'That's the infallible sign of true affection. According to your book.'

'Really?'

' "No opposition between interior solitude and friendship." ' He had ventured this far, and now, tremblingly, took one step further. 'But you'd still rather be with her than with me?'

Sarah held his gaze for a second or two, then smiled, and turned back towards the water. 'Since you ask, I was thinking about Cleo.'

'Cleo?'

'Specifically, I was thinking . . . I was thinking that if I'd had a twin sister, and she'd disappeared when I was very small, before I'd had the chance to know her, then there would hardly be a day, hardly a moment, when I didn't think about her. Wonder where she was. What she was doing. Is that what it's like?'

Robert couldn't answer. This time, the words refused to come. 'I suppose so,' he forced himself to say, eventually.

'Do you ever mention her at home? Talk about her with your parents?'

'No,' he said. 'No, never.' He seemed uneasy with the subject, and picked up the copy of *Gravity and Grace* again, adding: 'It says something else in here . . .' He thumbed through the book, but failed to find the relevant page. 'Something about loss: that when you lose somebody, when you miss them, you suffer because the departed person has become something imaginary; something unreal. But your desire for them isn't imaginary. So that's what you have to fasten on: the desire. Because it's real.'

Sarah frowned. 'Perhaps you'll meet her one day, though. She'll seek you out; or you'll start looking for her.'

'I might.' He blew a few grains of sand away from the pages of the book, and closed it. 'It would be a bit silly, wouldn't it, to go through your whole life desiring something, and not doing anything about it?'

'I'm sure it happens.'

'Yes. I'm sure it does.'

The shadow cast by the cliff lengthened, stealing over them. It was getting cooler, and Sarah's arms were covered with goosebumps. Ruby, lying curled against her thighs, stirred for a moment: shifted and kicked against Sarah's legs in ineffectual spasms. A few words gurgled, brokenly, from her mouth. It sounded like 'biscuits' or 'quickly' or 'Timothy'.

'Do you think she's all right?' said Robert.

The words swelled into a quiet, uneven, murmurous stream. Sentences formed and dissolved; strange polysyllables and indecipherable neologisms ebbed and flowed from Ruby's barely parted lips. Her body was at rest and her eyelids were closed, but for a few minutes she continued to talk hummingly in her sleep. Together, Sarah and Robert listened to her somniloquy, anxious but oddly enthralled, until she fell silent.

'Do you think we should wake her?' said Robert, then. 'You don't think she's having a seizure or anything?'

'She's fine.' Sarah felt Ruby's cheek and forehead. Her breathing was slow and regular. 'It might be a mistake to wake her. We'd better be going back soon, anyway. We'll wake her then.' Gently, carefully, she eased away from Ruby's sleeping body and rose to her feet. 'I suppose I'd better go and look at this creation of yours. Before the water gets to it.'

'I wanted to give you a guided tour —'

'No. You stay here, and look after her.'

Robert watched her walking down towards the sandcastle, the pastel colours of her skirt and cardigan washed greyer and bluer by the encroaching shadows; he watched her walking around the castle, inspecting it from different angles, her arms folded; watched her squat beside it, examining the craftsmanship even more closely, the decorative arrangement of shells and the fine, chiselled detail on the battlements. And as he watched her, his hand reached out to touch Ruby's lobster-red hair while she slept, and he began to speak. Aching to tell somebody, at last, of his feelings for Sarah, aching to unburden himself of an emotional weight which he could now barely support, he settled upon this small, sleeping child as the best available recipient of his confidences.

And he said: 'I can't see . . . How this will ever . . .'

Ruby had cried, briefly, upon seeing the sandcastle half-washed away, its turrets and gateway reduced to a shapeless mass by the hissing, invading water; but she had been very brave about it, on the whole, and found other things to think and talk about as Robert and Sarah escorted her back up the cliff path. She was very tired, by now, and Robert carried her up the final stretch, where the path was broad and even enough to allow it. After that, the party split up. Robert went back to Ashdown, where he was meant to be meeting Terry, and Sarah walked with Ruby down the single-track lane to her parents' house. Dusk was falling, and the child held on to her hand tightly.

'I hope your mother won't be worried,' Sarah said. 'We're going to be a bit late getting home.'

'She won't be,' Ruby breezed.

'And have you enjoyed yourself today?'

'Yes. It's been the best day ever.'

'Good. I'm glad. Only perhaps we shouldn't have stayed so long.'

'I don't think we stayed long *enough*,' said Ruby. 'I think we should have stayed there all night.'

'Don't be silly. You're much too tired.'

'I'm not tired at all.'

'So that's why you went to sleep on the beach, is it?'

Ruby was momentarily chastened; then said, in a tone of mild curiosity: 'I didn't know I'd been asleep.'

'Well you were,' said Sarah. 'And you were making noises, too.'

'Making noises? You mean I was talking?'

'I suppose you could call it talking.' She was surprised that Ruby seemed to be taking this in her stride. 'Why, have you done it before?'

'I do it all the time, Mummy says. She was worried about it, and she took me to see the doctor, but he said she needn't be.'

'And what do you talk about, in your sleep?'

'Mummy says it's just nonsense.'

They turned a corner, and the cottages were visible now, only a few hundred yards away.

'If I had a bicycle,' said Ruby, turning and looking back towards Ashdown, a bold silhouette on the horizon, 'I could come and see you all the time, couldn't I?'

'But you don't have a bicycle,' Sarah pointed out.

'I've asked for one. It's my birthday soon.'

'And what did your parents say?'

'They said it was a lot of money.'

'Well, it probably is.'

'Yes, but I really, *really* want one. Not just a bit. If I had a bicycle,' she said, 'I could come up to your house, and you and Robert could take me to the beach every day. Except when I was at school.'

'You'd soon get bored if we went there every day,' said Sarah. 'But we will go again. Next time we might go with Veronica.'

'Can she make sandcastles?' Ruby asked.

'I'm sure she can.'

'As good as Robert's?'

'Bigger and better, probably.'

Ruby clearly found this hard to believe. In any case, she would not be deflected so easily from her theme. 'Well, I *still* want a bicycle,' she said. 'I'm going to ask them again tonight.'

Sarah had an idea: a rather mischievous idea. It came to her quite suddenly, and then she toyed with it, turning it over flirtatiously in her mind — slightly shocked at herself — until they reached the gate at the bottom of the Sharps' garden. Ruby swung the gate open and was about to run up to the front door when Sarah stopped her, tapping her shoulder. 'Listen,' she said, and sat down on one of the low walls which ran on either side of the garden path, so that she and Ruby found themselves face to face, in conspiratorial closeness.

'What?' said Ruby.

'Here's what you should do,' Sarah whispered, 'if you want that bicycle.'

Ruby waited breathlessly.

'You should ask for it *in your sleep*.'

A baffled pause. 'In my sleep?'

'Yes. Your mother's heard you talking in your sleep, hasn't she?'

'Mmm . . .'

'So the next time she comes to your bedroom at night, you *pretend* to be talking in your sleep — yes? — and you say lots of stuff about how much you want this bicycle.'

Ruby met her gaze evenly. 'But why can't I ask for it when I'm awake?'

'Because if you talk about it in your sleep, then your mother will know that you mean it. She'll know how important it is to you. So she'll *have* to get it.'

Comprehension was beginning to dawn, making slow progress across Ruby's freckled face: so Sarah pressed the point home.

'She'll have to believe you. She'll know it's the truth. Because nobody —' (and of all the many strange things Ruby had heard that day, this was the second that she would never forget) '— nobody would ever tell a lie in their sleep. Would they?'

The other thing Ruby would never forget was the sound of Robert's voice as he talked to her, late that afternoon, believing her to be asleep when in fact she had just been woken up by the careful movement of Sarah rising to her feet. The sound of his voice as he spoke to her, softly, almost inaudibly, of something which she didn't understand. The sound of his voice as he said:

'I can't see . . . How this will ever . . .'

And then: 'I have never wanted anything . . .'

And then, after a deeper and longer breath: 'I have never wanted anything so badly, Ruby . . . You don't mind if I tell you this, do you? . . . I may as well tell you . . . While you're asleep, because then . . . My secret will be safe . . . Though I wonder if it is a secret, from her . . . Or anybody . . . Not that anybody else matters . . . What they think . . .

'Ruby . . .

'I'm only young . . . Though to you I must seem old, quite old . . . But I feel young . . . Or did, until . . . Recently . . . But even so . . . Even so, I *know* . . . Or at least imagine . . .

'I can't imagine . . . Ever . . . Not wanting her . . .

'*Ever* . . .

'Though perhaps . . . In the fullness of time, at the end of the day . . .

'But then this *is* the end of the day . . .

'The point is . . .

'You're right, of course . . . I *am* young, there *may* be others . . . But personally . . . I can't see it . . . And in any case . . .

That's not what I want . . . I want . . . I *have* to win . . . To *earn* her, somehow . . . And if . . .

'You see . . . If she doesn't love me, now . . . If she *can't* love me, as I am . . . That's all right . . . Because neither can I . . . If she can't love me . . . Then I can't love myself . . .

'And there are *no* limits . . . None at all, Ruby . . . There is *nothing* I wouldn't do . . . To make her want . . .

'Do you understand? Do you believe that? Do you know what I — ?'

And then Robert fell silent, having looked down, and having seen that Ruby, whom he had imagined to be asleep, was not asleep at all. She was lying quite still, but her limbs were stiff and tightened, and her eyes were open, as wide open

Stage Three

open and ush-
ered Terry into a darkened room in which two sounds competed for precedence: a low hum, as from some unidentified
electrical device, and a sort of quiet scuttling, the continuous
patter of small frantic footsteps which seemed to be coming
from every direction. Then Dr Dudden switched on the overhead lighting, and the following scene presented itself.

The room was not extensive — it was about the size of
Terry's room overlooking the ocean — and it contained twelve
small tables, arranged in three rows of four. On each of these
tables stood a large glass tank. Terry looked closer at the first of
these. Its floor consisted of a shallow basin of water, and just an
inch above this was something resembling a turntable, about
one foot in diameter. The tank was divided in half by a glass
partition, and in each half there was a white rat, its head wired
up to electrodes which in turn were connected to a single master computer standing in the centre of the room. The turntable
was revolving slowly, so that the rats had to keep in constant
motion: otherwise they would have been swept into the water
when they came into contact with the glass partition. The two
rats appeared to be in radically different states of health: one
was clean, sleek and bright-eyed, the other had ragged and
thinning fur, and its eyes were haunted and bloodshot.

'Well, Mr Worth, what do you say?' asked Dr Dudden, beaming proudly as he paraded between the glass tanks. 'Your initial
impressions would be of great interest to me.'

'Remarkable,' said Terry in guarded tones, as he crouched
down to inspect the distressed animals more closely. 'I don't
think I've ever seen anything . . . quite . . .'

'The principle of the experiment is quite obvious, I assume. Elementary, really.'

'You forget that — unlike yourself — I have never been a man of science. You may have to give me a little help.'

'Of course.' Dr Dudden switched on the monitor attached to the computer, and in a few seconds the screen was filled with ragged, constantly shifting lines, scrolling horizontally against a blue background. 'All twenty-four of the animals in this room have been wired up to the computer,' he explained. 'It records the electronic impulses from their brains, just like the machine which has been recording your own brain activity every night. This one, however, is slightly more sophisticated. I imported it from America myself at great personal expense. It monitors each of the animals simultaneously. With a few key-strokes —' he tapped a few times on the computer's keyboard, by way of demonstration '— I can switch from one reading to another.'

'Yes, I can see that: but what makes the turntables go round?' Some of them were revolving, others were stationary.

'It's a simple experiment, once you understand the principle. And I can't claim any credit for inventing it: like most of the great innovations in sleep research, it originated in America. Let me explain.' He pointed at the healthier-looking of the two rats in the glass tank. 'This rat here is the control. The other one is the test animal. When both rats are awake, the turntable is stationary. When the test animal falls asleep, the computer recognizes its slower brainwaves, and the turntable is automatically activated. Both rats have to start moving, to avoid being pushed into the water. *But*, when the test animal is spontaneously awake, on the stationary turntable, the control animal is able to sleep, because *its* brainwaves don't activate the mechanism. And so the control animal is allowed a reduced but still significant amount of sleep, while the test animal is allowed no sleep at all.'

'Until it dies, presumably.'

'Precisely.'

'And how long does that take?'

'Usually two to three weeks. This little fellow,' he said, pointing at the emaciated, wide-eyed creature, 'still has several days to go. Whereas this one —' walking to the furthest tank '— is on his way out, I'd say. Another few hours: six or seven at the most.'

Only at this point did Terry realize that not every tank contained a pair of rats. The middle four each contained a pair of white rabbits; and the last four contained Labrador puppies. It was to one of these that Dr Dudden had just directed his attention: a pathetic, skeletal, slavering creature, its eyes pools of exhausted blankness.

Terry swallowed hard. 'Why don't they bark?' he asked.

'A simple injection neutralizes the vocal cords,' said Dr Dudden. 'A precaution which slightly contaminates the experiment, in the case of these animals, but a necessary one.'

'I still don't quite understand,' said Terry — the words coming with some difficulty now — 'the role of the control animal in this experiment. Why must there be two of them?'

'That's easily explained,' said Dr Dudden. 'Come with me.'

There were two further adjacent doors at the back of the laboratory. From the inside of his jacket Dr Dudden produced two golden keys on a fine chain, and unlocked the left-hand door. It swung open to reveal a large and curiously furnished room. There was no bed, and only one chair, with a straight back and a thin, uninviting cushion to sit on. But there were, in addition, numerous pieces of exercise equipment: a treadmill, a rowing-machine, an exercise bike, and even a basketball hoop fixed to one of the walls. Another wall was covered with shelves full of books and magazines, while further shelves were stacked with computer and board games. There was a television, video and stereo system, along with racks of videotapes and CDs.

'This, as you've probably guessed, is our sleep deprivation room,' said Dr Dudden. 'It's where we experiment on human subjects. Not too Spartan, is it?'

'No, not at all.'

'You'll notice that my priority in equipping this room has been to find ways of stimulating the subject. It's essential, you see, that he finds plenty of ways to keep his mind and body fully occupied.'

'Very impressive,' said Terry, absently: his eyes were drawn, as usual, to the shelf of videos, and he was busy checking out the titles.

'Superficially, yes,' said Dr Dudden. 'But this is really rather a primitive way of studying sleep deprivation. Do you see why? Supposing, after three days in here, the subject shows all the signs of physical exhaustion. Is that due to lack of sleep, or because he has spent so much time on the rowing-machine? His mental responses are slow and erratic. Is that due to lack of sleep, or because he has been watching eight hours of television? Do you see the problem? Is it the lack of sleep that has exhausted him, or *the activities required to induce that lack of sleep*?' He led Terry out of the room, and locked the door carefully behind him. 'That,' he said, gesturing again at the twelve glass tanks, 'is the problem which this experiment so ingeniously solves. Both animals are stimulated equally, but only one of them is subjected to constant sleep deprivation. In this way, we succeed in isolating those symptoms which are the result of sleep deprivation alone.'

'Yes, I can see that now,' said Terry. 'So all you need to find is a version of the experiment which works for human subjects.'

'Correct.'

Terry indicated the second door; the one which had so far remained locked.

'Are you going to show me what's in there?'

Dr Dudden smiled, and toyed with the second of the golden keys on his chain. 'Have you thought about my proposal yet?'

he asked. 'When you have — and if you decide that you'd be willing to stay on here — then I would like us to sign a little contract, giving me certain . . . rights over your case. When we've done that, then I might show you the contents of this room. I think you'll find them interesting. In the meantime, however,' he concluded, looking at his watch, 'I see that we're in danger of missing supper.'

Terry was glad to leave the laboratory, but he made the mistake of looking back, just before Dr Dudden turned off the light, at the twelve glass tanks and their wretched occupants. Even he, who had happily dispensed with sleep for the last twelve years, could see the cruelty of these methods. Surely, he thought, no state-sponsored torturer, employed under however despotic or vindictive a regime, could devise a punishment quite as malevolent as this: to design a system whereby it was the very manifestation of their craving for rest — the appearance of the slow brainwaves associated with sleep — that should condemn these animals to perpetual motion and endless wakefulness. He shuddered at its diabolical ingenuity.

'Forgive me for asking,' he said, as they climbed the stairs to the ground floor, 'but how do you persuade your subjects — your human subjects, I mean — to take part in these experiments? I wouldn't have thought it would be much fun for them.'

'Oh, it's not that difficult,' said Dr Dudden, 'when you think about it.'

The dining-room at Ashdown had been used as a games room during Terry's student days. Now it provided just enough space for a long oak table capable of seating twenty. It was supposedly the custom here, at six-thirty sharp every day, for staff and patients to sit down together for the evening meal, but by the time Terry and Dr Dudden arrived, most of the diners had left: only Dr Madison remained, accompanied on one side by Maria Granger (who suffered from narcolepsy) and on the other by a somnambulist called Barbara. Dr Dudden pointedly avoided this group, and went to sit at the other end of the table, where he and Terry were presented with two bowls of tomato soup. After taking a couple of sips and adding copious amounts of salt and pepper, Dr Dudden resumed his explanation.

'Luckily, the university presents us with a large pool of willing participants. Many students have found the sleep deprivation room to be a rather pleasant environment, compared to most of the accommodation on campus. And then, of course, we pay them to take part in the experiments. Pay them a good rate, I might say.'

'All the same . . .'

'You and I, Mr Worth — or can I call you Terry, by now? — you and I, Terry, were educated during those halcyon days when students received full government grants to cover their fees and living expenses. We were pampered; spoon-fed. Measures have had to be taken since then: necessary measures, in my view. Nowadays students never tire of bleating about how poverty-stricken they are; how difficult it is to sustain their wasteful, hedonistic lifestyles. Surely you read your own newspapers, now and again? They're awash with heartbreaking tales of hapless scholars reduced to dish-washing, windscreen-wiping, or worse. Life-modelling, for instance. Lovely young female undergraduates at London University, forced to earn a crust in the topless bars of Soho. Lap-dancing; working as Strippograms; prostitution, in some cases. The massage parlours of this town are full of our students, you know — and you should see the prices they charge.'

'Really?'

'Well, so I'm told,' said Dr Dudden hurriedly. 'Anyway, I seem to have strayed from my point . . . And my point is, you see, that we provide an acceptable alternative to that kind of drudgery. Would you care for some wine, by the way?'

He poured a generous glass of Burgundy for himself, and one for Terry — seemingly unmindful, this evening, of the fact that his patients' alcohol consumption was supposed to be strictly regulated. They clinked glasses, and Terry said:

'So you're providing a social service, in other words.'

'Quite. I'm a public benefactor. A hero of the bloody community, not to put too fine a point on it. Ah, splendid, splendid.' He rubbed his hands in pleased anticipation as Janet, one of the cooks, served him a plate of beef, roast potatoes and runner beans. 'Red meat. There's nothing like it, is there? Scottish beef. God, it makes my mouth water just looking at it. What about you, Terry? Are you a meat-eater? A good old-fashioned, red-blooded carnivore? I bet you are.'

'Absolutely. Haven't been eating so much of this stuff, though. You know, a lot of places aren't serving it any more.'

'Because of BSE, you mean? A lot of hysterical rubbish whipped up by members of the most worthless and unscrupulous profession of all: journalists.' He drained his glass of wine in a single draught, refilled it and, to Terry's alarm, touched him jokingly on the arm. 'Present company excepted, of course. No, you won't find any credence given to that kind of unscientific panic-mongering here.' He gestured with his fork at Dr Madison, who was deep in conversation with her companions at the other end of the table. 'Of course, Miss Sourpuss down there will be tucking into her nut cutlets, or whatever nutrition-free alternative she has insisted upon tonight, to satisfy her own opaque ideological requirements.'

'I suppose,' said Terry, 'everyone has the right to their —'

'Tell me about your political views,' Dr Dudden interrupted. 'I imagine you're predictably left-wing, like everybody else in the media these days.'

'Politics are of no interest to me, I'm afraid. Left and right have become meaningless concepts. Capitalism has proved itself unassailable, and sooner or later, all human life will be governed only by the random fluctuations of the market.'

'And this is how it should be?'

Terry shrugged. 'This is how it is.'

'But surely, if you have a political leader of sufficient will, sufficient strength of character . . . Did you not think, for a while, that with Mrs Thatcher in charge, Britain stood poised on the edge of greatness again?'

'She was a remarkable woman, obviously. I couldn't tell you what any of her policies were: I took no notice of them.'

'And yet you and she have something in common, of course.'

'We do?'

'Absolutely. Didn't she attribute her success to the fact that she only needed two or three hours' sleep a night?' Dr Dudden took another slug of wine, and sat for a moment in abstracted thought, a skewered slice of blood-red beef poised in front of his half-open mouth. 'I wrote to her, you know. Numerous times, in fact. Asking her if she would agree to some simple tests. Her office always took the trouble to reply. Courteous refusals. Polite but firm. I'll keep giving it a shot, though. She must have more time on her hands these days. *She* would understand what I'm trying to do here,' he added, turning to Terry now, his voice swelling. '*She'd* have the vision.'

'Yes, I'm sure,' said Terry, spearing a potato.

'Napoleon was a light sleeper, too. And Edison. You'll find it's true of many great men. Edison *despised* sleep, we're told, and in my view he was right to do so. I despise it, too. I despise myself for needing it.' He leaned closer to Terry and confided: 'I'm down to four hours, you know.'

'Four hours?'

'Four hours a night. I've kept it up for the last week.'

'But that can't be good for you, surely. No wonder you look so tired.'

'I don't care. My target's three, and I'm going to get there. It's a struggle for some of us, you know. We don't all have your gifts. That's why I envy you so much. That's why I'm determined to discover your secret.'

Terry took a modest sip from his glass. 'Why despise it, any-way? I don't understand.'

'I'll tell you why: because the sleeper is helpless; powerless. Sleep puts even the strongest people at the mercy of the weak-est and most feeble. Can you imagine what it must be like for a woman of Mrs Thatcher's fibre, her moral character, to be obliged to prostrate herself every day in that posture of abject submission? The brain disabled, the muscles inert and flaccid? It must be insupportable.'

'I hadn't thought of it like that before,' said Terry. 'Sleep as the great leveller.'

'Exactly. That's exactly what it is: the great leveller. Like fuck-ing socialism.' The wine, Terry noticed, was starting to make Dr Dudden turn sour, and a burst of guttural laughter from Dr Madison's end of the table was enough to attract a poisonous look in her direction. 'Listen to that loud-mouthed witch,' he muttered. 'Huddled with her female cronies at the other end of the room. Have you not noticed, Terry, how this table tends to di-vide up on the basis of gender? That's her doing.'

'I'm sure it's only —'

'Dr Madison, you see, tends to prefer the company of women to that of men.'

Terry said, reasonably: 'But that's true of many women, isn't it?'

Dr Dudden lowered his voice. 'I don't think you've quite un-derstood my implication,' he said (wrongly, as it happened). 'Dr Madison,' he explained, whispering now, 'is a daughter of Sappho.'

'Sappho who?'

'She is,' said Dr Dudden, the whisper growing more sibilant and, as a consequence, louder, 'a sister of Lesbos.'

Terry had no idea whether this euphemism was in common usage, or whether Dr Dudden had just made it up. 'You mean she's a friend of Dorothy?'

'Precisely. She's a fucking muff-diver. Or, more accurately, a non-fucking muff-diver.'

'How do you know?' asked Terry.

'Oh, for God's sake, man, just look at her. It's in her whole demeanour. It's written all over her. I mean, has she spoken to you since you arrived here?'

'Not since that first evening, no.'

'Of course not. And she never says more than two words to me if she can help it. She's one of those women who chooses to ignore men because they're of no interest to her as sexual beings.'

'I have noticed a slight animosity between you . . .' said Terry.

'She's a competent psychologist,' said Dr Dudden. 'I have a certain respect for her on that level. But personally, we have nothing in common. Nothing at all.'

'Are you close to any of your colleagues? Personally, I mean.'

'Not really, no. Friendships form, among my staff, but I tend to be excluded from them.' He leaned forward confidingly. 'This might astound you, Terry. It certainly baffles me. But the truth is, I'm not very popular at this clinic.' He sat back with a martyr's smile. 'Explain that if you can.'

Ever since Terry had seen that second, locked door at the back of Dr Dudden's basement laboratory, he had conceived a specific plan for this evening, and listening to several more hours' worth of this stuff was unfortunately an integral part of it. After dinner they withdrew to the doctor's sitting-room, where brandy was poured, consumed, poured again, and followed by a second and then a third bottle of red wine. Terry managed to keep his intake down to a minimum, but was still feeling rather muddle-headed when the clock on the mantelpiece struck ten o'clock. He realized that most of Dr Dudden's latest diatribe had passed him by.

'. . . do these things differently in the United States,' he seemed to be saying. 'The state of sleep research there is infinitely more advanced. My clinic is the only one of its kind in

Great Britain, and yet there are dozens like it in America. Fully resourced, well staffed, and equipped with all the latest technology. In America, computer programs designed purely for polysomnography are written and marketed in the commercial sector. They can even monitor patients who are sleeping in their own homes, with the brainwaves being transmitted to the research centre down the telephone lines, via a modem. Imagine that! Just think of it! That's the sort of enterprise and innovation I'm trying to foster here, but the amount of encouragement I get is precisely nil. It's the bloody something-for-nothing culture in this country, I'm telling you. The Americans can afford to do what they do because they have an efficient system of private medical insurance supporting the whole structure.'

'Sure, sure,' said Terry.

Dr Dudden put down his glass. 'You're not looking well,' he said. 'We've both had too much to drink. Let's go for a walk.'

Before Terry had time to protest, they had swept through the hall — stopping only to pick up a torch from one of the cupboards — and were marching across the moonlit terrace on their way towards the clifftop.

'Where are we going?' said Terry. 'Isn't it a bit dark for this sort of — ?'

'It's not that I object to my lack of status in this community,' Dr Dudden continued, ignoring him. 'I don't mind being regarded as a maverick, an oddball. This is often what happens to men of vision. I don't care if they won't let me join the masons, for instance. I didn't want to join the fucking masons in the first place. Why should I want to join the fucking masons? I don't care about any of that crap, because I know for a fact that when I'm dead and gone, my work will be remembered. Because I'm the *only one*, you see, Terry.' He turned and stared him in the face. A strong wind had risen up and the ocean was roaring beneath him. 'I'm the *only one* working in this field, who sees sleep for what it really is.'

'And what's that?'

'A disease, of course.' He began making his way along the path — which at this point ran perilously close to the edge of the cliff — while declaiming over his shoulder: 'A disease, Terry — the most widespread and life-curtailing disease of all! Forget cancer, forget multiple sclerosis, forget AIDS. If you spend eight hours a day in bed, then sleep is shortening your life by a third! That's the equivalent of dying at the age of fifty — and it's happening to all of us. This is more than just a disease: this is a plague! And none of us is immune, you realize. Not one of us, except . . .' He turned to look at Terry and to draw breath, for he was panting now, either with emotion or exertion. '. . . Except for you.'

'Gregory,' said Terry (it was the first time he had used this name, and only wrung it out with the greatest effort), 'where are we going?'

'Well, I don't know about you,' Dr Dudden replied, 'but I'm going for a swim.'

He switched on the torch and suddenly, alarmingly, seemed to disappear over the precipice. What they had arrived at, in fact, was a steep, narrow path cut roughly into the sheerness of the cliff; a path Terry now remembered as leading down to a sandy beach, which he himself had occasionally visited as a student. He hesitated at the top of this hazardous-looking descent and then began to follow the bobbing light of the torch, cursing softly under his breath.

'So,' Dr Dudden continued, from some way in the night-shrouded distance, 'they call me an oddball, do they? Fine. Well, I'm only trying to give mankind one-third of its life back, that's all. I'm only trying to increase the life expectancy of every man, woman and child on this bloody planet by thirty-three per cent. For Christ's sake, doesn't that justify making a few rats suffer? A few cute-looking puppies?' He paused for a moment to negotiate some sudden declivity, some breach in the pathway where the dry, sandy soil had crumbled away. He was shouting now, to make himself heard above the crashing of the waves. 'And what about a human fatality, if it comes to that? One fucking fatality. Is that such a terrible price to pay?'

Terry paid barely any attention to this speech, since he was having great difficulty keeping his footing, and was already lagging further and further behind. Finally, the ground began to level out and he felt sand beneath his feet. Now he caught up with Dr Dudden and discovered, slightly to his surprise, that he had stripped completely naked.

'What about it, then?' the doctor said. 'Are you game?'

'Pardon?'

'For a swim, man, for a swim.'

'Isn't it a bit cold?'

'Come on, you big Jessie: off with your kecks. Two fine, full-grown men, naked beneath the moonlight: wouldn't that be something for the heavens to look down on tonight?'

'It's pretty rough out there.'

'I'm not a bum-bandit, you know. You've nothing to fear on that account.'

'I can't swim,' Terry protested. It was an unoriginal lie, but an effective one.

'Well, you'll be missing a treat. Keep an eye on my clothes.'

This was an odd request to make, late at night on an empty beach, but Terry nodded his assent and then watched as his companion trotted down towards the sea. As soon as that pale, furry backside was out of sight, he made a grab for the doctor's jacket, found the two golden keys and removed them from their chain. It was a good job he did this quickly, because in less than two minutes Dr Dudden had returned, shivering violently and wheezing harder than ever. His lips had turned blue and his penis was shrivelled to the size of a button mushroom.

'Ye gods,' he moaned, struggling into his wet underpants, and forcing his sand-encrusted feet into the legs of his trousers. 'That was bracing. That's the sort of thing that puts a man's mettle to the test.'

'Are you all right?' said Terry, helping him on with his shirt. Dr Dudden's hands were shaking so much that he could hardly do up the buttons.

'Me? All right? Of course I am. They make them tough in Tayside, you know. It's not the first time I've done this.'

'It may be the last if we don't get you home soon.'

'Nonsense, man,' said Dr Dudden. But he lost no time in climbing up the path, all the same, and was still shivering when they reached the hallway of Ashdown and it was at last time to say goodnight.

'You'll be late getting to your bedroom,' he said, dripping pools of salt water on to the flagstones. 'Apologize to Lorna for me. Tell her that I kept you talking.'

'I will.'

'And think about what I've said to you. I'll be away tomorrow, just for a couple of days: so you don't have to rush into a decision.'

'All right,' said Terry. 'I'll think about it.'

Dr Dudden held out his hand, yawning loudly. 'Goodnight, then.'

'You're going to bed already?'

He looked at his watch. 'Only for four hours. I shall be setting the alarm for three o'clock. Three-ten, to be precise. It *can* be done, I know. You've proved that to me.'

Terry smiled, shook the doctor's hand, and watched as he disappeared up the staircase and along the first-floor corridor. He waited for another minute, hearing the bedroom door open and close. Then he crossed the hallway and stealthily descended the stairs that led to the basement.

He had taken the precaution, of course, of memorizing the eight-digit code that unlocked the door to the laboratory, although it had been hard work keeping it in his head under the combined onslaught of the alcohol and Dr Dudden's ranting. The laundry was deserted now and it seemed quiet, shockingly quiet, in the basement corridor as he keyed the number in. He sensed the flurry of animal excitement as soon as he opened the door, but tried not to look at the tanks while passing between them. He could hear the slapping of tired feet against the turntables. Then, having reached the furthest wall, he ignored the left-hand door and made straight for the one that Dr Dudden had declined to open for him earlier in the day. It unlocked easily, and when the latch clicked back, an overhead light turned itself on.

At first Terry did not understand what he saw, for he seemed to be looking at some sort of room-within-a-room. Immediately in front of him was a thick sheet of perspex, and about ten feet beyond that there was a partition — made of chipboard, by the looks of it — upon which three appliances were ranged: a fridge, a washbasin and a toilet. An inch or so beneath the partition, there was a large, semi-circular wooden platform, raised some two feet above floor level. The area between the platform and the floor was filled with blue, chlorinated water.

What Terry was looking at, he soon realized, was an enormous perspex tank or cage, almost as big as the room in which it was housed. It was possible to walk all the way around the tank, thereby discovering — as he might have expected — that it was divided into two identical chambers, each containing the same basic equipment designed to render them fit for human occupation. High up in the partition a hole had been drilled, from which there dangled, on either side, a long cat's cradle of wire, culminating in a set of electrodes. This, in other words, was a large-scale version of the apparatus in the laboratory, holding a turntable big enough for two human subjects.

'Insane,' Terry whispered to himself, as he completed his third circuit of the tank, peering into it with a mixture of awe, fear and stupefaction. 'Totally, totally insane . . .'

He reached into his trouser pocket and pulled out a crumpled note: the note that had been sent to him anonymously, almost a week ago, in the form of a paper dart. 'ASK HIM ABOUT STEPHEN WEBB'. Instinctively, Terry knew that there was a connection between this message and the monstrous room in which he now found himself. Stephen Webb — whoever he was — had been here, had taken part in one of Dr Dudden's experiments. And then what? An accident, perhaps, or even a fatality (yes, Dudden had used that word) which someone was now urging Terry to investigate. The doctor had enemies in this clinic — many enemies, probably — and Terry was being asked to align himself with them. It seemed that they were, in some sense, counting on him.

He left the room, and left the laboratory, closing both doors behind him. He decided to try to forget the eight-digit code. He didn't want to go down there again.

As he tiptoed up the stairs towards the ground floor, Terry thought, instead, about his missing photograph. He thought about the possibility that he might soon begin to sleep and dream again. Doubtless there was an important story to be told about Stephen Webb: but he was a film critic, not a news journalist. He simply wasn't the man for the job.

Besides which, he was already an hour late for bed.

ANALYST: *Describe your feelings for Robert.*

ANALYSAND: *He was the only person I could be completely honest with. I trusted him and [. . .] felt I could tell him anything.*

ANALYST: *And yet he was never your boyfriend?*

ANALYSAND: *No. He was more like a sister to me. I mean a brother.*

ANALYST: *You said like a sister.*

ANALYSAND: *I meant brother.*

ANALYST: *Do you have any brothers and sisters? You never talk about them.*

ANALYSAND: *One sister, yes. She's eight years older than me, and she emigrated when I was only thirteen. It was rather a sudden decision.*

ANALYST: *And Robert, I think, also vanished abruptly from your life.*

ANALYSAND: *Very abruptly.*

ANALYST: *Well, now we are making progress.*

From the cliff path, they could see Terry sitting at his bedroom window, crouched over his desk, the gleam from his desklamp shining out like the beacon of a tiny lighthouse. They waved up at him but he didn't see them, or didn't feel like waving back.

They walked on. From time to time, Robert ventured a glance at Sarah's eyes: not because he wished to look into them (although he never tired of doing that), but because he wanted to mention them in his poem, and was stuck for a description.

In your something something eyes I spied . . .

In her . . . soft and gentle eyes? Warm and sparkling? Clear and present? Hale and hearty?

No, these wouldn't do at all. He tried to shake the problem from his mind and concentrate on what she was saying: something about an item of clothing Veronica had bought recently, to which Sarah appeared to have taken exception; and something about a letter Veronica had received, which she had then hidden, refusing to discuss its contents. Sarah was quite agitated by both of these developments, obviously. Robert was doing his best to understand why.

'Have you told anybody else about this?' he asked.

'Of course not. You're the only person I can talk to. Who else could I tell?'

'I thought you might have said something to Terry.'

Sarah laughed humourlessly. 'I couldn't get him to listen to *anything* unless it was about a film. You won't mention it to him, will you?'

'Of course I won't,' he said.

'Only I know how close you are.'

He looked at her eyes again and tried to decide whether they were blue or grey. Blue, definitely.

In your blue and something eyes . . .

They climbed over the stile and came to a fork in the path. One route led along the cliffs and into town, a distance of about two miles. The other led towards the main road, where they would be able to get a bus. They decided it was too late to walk all the way, and headed off towards the road.

Blue remembered eyes?

No, it was hills that were blue and remembered, not eyes. Anyway, they were probably more grey than blue.

'I'm sure there's nothing in it,' he said.

'You're right. I dare say I'm overreacting wildly.'

'After all, all she did was buy some clothes, without asking your opinion. There's no real harm in that.'

'Yes, but it was a *suit*, Robert. A horrible, prim, formal little suit. She knows that's the last thing I'd want her to wear.'

It was details like these — the small ones — that Robert found hardest to bear. The idea that Sarah and Veronica even dressed to accommodate each other's taste maddened him, and he found that he couldn't keep the words back: 'That's a pretty trivial issue, though, isn't it?'

'No, Robert, it isn't *trivial*.' All the sharpness in her, the part of her he feared most and yet was most fascinated by, rose to the surface at once. 'It's a symptom of something. It's a sign we're getting further apart. I've put everything I have into this relationship and if it's starting to collapse . . . I don't know what I shall do.'

'I'm sure it isn't starting —'

'This isn't some *fling*, you know, Robert. This is my future we're talking about. It was a big decision for me, going out with Ronnie. The biggest I've ever taken.'

'I know that. I know.'

In your grey, reflecting eyes . . .

Reflecting? Reflective? Neither seemed especially suitable, now that he thought about it.

'I mean, it's not just this stupid suit,' Sarah continued. 'We hardly communicate about anything at the moment. All those ideas for next year . . . I can't seem to get her interested in them.'

Sarah was still hoping to find a job at a local school, and to rent a house with Veronica who would then, in theory, try to get her much-discussed theatre group off the ground. But it was getting late to put these plans into action. Term was officially over, finals had been taken, results announced, and in just a few days they would all be leaving Ashdown for good. Time was running out: not just for Sarah and Veronica, but for Robert as well.

Trying to ward off this realization, and the panic associated with it, he said: 'Well, I don't think you have to worry about that. She seems more keen on the theatre than ever, as far as I can see. Last time I spoke to her — it was just the other night, down at the Café — it was all she'd talk about. This woman who'd given a workshop at the Arts Lab — Celia something . . .'

'Celia Blake!' Sarah rounded on him and almost shouted this name. He was startled to realize how tense she had become lately, how quick to anger. 'Oh yes, she's keen on *her* all right. Keen enough to go all the way to bloody London last week to see her in some play; and meet her backstage afterwards, probably.'

'Who is she, anyway?'

'They were at school together. Three years apart, or something. And now Celia's semi-famous and so she came down here to give this workshop, and when it was over Ronnie introduced herself and she remembered her and now we're never going to hear the end of it.'

'Is she gay? Celia, I mean.'

'I expect so.'

There was little traffic on the road. Sarah leaned against the bus stop, sighed deeply and raised her face towards the setting sun. Now her eyes looked neither blue nor grey. There almost seemed to be a greenish tint to them.

In your multicoloured eyes . . .

No, that was awful. He quite liked the rhythm of it, though: he liked the idea of using a single, four-syllable word, instead of those two flimsier, weightless ones.

In your polymorphous eyes . . .

In your diatonic eyes . . .

Getting closer, maybe. But before he could think of any more alternatives, Sarah had turned towards him again: she was still brooding over Veronica's behaviour and her expression was now narrow and accusing.

'Shit, *that's* why she bought the suit, you know. To go and see her in London. I bet she got herself all tarted up just so she could go backstage at some West End theatre, and then on to a swanky restaurant.'

'Was she wearing it when she left?'

In your antiseptic eyes . . .

'I didn't see her that morning. Nor when she got back.'

'Did she stay overnight?'

'With her cousin. So she said.'

Or even—

In your narcoleptic eyes . . .

Yes, that was a possibility. He was by no means certain, yet, that Sarah suffered from narcolepsy, but the thought had once or twice occurred to him, when he contemplated her disturbed nocturnal sleeping patterns, her strange hallucinatory dreams, and her occasional tendency to drift into sleep at odd times of the day. The word fitted nicely into this line, at any rate.

'I mean — supposing that's who the letter was from?'

She had lost him now: his concentration had lapsed for too long.

'Pardon?'

'Supposing the letter was from her — Celia?' said Sarah, her voice taut with exasperation.

'Well . . .' Robert knew it was unfair of him to feed this suspicion, but found that he couldn't help himself. 'I suppose it might have been. Did you see the postmark?'

'I barely even saw the envelope. She snatched it off Terry as soon as he brought it into the kitchen, and stuck it in her pocket. Then when I went upstairs and found her reading it . . .' Everything was falling into place: it was all too horribly plausible. 'Yes, it probably *was* from her. Her face was flushed. It was glowing. I've never seen anybody look so happy.'

'Then what happened?'

'I asked her who it was from, of course. And she just said that some things were private and put it away in her desk. Very purposely. I didn't want to get into a row so I said I'd only asked because I thought it might be something to do with the theatre group. I knew she'd been writing away for funding. And she was obviously really embarrassed because then she started rambling on and we got into this weird conversation about —'

'About history?'

Sarah laughed, with the self-mocking laugh he knew so well but which never failed to take him by surprise: it was uncanny, mercurial, this ability to turn on herself in an instant, irrespective of mood. It was a quality only women seemed to be blessed with, and Robert envied it fiercely.

'Oh God,' she said, smiling. 'I'm turning into an old bore, aren't I? I've probably told you all of this before. You're going to tell me now that we've had exactly this conversation a couple of days ago, word for word, and you've just been humouring me.'

'No, it's not that. Not at all. Only Terry did mention — yesterday, I think it was — that you'd asked him a funny question. To do with Zeitgeists and . . . historical moments, or something.'

'That's right. I had to ask him what a Zeitgeist was. Embarrassing, isn't it? Nearly as embarrassing,' she reflected, 'as going out with someone who uses words like Zeitgeist in everyday conversation. Anyway, all of a sudden this is the main problem about setting up the theatre group, apparently. The Zeitgeist. According to Ronnie, this may not be the right quote historical moment unquote.'

'She's having second thoughts?'

'From what I can gather, her thoughts don't enter into it. History's against her: it's as simple as that. Priorities are changing. Values are in a state of flux.'

' "A state of flux"? She said that?'

'Incredible, isn't it? I wondered if she might have been stoned, actually. But it was a bit early in the morning, even for her.' The flippancy in her voice was strained. She dropped it quite abruptly. 'Oh, Robert, what am I going to *do*?'

A bus appeared over the horizon and rattled its way towards them. It was almost empty, so Robert was to be denied the pleasure of sitting next to her. Instead, she took the seat in front of him, reclining with her back against the window, her legs stretched out into the aisle, staring past him vacantly.

'Do you think I should sneak in, and take a look at the letter?' she asked.

Narcoleptic eyes, Robert thought: that was definitely the phrase. He still didn't know if it was quite accurate — medically speaking — when applied to Sarah, but the rhythm and the sound of it were perfect. Which meant, at long last, that the poem was finished. It had taken him months, but now he could take it down to the Café, and tell her to look for it between the pages of their special book. She was bound to go there in the next few days, if only for old times' sake.

'Yes,' he said; and wondered, in passing, whether he would ever cure himself of this vice — this refusal to say to her anything but what she most wanted to hear. 'In the circumstances, I think that would be fully justified.'

'Good.' She rewarded him with a wide, grateful smile. 'Then that's what I'll do.'

On the train, Terry tried to concentrate on looking for errors and misprints in his article for *Frame*, the proofs of which had arrived that morning. But he was too distracted by the presence of his companion, Joe Kingsley, who was sitting across the table from him. For one thing, there was the hat. If there was one kind of hat Terry despised above all others, it was the baseball cap. There was nothing wrong with children wearing it, of course, but whenever he saw it on the head of an adult it seemed to symbolize everything that he most hated about America, even more potently than the figure of Mickey Mouse or the latest Coke adverts or the hordes of giant yellow 'M's which were even now beginning to advance across Britain like an unchecked virus. And even worse, Kingsley was *wearing it back to front*. This, without doubt, was the ultimate badge of imbecility. On this account alone, Terry felt personally embarrassed to be sitting with him. And the other thing distracting him was the way Kingsley sat there reading a film magazine — not a proper film magazine, but the sort you got given free at the cinema, full of colour pictures and semi-literate articles lifted from press releases. His lips were moving as he read, and when scanning a particularly dense paragraph he spoke the most difficult words aloud in a slow whisper.

'Hey, Kingsley,' said Terry, unable to bear it any longer. 'Shut up, will you? I'm trying to work.'

'I wasn't saying anything.'

'You were muttering to yourself. I can't concentrate.'

Kingsley glared at him, then went back to his magazine, saying: 'Loosen up, why don't you? I'm doing you a big favour here.'

Terry was aware of this, but he wasn't going to let his gratitude show. He rebelled at the thought of being indebted to Kingsley, who had been his personal *bête noire* ever since his arrival in the Film Department at the beginning of the spring term. Young, unshaven, spotty and possessed of a peculiar vocal whine, he was the son of an American businessman currently working in England on a six-month contract. Kingsley Jnr, who had been midway through a film-making course at some minor Midwestern college, took the opportunity to accompany his father on this trip and was promptly billeted on the university for two terms, the arrangement being secured — as was well known — by the gift of substantial funds towards a new hall of residence. He was loud, self-confident, inarticulate, rich, and universally despised by the other students. He had also (and this was where an element of envy crept in) already made two short films back home, financed in part by his father: and judging from the video copies he had brought with him to England, they gave every indication — on a technical level, at least — of being gallingly proficient. In fact the second of these, a thirty-minute stalk-and-slash movie with a loud and violent climax, had impressed even that select band of film pundits who liked to gather round the corner table at the Café Valladon: with the single exception of Terry, who maintained that all the spectacular closing sequence amounted to was 'just a lot of buildings exploding', and that there was 'no coherent vision' behind the film as a whole. (If the others thought that he was being self-important, they kept quiet about it.) He was all the more annoyed with himself, therefore, for having got drunk one night in the Union bar and told Kingsley all about his ambition to write a screenplay that could be shot over a period of fifty years. From this brief, alcohol-sullied conversation, Kingsley had formed the impression that Terry was something of a visionary, and thereafter insisted on referring to him simply as 'the writer' whenever his name came up in conversation. And it was for this reason, it transpired, that he had asked to see him so unexpectedly a few weeks ago.

'My dad's been getting friendly with this producer,' he had explained. 'Seems he's in London to shoot this film, and Dad's shown him my stuff, and now he wants to meet.'

'Well, that's great, Kingsley. I'm really happy for you. Why are you telling me this?'

'Because now I need a writer. It's Joe, anyway. Joe Kingsley.'

'I still don't quite see where I fit in.'

'You're a writer, aren't you? You write.'

'Well, yes, but what — you mean my screenplay, the one I told you about?'

'No, this guy, he's already got a couple of properties. We just need a writer. Someone who writes.'

Terry was still not sure why he had accepted this invitation. He was convinced that it would end in disaster. In the end he had succumbed to pressure from Robert and Sarah, who had done their best to argue that it might provide him, at the very least, with the opportunity to show some of his own work to an influential figure within the industry: for which an entire day spent in the company of Kingsley did, on reflection, seem a small enough price to pay.

'What are you staring at me for?'

Terry shifted guiltily in his seat, aware that for the last few minutes his eyes had been fixed in a hypnotic gaze on the offending item of headgear.

'Sorry,' he said. 'I was miles away.'

Kingsley snorted and turned a page of his magazine. A few minutes later he said, frowning: 'They're talking here about this thing called *The Third Man*. Have you heard of that?'

'Yes, it's a film.'

'I never heard of it. It must be really old.'

'Nineteen forty-nine.'

'Wow. You mean it's like a silent film?'

'Not quite that old, no. I'm surprised you never heard of it, actually. It's quite famous. Directed by Carol Reed.'

'I didn't even realize they had women directors in those days.'

In truth, Terry wasn't at all surprised that he'd never heard of it. The depth of Kingsley's ignorance of film history (pre-*The Godfather*) never ceased to fascinate him.

'By the way, I was meaning to ask you,' he said, 'what do you think of Hawks?'

Kingsley put the magazine down, looking pleased that they were about to have a proper talk at last.

'I like them,' he answered, after a little consideration. 'Hawks, buzzards — especially eagles. All the birds of prey, I think.'

'Uh-huh.' Terry drummed his fingers on the table, and waited a while before asking: 'Don't you think that Welles is rather overrated?'

'Definitely. I went there with Dad last month, and Bath's a lot nicer. No contest.'

'That's very true.' The train flashed through a station. 'Tell me, Kingsley — do you think that the answer to the crisis in the British film industry lies in a return to the principles of Free Cinema?'

He had to think about this one. 'No, not really,' he said finally. 'I think people should be made to pay for their seats here just like everywhere else.'

Terry burst out laughing. 'You're priceless, you know. You really are.'

'What are you talking about?'

'Hawks and Welles are film directors,' said Terry, still laughing. 'And Free Cinema is the name of an influential movement from the nineteen-fifties.'

'And *you*,' said Kingsley, rising to his feet angrily and giving him the finger, 'are a stuck-up prick.' He stormed off to the buffet car.

Delighted to be left alone for a while, Terry turned his attention to the proofs of his article.

He had good reason to feel pleased with his first foray into journalism: not only had *Frame* immediately accepted it for publication, but it had led the editorial board to offer him a job as a staff writer on the magazine, starting in a few weeks' time, at the beginning of September. They seemed to be quite satisfied that, despite his complete failure to locate a print of *Latrine Duty*, or even to have found any production stills or a copy of the screenplay, Terry had written an interesting and worthwhile piece which brought together for the first time a great deal of previously scattered information. There was, for example, the curious case of the British film reviewer who had flown to Italy for a private screening of the film, only to be found twelve hours later dead in his hotel room on the outskirts of Rome, shot clean through the head, with a revolver by his side and clutching in his hand a sheet of notepaper on which was scrawled the brief message: 'Life cannot be endured.' *Variety* had reported this incident later in the week, under the headline 'Sick Pic Nixes Brit Crit', and although it added that there was an alternative explanation for the suicide (the reviewer had recently been abandoned by his wife and children), there seemed little doubt that exposure to Ortese's nihilistic *tour de force* had been a major contributing factor. Terry was baffled and tantalized by this report, which still gave very little indication of what exactly was shown in the film or why it might have had such a profound and immediate impact on one of its spectators. Equally mysterious was an eight-year-old article from a Canadian academic journal called *The Quarterly Review of Urinary Medicine*. This presented the case history of a representative (since retired) of an Italian distribution company who had seen the film and, while he adamantly refused to disclose its contents, had forever afterwards suffered from a bizarre bladder complaint which made him unable to urinate in the company of other men.

The more Terry read about this movie, the more fascinated he became. What perverse mixture of scatology and radical politics could Ortese possibly have contrived, to give rise to all these strange myths and rumours? He was not the first person to have become interested in this question, but previous researchers seemed to have uncovered very little. The film's alleged director of photography had since denied any connection with it; its editor steadfastly maintained that it didn't exist; its costume designer, now well into her eighties and no longer in full possession of her faculties, believed that every print had been destroyed but remembered it as 'essentially a tender and romantic film'; while in 1973 the leading actor — apparently in direct response to the experience of making the movie — had joined a remote monastic order which observed a strict vow of silence.

The subject was still uppermost in Terry's mind at lunchtime.

'No, I never saw that picture,' said the producer, who turned out to be a lean, energetic, apparently genial man in his mid-thirties. His name was Bruce Logan. He had kept Terry and Kingsley waiting for fifteen minutes in the lounge bar of the Athenaeum, and had then taken them to an Italian restaurant round the corner in Mayfair. 'I heard about it, of course. I know the stories. But I saw the uncut version of *Salò* once in Paris, and that was enough for me.' He helped himself to ciabatta and offered it round. 'Ortese was a big influence on that movie, of course. I'm told they even used some of his footage.' He turned to Kingsley. 'Are you fond of Pasolini?'

'Actually I was just going to have a burger.' He was studying the menu intently.

'He's such a kidder,' said Terry, laughing without enthusiasm and kicking his companion under the table.

Logan waved his hand in an airy, dismissive gesture. 'So the boy's never heard of some faggot Italian director who made a few arty movies. Who cares? The European art movie's had its day, in any case. Ten more years and it'll have died off altogether. Another ten and you won't be able to find a single member of the paying public who can tell you who Renoir was. Besides, I'm not here to test you boys. This isn't some sort of exam.'

'He doesn't know shit about American movies, anyway,' said Kingsley, in his most sullen whine. 'He didn't even see *Ghostbusters* all the way through. Walked out in the middle of it.'

Terry snorted. 'That heap of juvenile, meretricious —'

'You liked it, then?' Logan said to Kingsley.

'Saw it seven times. One of the greats. One of the all-time greats. Fabulous effects.'

'Yes, I think Compsy really came into its own on that one.'

'Compsy?' said Terry.

'The Computerized Multiplane System,' Kingsley explained. 'You use it as a matte camera on a pan-tilt-roll system. They say it's actually better for rear projection than Automatte.' He turned to Logan. 'The *look* of that film was so clean, that's what was so incredible. How did they do that?'

'I think they were shooting in sixty-five mill and then compositing in thirty-five mill anamorphic. That at least was my understanding.'

'Wow. Well that explains a lot.'

'This gentleman seems to be waiting to take your order,' said Terry, indicating an expectant waiter.

'Oh.' Kingsley picked up his menu. 'I haven't quite decided yet.'

Terry could see that he didn't have a clue what to choose.

'Do you like tortellini?' he asked.

Kingsley stared at him defiantly. 'Sure I do,' he said. 'Especially the early, black and white ones.'

While they were waiting for the main course to arrive, Logan outlined his proposal. He worked for one of the major Hollywood studios, and was currently trying to get at least ten or twelve projects into development, all aimed squarely at the mainstream American market. Having seen Kingsley's two short films and been very impressed, particularly by his handling of action sequences, and having heard Terry's creative abilities being lavishly praised by his fellow student, he was hoping they would agree to work for him on one of two properties he had recently optioned: the first being a popular cartoon strip called *Spy and Son*, which he wanted to adapt for the screen.

Kingsley's eyes lit up when he heard this title, although Terry had never heard of it, or even the supposedly famous comic book in which it appeared.

'You've never heard of *Spy and Son*?' Kingsley said. 'But it's just *so* great: I can't believe it's not popular over here. This guy, right, he's like an American James Bond. But get the twist — he's a widower, and he's got this thirteen-year-old son, really cute and wisecracking, who has to go with him on all his assignments.'

'That's right,' said Logan. 'His wife dies in a car crash, before the film opens: obviously we don't show any of that, because we're not going to start on a downer. So basically what we're talking about here is a sort of American James Bond for the eighties, only with more reality.'

'More reality,' repeated Terry, almost tonelessly.

'Exactly. Because this is a guy who doesn't neglect his family responsibilities. OK, so most of the time he's out there, risking his life for his country and defeating Communism and what have you, but at the end of the day he's got time to come home to his boy and share some pizza and maybe watch a ball game. Real family stuff.'

'And the cool thing is,' said Kingsley, 'that when they're out on a job, right, it's always the kid that defeats the bad guys. Like that time when the two Russian spies want to come running after them, but they've trod on his bubblegum and their shoes are stuck to the floor?' He and Logan laughed uproariously. 'Or when he's firing his gun at all those Arab guys, but it only fires ping-pong balls and they all get them stuck in their mouths?'

'Do you get the picture?' Logan asked. 'It's a very visual sort of idea. Very filmic.'

Terry drew in his breath. 'Tell me the other one,' he said.

Logan regarded him curiously, but if he was offended, he didn't let it show.

'OK,' he said. 'Maybe this is more in your ball-park. I've taken an option on this novel, which is about two New York cops working on the same case. Now, you can do whatever the hell you like with the book, because all I want to keep is the title: *Chalk and Cheese*. Great title, isn't it? You see, those are actually their names: Officer Chalk and Officer Cheese. And the hook is this: not only are they working on the same case, but independently they answer the same ad in the newspaper, and so they end up living together in the same apartment.'

'This is great,' said Kingsley. 'I love this.'

'One of them's a little older, and, you know, a bit eccentric, a bit maverick, a bit of a slob . . .'

'So we could be talking . . . Jim Belushi here?'

'Exactly. Right. And the other guy's young, he's naïve, he's idealistic, he plays by the rules . . .'

'So we're looking for, say . . . Tom Cruise?'

'Could be. Could easily be. And what I'm thinking of here is a sort of cross between . . .'

'. . . between *The Odd Couple* and, say, *Dirty Harry*.'

'Brilliant. You've got it. And of course there's the boss, who's, er . . . crusty, but lovable. Firm but fair.'

'And black, obviously.'

'Goes without saying.'

'A sort of . . . James Earl Jones figure.'

'Got it in one. And then of course we need a sort of romantic, sexual entanglement thing . . .'

'OK, so Tom Cruise has this girlfriend, right? A little bit older, a little bit more experienced. I see a role here for, maybe, Jamie Lee Curtis.'

'Yes. In a tight black dress.'

'A tight, *tight* black dress. Tits out to here.'

'You're talking my language, Joe. Only how's this: what Tom Cruise doesn't know is she's really a hooker, and Jim Belushi's been balling her.'

'Is Tom Cruise balling her?'

'Of course Tom Cruise is balling her.'

'Or perhaps she's a stripper.'

'Could be. She could be a stripper.'

'And is he still balling her?'

'Of course he's still balling her. *And* Jim Belushi's balling her. Everybody's balling her.'

'What about the boss — is he balling her?'

'Hey — didn't we say the guy was black? Keep it clean, Joe, for Christ's sake.' Logan turned to Terry, who had so far taken no part in this impromptu script conference. 'I'm not getting a lot of input from you here, if you don't mind me saying. Joe and I seem to be making all the running.'

Terry was sitting back in his chair, his arms folded.

'I think it's a terrible idea,' he said. 'I already feel like I've seen this film about twenty times before.'

There was a long silence, broken only by the slurping of Kingsley as he attempted to transfer a gigantic forkful of pasta into his mouth.

'You think it's terrible, huh?' Consciously or not, Logan himself now sat back and folded his arms, imitating Terry's posture. 'Well, of course, if you've got any better ideas of your own, then I'd love to hear them. Joe here was telling me that you're working on an original screenplay, in fact.'

'Yes. Yes, that's right,' said Terry, rather hesitantly.

'Can you tell me what it's about?'

'Sure. It's about . . . well, it's about this man, and — and his life, basically.'

'His life?' Logan raised his eyebrows. 'Sounds good. So, does anything — does anything happen in this life, that we should know about?'

'Well, yes.' Terry sat up and dabbed at the corners of his mouth with a napkin. 'He passes — you know, he . . . *matures*, if you like, from a young man, to a — well, initially, to a middle-aged man.'

'Uh-huh. And then what?'

'Well, then he grows old, and eventually, I suppose — he dies.' Somehow, in the telling, this scenario did not sound quite as impressive as Terry had always imagined. 'The thing is, you see, the really original thing, is that this character would be played by the same actor all the way through.'

'Really? And who did you have in mind? Because you know, with a pitch like that, Hoffman and Nicholson and Redford are going to be fighting for this role. It's going to be a real blood-bath.'

'Well, obviously it needs a little fleshing out, at the moment . . .'

'Shall I tell you the problem I have with that idea, Terry? One of the problems, anyway. To me, somehow, it all sounds a little bit small. A little bit British.'

'But that —'

'Don't get me wrong. I've got nothing against the British. I'm half-British myself, as it happens. Did you ever hear of a man called Henry Logan?'

'Sure, he was a . . . he was a producer too, wasn't he?'

'That's right. He's my father. He wrote, directed, produced — a real journeyman. Came to the States for a while in the late 'forties, early 'fifties, married his first wife — my mother, that is — but worked most of his life in Britain. Did a lot of comedies, a lot of low-budget thrillers. Didn't aspire to any great . . . aesthetic status, you know, but he got films made, and every so often a good one slipped through. Finished up in the 'seventies making soft porn — it was the only work he could get.'

'That's a shame,' said Terry, not sure where this was leading.

'Well, there's a reason why that was the only work he could get. Do you know what it is?'

Terry shook his head.

'It's people like you.'

Suddenly he struck the table with his fist and sent the cutlery flying. Terry and Kingsley almost leaped out of their seats.

'*God*, people like you get up my nose, Terry. You would still have a proper fucking film industry if it wasn't for people like you. When you boys started moving in — when was it, late 'fifties? — that was the beginning of the end. Intellectuals: angry young men: John Osborne, Woodfall Films, middle-class lefties. Suddenly we were all meant to go around proclaiming that film was an art form — as if nobody had believed that before — and every other movie was made by some public school-educated romantic giving us his view of working-class life. And it's been the same ever since. Christ, I've never known a country like England for bowing down to people just because they claim to be artists! And writers! God, how you worship writers! Why else would someone like you have such an amazing opinion of yourself — even though, from what I can make out, the only thing you've managed to write so far could be written on the back of an envelope and still leave room for the Gettysburg Address!'

Terry stood up. 'Have you finished?' he said. 'Because I thought I'd do some shopping while I was in London.'

'No, Terry, *I* haven't finished,' said Logan. 'Nor has Joe, actually. But I think you'll find that *you've* finished. You've finished your business here, so any time you want to leave . . .'

'If these films of yours ever get made,' said Terry, struggling for a parting shot, 'it will be a sad day for cinema.'

'And if this film of *yours* ever gets made, it'll be a fucking miracle!'

'If every producer in the world was like him —' Terry turned to Kingsley now, while pointing an accusing finger in Logan's direction '— then just imagine it! There would have been no Eisenstein, no Mizoguchi, no Wenders . . .'

Kingsley's face, carbonara-spattered as it was, betrayed little emotion at this prospect.

'I mean, think about that for a minute. Can you even *imagine* the history of the cinema without Wenders?'

'No, I can't,' said Kingsley, truthfully. 'I mean, someone's got to sell you the Coke and the popcorn.'

Logan burst into delighted laughter.

'You deserve each other,' said Terry, and walked out of the restaurant in a glow of righteousness which intensified as he walked through the streets of Mayfair towards the nearest tube station, and continued to keep him warm throughout the many hours he sat, alone, on the train back to the coast.

ANALYST: *And why do you think you felt entitled to read your lover's letter?*

ANALYSAND: *Because I knew that she had betrayed me.*

ANALYST: *It wasn't simply because Robert had given his blessing?*

ANALYSAND: *No, not at all. That had nothing to do with it.*

ANALYST: *And what were your feelings when you read the letter?*

ANALYSAND: *[. . .] I don't know how to describe them. It was like the world being turned upside down, or suddenly not making any kind of sense, finding that there was someone you thought you knew and then finding that you didn't know them at all. I suppose it's how a woman must feel if she goes through a cupboard and finds that her husband's been hiding an inflatable doll or a pile of bondage magazines. Or a mother who finds out that her son's a rapist, or something.*

ANALYST: *You don't think you're exaggerating?*

ANALYSAND: *No. It was worse. It was worse than any of those things.*

Irresolute, Sarah waited for three more days before acting on Robert's advice, and her own jealous impulse, by opening Veronica's letter. She waited until Friday morning, the day of the leaving party.

She crossed the bedroom on tiptoe, even though the house, as far as she could tell, was empty, and even though she knew that Veronica wouldn't be back all day. For a while she sat down on the bed, waiting for the courage to come to her. The weather had turned: flecks of rain speckled the window, and she could hear the waves breaking in a long, muted roar. It was eleven o'clock in the morning.

Finally she opened the desk and took out the envelope. It was franked, not stamped, and bore a London postmark. Veronica's name and address were typed. It had been opened cleanly, with a knife, and inside was a single sheet of thick, embossed paper.

At the top was a printed letterhead, which gave the name of a well-known London merchant bank.

The letter said:

Dear Miss Stuart,

  Thank you for coming to see us last Thursday. We are very pleased to offer you a position as junior dealer in our foreign exchange room, at a starting salary of £43,725 per annum, plus commission and bonuses as previously discussed.

We look forward to seeing you here at 8.30 a.m. on Monday September 3rd, and would like to offer our best wishes on the start of what we hope will be a long and profitable career in financial services.

Her first thought was that she was going to be sick. She felt the gorge rising in her throat and leaned forward, clutching her stomach, ready to run for the bathroom. But this soon passed. She replaced the letter in the drawer of Veronica's desk and went to the window, staring out over the ocean and trying to push aside her fury, her slow-burning anger at having allowed herself to be deceived, so that she might see past it and try to remember any small detail, any potential clue which might have warned her that something like this was going to happen.

She could remember nothing. All she could remember was that she and Veronica were meant to be meeting in the Café Valladon at three o'clock that afternoon. It was to have been their last visit, but Sarah knew now that she wouldn't go. It was no place to have an argument. It was no place to split up with someone.

The next morning, Terry awoke.

An ordinary enough event in the lives of most people, perhaps: but not for him. The sensation of passing from sleep to wakefulness had eluded Terry for more than a decade, and although today he could not have identified it as such with any certainty, he was at least aware, as soon as dawn began to glimmer around the edges of his bedroom's small, thickly curtained window, that something new and exceptional had taken place. He felt profoundly refreshed, and was convinced that he had been unconscious for much longer than usual. Carefully ungluing and disentangling himself from the electrodes, he left his bedroom, waved good morning to Lorna (crouched bleary-eyed over her computer screen and habitual cup of tea) and went out on to the terrace to watch the sun rising over the headland. It was five o'clock. His brain coursed with energy, like a recharged battery; his limbs felt strong and supple; each one of his senses was primed, alert. Life had never seemed so brimful of potential.

Dr Dudden, on the other hand, did not emerge from his bedroom that morning. He had drunk far too much red wine and brandy the night before, and having slept straight through his alarm at ten past three, would remain in a deep, unwavering sleep for the next nine hours (very nearly missing the train he was scheduled to take in the afternoon). And so it was Lorna herself, her reams of computer paper billowing in the sea breeze, who came out to inform Terry that at one point during the night he had spent no fewer than eighty-seven minutes in Stage 3 sleep: his first passage through a genuine, restful, delta-wave sleep stage.

'You seem to be starting to normalize,' she said. 'I'd say that as far as your sleep patterns were concerned, you're about to join the rest of the human race again. How do you intend to celebrate?'

'A day trip to London, I think,' said Terry cheerfully. 'There's something I have to find.'

Sarah slept badly, having spent much of the night replaying in her mind the more acrimonious highlights of her telephone conversation with Alison's mother. Their argument had ended with the promise that an official complaint about Sarah's conduct would be lodged with her headmistress first thing to-morrow morning. Sarah was therefore not surprised to find a message waiting for her in the staff room as soon as she arrived at school.

'I know exactly what this is about,' she said, on entering Mrs Palmer's office and being waved into a chair. 'It's Alison, isn't it? Her mother's been on the phone to you already.'

'Yes. She phoned about ten minutes ago. She seemed rather agitated.'

'What did she say?'

'It was all a little confused and overwrought, to be honest. Something to do with your having taken Alison to see a porno-graphic film. Which strikes me, I have to admit, as unlikely. Per-haps I'd better hear your side of the story first.'

During the course of this speech, Sarah began to relax slightly. She remembered that Eileen Palmer had never treated her with anything other than fairness and generosity; and that, in the three years they had worked together, they had fought so many battles side by side, worked so hard to clear for each other a pathway through the new legislative and administra-tive jungle that had sprung up around them, that they had forged for themselves an indissoluble alliance. She knew that if she told the truth, she had nothing to fear from her.

'I found Alison Hill sitting by herself in Finsbury Park yesterday afternoon,' she began. 'I asked her what she was doing there and she said that she couldn't go home because her mother wouldn't be back from work until seven o'clock, and she'd lost her key to the house. In the circumstances I thought that I had no option but to take her home with me. We went to a café and after that we were walking past a cinema, and it occurred to me that she might like to go and see a film. I remembered the title of one of the films from a review in the newspaper, which had made it sound like something suitable for the whole family. It had a certificate which seemed to confirm this view. Anyway, when we got inside and the film started I found that it was extremely sexist, and very violent and . . . generally objectionable, on every level. So I decided that we should leave. I went to the toilet and then came back, ready to take Alison away, but she'd gone. Disappeared. Run off.'

Eileen was listening attentively. She was frowning, but it was an encouraging frown: a pucker of concentration.

'Then what?'

'That was when I realized that I'd been stupid. The first thing I should have found out was Alison's address, but I didn't have it. So I had to come all the way back here, get Derek to let me into the secretaries' room, and look it up in the files. I phoned Alison's home from here, and her mother answered. She'd found her sitting on the front doorstep when she got back from work — very upset, apparently. The film seemed to have disturbed her quite a lot and she cried about it for some time. So her mother gave me a bit of an earful about that and accused me of making a serious error of judgment, and I told her that she obviously wasn't looking after her daughter properly if I'd found her wandering around a public park for three hours by herself without supervision, and it all got . . . quite nasty, I suppose.'

'Well, you obviously put her on the defensive. She is, in my experience, quite a combative woman.'

'Oh, so you have . . . you have met Mrs Hill?'

'*Ms* Hill is her preferred designation, I think. Yes, she's been to several parents' meetings this year.'

'And Mr — I mean, her husband, partner, whatever?'

'No. I know nothing about him. I don't even know if there is one.'

'I've got this feeling . . .' Sarah leaned forward, more confident now, feeling herself drawn in by the mystery surrounding this family. 'I've got this feeling that he may be dead. That he may have died only recently.'

'Really? What's given you that idea?'

'It's just something about Alison . . . she seems to have this thing about death. She read out a poem she'd written in Norman's class the other day, and it was . . .'

'Morbid?'

'Not morbid so much as — well, desolate. It was about a star dying and turning into a black hole and leaving the other stars feeling bereft and lonely. And then yesterday, I caught her carrying a mouse in her satchel. A dead mouse. She'd found it on the playing fields and said she wanted to take it home and bury it.'

'That does tend to support your hypothesis,' said Eileen. She was prone, occasionally, to these rather dry formulations. Now she looked at her watch and rose to her feet: it was almost time for morning assembly. 'Well, Sarah, I shall be writing to Ms Hill this afternoon, to tell her that I've looked into her complaint and I'm satisfied that my staff behaved properly on this occasion.'

'Thank you.'

'I'd have been very surprised to find otherwise, in your case.' She smiled warmly. 'At the same time, it might be a good idea if you tried to patch things up with her yourself. Especially if it gives you a chance to satisfy our mutual curiosity about the family.'

'You mean . . .' Sarah decided to risk an irreverence: 'You mean I should turn up at the house and have a nose around?'

'Something like that,' said Eileen, and ushered Sarah into

the corridor, already thronged by children making their shrill, erratic way towards the assembly hall.

Sarah had arrived at Rebecca Hill's house that evening armed with prejudices: class prejudices, mainly, because it had never occurred to her that a woman who adopted (in her view) such a cavalier approach to childcare would be so prosperous. She had braced herself for something like squalor, and instead was confronted by all the hallmarks of middle-class taste. As she waited, alone, in Rebecca's sitting-room, her initial surprise quickly gave way to self-reproach; following which, another, even more unexpected sensation began to steal over her. She realized that she was beginning to feel at home — more thoroughly at home than she had ever felt in her own house, since Anthony walked out — and couldn't understand why. She had, after all, only been sitting there for a few minutes, waiting for Rebecca to reappear with the wine that had been frostily, grudgingly offered once Sarah had introduced herself and the shock of her appearance on the doorstep had been assimilated. Surely it was absurd to be feeling so very much at home in a stranger's house, within such a short space of time, when that stranger appeared to be in a substantially higher income bracket than herself, and when she was anticipating, besides, an extremely difficult conversation. None the less, there was something about the furnishings, the paintwork, the pictures on the walls, the play of light from the French windows on to the carpet, the rows of hardback books, the vases of gypsophila and delphinium, which instilled in Sarah a blanketing, if inexplicable, sense of familiarity and reassurance. She even wondered, for a moment, if she was experiencing *déjà vu*, or if she might have seen this room years ago in one of her all-too-vivid dreams. But she thought not. The explanation for her strange, pleasurable sense of homecoming (there was no other word for it) lay somewhere deeper.

'It's only from Sainsbury's, I'm afraid,' said Rebecca, presenting her, in an offhand way, with a glass of greenish-yellow Australian wine. 'Alison's upstairs doing her homework. I could ask her down, but perhaps we'd better thrash this out by ourselves.'

Sarah was alarmed at the thought of thrashing anything out with this woman. She had already noticed the collection of legal textbooks on the shelves and had guessed that Rebecca must be a barrister. She took three rapid, nervous sips of the wine.

'Why exactly are you here?' Rebecca now asked, bluntly. 'I made my complaint to your headmistress this morning. I would have thought the matter rests with her.'

Sarah half-laughed, half-gasped at the audacity of this gambit. 'Well, she doesn't seem to think so, and to be honest neither do I. *We're* rather more concerned about the fact that I found your daughter sitting in Finsbury Park yesterday afternoon, locked out of her house, with nowhere safe to go for nearly four hours.'

Rebecca sighed. 'Look, I'm as upset about that as anybody. It should never have happened. I had to be out of London on a case, and Alison told me that she was going to be watching the sports until after five o'clock. I thought she could walk home with some of her friends, and let herself in. Then the silly girl goes and loses her key.' In an undertone, as if to herself, she added: 'Much as she seems to lose everything at the moment.'

'I'm sorry,' said Sarah, 'but that isn't good enough. For one thing I'm not sure that Alison *has* any friends at school, to be honest. She doesn't seem to be very good at making them. And it doesn't surprise me that she loses things all the time, because she's obviously going through a very unhappy and vulnerable period.'

'Putting aside the pop psychology,' said Rebecca crisply, 'I'd love to know how that fits in with your decision to make her sit through a film which sounds violent and unpleasant enough to upset any girl of her age.'

Her voice had risen in both pitch and volume. Sarah had no wish for the confrontation to grow so heated, so early.

'This isn't — or shouldn't be — about blame,' she said. 'We're both interested in Alison's welfare, so let's not forget that we're on the same side really. Having said that —' and here she allowed a steelier note to insinuate itself '— I need an assurance from you that this isn't going to happen again. Otherwise I'm going to have to report it.'

'Yes, of course.' This was agreed testily, without grace, and Rebecca immediately followed it up with: 'And I'd like you to think a little more carefully before inflicting any more . . . unsuitable entertainments on my daughter.'

Sarah left a short silence, which seemed to her a more than adequate response. Then she asked: 'Is Alison's father at home tonight?'

'Alison's father doesn't live here,' said Rebecca.

'Ah. What does your husband do, if you don't mind my asking?'

'My what?'

'Your husband.'

'I don't have a husband.'

'Your partner, then.'

'My partner,' said Rebecca, placing a neutral stress on the word, 'is dead.'

It was exactly what Sarah had been expecting to hear. Even so, the words were shocking: both in their finality and in the quiet, almost emotionless candour with which they had been spoken. She bowed her head.

'I'm sorry.'

'Well . . . there you go.' Rebecca drank deeply from her wine.

'I suppose that explains . . . one or two things . . .' Sarah looked up. 'Did you see that poem she wrote for her homework? The one about stars?'

'Yes.'

'I suppose — I suppose in a way Alison might have written that about her father.'

Rebecca flashed her a sharp look: scathing, impatient. 'Alison's father isn't dead.'

'No? But I thought you said . . .'

'I said her father didn't live here. He's very much alive, all the same. He's my brother, in fact.'

Sarah was having difficulty taking all of this in. 'Your brother? But in that case — I mean, how . . .?'

'Don't worry. You haven't stumbled upon a case of incest: one more thing to be reported to the social services. You see, I'm not Alison's biological mother. Technically speaking, I'm her aunt.'

'Her aunt. Right. So who — who *is* her biological mother?'

'My partner. Who, as I told you, is now dead.'

Sarah willed her brain into faster motion. She couldn't understand why she had begun to feel so sluggish, so inept.

'She was a woman, then: your partner.'

'Yes.' Rebecca stood up and looked out of the French windows. 'I'm not absolutely convinced that this is any of your business, you know.'

'No. No, you're right. It isn't.'

'Somehow you don't strike me as the kind of person who's going to take a very enlightened view of these matters.'

Sarah ignored this; or rather, it failed to reach her. 'How long were you together?' she asked.

'It would have been eleven years this August. She died almost a year ago.'

Neither of them spoke for a while, and when Rebecca sat down again Sarah thought she could sense a softening, a perceptible easing of her tension. It occurred to her that perhaps there had been very few people with whom Rebecca could have shared these painful confidences, over the last few months. When she asked the next question her voice was tentative, gentle, as if she was offering up a fragile gift.

'And how did she die?'

'Messily,' said Rebecca. But this was her last stab at bravado. Abruptly the mask slipped, her face collapsed in upon itself,

and then there was nothing but misery, shameless and uncompromising. 'She took her own life.' Still, however, she would
not allow herself to cry.

Sarah said nothing at first. She could not bring herself to ask
any more. She knew that the rest would come anyway.

'The newspapers have got a name for it,' Rebecca continued,
brokenly. ' "Yuppie burn-out". It's a syndrome, apparently. You
work your rocks off in the City for ten years, you make pots of
money, and then one day you look at your life and can't remember what any of it was for. She was a textbook case. Driving around South London late one Friday night — God knows
what she was doing in South London — she finds a nice long
cul-de-sac with a brick wall at the end, revs up to ninety miles
an hour, and drives straight into it. Writes off the company
BMW. Writes herself off into the bargain.'

'That's . . . that's dreadful,' said Sarah, cringing at the inade-
quacy of her own words. 'I can't imagine anything like that. I
mean, I can't imagine anything like . . . having to be told that.'

'It wasn't so hot.' Rebecca stirred herself, smiled a tough
smile. 'I think I'm going to have another glass of wine, at this
point. D'you want some?'

'That would be lovely.'

'I might as well bring the bottle.'

She was away for some minutes: long enough for the realization to creep up on Sarah slowly, biding its time, pacing itself, so that the thunderclap, when it came, would be all the
more brutal, all the more devastating. It started with the return
of that odd sense of familiarity: general at first, to do with
shapes and textures and colours, before the real specifics began
to announce themselves. Then, initially, it was the books. Her
eyes were drawn to the row of novels by Rosamond Lehmann:
hardbacks, first editions, unmistakably, their original dustjack-
ets protected by plastic wrappers, but missing one title: *Invitation to the Waltz*. Yes, she had always said that one would be

hard to find . . . And as this thought broke in upon her, everything else followed at once, the whole impossible truth of it made suddenly clear, the world turned upside down in one infinitesimal movement . . . The African figurine on the mantelpiece, souvenir of a family trip to Ghana . . . The tiny framed photograph on the bookcase, arms around Rebecca, beaming blissfully, the happy couple . . . And just outside Sarah's field of vision, the sight of it not yet to be trusted, but irrevocably *there*: another book, *the* book, that well-remembered green spine . . . These were hers. These were her things. This had been her house, her room . . .

Rebecca came back with the bottle. Sarah could just about see her through the mist.

'What was her name?'

'Pardon?'

'Her name: it was Veronica, wasn't it?'

And everything else was blank, until she recovered and found herself on the sofa, sobbing uncontrollably, Rebecca's taut arms holding her in an awkward, uncomprehending embrace. It seemed for a while that she would never be able to stop crying, and the explanation she offered Rebecca through her tears must have been wildly incoherent, for she had to repeat it, again and again, and there were gaps in the explanation, there were intervals, when Sarah had to go into the toilet to pull herself together, for instance, and when Alison appeared, drawn by the noises and the voices, and Rebecca had to take her upstairs and put her to bed.

As the evening drew on, things became calmer. When the light began to die down outside, Rebecca brought in candles and placed them around the room. She opened the second bottle of wine, and they started to talk about Veronica.

What seemed most incredible, to Sarah, was that in all the years Rebecca and Veronica had spent together, her name had never once been mentioned.

'But that was how she was, in a way,' Rebecca insisted. 'Absolutist: don't you think? I mean, when she was going out with you, did she ever talk about any of her previous girlfriends?'

'No, I suppose not.'

'She never dwelt on things. She was less tied down by the past than anyone I've ever known. I tried to be like that, as well, when I was with her. It's only now, really, that I've started to wonder whether it's actually any kind of way to live your life.'

'Well . . . You knew her much better than I ever did, obviously. In fact I hardly knew her at all. We were only together for . . . well, for about nine months. You must think it's very odd, in a way — you must wonder why I'm so upset about this.'

'No. No, not at all.' Their eyes met, briefly, but Rebecca was quick to look away, and flicked back a short lock of her auburn hair in a rather self-dramatizing gesture. 'Why did you split up, anyway? Was it mutual?'

'No,' said Sarah. 'No, it was my fault, entirely. It's funny, isn't it, still to be talking of faults at this kind of distance? But it *was* stupid to split up with her: that's what I think now. It wasn't even for personal reasons. It was . . . political, almost. Something to do with the spirit of the age . . .'

'The Zeitgeist: Ronnie's favourite word.'

'Yes,' said Sarah, surprising herself with a smile. 'Yes, it was one of her favourites. I used to make fun of her at the time, but in a way I was the one who was . . . too solemn about all that sort of thing. Everybody gets it wrong about the nineteen-eighties, don't they? They think it was all about money, and maybe it was, for some people, but for the people *I* used to hang about with, the students and people like that, there was a different set of values, just as severe, just as intolerant, really. We were so *obsessed* with politics all the time: gender politics, literary politics, film politics . . . there was even that phrase, wasn't there, that awful phrase, "political lesbian".'

'And is that how you used to think of yourself?'

'On the surface, maybe. God, I probably even described myself that way to some people. And yes, we were reading our Julia Kristeva and our Andrea Dworkin and we never passed up an opportunity to complain about patriarchy, but . . . you know, that wasn't the real reason. I can't even remember how it all started, now. I just remember that I really liked Veronica . . . I thought she was just a lovely and fascinating person. Which made it all the more ridiculous that it was *my* political puritanism that split us up, in the end. I couldn't cope with the idea of her going to work in a bank. I saw it as a personal insult, an affront to all the things we stood for, as a couple . . . She was supposed to be starting this theatre group, you see. That was always going to be the plan.'

'She was still talking about that. She never stopped talking about it.' Rebecca's hazel eyes glowed with the reflected candlelight; these recollections were warming her. 'It was one of the things that kept her going.'

'Did she not like working in the City, then? I never thought she'd be able to stick at it, somehow.'

'She must have liked it a bit — or part of her must have liked it. I'm sure the work excited her, even though she despised it too. I think she enjoyed it on the level of a highly abstract, highly intellectual game, but probably knew — certainly knew, I suppose, considering what she did in the end — that this was a fiction, and that she'd lost something by trying to sustain it for so long: lost something of herself. And of course, she hated all of the people she had to work with — that goes without saying. I noticed that right at the beginning. We met at a ghastly office party — I was acting for her firm at the time — and we clocked each other at once, got chatting, realized we'd found kindred spirits, left early, and . . . that was that. It all followed from there.'

'And Alison? You must — I mean, Veronica must have had her really soon afterwards. Which amazes me, because she never, *never* said anything about wanting children, or even liking them.'

'Yes, it was a very sudden decision. She knew the dangers, you see, of doing that job: she knew what it was going to cost her. And Alison was a sort of insurance policy against that. She thought — we thought — that if we had a child, then we'd be less likely to lose sight of — the fundamentals, if you like. Does that make any sense?'

'Yes, I think so.'

'So, first of all we had to find a donor, which didn't turn out to be very difficult. My brother helped us out there. But things seemed to go wrong after that. It was a terrible birth — twenty-four hours in the delivery room, very nearly a Caesarean — and then Ronnie went into a major depression which lasted . . . lasted for years, in effect. It's a miracle she didn't lose her job in that time.'

'Poor Veronica . . . I can see it now, as well: the resemblance. It's been staring me in the face all this time. Just the other day I started thinking about her, for no apparent reason, but now I know why: because I'd noticed something about Alison recently — something about her mouth . . .'

'They were alike in lots of ways. Which was ironic, sadly, because Ronnie never took to Alison, never seemed to bond with her at all. I did all the childcare, saw her through the nursery, got her into primary school; played with her, read to her; slept with her, most nights. I thought this was the right thing to do — and it was, in a way, the only thing to do: I mean, somebody had to be giving the child some attention — but I never noticed the effect it was having on the two of us; how edgy she was becoming, how remote. Everything had gone very stale, very suddenly. So we started trying the usual sorts of tricks — we moved to this house a couple of years ago, thinking it would give us a new start, maybe, but . . . well, it was too late by then.'

Sarah nodded. 'Yes, I can see . . . I can see exactly how something like that might happen.'

Rebecca drained off the last of her wine. 'I'm sorry,' she said, upending the bottle over her glass. A few droplets spilled out. 'I'm sorry I was so hostile to you earlier. I underestimated you. You get used to assuming that everyone else is going to be conventional; censorious.'

'That's OK.' Sarah looked at her watch. 'I should go now, anyway. I've got forms to fill in before tomorrow. The never-ending nightmare.'

'Yes, of course.'

As they stood in the centre of the room, facing one another, there seemed to be no obvious way of bringing this extraordinary evening to a close. Finally Sarah remembered the business which had brought her there in the first place.

'I don't know if we have anything more to discuss,' she said. 'About Alison, I mean.'

'Look, I'm sorry I complained about that. I went way over the —'

'No, it's good that you did. Now we'll both be looking out for her. I'm sure she's going to be all right.'

'I hope so,' Rebecca murmured. 'I'm doing my best.' She waited for a shy moment, before admitting: 'There is one thing, anyway . . . One bright spot on the horizon.'

'What's that?'

'I think I may have met someone. Someone new.'

'Oh?' Sarah felt a quick, tiny sense of deflation: the premature thwarting of some unacknowledged hope.

'She works in publishing,' Rebecca said. 'So far we've only seen each other a few times, but . . . it's been good. You know, we're taking it slowly.'

'That's wonderful,' said Sarah: and meant it.

They fell silent, until Rebecca added brightly, changing the subject: 'I like your hair, by the way.'

'Really?' Sarah was pleased, and found herself blushing; she was not used to compliments. 'I keep thinking about dyeing it, but people seem to like it like this.'

'It looks great.'

They walked to the front door together, and said goodnight on the steps with a hug: longer, probably, and more charged than either of them had intended. It was a warm night, humid and starry. Sarah said that she would walk home. It would only take fifteen minutes or so.

Just as she was leaving, Rebecca asked: 'What was it — what was it exactly — that made you realize it was her? You said you recognized some of her things . . .'

'It was a book,' said Sarah. 'You've got a book on your shelf called *The House of Sleep*. We used to read it together. It was something we shared.'

Rebecca hesitated. 'Can you find it for me? I don't know her books very well.'

So they went back inside, and Sarah stretched up on tiptoe to reach the copy of Frank King's novel.

'This is it.'

She tried to hand it over, but Rebecca pushed it back towards her.

'I don't want it,' she said. 'I'd like you to have it. You should have something of hers, and if it was special to you, then . . .'

Sarah said nothing; just clasped the book tightly.

'Call me, will you? Some time soon.'

'Yes,' said Sarah. 'Yes, I will.'

And as she set off down the tree-lined street, packed densely at this late hour with parked cars, their roofs glinting with the silver glow of the street lamps, she thought to herself that Veronica could not have forgotten her, not completely, in the intervening years, because a copy of this book would not have been easy to find: she must have searched diligently for it in the secondhand shops. 'She was less tied down by the past than anyone I've ever known,' Rebecca had said, but some small voice within Sarah wanted to question the truth of this. Against her will — because the fact of her suicide was still intolerable, unthinkable — she found herself imagining Veronica as she might have looked that night, the last night of her life: the car rushing towards the wall of the cul-de-sac, white and brilliant in the glare of the headlamps. Might the faintest memory of their friendship, some thin reminiscent flicker, have passed through her mind during that instant? Sarah's eyes were stinging with tears again, as she wondered

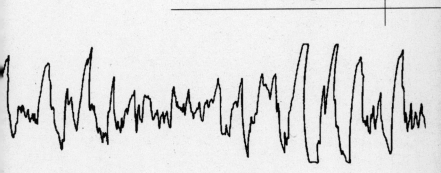

Stage Four

wondered where she could possibly be. They had arranged to meet at the Café Valladon at three o'clock, but when Veronica arrived, the place was empty. She sat at the table nearest the door, smoked two cigarettes, and drank a mug of coffee.

It wasn't like Sarah to be late.

At three forty-five, Veronica decided she might as well return to Ashdown. Tomorrow was Saturday, the day they would all be leaving, mainly back to their parents' homes for the early part of the summer. She had her cases to pack, and the evening's farewell party to prepare for. Perhaps, in the organizational fluster and confusion, Sarah had simply forgotten about their appointment: but this was surprising, since they had both agreed that there were sound sentimental reasons for paying a final visit to the Café, the place where they had first met, all those months ago.

In any case, it was clear that she wasn't coming. Veronica went over to the counter and dropped a fifty-pence piece into the little sugar bowl next to the till.

'Keep the change,' she said, as usual.

Slattery, engrossed in a copy of Richard Rorty's *Consequences of Pragmatism*, looked up and grunted.

Veronica paused as she reached the door.

'I shall miss our conversations,' she said.

This produced no response.

'The cut and thrust,' she added. 'The give and take. The easy repartee.'

Crushed, finally, by his silence, she started to turn the door handle, only to hear him say: 'You're going, then?'

She wheeled around, disbelieving, sensing a minor victory.
'What?'

'You're leaving town. You've finished.'

'That's right. All of us.'

Slattery had done the impossible: laid his book down, and risen to his feet. Veronica realized that this was the first time she had seen him standing. He was surprisingly short.

'Take something, if you want,' he said. 'A souvenir.'

Veronica suspected some inscrutable Slattery-esque joke.

'Do you mean that?'

'A book or something.'

She looked into his impassive, bristly face, and decided that he was sincere.

'Any book?'

He waved his arm, in an all-inclusive gesture.

With no need for reflection, Veronica went to the shelf above her regular table and plucked down *The House of Sleep*, by Frank King.

'This was always my favourite,' she explained.

'It's yours,' said Slattery.

She opened the door, stepped out, blinking, into the sunshine, and walked down the High Street with the book clutched to her heart, which for some reason was thumping wildly.

She had intended to tell Sarah about this incident, but never did. When she opened the door to their bedroom, Sarah was sitting on the bed, staring up at her. In her hand was the letter from the merchant bank.

Veronica took a deep breath and said: 'Let's just try and talk about this reasonably, shall we?'

ANALYST: *Why do you find it such a hard evening to talk about?*

ANALYSAND: *I don't find it hard to talk about.*

ANALYST: *... I have the impression that you're holding something back.*

ANALYSAND: *I'm not holding anything back. I just don't re-member much about it, to be honest.*

ANALYST: *There's a fine line between forgetting an event, and suppressing the memory of it.*

[ANALYSAND's *response unrecorded.*]

It was some time now since Robert had stood up when going to the toilet. Even at moments like this, when he was in a hurry, and bursting to go, and there would probably be someone else waiting outside, he preferred to sit down and take his time over it. The idea of standing over the toilet and pointing in the vague direction of the bowl and splashing everywhere repulsed him. He hated the thought of it.

He sat on the toilet with his head in his hands, leaning forward, rocking slightly. It had been a long evening, and an excessive one: everyone seemed overwrought, and everyone had had too much to drink. The sensible ones had already gone to bed, a little while ago. Terry was holding court in the kitchen, now, drawing upon his repertoire of jokes which were gradually getting dirtier and funnier. He could hear the laughter. Sarah's laughter among them.

But Sarah and Veronica had split up, that was the incredible thing. She had told him this evening. It was over. Their affair, and his ordeal, were over.

Where did this leave him, exactly?

On his way back to the kitchen, he had intended to stand in the doorway for a while, to take in the scene with a modicum of objectivity and decide whether he wanted to rejoin it or whether it was time to slip quietly upstairs to bed. But there now appeared to be little question of standing, either in the doorway or anywhere else: the moment he tried to stop still, or relinquish the momentum of walking, he could tell that he was about to collapse; and so, pushing to the back of his mind the realization that he was by now *very* drunk indeed, drunker perhaps than he had been in his entire life, he lurched back towards the kitchen table and sank gratefully into the seat next to Sarah. There were still at least ten or eleven of them around the table, and it was crowded, so that he and Sarah were sitting squashed together, leaning drunkenly into each other as Terry continued with his story and laughter rippled from person to person.

'. . . so he decides to buy his wife an anniversary present, it's their tenth anniversary, and he thinks to himself — I know, I'll buy her a pet . . .'

The table was covered with half-empty bottles and glasses. Robert couldn't remember which glass was his. He tasted the liquid at the bottom of one glass, found that it was whisky, and refilled it. It tasted unbelievably sour.

'. . . so he goes into a pet shop and the pet shop owner says, Well, why don't you get her a puppy? and he says, No, she's already got a puppy; so then the man says, Well what about a parrot? and he says, No, she's already got a parrot . . .'

He was conscious of Sarah's arm brushing against his, and her shoulder weighing heavy against him as she reached across for a bottle. She was drinking gin, neat: all the mixers had long ago disappeared. She was already leaning forward in anticipation of Terry's punchline, laughter straining at the corners of her mouth: but her eyes were dull, tired.

'. . . so he says, Well, how about this then? and he gets this creature and puts it out on the counter. And the man says, What is it? and the pet shop owner tells him, and he says, That's perfect, so he puts it in a box and he takes it home to his wife . . .'

Veronica was sitting at the far end of the table from Sarah, so there was little eye contact between them. Nor had they spoken to each other all evening: but each was clearly determined to prove a point by staying until the end of the party. Veronica was drinking tap water. From time to time, unobserved, she looked across sharply at Robert and Sarah as they sat wedged together over their drinks.

'. . . so he gets home and gives her the present and she unwraps it and there, sitting in the box, is this enormous green frog, with a huge mouth and puffed-up lips, just sitting there and staring at her . . .'

Robert wanted to leave. He badly wanted to leave, but he couldn't bring himself to move from Sarah's side. How had they come to be sitting together like this? Whose decision had it been?

'. . . so she takes one look at this animal, and says, What the *fuck* is that? And he says, That, my dear, is a South American cocksucking frog . . .'

Everyone was laughing, by now, but Sarah's laughter was the loudest. It was almost hysterical. Robert looked at her, saw her quivering jaw and heaving shoulders, and was suddenly alarmed. There was something wrong.

'. . . and she says, What am I supposed to do with it? And he says, Well, you can teach it to cook, and then fuck off.'

In the new eruption of laughter, the second wave, Sarah and Robert were thrown against each other, and for a few seconds they clung together, limp with hilarity: but when he tried to raise her from this position, to push her away slightly, he found that her body was inert. Her limbs drooped uselessly, and she flopped over him like a rag doll, her eyes wide open and her mouth fixed in a grinning rictus. He started shaking her.

'Sarah! Sarah, what's the matter?'

All around the table, the laughter died down as people stared at her flaccid body in Robert's arms.

'My God, I thought *I* was pissed,' someone said: but the joke provoked no amusement.

'Has she passed out?'

Veronica stood up and came to Robert's help. 'She'll be all right. I've seen this happen before. It won't last for long.' She sat beside Sarah, took one of her arms and, together, they gently eased her into an upright position, so that she sagged between them. 'Have some water ready for her. Cool water.' Then she murmured softly into her ear: 'It's all right, Sarah. Come on. It's OK. Wake up now . . .'

Slowly, after only a few more seconds, the life started to return to Sarah's eyes, and her body tautened as she regained control of her muscles. She blinked and yawned, like someone waking from a sleep filled with absorbing dreams.

'Oh God, I . . . oh, that was a bad one . . .'

'Are you all right?' said Robert, leaning over her. 'Are you OK?'

'Did you know what was happening?'

'Of course she knew what was happening,' said Veronica. 'She —'

'Yes. I could hear what you were all saying. There was just nothing I could do about it. I couldn't move.' Placing both hands on the table, she pushed herself gingerly to her feet. 'Listen, I'm sorry to break up the party, but — I have to get to bed, I think . . .'

Whether because Sarah's odd behaviour had shattered the mood, or from a more general sense that the evening had run its natural course, there was now a collective sliding-back of chairs as people followed her lead, with yawns and nods of agreement and murmurs of assent; so that within a few minutes the party was broken up, and ragged groups of people were dispersing down the various corridors with scarcely a word of goodnight to one another.

Climbing the staircase to the first floor, Sarah still found herself flanked by both Robert and Veronica, hovering solicitously even though she no longer looked any more frail or unhealthy than the rest of them. Terry was just a few steps behind.

At the top of the stairs, Sarah turned to Veronica and said, in a tense flurry of words: 'I think Michèle's room's empty tonight. I'll sleep there.'

Veronica muttered something inaudible, and walked off in the direction of her room. Then Terry said goodnight, adding that he would speak to them both in the morning before he left. And then they were alone.

The house was very quiet. It seemed to have taken no time at all for everyone to go to bed.

'That was quite an evening,' Robert said, feebly, when the silence began to seem oppressive.

Sarah had started to look at him in a strange way: with an unsteady, birdlike intensity. She showed no sign of wanting to move. Robert struggled to remember where Michèle's room was, so that he could guide her there. Soon he remembered that it was at the top of the staircase: exactly where they were already standing, in fact.

'Are you sure you're feeling all right now?' he asked.

'Yes, thanks: I'm much better,' said Sarah; her eyes never leaving him.

'Good. You had us all worried back there. And this has happened before, has it?'

'Once or twice, yes.'

'You should see a doctor about it.'

'It's nothing, really. I just get a bit carried away if I laugh too much.'

Someone was still around: there was a small bang and a crash of glass from the kitchen, and then a light went off in the corridor downstairs.

'Do you want me to help you into bed?'

'Not exactly,' said Sarah. It was quite dark now, but her eyes continued to shine, lit by a pale, listless gleam. 'I'd like you to come to bed with me, actually.'

Robert's next words, although he would never be able to remember them, were: 'That maybe isn't such a good idea.'

The light in Sarah's eyes was at once extinguished. She said: 'No,' and the word hung between them in the darkness and the silence, final, irrevocable.

'I mean,' Robert said, 'this might not be the best time, or —'

Sarah had reached the door, had eased it open, was about to disappear.

'Goodnight, Robert,' she said.

He cried out her name; or imagined that he did. Then the door closed, and was locked.

Dumb with shock, Robert stood in the darkness, staring at the closed door. No beam of light issued from beneath it: Sarah had not turned on any of the lamps in her room. He did not know whether to move forward and knock on the door, or turn and go back to his own room. He turned, and took a few steps back along the corridor; then stopped, and stood bewildered again in the darkness, shivering, paralysed by indecision, clenching and unclenching his fists. He took a few steps backwards, turned, then tiptoed towards Sarah's door. He stood beside it, listening, holding his breath. After a second or two he began to suspect, and was then absolutely certain, that she was standing just on the other side of the door, leaning against it, listening to his own irresolute movements in the hallway. It seemed extraordinary then that he could not reach out and touch her, separated as they were only by an inch or two of wood. He listened closely and thought that he could hear her breathing: deep, excited breaths. The brush of a hand, or a body, against the door panel: the texture of cloth against wood. But then another noise — a bump from somewhere deeper in the room, which could have been someone knocking against a bed, or the sound of a shoe falling to the floor — made him think again. He reached up his hand to knock on the door; wondered what he would say when she answered; shook this thought away as neurotic, irrelevant; made as if to knock, then faltered. His knuckle, instead of rapping on the door, made contact with his eyeball, which he rubbed fiercely. A sob shook his body: he was so drunk, and so tired. He turned and made off swiftly down the corridor, back towards his room.

The next sensation he could recall was a sharp pain in his left hand. He looked at the hand and saw that it was scored with deep toothmarks. He was sitting on the single bed in his room and had been biting his hand, sinking his teeth into the ball of his thumb, almost but not quite to the point where blood might be drawn. He had turned on the light and taken his trousers off. They were thrown on the floor, over by the wardrobe.

He stood up and immediately reeled, partly with drunkenness, partly with disbelief. The scene he had just acted out with Sarah seemed to defy comprehension: half of him wanted to erase it at once from memory, while the other half struggled to revive and dwell upon every detail. Had she really, *really* asked him to do that? And had he really refused?

This will never happen again, he told himself. *She will never ask you again.*

He picked up his trousers. Should he put them on, and go back to her room?

Where were his shoes?

Go back.

But he had said no; and as soon as he had said it, the invitation had been withdrawn, absolutely.

Another lifetime is the least you'll need . . .

He struggled into one leg of his trousers; then, on the second leg, he lost his balance, hopped and capsized. Falling, he caught his head against the corner of the bedside table, and a sudden ache spread through his skull and neck. Collapsed foetally on the floor, he touched his upper cheekbone, between eye and ear, and felt a melted rivulet of blood.

To trace the guarded secrets . . .

'There'll be no going back,' he said to himself, aloud.

He disentangled himself from his trousers, retrieved a handkerchief from one of his pockets, and held it to the cut while sitting on his bed. It was a shallow abrasion, and the blood soon dried. In the process he sobered up, with what seemed to him unusual rapidity. Shivering, trouserless, he now felt a sudden urge to write something, and with this in mind he crossed over to his desk, picked up a felt-tip pen and opened his notebook at the first blank page, where all the various drafts of his poem ended.

It was the sight of these literary efforts, probably, which concentrated his pain, and confusion, and tiredness, and fused them, at last, into a single emotion: rage. All these difficult, tentative utterances, these early versions, revisions, alterations and rethinkings, pondered and erased, rephrased and agonized over, now appeared to Robert as objects of contempt. What was the point of all that secret labour, that time-consuming, interiorized donkey-work, if, when the opportunity to act upon his desires was offered to him on a plate, he had neither the courage nor the presence of mind to seize it?

He stared at the words on the page until they looked like random, meaningless scribble; until they made no sense.

He took the pen and drew a thick line through the finished version of the poem. Then he drew another line, making an 'X'. He pressed so hard, this time, that the tip of the pen, even though it was soft, tore through the page. He liked the sound and the feel of the page being torn. He scribbled obscenities over the earlier drafts of the poem, and again tore through the pages with the tip of his pen, and then finally tore the whole book apart with his hands and scattered its pages over the desk and the floor.

Still clutching the pen, he stood up, lurched and collided with the wall. He was not as sober as he had thought.

Sarah was lying in bed now, a few yards down the corridor, asleep probably, her room in darkness, her door locked. And she would never ask him again.

Stupid, stupid, stupid . . .

He banged his head against the wall, softly, as he said this, smearing it with blood in the process. The wound must have opened again. He scrawled the word on the wall with his felt-tip pen.

FUCK FUCK FUCK FUCK FUCK

He was standing close to the wardrobe as he added this word in quavery capitals, and then felt his legs giving way and realized that he was sliding down the side of the wardrobe towards the floor. He looked across at his bed and with one final effort managed to propel himself towards it. Then he passed out.

Robert awoke only a few hours later, with a raging thirst. Had he been a more experienced drinker he would have known that this was not really the time to get up: that it was no more than a momentary interruption to the process of rest, a time to gulp down several glasses of water before staggering back to bed and sleeping again for another three or four hours, until midday at the earliest. But he mistook the unnatural feverish enthusiasm with which he registered the morning sunlight for genuine wakefulness; and was drawn, besides, by the sound of voices downstairs in the kitchen. He splashed his face with cold water, stepped out of yesterday's clothes and put on some new ones. Shortly before leaving the room, he looked at the words he had written on the wall a few hours earlier. Ashamed, he took hold of the heavy teak wardrobe, braced himself against it, and dragged it a few inches in the direction of the window. The words were hidden, and he was ready to go downstairs.

In the kitchen, he found three of his drinking companions from the night before, making toast and coffee and in one singularly intrepid case a cooked breakfast, and all wearing the same shell-shocked, abnormally bright-eyed expressions. After they had asked him what had happened to his face, and after he had said that it was nothing, conversation was kept to a husky minimum. Neither Terry nor Sarah had surfaced yet, although Veronica was the next to appear, nodding curtly at Robert and heading straight for the fridge, where she made short work of a litre carton of orange juice.

'Thirsty?' he said, stupidly, when she had finished.

She ignored the question and said merely: 'Did somebody hit you last night?'

'No. I had an accident.'

'I thought it might have been a lovers' tiff,' said Veronica, and started to cut thick slices of bread.

Terry entered in his pyjamas.

'I've just been sick,' he announced, to no one in particular.

'We forgive you,' said Robert.

'All over the telephone. I was trying to call home.'

Terry was not the only resident of Ashdown whose parents were supposed to pick him up that morning. Several of the others were expecting lifts; some had their own cars, and were intending to pack up and drive off as soon as they felt well enough. Beneath the general fragility and queasiness lay a peculiar, apprehensive sense that they had only a few more hours to spend together before parting; perhaps never to meet again.

'I need some fresh air,' somebody said, after the heat from the fried egg and bacon had steamed up the kitchen windows.

'Good idea. Let's walk.'

There were eight of them, now, as they made their way along the cliff path towards the highest promontory. It occurred to Robert that it was still too early for the effects of the alcohol to have worn off, so that they were all still, technically, drunk. A warm, wet mist hung in the air, and a pale sun was shining, stifled by clouds and managing only to wash a thin, pale, yellow-grey light over the swelling ocean.

As Robert strode ahead of the group, Terry caught up with him and said: 'So — was Sarah OK last night?'

'I think so.'

Terry shook his head. 'Funny business, that. What happened to your face, by the way?'

Robert didn't answer; and Terry hesitated now, as if fearful of the impact his next words might have. 'And did she mention — did she say anything, at all, about our . . . arrangement?'

'What arrangement?' asked Robert: rather too quickly.

'She didn't tell you?'

'I don't know what you're talking about.'

'All right, then . . . You know how I'm going to start working for *Frame* in September?'

'Yes.'

'And you know how I'm going to be renting this flat in London?'

'Yes, of course.' Robert had, as it happened, already refused Terry's offer of a spare room, preferring to find out what Sarah's plans were.

'And you know how Sarah and Veronica have split up, so they're not looking for a house round here any more?'

'Get to the point, Terry, for God's sake.'

'Well . . .' He took one final, searching look at his friend, and then ploughed on: 'She's going to come and live with me.'

Robert stared at him in horror. '*Live* with you? What do you mean?'

'I mean she's going to have one of the spare rooms.'

'But . . . when was this decided?'

'Yesterday evening: before the party.' He grasped Robert's shoulder, and shook it clumsily. 'There's nothing sinister about this, you know. Nothing going on. And the best thing about it is, there's still room for you to come and live with us as well. There are three bedrooms. It'll be just like Ashdown, only in London.' Robert was still dumbfounded. Terry could see that he was going to get little more out of him, for the time being. 'Think about it,' he concluded. 'We'll talk about it later.'

He moved on, and the others soon joined him, pushing past Robert as he remained standing in the centre of the path, his back to the ocean, his gaze fixed on the grey towers of the enormous house. After a few minutes he saw Sarah emerge from the front door. He turned and began to walk away from her, but slowly, so that it did not take long for her to reach him. Her unwashed hair seemed darker and sparer than usual. She had taken off last night's makeup but hadn't applied any more. Her skin seemed pallid, and a cold sore was forming on her upper lip. Her eyes had lost their flame; the lids were hooded. She was wearing her usual denim jacket, and a thick cotton blouse and a pair of bottle-green corduroy trousers.

'Thanks for waiting,' she said, not meeting his eye.

The others, in fact, had also slowed down, and were not far ahead.

'You don't look too good,' said Robert.

Sarah laughed. '*I* don't look too good? What happened to you?'

'I had an argument with a piece of furniture.'

Sarah seemed hardly to hear this. She seemed uneasy, almost distraught.

'Everyone looks terrible this morning,' Robert added. 'Perhaps it wasn't the best note to end on.'

They were absorbed into the group, but somehow managed to retain their separateness, so that the intimacy between them continued, even as their friends chatted aimlessly on either side.

'Last night . . .' Robert began.

Sarah bridled. 'I wanted to say something about that. Do you mind if I go first?'

'No, of course not. Carry on.'

'Well.' She made the gesture again: running a hand through her hair, taking hold of a clump and tugging at it lightly. As always, Robert was pierced by it: a sharp pang of tenderness. 'I just wanted to thank you, actually.'

'Thank me.'

'Robert —' they detached themselves from the group smoothly, almost unnoticeably '— I know how you feel about me. Of course I know. I've known for ages. I think everybody knows, actually.'

'Fine. Why shouldn't they?'

'So — in a way it was cruel of me to say . . . what I said last night.'

'Why? Didn't you mean it?'

'Yes, I did. Or at least I did — at the time.'

'I see.'

'I was terribly drunk. So were you.' She turned away, looked out towards the sea. 'So what I'm saying —'

'I know what you're saying. You think it would have been a dreadful mistake, and you want to thank me for not allowing it to happen.'

'Yes.' Sarah nodded unhappily. 'That is what I'm saying, I suppose.'

'Don't deceive yourself about this,' said Robert. 'It had nothing to do with strength of character. It was pure weakness, actually.'

'I don't believe that. You're not a weak person.'

'Yes I am. Weak and indecisive.'

The others had started to drift back towards the house. Veronica passed by, unable to stop herself from throwing a jealous, curious glance in their direction. Even when she was well out of earshot, Sarah spoke in a low whisper.

'It's good that we're leaving here. We've all got to know each other too well. We've become too close.'

'Oh? And how does sharing a flat in London with Terry fit in with that idea?'

'That's just a stopgap. A temporary thing. I don't know how that's going to work out.' She rounded on him in despair. 'Oh, Robert, you *can't* be jealous of me and Terry.'

'You'd be surprised.'

'Anyway, what's to stop you coming too? There's still a spare room in that flat. It would be lovely if you were there.'

Robert shook his head. 'It's not what I want.'

'Well, what do you want? To go back and live with your parents?'

'No. I thought I might stay on here for a while.'

'But you'll be all by yourself. It'll be awful.'

'Maybe.'

There was no fence, at this point, between the path and the edge of the cliff. There were a few boulders, and one or two clumps of wistful, persevering heather sprouting from the grass. Robert tiptoed to the edge and looked down at the water, which slapped at the cliff face in languid, haphazard motions.

'What did you do last night?' he asked.

'Pardon?'

'After we'd said goodnight. I'd like to know.'

'Come away from there,' Sarah insisted. 'You're too close to the edge. It's not safe.' Robert stayed where he was, so she sighed and said, tetchily at first: 'Well, I went into Michèle's room, and sat on the bed. I thought I could hear you outside. I thought you were going to knock on the door.'

'I nearly did.' He sat down, cross-legged, on the heathery grass. 'What would you have done?'

'Don't, Robert. Don't ask. There's no point.' She sat down beside him. 'It *would* have been a mistake, you know. I don't know what came over me. I was just trying to use you.'

'Use me?'

'Yes: to hurt Veronica. I mean, I probably couldn't have gone through with it. I don't even like sex with men —' she looked at him with sudden fondness '— *any* men, so I'm sure it would have been a disaster. It would have spoiled everything.'

'Our friendship, for instance,' said Robert, flatly.

'Exactly. Our friendship. And that's *so important* to me, Robert: especially now. I really need a friend at the moment. A good friend. And you've always been the best: the best I've ever had, in a way.'

'Well, that's too bad,' he said, averting his eyes, 'because I don't want to be friends with you. I can't do it any more.'

It took Sarah a few seconds to absorb this. Then she said: 'Well, you'll just have to. Because that's all there is. That's all there's going to be.'

'Ever?'

'Ever.' She put a hand on his knee. He looked down at it, mildly incredulous, but feeling no emotion. 'Ronnie and I aren't on very good terms at the moment,' she continued, 'but I shall always owe her something. Because — she did something amazing, really. She introduced me . . . to my nature.'

'You're sure of that, are you?'

A long time seemed to pass before Sarah said: 'Yes, I am.'

Robert nodded, and plucked at the grass. 'I thought she might have been . . . I don't know: a one-off.'

'No. She just wasn't right for me, in the end.' Sarah smiled. 'I spent a lot of time, in the last few weeks, wishing that she was more like you.'

'Like me?'

'Of course. You'd be perfect for me — don't you think? If it wasn't for . . . a certain something, that is.'

'Don't play with me, Sarah. Please. I'm not up to it.'

'I'm not. I'm serious. I think you're wonderful: I always have. And you know that, as well.' She squeezed his knee and again he looked down, like a sleepy cat responding to a stroke, curious but nonplussed. 'You know, it should really be me who goes off looking for Cleo. Just imagine it — your twin sister: a female you. That would be my ideal partner, wouldn't it?'

Robert stared at her now. He stared at her calmly, searchingly, for a long time, while she stared back, embarrassed, hoping to catch a hint of amusement in his eyes. But there was no trace of humour in Robert's stare. He could scarcely have looked at her more solemnly, or with more intensity: though if he had known how long it would be before he would look at her properly again, he might have tried.

'We should go inside,' said Sarah at last. 'It's getting cold.'

'You go in,' said Robert. 'I'm going to stay here for a while.'

She stood up stiffly. 'Are you sure?'

'Yes.' He noticed the concern on her face. 'Don't worry,' he said. 'I'm not going to jump.'

Sarah bent over and kissed the top of his head. 'Good.'

Before she had walked more than a few yards, Robert called after her: 'Sarah!'

She turned.

He was on the point of telling her about the poem; telling her to go and look for it in the Café, in the book, on page 173. But he realized now that it was no use. He had left it too late.

'Goodbye, then,' was all he said.

She smiled again, and carried on walking back towards the house.

Terry was very late getting back from London that evening. The search for the photograph had lasted for more than five hours, at the end of which he was in a condition of breathless near-despair. At last, however, he had found it: by some evil quirk of fate, it had worked its way down to the very bottom of the very remotest cardboard box in the second of his two overcrowded lumber rooms. When he finally saw the picture, he clutched at it as if it were the hand of his dearest, long-lost friend, and had to fight back tears of triumph and relief. Then he looked at his watch, made a swift calculation and realized that he just had time to catch the last train to the coast, even though it meant leaving his flat in a state of rubbish-strewn chaos, as if it had just been ransacked by the security services or a posse of incompetent burglars. The strength of his desire to return to Ashdown that night took him by surprise. Forty minutes later he was sitting on the train as it rattled out of London, and he had the photograph on his lap in front of him, safely enclosed within the latest issue of *Sight and Sound*: every so often he would open the magazine and sneak a glance at it, this redis-covered symbol of everything in his life that was most valuable, most worth pursuing. He was resolved that it should never be mislaid or forgotten again.

He had to wait several minutes at the station for a taxi, and it was after eleven o'clock by the time he was deposited on the front steps of Ashdown. At this hour of the night, he would have expected the house to be darkened and quiescent, the patients all at rest in their bedrooms, the only real activity being the frantic scratching of the polysomnograph pens as they traced their electrically determined patterns (and, of course, the ceaseless pattering — just as frantic, even though hidden — of the unwilling participants in Dr Dudden's experiment). Instead, a rather different scene awaited him: there were three women sitting outside on the brightly lit terrace, and the warm night air rang with the sounds of their laughing voices and the clinking of bottles and glasses. The women were Dr Madison, Maria Granger, and Barbara Daintry, the sleepwalker.

Seeing him climbing the steps, Maria called out: 'Hey! Harry — what are you up to?'

'The name's Terry,' he said, strolling over.

'Terry — Harry — whatever: what are you doing sneaking in at this time of night?'

Maria was a cheery, outgoing, middle-aged Londoner who had already made several friendly overtures towards Terry during the last few days. She was a big woman, with many chins and a mouth that seemed poised permanently on the edge of a subversive smile. Her stomach was vast, and her breasts enormous. Partly, he had been told, her size was the result of the drugs she was obliged to take to counteract the symptoms of her chronic narcolepsy; but Maria was also the first to admit that her marked *penchant* for chocolate doughnuts and strawberry cheesecake was a contributing factor. Terry liked her; as did everybody at the clinic, with the exception of Dr Dudden.

'I've been to London for the day,' he said.

'I see: playing truant.'

'In a manner of speaking, yes.'

'Are you going to have a drink with us, then? We could do with some male company.'

'Aren't we all supposed to be in bed by now?'

'He's not here, though — Doctor Death. He went off to a conference this afternoon. And besides, it's my last night tonight, so I'm celebrating. You know — while the cat's away . . .'

'. . . the mice can relax a little bit,' Terry concluded. For Dr

Madison's benefit he added: 'As can the rats, I hope.' She didn't reply, and her face betrayed no complicity. 'All right, then,' he said. 'I'll just take these things upstairs, then I'll come and join you.'

By the time he returned, Dr Madison had disappeared.

'She's gone to bed,' said Maria.

'She works too hard, that woman,' said Barbara. 'He drives her into the ground.'

Maria passed Terry a paper cup, filled almost to overflowing with white wine.

'So,' he said, after his first sip, 'are you looking forward to re-entering the real world?'

'I'm looking forward to seeing my kids again. And my husband. I've missed them. But I've enjoyed it here, actually. Two weeks by the seaside. It's been a laugh.'

'She loves a laugh,' Barbara said, and they both giggled. 'You should see what happens to her when she laughs. She goes all peculiar.'

'Oh, don't get me started,' said Maria, the giggles giving way to something throatier, more deeply rooted. 'Don't start telling me jokes. You know I can't stand that.'

'Why?' said Terry. 'What happens when you laugh?'

'She goes all limp,' said Barbara. 'She goes limp and strange all over. You know when you say someone's helpless with laughter? Well that's what happens to her.'

'Now don't start winding me up,' said Maria, already fighting for control of her facial muscles. 'Don't you dare get me going with one of your jokes.'

'What about that one you told me?' said Barbara. 'About the man with the banana.' She turned to Terry. 'There was this man, and he had three bananas, you see. He gets on to this crowded bus in the rush hour, and he doesn't want them to get squashed, so he puts one in his breast pocket, one in his side pocket, and one in his back pocket . . .'

With what seemed to be a serious effort of will, Maria stifled her own laughter and interrupted Barbara forcefully, saying: 'Come on, knock it off, will you? Give me a break here. I don't want to do it in front of Harry —'

'Terry.'

'Terry. I mean, I'm not proud of it, you know. I don't like people seeing me that way.'

'I'm sorry, love,' said Barbara, chastened, full of contrition. 'I just thought he'd be interested.'

'Yes, well, I'm not a bloody exhibit.' For Terry's benefit, she explained: 'When you're narcoleptic, you see, you have this thing called cataplexy. So when you laugh — it's usually laughter that brings it on — you go into a sort of faint. You lose control. You can feel it happening. It's been happening to me for thirty years or more, but they only worked out what was causing it a couple of years ago. So I've got to cut down on my laughter, now, because it tires me out, going funny like that all the time. All my friends and family and that, they all think it's hilarious, seeing me fall over and pass out, they're always winding me up, always trying to set me off, get me giggling. Well, it's a way of life with me, isn't it? Always has been. I've always loved a laugh. I mean, how do you get through life otherwise? You've got to laugh to survive . . .'

And Terry was reminded, at this point, of the farewell party at Ashdown all those years ago, and suddenly he realized what had happened to Sarah that evening, when she had reacted so strangely to his jokes and they had all assumed that she had collapsed from drinking too much. And all at once this memory of the past reached into the present, colouring it, transforming it, so that something happened to Terry which had not happened for many years: a change took place within him, and he was able to look at Maria and to sympathize with her — to feel real sympathy, after all this time, with another human being — watching her face and reading its mixture of sadness and glee, thinking what it must be like to crave laughter, to crave it more than anything else and yet always to deny yourself, knowing that it was the instrument of your destruction, just as the rats on Dr Dudden's turntables were forced to deny themselves sleep every time they showed a yearning for it . . .

'And has it helped?' he asked. 'Has it helped, coming to this place?'

'Well, they've given me some new drugs,' said Maria. 'I don't know how much good they'll do. The main thing's being able to talk about it. Cleo's been great, actually. I could talk to her for hours. I think I could tell her anything.'

'Sorry,' said Terry, 'who's been great? Who did you say?'

'Cleo. Dr Madison.'

Terry stared at her for a long time.

'Look, I really must get to bed,' he said, eventually. 'I've been travelling nearly all day, and it's after eleven-thirty. I really must go.'

He pushed back his chair and stumbled towards the house, and it wasn't until the next morning — after a night in which he drifted into Stage Four sleep for more than an hour, and even experienced, momentously, the first, tenuous stirrings of a dream — that he allowed himself to ponder that name again, and to analyse the dizzying sense of wonder it had aroused in him. Then he remembered its significance, and remembered, at the same moment, why Dr Madison's face had for the last week been teasing him with a distant familiarity.

He went to find her at once.

As Terry was searching the corridors of Ashdown for Dr Madison that Thursday morning, Sarah was eating a slice of toast and looking warily at the copy of *The House of Sleep* which lay on her kitchen table like an unexploded bomb. She had not yet opened it.

It was absurd, she told herself, to be so superstitious about this book. Where was the harm in flicking through it again, in reading a few pages? Did she really think that this penny-dreadful yarn, which she and Veronica had always regarded as the most delicious joke, would have acquired some mysterious power to wound her?

She looked at the clock: there were only five minutes left before she had to leave for work.

She wiped the butter off her fingers with some kitchen towel, picked up the book, and opened it slowly. It seemed to open very naturally at a particular page, a little more than half-way through, and when it was open, a sheet of paper fell out. A folded sheet of lined notepaper, covered on one side with handwriting.

It had never occurred to her that it would have been the same copy. It had never occurred to her that neither Veronica nor Rebecca had once opened the book in twelve years.

With trembling hands, she unfolded the sheet of paper, and recognized Robert's handwriting immediately. His words, forgotten for so long — completely forgotten — drifted back into her mind.

If ever I want to leave anything for you, I'll put it here. In this book.

Page 173.

Then you'll always know where to find it.

She laid down the paper without reading any of it, and took deep breaths. She could feel all the strength, all the responsiveness, draining from her muscles. She could barely move her arms. She was slumping forward in the chair.

No. She could stop this. She could control it.

She sat upright. She forced her hand towards the sheet of paper again. She forced her fingers to grasp it, to turn it over. She would read it. She would read it quickly, in one go, and then it would be over.

One more deep breath. Then:

Gravity and grace . . . yes, of course, that was the book they had been reading, on the beach, they had talked about affection, and about loss, about what you do if you lose somebody . . . *your narcoleptic eyes* . . . but how could he have written that? How could he have known? Nobody knew, back then . . . *a disregard* . . . *a disregard that made me feel* . . . he meant the Café, that time in the Café, when she and Ronnie had taunted him . . . *'as still, as carved, as death'* . . . the beach again, she had read that line aloud, it was from Rosamond Lehmann . . . *an oblivion so deep it ends* . . . *drown the ghosts* . . . *another lifetime* . . . *another lifetime is the least you'll need* . . .

She finished reading, and the paper fell from her hand. She looked ahead of her, unseeing. She forgot that she was supposed to be leaving for school. She had no awareness of the passing of time. Time seemed to have been suspended.

It was in fact nearly thirty minutes later when she walked across the room and picked up the receiver of the wall-mounted telephone. She dialled a number which was scribbled on a notepad next to the phone.

An unfamiliar voice answered the call after ten or eleven rings.

'I'd like to speak to Ruby, please. Ruby Sharp.'

'Hold on a minute. I'll see if she's in.'

The acoustics at the other end of the line called to mind a hallway or corridor. Sarah could hear footsteps and far-off voices. She imagined some dowdy institutional building, cheap parquet flooring, notices pinned to a cork-lined noticeboard. Then she heard the approach of one set of footsteps, and the crack of the receiver being picked up again.

'Yes, hello?'

'Ruby, this is Sarah. Sarah Tudor.'

'Oh.' A pause, filled with pleasure and surprise. 'Hello, Sarah. How lovely to hear from you.' Then a longer pause: puzzled, expectant. 'Sarah? Are you all right?'

'I need to talk to you.'

'Yes, of course.' Ruby waited. 'What about?'

'I need to come and see you.'

'Has — look, has something happened? Is something the matter?'

Sarah broke her own long silence, by saying: 'You were right.'

'I was right? What was I right about?'

'You said that he really cared for me. You were right.'

'Who really cared for you?'

'Robert did. You said it the other day and I didn't believe you; didn't want to believe you. But now I've remembered.'

'Sarah . . .' Ruby sighed, exasperated. 'You sound very strange. I think you should —'

'I found something of his.'

'What did you find?'

'Something he wrote to me. *For* me.'

'You mean — recently? He wrote this recently?'

'No. Years ago. Listen, can I come and see you? Can we meet somewhere today?'

'Don't you have to be at school?'

'Oh, yes. Of course.' Crestfallen, Sarah looked at the wall-clock. She passed a hand over her eyes. 'This evening, then: can I see you this evening?'

'I'm going home today. I'll be staying with my mother for the weekend.' She could sense Sarah's disappointment. 'I'm sorry.'

'That's OK. I'd better go to school now.' But Sarah did not move; neither did Ruby. When Sarah managed to speak again, her voice was quieter, as if she was talking to herself now; thinking aloud. 'Why did he just leave like that? Without saying anything. Running off into the night.' Then she seemed to remember that Ruby was still listening. 'That was the last time I saw him. And before that — a few years before that — there was a letter. One letter.'

'What did the letter say?'

'Nothing.'

'Nothing at all?'

'Not really. It mentioned a dream he'd had. But apart from that — well, it didn't even tell me where he was writing from. Or what he was doing. I wondered at the time whether . . .'

'Yes?'

'Did you know that Robert had a twin?'

'No. No, I didn't. I barely knew him at all.'

'He had a twin sister called Cleo. She was given up for adoption when they were just a few weeks old. He'd never seen her again. Perhaps he was going to look for her. He always said that he would.'

Ruby was lost. 'Look, Sarah, I have to go. I really have to go.'

'I know. I'm sorry.'

'I'll be back after the weekend. I'll come round and see you then, shall I? Monday evening.'

'You don't have to. I don't know why I should be bothering you with this. It's just that . . . you brought it all back, talking about him the other day.' She sniffed, rubbed her eyes, began pulling herself together. 'I'm sorry, really I am. This isn't your problem.'

Then, softly, Ruby said, 'No, it is my problem, actually,' and hung up.

Even though it pained Dr Dudden to leave his clinic in the care of Dr Madison for two days, he would not have missed this conference for anything. Hingleton Pendlebury was one of the country's most prestigious firms of management consultants, and this short, intensive, residential course, 'Motivating for Change', promised to do something which he felt was long overdue: namely, to introduce leading members of the psychiatric profession to some basic business concepts, in keeping with the Health Service's painful but inevitable transition to a management culture.

Along with the other delegates, he had arrived at the designated London hotel early on Wednesday evening. It was a five-star hotel, and its rooms seemed to have been designed —

annoyingly — with extremes of comfort, rest and relaxation in mind. His bed had a soft goose-down mattress, and the armchairs were plump and well upholstered. Not to be deterred, Dr Dudden had settled down on the floor at midnight, with his latest lab results spread out before him, and had resolved to occupy himself with work until four-thirty at the earliest. How long he managed to stay awake, he would never know. He woke up at nine-fifteen, flat out on the carpet with a sore back and a terrible crick in his neck. Just as Ruby, therefore, was replacing her telephone receiver on the other side of London and walking thoughtfully back towards her room, Dr Dudden was rushing through the hotel corridors, unshaved, unwashed and wearing last night's clothes, desperately trying to locate the main conference chamber.

Despite his fatigue and his dishevelled state, however, he was anticipating the day's opening session with a good deal more enthusiasm than the other participants; all of whom, it transpired, were there under duress of one sort or another. Mostly they were London-based psychiatrists, whose attendance seemed to be a contractual obligation rigorously insisted upon by the managers and non-executive directors of their new hospital trusts.

'It's bloody ridiculous,' one of them was already saying when Dr Dudden entered the room. 'I've had to cancel five lectures and six consultations, all at the behest of some pimply-faced accountant who thinks he knows what's good for me.'

Now the two course trainers appeared. Their faces were fresh and unformed, and they wore identical, closely-fitting Jaeger suits. Each appeared to be in his early twenties and had the vacantly shining eyes of the evangelical zealot.

'Hi: I'm Tim Simpson,' the first one said.

'And I'm Mark McGuire.'

Tim Simpson explained that he had recently returned from a year in Minnesota, where he had majored in Organizational

Change at Duluth University. Mark McGuire, on the other hand, boasted a diploma in Group Relations, Meeting Planning and Human Resource Development from the University of Milton Keynes.

'And we're here to talk about change,' said Tim Simpson. He turned over the first page of a flip-chart, and pointed at the word 'CHANGE', which was written in foot-high capitals.

'That's right,' said Mark McGuire. 'Change is a scary word. And for many of you, these are scary times.' He turned over the next page of the flip-chart, and pointed at the words 'SCARY TIMES'.

'Many of you will be afraid of change,' said Tim Simpson. 'Some of you will even be angry about it. But our message to you over the next two days is going to be — *use* that fear; *work* that anger; and above all —'

He glanced at Mark McGuire, who turned over the flip-chart again as they both chanted, in unison: 'EMBRACE THE CHANGE.'

'As qualified facilitators,' said Mark McGuire, 'our task during these sessions will be to engage you in a series of role-playing modules and creativity enhancement procedures.'

'These methods have been tested and approved by some of America's most successful corporations,' said Tim Simpson.

'The exercises you will be performing should not be regarded as a training programme *per se*,' said Mark McGuire.

'Our aim is simply to open up your minds . . .'

'Stimulate creative thinking . . .'

'Engage your attention . . .'

'Embed key points and concepts for long-term retention . . .'

'And above all . . .'

One more turn of the flip-chart, and then, in unison: 'MOTI-VATE YOU FOR CHANGE.'

'Now,' said Tim Simpson, 'does anyone have any questions?'

Most of the audience seemed too dazed and bewildered to

ask questions at this stage, so the facilitators divided them up into groups of five and explained that the first exercise would provide a relaxed forum in which introductions could be made.

'All you have to do,' said Mark McGuire, 'is to address the group, tell them your name — and your age, if you feel like it — and any job description that you consider relevant.'

'Is that all, Mark?' said Tim Simpson. 'That sounds kind of dull and conventional to me.'

'You're right, Tim. I've forgotten something,' said Mark McGuire. 'And do you know what I've forgotten?'

'I think I do, Mark. I think you've forgotten —' and here Tim Simpson produced a cardboard box from behind the flip-chart, whereupon they both exclaimed:

'— the SILLY HATS.'

A number of party and fancy-dress hats were now extracted from the box and distributed at random among the astonished delegates, while Mark McGuire explained that they might find it easier and more liberating to assume a role appropriate to each hat when making their introductory speeches.

The five members of Dr Dudden's group sat in a circle, donned their respective hats and regarded each other mournfully before proceeding.

'Well, I suppose I might as well start,' said one bespectacled, grey-haired delegate, upon whose head was perched a papier mâché policeman's helmet. 'My name is Dr Christopher Myers, I'm forty-eight years old, and I'm a Senior Lecturer in Liaison Psychiatry.'

'My name,' said the woman sitting next to him, wearing a Valkyrie helmet, complete with horns, 'is Dr Susan Herriot, MRC Psych. I'm forty-two years old, and I lecture in Perinatal Psychiatry.'

'I'm Russell Watts,' said the next man, who sported a deer-stalker. 'Self-employed counsellor and psychotherapist. Thirty-nine years old.'

'Avast there, me hearties!' Dr Dudden now shouted, pound-

ing the table with a violence that made the others jump. He was
wearing a pirate's hat. 'Hoist the Jolly Roger, splice the mainsail
and man the poop. Fifteen men on the dead man's chest, Yo-ho-
ho and a bottle of rum!' His colleagues were staring at him in
amazement, so he finished by announcing, in more subdued
tones: 'Dr G. K. Dudden, MRC Psych. Founder, manager and
team leader of the Dudden Clinic. Aged thirty-six last birthday.
At your service.'

The others did not seem to be curious enough about his first
name to insist upon hearing it. Besides, this reference to the
clinic itself was enough to spark a glimmer of recognition in the
last member of the group, who remarked, 'Ah! The sleep man,'
before proceeding to address them all. He was the oldest of the
five, with a mane of white hair and a fine, aquiline face, partially obscured at this point by the veil hanging down from his
broad-brimmed wedding hat, which was topped with a multi-
layered arrangement of pink and blue plastic roses. 'My name,'
he said slowly, 'is Marcus Cole, FRC Psych. I'm fifty-eight years
old, I'm a Professor of Forensic Psychiatry, and I had to cancel a
meeting at the Home Office to be here today. Now, shall we take
these ridiculous things off?'

As the morning's activities continued, tensions between
these five group members seemed to intensify rather than dissolve. Professor Cole and Christopher Myers already appeared
to be quite well acquainted: they were on first-name terms, and
treated each other with evident mutual respect. They were
both openly suspicious of Russell Watts, however, and notice-
ably cool towards Dr Dudden. The next game, in which they
had to find ways of arranging six matchsticks so as to make different combinations of equilateral triangles, passed relatively
without incident. After that, in order to unblock their latent
creativity channels (Mark McGuire's phrase) they were asked to
make personalized sculptures out of pipe-cleaners. This aroused
some controversy, since Russell Watts's sculpture was judged
to be obscene and suggestive; as indeed were the gestures

he started making with it towards Dr Herriot, which she did her best to ignore. Finally, just before lunch, they played a game called 'Modify That Paradigm!' which required them each to cut up a colour advertisement from a newspaper or magazine, and arrange the pieces into an original collage. The new pictures, they were told, should be representational rather than abstract.

'Is that the best you could do?' Dr Myers said at the end, looking over at Professor Cole's collage.

'What do you mean?' said the Professor irritably. His fingers were covered with glue.

'Well, it's a bit basic, isn't it?'

'It's a perfectly good picture of an aeroplane, if you ask me.' With a disparaging glance at Dr Myers's effort, he added: 'At least you can tell what mine is.'

'What's that supposed to mean?'

'Well, what do you call that? Is it meant to be an elephant or something?'

'It's a horse, for God's sake.'

'It's the wrong shape.'

'What are you talking about, the wrong shape? It's bloody . . . horse-shaped, that's what it is. At least I took on a bit of a challenge. Anybody could do an aeroplane.'

'Oh, fuck off, Myers. You always were a pompous old sod.'

Their collective tempers did not improve over lunch. After washing the glue from his hands Professor Cole seemed slightly less fractious, and merely sat with a resigned, melancholy expression on his face, eating his meal in silence. Dr Myers was a good deal more vocal.

'It's like being back in a bloody kindergarten,' he complained. 'How much are these pre-pubescent clowns being paid to waste our time like this? I mean, has anybody ever heard of this company — Higgledy Piggledy, or whatever they're called?'

'Hingleton Pendlebury,' said Dr Dudden, 'is a firm with a considerable reputation within the business community. Personally, I've found this morning's activities to be extremely stimulating. We shouldn't knock these methods just because they seem to be a little juvenile at first. The success of American business is built on events like this.'

'Oh, what bullshit,' said Dr Myers. 'For one thing, providing health care is not a business. And secondly, American business success is a myth. Look at their national debt. You don't find the Germans or the Japanese messing around with matchsticks and pipe-cleaners during their working hours. On the contrary, this sort of thing shows you exactly what's wrong with the Americans: their pathetic infantilism.'

'What do you think, Professor?' asked Dr Herriot. She was sitting next to Russell Watts, and leaning visibly away from him.

Professor Cole laid down his knife and fork, and said dreamily: 'In two years' time, I shall be retiring. I shall have been in the profession for more than twenty-five years, and in that time I shall have seen psychiatry being transformed, in the public eye, from a serious medical science into a discredited wing of the civil service; the scapegoat for every ill which society happens to throw up. It seems to me entirely appropriate that I should end my career making collages out of paper and glue, under the supervision of a man ten years younger than my youngest son. Today,' he continued, as the others listened with shocked concentration, 'I should be meeting with the Home Office and with my trust managers to discuss the case of a young schizophrenic on one of my wards. I am the only person qualified to give a medical opinion on this case, but the meeting will proceed without me. Such are the realities of psychiatric practice in London today.'

'The managers want to release him, I suppose?' said Dr Myers.

'Yes. There's a shortage of beds, and his condition has stabilized in the last few weeks.'

'Permanently?'

'No. Only thanks to our efforts.'

'They won't let him out, will they?'

'I hope not. It's possible.'

'Is he dangerous?'

'Very.' Professor Cole rose tiredly to his feet, and said: 'I'm going to lie down for a little while, I think. I'll see you all in half an hour or so.'

When he had gone, Dr Dudden began to pour coffee for everyone and snorted: 'Bit of a dinosaur, that one. He needs to move with the times.'

Christopher Myers bridled. 'You should remember,' he said, 'that not all of us have embraced the free market with quite your enthusiasm, Dr Dudden.'

'You will,' he said. 'You'll have no choice.'

'The clinic is thriving, I take it?'

'We're getting by, we're getting by.'

'Not too much adverse publicity?'

Dr Dudden paused in the act of stirring his own coffee. 'Meaning?'

'I just wondered about the little spot of bother you had down there last year with that young man: the name was Webb, wasn't it?'

'Stephen Webb died in a road accident. Nothing to do with my clinic.'

'Yes, of course. Still, it did attract a certain amount of attention, you know . . .'

Dr Dudden shrugged. 'That doesn't surprise me. Or disturb me, to be perfectly honest.'

'Maybe not.' Dr Myers hesitated, as if about to raise a delicate topic. 'All the same, I think you should know that I've been asked to chair a committee to look into that incident. You'll be told about it soon, officially, by letter.'

Dr Dudden paused, open-mouthed, in the act of sipping his coffee. His face was pale.

'I see,' he said quietly.

Noticing the silence that had descended on their table, Dr Herriot turned to Russell Watts and asked him to pass the sugar.

He handed her the little basin of brown and white sachets, and slipped his hand purposefully on to her thigh.

'I put it to you,' he whispered, 'that your cunt is on fire.'

'Time to go back to the conference room, I think,' said Dr Herriot, standing up in a sudden, startled movement. Her voice was unusually high and strained.

Most of their time, that afternoon, was spent playing a long and elaborate game called 'Alien Babies'. For this purpose, Tim Simpson and Mark McGuire had pegged out a number of circles in string on the floor of the conference room. These circles were some twelve feet in diameter, and in the middle of each one was a small bucket filled with jelly babies.

'Now, they may look like ordinary jelly babies to you,' said Tim Simpson, 'but in fact these are the embryos of an alien life form. They've just landed in your back garden, and in thirty minutes' time they're going to hatch out and turn into enormous, life-threatening monsters, capable of destroying the world.'

'What's more,' said Mark McGuire, 'they're already giving out a powerful and deadly radioactive energy, so that anyone who steps inside one of these circles is going to be killed.'

'There's only one way of destroying these aliens,' said Tim Simpson. 'They have no immunity to water. Immerse them in water, and they die instantly.'

Each group was provided with a bucket of water and five eight-foot lengths of rope. They were then told that they had thirty minutes to find a way of transferring the jelly babies from one bucket to the other, without stepping inside the dangerous radioactive field, without laying hands on the alien bucket and without bringing it out of the circle.

Dr Dudden assumed command of his group.

'Now, we're not going to rush into this,' he said. 'Let's keep a cool head, and allow five minutes to think of a strategy.'

'Well, it seems clear enough to me,' said Dr Myers. 'One of us should walk into the circle and tip them straight into the bucket of water.'

'But he'll be killed,' said Dr Dudden.

'So? He'll have saved the entire population of the world. That's worth dying for, isn't it?'

'Let's draw lots,' said Dr Herriot. 'Or toss for it.'

'But you die as soon as you step inside the circle.'

'They didn't tell us that you died immediately. You might have ten seconds, or thirty seconds, or even a minute.'

Dr Dudden consulted with Mark McGuire, who told him that once anyone stepped inside the circle, death was instantaneous; furthermore, individual sacrifices were not in keeping with the spirit of the exercise. He then returned to find that Professor Cole was busy tying a knot in his length of rope.

'What are you doing?' he asked.

'It's perfectly obvious,' said the Professor. 'We're going to have to put lassoes around the buckets. We put one around the bucket of water, and pull that into the centre of the circle. Then four of us have to lasso the bucket full of jelly babies, and if we all pull the ropes tight, we ought to be able to raise it and tilt it so we can get them into the water. Look —' he pointed at the other groups '— they've already started.'

Dr Dudden frowned judiciously. 'That might work,' he said.

It was a surprisingly difficult operation, and more than twenty minutes had gone by before they had secured the central bucket with four ropes, and were preparing to pull them tight under Dr Dudden's supervision.

'All right,' he said. 'Now, on the count of three, we're going to raise the bucket, and then —'

'Can I just say something at this point?' said Russell Watts.

'What?' Dr Dudden snapped. He was sweating profusely, and beginning to find the whole activity rather stressful. 'We've only got another six minutes, you know.'

'Well, I was just thinking: perhaps we're going about this in the wrong way.'

'How do you mean?'

'Well, we're assuming that these creatures have to be destroyed.'

'Yes?'

'But perhaps we should try reasoning with them.'

Christopher Myers and Susan Herriot put down their ropes and looked at each other despairingly. Professor Cole, on the other hand, appeared not to be listening. The dreamy expression had returned to his face. He was thinking, in fact, of the meeting he had been forced to miss that afternoon; thinking about the schizophrenic patient who had been in his care for the last few weeks, and wondering what would happen if the hospital managers decided to release him.

the assailant was six feet two inches tall, wearing black jeans and a green combat jacket

'Reason with them? What are you talking about?'

'This could be our first contact with an alien civilization, and we're just going to kill them off without even trying to communicate with them?'

he was pacing backwards and forwards along the platform, muttering to himself and occasionally shouting

'For God's sake, man, these are jelly babies, not real aliens. It's only a game.'

'Well if it's only a game why are we taking the rules so seriously?'

'Let's just tip the bloody things in the water and be done with it.'

the blade of his knife glinted in the evening sunlight

'How do we know that water kills them anyway?'

'What?'

'They've just landed in our back garden. We know nothing about them. How do we know that the water's going to kill them?'

the victim remains in a coma, after receiving multiple stab wounds to the chest and throat

'Look, just grab hold of the rope and get on with it.'

'Yes. Stop being childish.'

'Are you ready, Professor?'

the patient's release ran contrary to my own professional judg-
ment, and contrary to the advice contained in my memo to the
Home Office

'Marcus, are you ready?'

since there seems to be no prospect of improvement in your son's
condition, I can offer only my condolences for the grief this must
have caused to you and your family

Professor Cole realized that he was being spoken to, and
looked up at the expectant faces of his colleagues. He found
that he was sitting on the floor of the conference room, although he had no memory of getting there. Before struggling to
his feet he took out a pocket handkerchief and wiped some
pearls of sweat from his cheeks and brow.

Professor Marcus Cole, FRC Psych., said reluctantly: 'Yes,
I'm ready.'

Then the four rope-pullers took up their positions, and Dr
Dudden counted to three in a careful but excited monotone.
When they had successfully completed their task, they were al-
lowed to eat the waterlogged jelly babies.

There was never any question of Terry hitting her, as Sarah was always careful to emphasize, whenever she discussed the incident later with one of her friends, or even with her analyst. All the same, she was frightened. She had never seen anger quite like it, not even from Gregory on the night they split up. Tables and walls were thumped. Short, high-pitched, inarticulate noises of rage were emitted. Small items of furniture were kicked and thrown around the room.

'But it's not my *fault*,' Sarah had protested, repeatedly. 'It's not my fault. I couldn't help it.'

Terry didn't speak to her for almost a week after that. The flat they were sharing was not large, and it would have been difficult to avoid contact altogether, but he made his point by removing all his books and papers from the sitting-room, where he usually worked, and setting up a makeshift office in the dark and unheated spare bedroom. It was to no avail, anyway, because at the end of the week he was called into his editor's office and told that he had lost his job; and since he had been paying the rent for both of them, that was the end of their flat-share. *Frame* had only employed him for three months.

A few days later they moved out: Terry to begin an extended period of sleeping on friends' floors, Sarah (who had not yet found a teaching job) to stay in the spare room of a much-disliked aunt in Crouch End. But Terry's anger had subsided, by now. He was able to see that the incident had, if not quite a funny side, then at least a certain ironic dimension which he would come to relish more and more over the ensuing years. And he kept in touch with Sarah, and kept taking her out for drinks and meals, and occasionally asked her to tell him the story again, just so that he could be clear in his mind about how the disaster had happened.

'It was a dream, Terry. I must have dreamed that I'd done it.'

'But how is that possible? Nobody has dreams like that.'

'They do. *I* do. It's been happening all my life.'

And even now, looking back on that day, Sarah found it impossible to distinguish the dream from the reality: the transition from one to the other remained perfectly seamless. Each was characterized by the same elements: the frail afternoon sunlight, dimming and brightening on the surface of her desk as the clouds went by; the sound of trains rattling past every few minutes; and beyond the railway line, on the fringes of the cemetery, the sea of treetops undulating in the breeze. It was mid-November. The flat was ghostly quiet, and had been for the last two days, ever since Terry's departure for Italy. Since then she had spoken to no one, apart from Terry himself when he had phoned from Milan that morning, full of stories about the famous director he had been sent out to interview, and wanting to know if the proofs of the Henry Logan speech had arrived yet. Yes, said Sarah, they came in today's post. And Terry had said, Good: because there's something I want you to change.

Frame was by now, in this last year of its existence, an austere, rather intimidating-looking publication with a small but influential academic and general readership. Articles tended to be long, sparsely illustrated and freighted with heavy footnotes. Normally its editorial board would never have contemplated running anything as thin or anecdotal as the text of an after-dinner speech given by Henry Logan; but this infamous British mogul and ex-producer had recently announced his retirement from the film business and simultaneously — for reasons best known to himself — come to the rescue of the magazine during its latest near-fatal financial crisis. Now that he was their benefactor and majority shareholder, there was no question, unfortunately, of not publishing the food-spattered manuscript he had proudly dropped on to the desk of the editor-in-chief one Monday morning. *Fragments from a Life in Movies* was his inspired title, and the appearance of these pages had immediately set in train an orgy of buck-passing, as successive members of staff frantically ducked the awesome responsibility of subbing them into some kind of shape. The job finally devolved upon Terry, as the newest and lowliest employee. He recognized at once that there was nothing much to be done about the substance of the speech, which comprised the expected mixture of trivial reminiscence and insufferable self-congratulation. None the less he did his best to set aside the personal animosity he had conceived towards Logan's son during their brief meeting, and applied himself to what seemed, in this case, to be the most useful editorial task: the provision of footnotes, to add something more in the way of biographical colour and to make the many specific British cultural references more explicable to the magazine's international readership.

With a newcomer's diligence, Terry spent at least a week working on these footnotes, and was still agonizing over which were necessary and which superfluous when a call came from the magazine, to say that a staff journalist had fallen ill. Terry was going to have to deputize for him, and this involved the pleasant responsibility of flying out to Milan, to prepare a location report on the shooting of a prestigious Anglo-Italian co-production. Before departing, he had submitted a more or less final version of his annotated manuscript which still, however, left him with some nagging uncertainties. And it was to resolve one of these that he phoned Sarah from Italy that morning and asked her if the proofs had arrived.

'Now, listen carefully,' he said, 'because those will have to go back in the post this evening, first class. So first of all you've got to read them through for typos. And then — are you listening? — and then I want you to take out the third foot-note.' He enunciated these words as clearly as possible, as the international line crackled and spat. 'Footnote number three. Delete it. We don't need it. It's fussy and it doesn't add any-thing.'

'OK,' said Sarah. 'That's easy. I can do that, no problem.'

'Yes, but make sure you do it properly,' Terry said. 'You'll have to renumber all the footnotes. Make sure they correspond.'

'Terry, I'll do it. Don't worry.'

He had hung up then, apparently reassured, muttering some-thing about an impending lunch appointment with Marcello Mastroianni.

Sarah waited until early in the afternoon, when she had fin-ished her shopping and the light would be better on the sitting-room desk. After making herself a cup of coffee, she took the sheets of paper from their envelope and arranged them neatly in front of her. Terry's footnotes were on a separate sheet; the third one would have to be deleted and the others renumbered, but she set them aside for the time being, and decided to look first of all at the main body of the text (five pages in all), read-ing it through carefully for sense and printing errors. This took twenty minutes or so. Then she went back to a sentence near the beginning. 'Who'd have thought,' Logan had written, 'that, only last year, I would have become managing director of a sub-stantial new country club and leisure centre situated just a stone's throw from those self-same studios — in Teddington, no less?' After the word 'Teddington' came a small superscript '3', directing the reader to a simple explanatory footnote on the sep-arate sheet, which read: 'A placid, respectable Thameside sub-urb of London, just south of Richmond.' This was the footnote Terry wanted deleting. She couldn't see why, at this late stage, but it was his decision, after all. So she crossed out the little '3' in the text, left a clear mark for the printer in the margin, and set about changing all the numbers which followed it: '4' became '3', '5' became '4', and so on. She left the footnotes themselves untouched at this stage. It was easy, mechanical work, and the flat was so quiet as she went about it that she could hear the scrape of her biro on the page, and each delicate slurp of coffee seemed like a shattering intrusion upon the silence.

She had just changed the final '16' to '15' when there was a noise from the hallway: something coming through the letter-box. It was late, but not impossibly late, for the second post. She went to look and found that there was a single letter lying on the floor. It was in a plain white envelope, bore a first-class stamp, and was addressed to her in what she immediately recognized as Robert's handwriting. Shaking, she tore it open with her forefinger and stood in the hallway reading it.

She had heard nothing from Robert since the day they had parted; the day she had left him sitting on the clifftop, his cheeks bruised and swollen from some bizarre, unspecified accident in his bedroom during the small hours. He had not followed her back into the house, and an hour later Sarah's parents had arrived to take her and her possessions away from Ashdown for good.

Since then, nothing.

Two letters addressed to Robert at Ashdown had gone unanswered. Then, six or seven weeks after the end of term, Sarah phoned the house, and some man whose voice she had never heard before told her that Robert had gone, more than a month ago. She phoned his parents and was told that he was on holiday, in Europe somewhere, Interrailing. The next time, they gave her an unlikely-sounding address, a town whose name meant nothing to her, some 200 miles from London. There was no telephone number. She wrote but he never answered. Terry wrote; and his letters, too, were ignored. Sarah gave up. Robert had said that he didn't want her friendship, for the moment at least. It seemed that he had meant it. There was only so much effort she was prepared to make.

And now, this letter.

It gave no address, and there was only one sheet of paper, which seemed to have been scribbled over hurriedly. Clearly she was not going to learn much in the way of news.

It said:

Dear Sarah,

> *Ashdown was bad. A bad idea. I only stayed a week or so. Too many phantoms.*

> *Then I went home for a while. Arguments with my father (we never got on), and lots of days in bed. Not much fun, so I tried a bit of travelling. Not much fun either.*

This was hopeless, Sarah thought. Worse than hopeless. But the next paragraph looked longer, at least.

> *Did I ever tell you about a dream I had when I was a child? I suppose I must have done — I told you everything, at some time or another. It was about being on a road, a very hot and dusty road, with a woman in a nurse's uniform pointing into the distance, towards a building which I could tell was a hospital. She was standing in front of a sign written in a foreign language.*

> *I've finally worked out the meaning of this dream. What it has been trying to tell me.*

> *So, here I am. You'll know where, roughly, because of the postmark, but I wouldn't try to get back in touch for a while. You wouldn't find me very good company.*

> *This is it, Sarah, for the time being. But you will hear from me again one day. I promise you that. And I hope everything goes well for you till then.*

> *I love you more than ever.*
> *Robert*

'What did the letter *say*?' Terry would always ask.

'Nothing,' Sarah would answer. 'Hardly anything. It didn't tell me where he was, or what he was planning to do . . . nothing.'

'And then what happened?'

'Well, I think . . . I can remember taking the letter into the sitting-room, and sitting down somewhere, and trying to read it again. And then half-way through, I started shaking, and I could feel it coming on but I couldn't do anything about it, and then I must have — collapsed, I suppose.'

'Collapsed? In what way?'

'You know, I've noticed that this happens to me sometimes. Like a faint, only I'm still conscious: there's no power at all in my muscles, and I can't move until it passes . . . It happened to me at the party — don't you remember?'

'You were drunk.'

'We all were. I was no drunker than anybody else. I know what it's like to be drunk, and this is different. It's completely exhausting, for one thing. Usually the first thing I want to do afterwards is go to sleep.'

And this is what she had done, just a few minutes later, lying full-length on the sofa with Robert's letter crumpled beneath her body. Sarah had fallen asleep that afternoon and started to dream; and like most of the dreams which came to her when she was upset or excited about something, this one was inspired by the events immediately preceding it. She dreamed about her corrections to Terry's article. She dreamed, fatally, that she had finished them. She even dreamed that she had double-checked them. So that when (a few minutes later? — it was impossible to tell) she awoke blearily, sat up, looked around her, put Robert's letter to one side and went back to the desk, she did not even so much as glance at the pages before slipping them into the already stamped, already addressed envelope, sealing it, and running out to the postbox on the other side of the street.

But the footnotes themselves had not been corrected, and had not been renumbered. And this is how it came about that Henry Logan's after-dinner speech would unwittingly attract at least seven libel suits, have a devastating effect on Terry's career and eventually go down in journalistic legend as 'the piece that closed down *Frame*'.

FRAGMENTS FROM A LIFE IN MOVIES

Producer, film-maker and bon viveur *Henry Logan takes a wistful look at the highs and lows of a long career.*

Now that I am easing myself into well-earned retirement, it seems incredible that I should have entered this mad, wonderful business almost fifty years ago, back in 1935 when I was first taken on as a runner at Twickenham Studios. The very first film I worked on was *A Fire Has Been Arranged*, with that cracking comedy duo, Bud Flanagan and Chesney Allen:[1] with a madcap pair like that on the set there was, as you can imagine, scarcely a dull moment! Though no 'classic', of course, it wasn't a bad little film, and somewhere down the cast-list you can spot the name of a young actor called Alastair Sim, who would soon progress to great things of his own.[2]

Life, I've found, has a way of turning full-circle. Who'd have thought that, only last year, I would have become managing director of a substantial new country club and leisure centre situated just a stone's throw from those self-same studios — in Teddington, no less? This club, the flag-ship of my chain I might add, has already played host to some distinguished visitors, and boasts among its attrac-

---

1. Popular British music-hall comedians, on stage together from 1931 onwards, and later members of the Crazy Gang.
2. Sim (1900–76) went on to star in such later hits as *Green for Danger* (1946), *The Happiest Days of Your Life* (1950) and, perhaps most famously, many films in the *St Trinian's* series.

tions no fewer than two rather challenging eighteen-hole golf courses.[3]

Those studios remain close to my heart in other ways, too, for it was at Twickenham, only a few years ago, that I first met my lovely (fifth) wife Marsha, who was filming there at the time. Now a distinguished actress, of course, Marsha is delightfully candid about her earlier career, and has never made any secret of the fact that she started out in the business by starring, under my own direction, in a series of sex movies.[4] What many people don't know about her, though, is that she is also a deeply religious woman, and a devout Catholic. Among the most prized possessions in our library are several books recommended to her during an audience with Pope Paul VI, who said that they were among the most inspiring and influential works he had ever read.[5]

Frankly, I have never seen anything wrong with films which depict the beauty of the sexual act in an open, honest and forthright manner. Nor do I see any contradiction between this and my early reputation as a powerful advocate of family films, which cannot be called into question. In the late 1940s, for example, I attempted to establish an Anglo-American production company for the making of family pictures with worldwide appeal. With a package of excellent books under option, I spent many fruitless months in Hollywood trying to set things up. Perhaps my

---

3. A placid, respectable Thameside suburb of London, just south of Richmond.

4. Much praised, recently, by Denis Thatcher, who said they had given him 'six of the most enjoyable hours of my life'. His wife Margaret later joked that he was 'stiff for hours afterwards'.

5. Their titles, for the record, were *Wet Knickers*, *Pussy Talk* and *Cream on my Face*.

mistake was in trying to insist upon a particular star — for I had spotted a young, handsome actor, then at the start of his career, by the name of Dean Martin — rather an odd choice of leading man, in retrospect![6] Anyway, it all came to nought.

If ever I'm disheartened by failures such as these, I simply reflect on my humble beginnings and marvel at the enormous distance I have travelled since then. My father owned a small sweet-shop in Market Harborough, and an amusing story attached to it which, although it has been often repeated, I hope I can be forgiven for telling again. One afternoon — in late 1929 or '30, I should think — I remember a large Rolls Royce drawing up outside it, and a small boy getting out to buy a ha'porth of liquorice allsorts, which he ate with great enjoyment. 'One day,' he told my father, 'I shall be very rich and famous, but I shall always remember this shop and its lovely sweets.' Sure enough, thirty years later my father received a summons to Buckingham Palace: for that small boy had been none other than Philip, the future Duke of Edinburgh![7]

Of course, there has been tragedy in my family, as well as good luck. I well remember the terrible night in August 1959, when my brother Jack was staying at my house and received a police telephone call to say that his three young children had gone missing. His beloved son Jimmy — the eldest of three brothers — was subsequently found to have been abducted and murdered by a brutal sex fiend.[8] I have always admired the enormous strength of character

---

6. The books in question are believed to have included the *Confessions* of St Augustine and *Revelations of Divine Love* by Julian of Norwich.

7. He later developed a distinctive public persona, based largely on his self-confessed drinking habits and enormous sexual appetite.

8. An incident which later became the basis of one of Norman Wisdom's less successful comedies, *The Candy-Shop Man*.

Jack showed in rising above this calamity and establishing for himself a successful career as politician and states- man; never once forfeiting his integrity in that sometimes corrupting arena. (As an example of his uncompromising standards, I recall him whispering warmly to me once — of one senior politician who shall for his own modesty's sake remain nameless — 'There are only three people I trust in public life: he is one of them'.)[9]

I think you will probably appreciate, by now, that I come from a close-knit family, and that the traditional family values of loyalty and mutual support have always been very important to me. Although I am separated from my first (American) wife, I keep in close contact with our son Bruce, who is now a successful producer in Holly- wood. The woman who instilled these values in us, and whom we all still remember with enormous fondness, was my dear mother: a woman of terrific warmth and vitality, who lived her life in a golden haze of laughter. Indeed, she died as she had lived — laughing: in this case, at a joke told by a comedian on the television (I wish I could re- member his name), about a housewife describing her new television set to a next-door neighbour: 'It's an eighteen- inch console,' she was supposed to have said. 'Well,' replied the neighbour, 'I should think that eighteen inches would console anybody';[10] whereupon my mother erupted into laughter, choked on a pork scratching and was dead within the half hour.

I have spoken of my family; but I should also speak of my friends. One of the things I love most about this crazy, magical business is the extraordinary diversity of talented

9. The other two, thankfully, were later found tucked up in bed to- gether at Jack Logan's house in Esher.
10. Believed to be a reference to the then Prime Minister, Edward Heath.

people who gather together under its benign umbrella, and who have blessed me, over the years, with their friendship and affection. This realization was brought home to me only two weeks ago, when a select group of conspirators — including, I am happy to say, many of tonight's illustrious guests — put their heads together to organize a surprise party in my honour at London's National Portrait Gallery. What a distinguished roll-call it was! After being welcomed at the door by my old and dear friend Jeffrey Archer,[11] who should I espy first of all — contemplating, with an amused but sceptical frown, a new portrait of himself in oils — but that doughty man of letters Kingsley Amis.[12] We had a fair old chat about matters cultural and political (his reminiscences about a recent encounter with Larry Olivier were, I have to say, brief but tantalizing[13]), but I had to break away all too soon in order to renew my acquaintance with the delightful Dame Vera Lynn.[14] Finally, I had an enthralling conversation with someone whom I have long admired, and whose film work has never, in my opinion, received the recognition it deserves — that great tunesmith and family entertainer, Cliff Richard.[15]

---

11. The origins of this particular joke remain obscure, despite our best endeavours.
12. Loyal supporter of, and propagandist for, the Conservative Party, whose novels, however, are not regarded with much seriousness in literary circles.
13. 'Extremely well-hung' was Amis's only recorded verdict on this occasion.
14. They had met for the first time only a few weeks earlier, to discuss their shared enthusiasm for Jamaican cigars and eighteenth-century erotic drawings.
15. Durable singer of uplifting ballads who has, for as long as most of us can remember, been regarded as one of the undisputed queens of British popular music.

All in all, then, a memorable evening — but one in many ways typical of what I have come to expect from this mad, wonderful business called the movies.

---

16. Performer of such hits as *Congratulations* and *Devil Woman*, whose film roles have so far been confined to minor youth musicals (*Summer Holiday*, *Wonderful Life*, etc.).

Terry and Sarah kept in touch for about a year after they had moved out of the flat. Their restaurant meals dwindled into drinks, which in turn dwindled into telephone calls. She sensed a growing coldness in him. Some months after being fired from *Frame* he managed to find work on a TV listings magazine, where one of his jobs was to write short, eye-catching résumés of the week's films. He was allowed an indiscriminate fifteen words per film, whether it was *Smokey and the Bandit* or *La Règle du Jeu*. Demeaning work, Sarah would have thought, but she couldn't help noticing, the last few times she saw him, that he seemed to be applying himself to it with ever more single-mindedness, and ever more manic energy. His eyes, which had always been hooded with the dead weight of his fourteen hours' nightly sleep, were soon red-rimmed and staring. He admitted that he didn't need nearly so much sleep any more. He admitted that his interest in Salvatore Ortese, *Latrine Duty* and the whole subject of 'lost' films was beginning to dwindle. His visionary, elusive, Edenic dreams were becoming less and less frequent: once a week, then once a month, if that. He no longer saw any point in spending half of his life asleep. He sat up most nights, until dawn sometimes, watching films on television or video. What sort of films? Sarah would ask; and Terry would shrug his shoulders and say, It doesn't really matter.

After they lost touch, Sarah disappeared from Terry's view, teaching being one of the more anonymous professions. But she continued to see his name in the magazines, and then the newspapers, his byline getting more and more prominent, his articles rising closer and closer to the top of the page. Sometimes she even saw him on television; and though her interest in film theory was never more than casual, she knew enough to realize that he had become one of the leading spokesmen for a form of criticism which jettisoned all the concepts of value that had been held dear, only a few years earlier, even by Terry himself. Beyond that, she had no idea what kind of person he had become, or what kind of life he lived now. Sometimes she liked to believe

REM Sleep

believe that I may have known your brother.'

Something seemed to flare in Dr Madison's eyes for a moment — some hint of circumspection, bordering on alarm — but she subdued it quickly and said: 'Really? You knew Philip?'

Now it was Terry who looked surprised. 'No, not Philip: Robert. Your brother Robert.'

'My brother's name is Philip. He's a geneticist. Lives in Bristol.'

This didn't sound promising. 'Was he a student here?' Terry asked.

'At this university? No. He went to Cambridge.'

'The guy I'm thinking of,' said Terry, persisting, 'was a student here. He was one of my best friends. He looked exactly like you, and he said that he had a twin sister called Cleo who was given up for adoption when he was very small.'

Dr Madison smiled. 'It's a nice story,' she said, 'but I think you must be imagining it. The resemblance, I mean. I never had a twin brother.'

'Were you adopted?'

Dr Madison looked at her watch. 'Terry, I have a seminar to conduct.'

She found him again, early in the evening, sitting out on the terrace with a notepad and pencil on his lap.

'Another film review?' she asked, pulling up a chair and sitting alongside him.

'No: I was just making some notes, actually. Memories, impressions, that sort of thing . . . I don't know why.'

'Where's the computer, then? Batteries being recharged?'

'No, I just felt like writing, for a change.'

'Ah.' Dr Madison crossed her legs, then uncrossed them, then sat forward in her chair. She seemed to be lacking her usual composure. 'I lied to you this morning,' she now said, unexpectedly. 'I *was* adopted. I was adopted when I was three weeks old. My new parents called me Sally but I always hated the name and years later they told me what my real name had been, so I've been using it ever since. And I did have a twin brother, and his name was Robert.'

Terry shook his head in disbelief — not at this story, but at the twists of chance that had now brought the two of them together.

'I knew it was you,' he said. 'I knew it had to be you. It's been so long, you see, since I've taken any notice of faces; been able to recognize people. And last night was the first time that I'd heard your name. But . . . but anyway — what happened? Have you ever met your real parents? Have you ever met Robert?'

Cleo nodded. 'Yes. I traced them, eventually. Curiosity got the better of me.' She appeared, for the time being, to have nothing more to say on this subject. 'You were good friends, you said?'

'Yes. Pretty close.'

'Did you keep in touch with him after leaving university?'

'I tried writing to him once or twice. But I don't think he wanted to stay in touch with any of us, for some reason. He just disappeared.'

'Did anyone know where he went? Did anyone ever wonder?'

'Yes, I'm sure they did.'

Cleo stared out to sea. Her spectacles were tinted, and the lenses grew darker as the evening sunlight shone full upon them, making the expression in her eyes unguessable. Something about her reticence was starting to make Terry nervous, and a black, nameless suspicion crept up on him.

'He is — he is still alive, isn't he?'

After a long pause, she said: 'No.'

Terry bowed his head. Somehow he had been anticipating this: the news was numbing, rather than revelatory.

'Oh shit,' he said; and exhaled deeply. 'You know, I always thought . . . I sometimes wondered if he would end up doing that.'

'Doing what?' said Cleo, with a sharp edge to her voice.

'Killing himself.'

'I didn't say that that's what happened.'

'No — but it is, isn't it?' She stared ahead, not answering. 'Do you know why?' Still no answer. 'How?'

'I think there was a woman,' she said: so slowly, so effortfully that the words were almost slurred. 'Some woman he was deeply in love with. As for how . . .' She took off her glasses, rubbed her eyes, then rushed on: 'He drove his car into a wall one night. A street in South London. No note, no farewells, nothing.'

'Poor Robert,' Terry mumbled; then fell into helpless silence. He knew that this conversation, or the memory of it, would stir some feeling in him eventually — some residue of grief, or regret — but for the moment his gaze remained fixed on the horizon, and gave nothing away. When a low sunbeam spilled out from behind a cloud he was dazzled by its reflections upon the water, and fleetingly he had a vision: the wall of some South London cul-de-sac, white and brilliant in the glare of the headlamps from Robert's car as he drove into it. He wondered if the faintest memory of their friendship might have passed through his mind: some thin reminiscent flicker . . .

'When was this?' Terry said at last.

'Eight years ago.'

'And had you known him long, by then?'

'No. We'd met for the first time, just a few months before.'

'That must have been extraordinary, though,' said Terry, trying — for his own benefit as much as Cleo's — to inject a cheerier note. 'To meet up with your twin — your other half, your counterpart — after so many years. You must have been, what, twenty-six, twenty-seven . . .?'

He tailed off as Lorna came hurrying out on to the terrace with a message for Dr Madison.

'We've got a rather strange girl in reception. I've tried talking to her but she says she needs to see you personally.'

'What does she want to see me about?'

'She wants to spend the night here. She says she's been talking in her sleep and she's worried about it.'

'Who's referred her?'

'I don't think anyone has. She lives locally and she's just turned up on spec.'

'Well, send her away. Nobody gets in here without a referral.'

'I told her that.' Lorna paused, then pointed out: 'We do have a bedroom free, though. Because of that cancellation.'

'Makes no difference,' said Dr Madison.

'Yes, but this girl . . .' Lorna persisted, uncertainly. 'She says that you met her recently and gave her your card and told her that she could come here.'

Cleo remembered, now, the young woman who had sat next to her on the beach, the day she returned from her holiday. In retrospect, giving her that card had been an embarrassing thing to do, and she had assumed that it was probably thrown away immediately. Even now, pleased as she was to hear of the woman's arrival, she was mildly shocked by her audacity in turning up unannounced.

Lorna said: 'She asked me to tell you her name, as well.'

'Her name?'

'Yes. She was most particular about that.'

Cleo frowned. 'Well, I can't imagine why. What is it, anyway?'

'Language is a traitor, a double agent who slips across borders without warning in the dead of night. It is a heavy snowfall in a foreign country, which hides the shapes and contours of reality beneath a cloak of nebulous whiteness. It is a crippled dog, never quite able to perform the tricks we ask of it. It is a ginger biscuit, dunked for too long in the tea of our expectations, crumbling and dissolving into nothingness. It is a lost continent.'

Russell Watts looked around at his audience impressively. He seemed to have won their attention. Dr Herriot and Professor Cole sat in armchairs on either side of his bed; Dr Dudden sat on the bed itself, as did Dr Myers, whose idea this informal seminar had been. 'It's absurd,' he had said over dinner, 'that we have five distinguished practitioners gathered together here, and all we're doing is playing games with jelly babies and pipe-cleaners.' He had suggested that they should round off the day by convening in somebody's room and having a group discussion on a serious work-related topic; at which point Russell Watts had intervened, inviting them all to his room and offering to read them a paper which he was intending to present at a conference of Lacanian analysts in Paris next week. It was entitled: *The Case of Sarah T.: or, an Eye for an 'I'.*

This invitation was accepted by the other four with varying degrees of alacrity, the least enthusiastic — by some margin — being Dr Herriot. There was a certain unwillingness, too, on the part of Professor Cole, who was once again not in the best of tempers. He had phoned his hospital just before dinner, only to be informed that the schizophrenic patient had not merely been discharged, but discharged that very evening; sent back to his council flat in Denmark Hill, where there was no one at all — to the best of the Professor's knowledge — who would be able to look after him. With this alarming development preying on his mind, he was not predisposed to listen with much sympathy to Russell Watts's paper. He had, in any case, spent his entire career working for distinguished London teaching hospitals, and was suspicious of this self-styled maverick, with his dubious professional status. These factors, combined with a pragmatic Englishman's thoroughgoing scepticism about Lacanian methodology, were enough to bring a battle-hungry glint to the Professor's eye.

'This is a story,' Russell Watts continued (reading from the screen of his laptop computer), 'about language and the games it plays with us; about how language colludes with the unconscious; about the unholy alliance between the signified order and the repressed contents of the neurotic mind.

'Sarah T. is a young woman who was sent to me for psychotherapy. Her GP was of the opinion that she was on the verge of a nervous breakdown. Her marriage was in crisis and she had recently been sacked from her job as a primary school teacher. She was not sleeping well, and this in turn was disturbing her husband's sleep and exacerbating the problems in their relationship. She suspected him of infidelity.

'At our first session she described to me the process by which she had lost her job. Exhausted from lack of night-time sleep, she had dozed off while teaching a lesson. When her headmaster arrived unexpectedly in the classroom a few minutes later, he found her sleeping soundly in front of an unruly class. This incident subsequently led to her dismissal. There had been other, similar ones, it transpired. There were two members of Sarah's class whom she had trusted, and who had been in the habit of waking her whenever she fell asleep in such circumstances. On this last occasion, however, they had decided to take advantage of her and to let her sleep on while the class enjoyed a period of unsupervised leisure. I asked her whether she had mentioned this to her headmaster and she said that she had not, because "I wanted to protect my pupils". I thought this a most remarkable turn of phrase, but naturally refrained from comment. As Lacan has so elegantly expressed it: "We must recognize, not that the analyst does not know anything, but that he is not the subject of his knowing. It is thus impossible for him to speak what he knows."

'At our second session, after a period of perhaps five or six minutes, Sarah fell into a profound sleep, which lasted for the remainder of the consultation. Even more interestingly, when she awoke she seemed to be under the fixed impression that we

had been engaged in animated dialogue for the last hour. Had
she dreamed this dialogue, I was forced to ask myself? It was
too early to reach a conclusion, but I decided to encourage her
in this fascinating delusion, by charging her my full fee for a
sixty-minute session.

'During the next few meetings our conversation ranged, in a
pleasingly haphazard way, over three central subjects: Sarah's
dreams, the continuing disintegration of her marriage, and her
sexual history.

'Sarah's dreams fell into two distinct types. Many of them involved no fantastic element at all, but were thoroughly rooted
in reality and mundane, often domestic detail. Mundane as
they were, however, these dreams could also be very vivid, and
she sometimes had difficulty distinguishing the events of her
dreams from the events of her real life. I asked her for an example, and she told me that once she had fallen asleep in the
course of proof-reading a magazine article, and dreamed that
she had "taken out" one of the footnotes, when in fact she had
not. She described to me the unfortunate consequences of this
dream, but they were of less interest, in my opinion, than her
choice of the ambiguous phrase "take out", which, as I'm sure
you are aware, can also refer to the act of escorting a prospec-
tive lover on a date — the prelude to sexual intercourse, in
many instances — or even to an act of assassination.

'On the other hand, Sarah also had more bizarre and imagi-
native dreams, bordering on nightmares: these frequently involved lizards, snakes, and in particular frogs.

' "Are you frightened of frogs?" I once asked her.

' "Perhaps I am," Sarah answered. "They repulse me, but I
also feel sorry for them."

' "Why such a complex reaction?" I asked.

' "Because of their eyes," she said. "I don't like the way their
eyes bulge out. It makes them look ugly and vulnerable."

'She then described to me a strange occurrence from her
student days. At an end-of-term party, one student had been

entertaining a group of his friends with an obscene joke about a frog that performed fellatio. He had described the frog, Sarah said, in striking physical detail. When he reached the "punchline" of the joke, Sarah had been joining in the laughter of the group, but had suddenly lost control of herself, and had collapsed into a sort of faint. Once again I refrained from commenting on this story, although the inference to be drawn from it was plain . . .'

'Of course: Sarah was narcoleptic,' said Professor Cole.

Russell Watts looked up in surprise. 'Pardon?'

'An obvious case of narcolepsy. She was exhibiting three of the classic symptoms.'

'I don't quite follow.'

'Excessive daytime sleepiness; vivid pre-sleep dreaming; cataplexy brought on by laughter. Three of the main symptoms of narcolepsy. Wouldn't everyone agree?'

He looked around for confirmation. Dr Myers nodded vigorously, and Dr Herriot said, 'Yes, absolutely.'

'And what about you, Dr Dudden? You're the sleep specialist, after all.'

Dr Dudden seemed to have something else on his mind at that moment. Most of the colour had drained from his face and he was taking small, nervous sips from a glass of water. Now, realizing that he was being directly addressed, he managed to murmur something along the lines of, 'Quite so — narcoleptic — no doubt about it'; after which, in an apparently casual tone of voice, he asked Russell Watts this question:

'Of course, purely as a matter of professional protocol, I'm assuming that you have changed all the names in this case?'

Russell Watts stared at him curiously and said, 'Actually, no. That isn't my practice. When you're working in a discipline which concerns itself so minutely with matters of linguistics and nomenclature, case studies can often become quite meaningless if the names are changed.'

'Do you make that clear to your patients?' asked Dr Myers.

'Of course.' He turned back to Professor Cole. 'On the subject of Sarah's narcolepsy, you may have a point, I suppose. That was something her GP should have spotted.'

'I'm amazed he didn't.'

'You realize that this was several years ago. There was far less awareness of the syndrome then.'

'But did it never occur to *you* at all?'

'It's not really that aspect of the case that interests me,' Russell Watts stammered, avoiding the Professor's eye and returning instead to his computer screen. 'This is actually a case . . . a story about . . . as I said before, a story about language, and . . . and discourse . . . As will become apparent if you just let me continue, without further interruptions.'

'By all means,' said Dr Myers. 'Do carry on. This is very intriguing.'

'Right.' He scrolled up and down the screen a few times, trying to find his place. 'Now where was I . . .'

'The inference was plain,' prompted Professor Cole, evenly.

'Yes, of course. All right, then — to resume:

'Sarah found it very hard to talk about the evening when this joke was told, and was evasive when I encouraged her to ask herself why. Eventually, however, certain interesting facts emerged. There had been two people present at the party, one of them a woman with whom she had recently enjoyed a sexual relationship, the other a man who, not content with being one of her closest friends, also fervently wanted to be her lover. This man's name was Robert, and he had disappeared somewhat mysteriously and abruptly from her life shortly after the evening in question.

'Now that I knew that Sarah had had sexual relations with both men and women, it was clear that we were making progress; and as she told me the details of her friendship with Robert, many things began to fall into place. She explained, for instance, that they had shared a communal bathroom as students, and once, not long after their first meeting, she had entered it to find not only that he was lying in the bath, but that he had a razor in his hand and the bath-water was full of blood.

'"What did you feel when you saw him like that?" I asked.

'"I was very disturbed."

'"Because you thought he was trying to kill himself?"

'"No," Sarah answered. "That's not what I thought."

'In fact — although she was never able to recognize this — it was clear to me that she suspected Robert of having guessed the secret of her sexuality, whereupon he was — or so she supposed — attempting to castrate himself in order to appeal to the homosexual aspect of her nature.

'At this stage in the analysis, Sarah's marriage came to a crisis. She had established beyond doubt that her husband Anthony was betraying her. What had particularly enraged her was the revelation that he had met this other woman, not through some chance, unplanned encounter, but by placing an advertisement in the "lonely hearts" column of the magazine *Private Eye* — a well-known method of arranging adulterous liaisons among the London middle classes. Sarah and her husband had quarrelled violently, and she had, in fact, assaulted him, following which he had packed his bags and left their marital home.

'"How exactly did you assault him?" I asked.

'"I kneed him in the balls," she said.

'I asked her to repeat this and she said once again, with great emphasis and satisfaction: "I kneed him in the balls."

'I suggest that you all remember these words and ponder them carefully, for they contain, in microcosm, the whole key to Sarah's neurosis.

'Meanwhile, further details of her friendship with Robert were being disclosed during every session. She talked repeatedly, for example, of an afternoon she had spent with him on a beach, in the company of a young girl who had been placed in their care for the day. On this occasion Robert, it seems, had constructed an elaborate sandcastle with the child's help, and she had started referring to him as "the Sandman" — an appellation which seemed to have lodged itself very firmly in Sarah's mind.

'It was this last detail which made me decide that it was time to confront Sarah with her obsession: an obsession which was now absolutely clear to me — as it will be to my distinguished audience — but of which she herself remained in complete ignorance. Sarah was, of course, obsessed with her eyes: obsessed with their vulnerability, fearful of their being harmed or violated. Was this not at the root of her fraught and ambivalent feelings towards frogs? Did it not explain her unusual choice of words when talking about her schoolchildren: "I wanted to protect my pupils"? Was this not the reason why she had felt so cruelly betrayed by her husband's means of committing adultery — the placing of an advertisement in a magazine called *Private Eye*? I put these questions to her, and asked her, as a matter of urgency, if she could recall any early traumatic experience which had involved her eyes, particularly in an erotic or sexual context. Under my careful probing, it was not long before the truth came out.

'During her time at university, Sarah told me, she had been deeply involved with a medical student called Gregory. He was her first . . . — I'm sorry, Dr Dudden, are you feeling all right?'

The others all turned to look at their colleague, who suddenly seemed to be choking on his glass of water. Dr Herriot patted him on the back, while Dr Myers took some tissue paper and tried to soak up some of the spilled liquid from the counterpane.

'Yes, yes, I'm fine,' he was saying, red-faced and gasping for breath. 'Just a little water went down the wrong way, that's all.'

'Shall I carry on?'

'Well, frankly,' said Dr Dudden, now regaining his power of speech, 'I'm beginning to find all this a little fanciful. Isn't it time we heard from someone whose methods are rather more rigorous, rather more, erm . . . scientific?'

'I've nearly finished. Just a few more pages to go.'

'I think we should hear it out to the end,' said Dr Herriot. 'I'm quite hooked, I must say.'

Professor Cole and Dr Myers agreed with her, and Russell Watts continued with his reading.

'He was her first serious boyfriend, and I asked her if the early stages of the relationship had been happy.

' "Yes," Sarah answered. "He took me out to dinner, and he took me to concerts. I used to enjoy being taken out by him." '

'There were, however, some aspects of Gregory's behaviour which began to alarm her. He liked to watch over her while she was sleeping, for instance, and was especially fascinated by the activity he claimed to be able to discern behind her eyelids during Rapid Eye Movement sleep. Sometimes she would awake suddenly to find him shining a light into her eyes, or even touching her eyelids and applying pressure to them. Her sleep patterns, never very regular at the best of times, became highly disturbed from this point onwards.

'It was to Gregory that Sarah had lost her virginity, and sex now began to play an increasingly important part in their relationship. He was, she told me, an energetic but also clumsy and unsatisfactory lover —'

This time a whole jet of water shot out of Dr Dudden's mouth and landed on Professor Cole's trousers. The Professor sprang to his feet with a cry of annoyance, and began wiping himself down with a pocket handkerchief.

'For God's sake, man, what on earth's the matter with you?' he shouted. 'Can't you just drink the stuff, like everybody else?'

Dr Dudden jumped to his assistance, and started using his own handkerchief to dab at the Professor's trousers. 'Look, I'm terribly sorry,' he said, his voice shaky with mortification. 'This is inexcusably careless of me. It's just that the — I don't know how much longer I can tolerate the . . . the rank *amateurism* of this man's approach . . .'

'Just hear him out, will you?' Professor Cole barked. 'That's what we're here for. There'll be plenty of time for argument when it's over. Now just sit down and give the man a fair hearing.'

Dr Dudden meekly resumed his position on the bed; and as soon as calm, of a sort, had been restored, Russell Watts read out the concluding part of his paper.

'He was, she told me, an energetic but also clumsy and unsatisfactory lover. Furthermore, he soon began to incorporate his fascination with Sarah's eyes into their performance of the sexual act itself. Central to their lovemaking was something they had come to refer to as "the game", in which he would touch both of her eyes with his outstretched fingers, applying more and more pressure as he approached his climax, this process being invariably accompanied by his ritual repetition of the phrase, "I spy with my little eye". (The word "spy", as I hardly need to point out to you at this stage, being almost synonymous with "private eye".)

'"Did he ever cause you physical pain?" I asked her.

'"No," Sarah answered, "he never really hurt me."

'"But you thought that he *might* hurt you?"

'"It could have been at the back of my mind."

'"And did he know that? Was that in fact the whole point of the game?"

'"Yes, I suppose it could have been."

'"For him? Or for both of you?"

'Sarah was unable — or unwilling — to answer my last question, but this was of little consequence, because I now had all the facts at my disposal, and was satisfied that the cause and extent of her problems were perfectly clear to me. And while it would have been highly irresponsible of me to share any of my insights with the patient herself, I shall conclude this paper with a sketch of the most salient points, for the benefit of my listeners.

'The "eye" is not only the instrument through which we view the world; it is also the "I", the innermost self, that stands at its centre. By eroticizing Sarah's eyes, by linking them inseparably in her psyche with the expectation of sexual pleasure, Gregory had given her an appetite for violation, for the penetration of her "I", the rape of her most intimate self, that neither he nor any other man or woman had ever been able to satisfy . . .'

'Oh, *please,*' said Dr Herriot.

'Let him finish,' said Dr Myers wearily. 'We might as well get to the bitter end.'

'Sarah did not know this, of course,' Russell Watts continued. 'And on one level, she was afraid of masculine desire; afraid, in fact, of the phallus itself and its awesome, delirious power. This is why she slept so badly at night, in bed with her husband: from the fear that, like Gregory, he would wait until she was powerless with sleep, and then seek to penetrate her "I". But was there not another level on which this was the very thing she most wanted? Why else would she regularly fall asleep during the daytime, in the company of strangers? For no other reason than to put herself at their mercy, to prostrate herself before them in the attitude of sleep; to invite them, man and woman alike, to play their own game of "I spy with my little eye".

'Yes, I am afraid there was something of the whore about Sarah.'

'I've had enough of this,' said Dr Herriot. 'I don't need to listen to any more of this rubbish.'

But Russell Watts was too caught up in his rhetoric to take heed of any more interruptions. He had not even noticed, for instance, that Dr Dudden was now sitting forward on the bed, his teeth clenched, his whitened knuckles clutching the water glass so tightly that it threatened to shatter at any moment.

'Clearly,' he continued, his voice rising in volume and the rhythm of his speech breaking into something like a crazed gallop, 'there had only ever been one man who, in her fantasies at least, might have satisfied her craving for violation: Robert —

the absent one, the missing, the mysterious Other who had so completely vanished from her life. No wonder she had been horrified, after surprising him in the bath that afternoon, to think that he had castrated himself, casting aside the phallus, his gender's magnificent, philoprogenitive signifier. For it was Robert she had really desired in all his thrilling, masculine glory: why else should she dignify him with the name of "Sandman" — that legendary figure whom children allow every night to *enter their eyes* and leave behind traces of his invading presence?

'And I could be certain of this for one very simple reason: because *Sarah had told me herself*. For remember — language is a cruel and faithless mistress; it is a sly cardsharp, who deals us a pack full of jokers; it is a distant flute on a misty night, teasing us with half-forgotten melodies; it is the light on the inside of the fridge, which never goes off when we are looking; it is a fork in the road; it is a knife in the water.

'What had Sarah said to me, after all, when I asked her exactly how she had assaulted her faithless husband? *"I kneed him in the balls,"* she had said. Was she really talking about her domestic argument at the time? Of course not: if so, she could just as easily have said, "I kicked him in the crotch." No, what she was doing, at that moment, was *articulating her desire for the phallus*. When she used the word "kneed", she did not mean "I attacked him with my knee", but "I *need*, I *crave*, I *desire*." And when she talked of "the balls", she did not mean the testicles, she was not referring to her husband's bruised and mangled organs of generation, she meant *the balls of her eyes*, her own eyeballs, those twin desiring globes which had become, in her strange, private, opto-erotic sexual universe, nothing less than two vaginas which some freak of nature had placed on either side of her nose.

'Yes, it was Sarah's misfortune — Sarah's tragedy, you might say — to have begun her sexual life under the perverse tutelage of a man who had not only made a fetish of her eyes, but had proved himself unable to satisfy the raging desires he had thereby aroused in her. Like all women, Sarah felt a longing for sexual pleasure which was also a longing for death: hence her fantasies of assassination, of things being "taken out". At the beginning of her relationship with Gregory, she used to enjoy being "taken out" by him; but as that relationship acquired a sexual dimension, it seems that he no longer "took her out", no longer assassinated her; his penis, apparently, was anything but lethal. And so the root of her problems lay in the unsatis-factory nature of that first sexual relationship — in Gregory's impotence, his phallic debility, the redundancy of his pistol, his failure to shoot anything but blanks, his crushing inability, in short, to bring her to orgasm or anywhere near it —'

Russell Watts broke off abruptly as Dr Dudden sprang to his feet with a final cry of contempt and made for the door. When he turned to address his four colleagues, they were shocked to see that his face was puce with rage, the veins on his neck and forehead standing out like knotted string.

'I know what this is about,' he said, pointing a quivering fin-ger at each of them in turn. 'I know what this is about, you bastards! You cooked this up together, you sad, pathetic, jeal-ous . . . mediocrities! And I know why, as well. Because you know what I'm trying to achieve. You know what I'm on the *brink* of achieving. And you think you can stop me, don't you? You think you can undermine me. Humiliate me. Well, you can't! No matter how hard you try. No matter how devious you are. Because I know one thing for a fact — a solid, incontro-vertible *fact*: that the name of Gregory Dudden will be remem-bered long after *your* names have been forgotten. Do you hear that? All of you? Completely —' (and here he opened the door) '— utterly —' (and now he stepped outside, gathering breath for the delivery of his last word) '— *FORGOTTEN!*'

After he had slammed the door behind him and stormed off down the corridor, the others sat for a few seconds in silent bafflement. Dr Herriot was the first to speak. Comprehension had begun to light up her face, bringing a slow smile in its wake.

'*Gregory* Dudden, did he say?' She turned to Professor Cole. 'Did he say his name was Gregory?'

But the other three had yet to catch up. Dr Myers merely shook his head sadly, and said: 'I think the sooner I start that investigation, the better.'

Darkness over Ashdown, where Ruby Sharp lies in Bedroom Three. Her head festooned with electrodes, she rolls and squirms in the bed, restless. Every so often a few words gurgle, brokenly, from her mouth. Above the bed a microphone is listening, and in the adjacent observation room, magnetic tape glides between two spools. Soon the words will swell into a quiet, uneven, murmurous stream. For a few minutes, Ruby will disclose her secrets to the microphone and the tape-recorder. In the morning Lorna will transcribe them, and Dr Madison will read them. But Ruby will have left the clinic by then, without explaining, without saying goodbye.

Darkness in Bedroom Nine, where Terry now lies, smiling a blissful smile. Behind his closed eyelids, his eyes are rolling busily: he is deep into Rapid Eye Movement sleep, and an exquisite dream is playing itself out in his brain. This dream is both sensuous and cerebral; it transports him glidingly, effortlessly to heights of physical pleasure and intellectual enlightenment such as he could never imagine in his waking life. Nothing that happens to him during the daylight hours will ever match the pleasure, the intensity, the joy of this dream. In the morning, he will have forgotten it almost entirely.

Darkness, too, in Day Room Nine — Terry's day room — where Cleo Madison sits at the desk, looking out over the water, as she has done every night for the last week, ever since the discovery of that curious, unexplained writing behind the wardrobe. She has been disturbed by her conversations with

Terry today. The lie she told about her brother Philip was foolish and trivial, a botched improvisation, born of confusion and
haste. The lies she told about Robert, though, were far more
considered; and yet she already regrets these, just as deeply. In
short, she cannot decide what to do about Terry. She cannot decide whether to tell him the truth.

   She has not yet noticed the photograph Terry has placed on
the bookshelf behind her; the photograph for which he scoured
an Italian film archive; the photograph he travelled all the way
to London to retrieve; the only surviving fragment of Salvatore
Ortese's lost film, which was once his great obsession. A single
black and white photograph, showing a road, a dusty, arid
landscape, and a woman, a woman in nurse's uniform, pointing off into the distance as she stands in front of a sign which
consists of one word, written in a foreign language. Perhaps
when Cleo does notice it, it will help her to make up her mind.

Late autumn, 1984

Everything about this city was different. That had been the idea, of course, but it was also what he found so disheartening, so hard to fight against. The people were different; the jokes, the humour, the accents; the buses were a different colour; the beer tasted different; the skies were different — bigger and greyer, somehow; the houses were packed together more tightly than he would ever have thought possible; the days seemed to be shorter here, and the nights longer; the names of some of the biggest shops were new and strange to him; the cinemas showed unfamiliar local advertisements and the evening newspaper seemed to be written in some inscrutable code; even the tea was different, and the cakes they served with it in the market café.

He was trying to get used to this café, though. He was trying to get used to its formica tables and plastic bottles encrusted with ketchup and HP sauce. He was trying to forgive it for the fact that it was not the Café Valladon.

The market always seemed to be busy on Wednesday afternoons. Robert sat at a window table and watched the crowds passing by, their patient, wind-chapped faces and ruddy hands. He wanted to take comfort from all this bustling humanity but instead it swamped him, making him feel smaller, even less noticeable, even more lost.

As he looked through the café window, he thought about what the psychiatrist had said to him.

Robert had been referred for psychiatric treatment more than seven years before Sarah would begin her own course of analysis with Russell Watts, and had been lucky enough to find a more helpful practitioner. Dr Fowler was approachable and sympathetic, a good listener but also generous with his advice and encouragement. They had met in his consultation room each Wednesday for the last month, ever since Robert was sent there as a matter of urgency following his third and most desperate call to the Samaritans. And now, while he was not exactly making a recovery, at least the feelings of hopelessness and self-hatred were beginning to come into focus: he was starting to understand them, and could almost bring himself to imagine, at the end of this particular tunnel, the glimmering possibility that they might prove containable.

Dr Fowler knew that Robert had been rejected by a woman, and he now wanted to examine why she had made him think of himself this way: why he had started to regard himself as fundamentally impossible to love. He wanted Robert to try to isolate this one specific aspect of himself: What was it about him that she had never loved — and which he, as a consequence, had started to hate?

This afternoon, the answer had become clear. He hated his gender: his body.

That was the only thing that Sarah had never loved about him.

'You hate yourself for being a man?' said Dr Fowler.

'Yes. I think I always have, in fact. All my life.'

'Have you ever had fantasies of being a woman? Of living as a woman?'

'No, I haven't. At last — not until now.'

That evening, it suddenly seemed the obvious solution. A breathtakingly easy solution. Drunk with excitement (and drunk on the two bottles of dry white wine that had recently become his nightly tipple) he wrote to Sarah for the first time. He wrote to her about his childhood dream, and how he had finally come to understand what it was telling him. He told her that he was certain they would meet again. He told her that he loved her more than ever.

At their next meeting, however, Dr Fowler explained that Robert's solution wasn't quite as easy as he appeared to imagine. It wasn't possible just to go off and have surgery at the drop of a hat, he pointed out. For one thing, unless he had the funds to do it privately, there was a waiting list of at least two years. And for another, he would have to prove — to Dr Fowler's complete satisfaction — that it was what he really wanted.

Robert now began to apply himself to this task with some energy.

The clothes he began to wear were androgynous, rather than specifically female.

He wore a modest amount of makeup, and kept his hair short, but had it permed and highlighted. People began to tell him that he looked like Annie Lennox.

The hormones he was prescribed were supposed to boost his hips and his bust, but mainly he just seemed to put on weight. Whenever he went out, he wore a padded bra.

Regular electrolysis helped to keep facial hair at bay.

He began to pick up technical translation work for local companies, anxious to meet the new challenges posed by the European Community. Later, feeling more confident in his female guise, he started to give private lessons in French and German. He lived carefully, and supported himself.

Judi was his first great success. As soon as he decided to start living as a woman, he moved to another part of town, where it transpired that Judi — a dental hygienist — was his new neighbour across the landing. She never once guessed that he was a man. They became close friends, and although he rarely invited her into his flat, they would often go out together, drinking or clubbing. Judi described these occasions as her 'girls' night out', and when she got herself a boyfriend and started seeing much less of Robert, he found that he missed her company very badly.

To Judi, to his landlord, and to his students, Robert was now known as Cleo Madison. 'Madison' was an easy choice, for it had been his mother's maiden name; and as for 'Cleo', how could he have used anything else? This, after all, was the name that Sarah had dreamed for him.

He never knew where it had come from; from what period in her early life or what little-visited corner of her unconscious she had retrieved it, so that it might play a new and transfiguring role in her dreams. Nor did he know exactly what he had said to her, more than a year ago, during that long, rapt, confessional encounter on the terrace at Ashdown, that had inspired Sarah to dream anything so unaccountable as the existence of a twin sister who had been separated from him shortly after birth. He had talked about the feeling — yes, he could remember this, at least — that he had a female *counterpart*, that the world contained some feminine soulmate with whom he longed to be united. He had actually been talking about potential girlfriends, potential life-partners (and thinking secretly about Sarah, even then), but might this have been the remark that prompted her fatal dream? He would probably never know. All he knew was that he had taken an irreversible step, a life-transforming step, when Terry and Lynne had told him about this dream, and instead of denying it, instead of joining them in their easy mockery of Sarah and her comical fantasies, he had come to her defence. He had invented Cleo, in order to protect Sarah from their laughter. But then, Sarah had invented her too. The fiction had been conceived by them both, it was their child, and all year they had raised it and nurtured it together, feeding it with anecdotes, watching it grow strong and healthy on the diet of their conversations. And now, Robert was ready to go one step further.

He would become Cleo. He would become Sarah's hallucination. He would, in the purest possible sense, make her dreams come true. Wasn't that the most that any lover could offer?

Summer, 1986

Dr Fowler said: 'Let me repeat that if you do this, you do it by your own decision, at your own risk, and on your own responsibility in relation to the civil authority — by which I mean the police. Do you understand?'

'Yes, I understand.'

'All right. Now I want you to listen carefully, because what I will say now has medical and legal significance. Two further things. Whatever is done to you, you won't be a woman legally. You can't change your birth certificate, because that is a definition of sex attributed at birth, however much it may contradict what you think of yourself now. Secondly, it is a criminal offence for you to attempt to marry another biological male.'

'Yes, I know that.'

'Good. Well, in that case — and if you're quite happy in your mind about this, if you're quite decided — I'll now refer you to my surgeon.'

Robert smiled: a huge, relieved smile. He couldn't help himself.

'You don't have the resources to pay for this privately, do you?'

'No, I don't.'

'Then I'm afraid you're going to have to wait for a little while.'

'That's all right,' said Robert, his blood pounding as he fingered the ladder in his tights. 'That doesn't matter at all.'

Autumn, 1988

It wasn't long before he was on friendly terms with the nurses: since choosing to become female, he found that his social skills had improved considerably. There was one that he liked in particular, called Rachel. She was the one who came to say goodbye to him on the night before his surgery.

'Big day tomorrow, then,' she chirped, sitting at the foot of his bed. It was the end of her shift, and she was wearing a raincoat over her uniform. Outside it was teeming down. 'How are you feeling?'

Without answering, Robert reached across to his bedside table for a book. As it happened, he was feeling terrified.

'Have you ever read this?' he asked.

Rachel looked at the title: it was *Gravity and Grace*, by Simone Weil. She shook her head.

'It's one of those books,' said Robert, 'where, no matter what situation you're in, you just have to open it at random and read a page or two, and you find . . . well, listen to this: this is the bit I read this morning.

' "To accept a void in ourselves is supernatural. Where is the energy to be found for an act which has nothing to counterbalance it? The energy has to come from elsewhere. Yet first there must be —" ' he looked up at Rachel ' "— a tearing out, something desperate has to take place, the void must be created." ' Robert closed the book. 'What do you think of that?'

She was struggling. 'I don't know. I don't know what it means.'

'Sometimes,' he said, 'I didn't think I'd be able to make it through the last few years. But there's something else I read in here this morning: "A time has to be gone through, without any reward, natural or supernatural." '

Rachel thought it best to move on to safer territory. 'They told me you had some visitors in earlier.'

'One visitor,' said Robert, replacing the book on the table. 'Just my mother.'

'Oh.'

'She's come to stay: you know, just while I'm in here. Booked herself a hotel in town.'

'That's nice. That's very nice. You don't see a lot of parents in here, for this kind of operation. They're not very supportive, usually.'

'She's been great.'

'What about your father. Is he not . . .?'

'He died last year.'

'Oh. I'm sorry.'

'I hadn't seen him for ages. There was no love lost. He didn't know anything about . . . this.' Robert lay still for a while, listening to the rain. 'It's odd: I always thought he hated me, in a way, but he left me quite a lot of money. Seems he'd been setting some stuff aside.'

'You could do with that, I expect,' said Rachel. 'What are you going to spend it on?'

'With any luck, I'm going back to university. I want to study psychology.'

'Sounds just up your street. Then you'll be able to help people . . . people like yourself. You can counsel them.'

'Maybe. That's not really the field I want to go into, though. I'm more interested in sleep.'

'Sleep?'

'Sleep disorders. Narcolepsy, mainly. I had a friend who was narcoleptic, once. At least — I wasn't sure, at the time, but I've been reading some books since then, and it's pretty obvious that that was her problem. It's one of the things I'm going to talk to her about, when I next see her.'

'Oh yes? And when will that be?'

'Soon,' said Robert, managing a smile now. 'Very soon.'

The strip lighting, passing overhead in blinding flashes as he is wheeled towards the operating theatre.

The confusion of doctors and nurses. The glint of electric light on the surgical instruments.

The eyes of the anaesthetist, neutral and inexpressive as he prepares to insert the needle into Robert's wrist.

A sightlessness . . . or something worse

The sweet vision of darkness, the loss of control, as he breathes deeply, and closes his eyes, and starts to

. . . pray for an oblivion so deep

It ends in . . .

. . . transformation.

When Cleo awoke, she felt a pain in her throat, in her breasts, in her abdomen and between her legs such as she never could have imagined, or believed endurable.

She was unable to walk for more than a week. The pain and nausea, the bleeding and the discharges would continue for several months.

This was the worst time. She had to call upon all her reserves of patience. But she had waited for so long, there was no point in hurrying, now. She wanted to be absolutely well when she saw Sarah again. She wanted to be ready for her.

Spring, 1989

Thin, ineffectual rain spattered the windscreen as Cleo drove her hired car along the once-familiar coast road. She had left the town behind and was beginning to climb towards the headland. Passing the row of cottages where Ruby Sharp used to live with her parents (and perhaps still did), she braced herself for the waves of feeling which the sight of Ashdown was bound to stir. Any second now she would be round the corner, and it would loom into view.

And there it was: huge, grey and imposing, a solid, weather-beaten gesture of defiance directed at the ocean and whatever rigours and inclemencies it threatened to sweep inland. Seeing that distinctive stonework again, those characteristic angles, contours, curves and lineaments, Cleo braked to a sudden halt and found herself blinking back tears. Who would have thought that mere form, mere architecture, could hold such sway over her emotions? She sat for a while irresolute, her car stopped dead in the middle of the deserted road, listening to the plaintive cry of the gulls and struggling to resist the tide of nostalgia and regret that pressed itself upon her.

She drove up to the house and parked outside the front door.

She had chosen to come here on Good Friday, knowing that the house would be empty over the Easter weekend. The door was locked, of course, but this presented no problem, for she still had a set of keys: she had never returned them to the university authorities, and the locks, she discovered, had not been changed in the intervening five years.

Cleo wandered through those glacial rooms and mazy, echoing corridors for only a few minutes. She did not attempt to gain entry to any of the bedrooms, for it was really the L-shaped kitchen she had wanted to see again. She put the kettle on and made herself a cup of instant coffee, then stood by the table and looked around her, thinking: Yes, this is the place. This is where it must happen.

Returning to her hotel room in town, she sat on the bed beside the telephone and opened her address book. The plan could still go wrong, she realized. If Sarah's parents no longer lived at this address, she would have to begin searching for her. That might take weeks, or even months. But somehow, she didn't think they would have moved. Luck, she believed, was finally on her side.

Her call was picked up by an answering-machine, which invited people to leave messages for Michael and Jill Tudor. Cleo replaced the receiver without speaking, and thought carefully about what she was going to say. Then she redialled the number. She said that she was trying to get in touch with their daughter, Sarah. She was calling with news of Robert, an old friend of Sarah's from her student days. There was going to be

a small reunion this weekend. She apologized for the short notice, but would Sarah be able to come to Ashdown, this Sunday,
at about seven in the evening?

   She was sure that the message would be passed on. She was
sure that Sarah would come.

The next morning, Cleo walked down to the supermarket to
choose the food that she would cook for Sarah; and on her
way, she visited the Café Valladon. It appeared to be under new
management — at any rate, Slattery's place behind the counter
had been taken by a helpful and talkative young woman — but
otherwise little had changed. The interior was still gloomy, the
coffee was still strong, and the walls were still covered with
second-hand books. She searched in vain for a copy of *The
House of Sleep*, however: perhaps Sarah had taken it after
all. She would find that out tomorrow. In the meantime, she
fetched down Terry's copy of *Great Expectations*, and was
pleased to see that there was a ten-pound note safely hidden
away at page 220. She left the money where it was, and read
the last few pages of the novel while finishing off her slice of
fruit cake. Then she replaced the book on the shelf, and took
her leave of the Café for the last time.

*A cold silvery mist had veiled the afternoon, and the moon was
not yet up to scatter it. But the stars were shining beyond the mist,
and the moon was coming, and the evening was not dark.*

   From her window on the first-floor landing, Cleo could see
the sweep of the approaching headlights even when the car
was more than a mile in the distance. She heard the crunch of
its tyres against the gravel drive, and watched it draw to a halt
beside her own car on the forecourt. Then a solitary figure
stepped out. It was her: it was Sarah. Her hair was turning
grey — she could make that much out, even in the gathering
dusk — but there was little else that Cleo could notice about

her in the short time it took Sarah to lock her car and walk up the steps to the open front door.

Cleo turned, hurried along the corridor and ran down the narrow, little-used staircase that led to the kitchen's back entrance. When she got there, Sarah was already in the hallway, calling:

'Hello? Is there anybody here?'

'Hello!' Cleo called back.

Sarah stepped into the kitchen doorway. 'Robert? Is it really you? Are you there?'

The kitchen seemed to be empty. The only light came from three candles, flickering warmly on the table, and a cleaner, ghostlier sheen issuing from around the corner: this was from the lamp over the oven, presumably. Lovely, aromatic cooking smells filled the room.

'Robert?' Sarah said, advancing a little further. 'What's going on? Where is everybody?'

'Come on in,' said Cleo. 'There's a drink for you on the table.'

'Yes, but where are you?'

'I'm round the corner here.' She could hear Sarah's footsteps approaching. 'Don't come round, please. Not for a minute.'

The footsteps halted. 'Don't come round? What are you talking about?'

'Please, Sarah. Please stay where you are.'

'But I want to *see* you, for goodness' sake. I haven't seen you for five years.'

'I'll be out in just a second,' said Cleo. 'I've reached a slightly delicate stage here. We're having okra dal with cardamom and coriander rice.'

'Well . . . that sounds wonderful,' said Sarah, with a touch of impatience. 'But food is hardly the first thing on my mind at the moment. I didn't come all this way for a meal.' There was no response from around the corner. 'I mean, could you not have left a slightly less cryptic message? Why all this drama?'

'Five years is a long time,' said Cleo. 'I felt that something special was called for.'

Sarah sighed crossly, then picked up one of the glasses of red wine from the table, and drank a little.

'Robert, this is so silly,' she said, coming even closer to the cooking area. 'I've just driven all the way here from London, and I'm tired out. I don't want to be messed around any more. I know it's ages since we were last together, and we've got . . . a lot of ground to cover, but let's at least *look* at each other.'

'No!' Cleo shouted, and such was the urgency in her voice that Sarah took several steps back. In more controlled tones, but no less earnestly, Cleo added: 'The thing is, Sarah, that I've changed a lot in the last few years. You're going to get a shock when you see me, and I want you to be ready for it. Just sit down for a minute, and then I'll come and talk to you.'

'All right,' said Sarah, and she sat down at the table, her thoughts racing with various possible interpretations of these ominous words. 'You . . . you haven't been ill, have you, Robert? I mean — you are all right? That's not why you suddenly wanted to see me?'

'I'm fine,' Cleo answered. 'In fact, I've never been finer.' She could not concentrate on her cooking any more, and leaned with her back to the oven, breathing deeply. 'There's so much I've got to tell you. So many things.'

'Me too,' said Sarah.

'We've got all evening, haven't we? You don't have to drive back to London tonight?'

'I'm not sure what I'm doing. Is there anyone else coming to this . . . reunion?'

'No. No, it's just you and me. I hope that's all right.'

'Yes, of course it is. You're the one I wanted to see.' Sarah drank more wine, and looked around her. The situation was so bizarre, she felt so tense and uneasy, that she began talking again simply in order to calm herself. 'It feels very weird being back here, I must say. Back in this house. In this kitchen.'

' "After so many years," ' Cleo quoted, ' "it is strange that we should thus meet again, here where our first meeting was." ' She picked up the kitchen knife, and began chopping some parsley. 'Do you remember that night, Sarah? When you were drinking soup — in your dressing-gown?'

'Yes, I remember,' she said. 'Of course I remember. There's barely a day gone by, in the last five years, when I haven't thought about it.'

'Really? You haven't forgotten me, then?'

'Oh, Robert, *why* didn't you keep in touch?' Her voice rose and pulsed, suddenly, with a multitude of resentments. 'It was horrible, saying goodbye to you on the cliff like that. And then the way you just disappeared, never answering my letters or anything . . .'

'I did write to you, once.'

'Yes, but that didn't *tell* me anything. It didn't say where you were, or what you'd been doing. And even *now*, you know, I get this peculiar message from my parents, and I drive all the way down here, and you won't even let me see you, you behave so . . . *strangely* . . .'

'In a minute,' said Cleo, 'you'll understand everything.'

'I hope so.'

'You're being very patient, Sarah. I do appreciate that.'

Sarah sipped her wine, almost but not entirely mollified. 'I had to cancel a dinner party to come here tonight, you know.'

'Really? That was good of you.'

'With my future in-laws, I might add.'

The sound of Cleo's chopping ceased abruptly.

'Pardon?'

'My fiancé's parents.'

'Your . . .? You mean you're getting married?'

'That's right. In three months' time.'

'To a man?'

'Of course to a man.'

'But . . .'

'But what?' said Sarah, when the silence began to seem interminable.

'But I thought you were gay.'

'Gay? What gave you that idea?'

'Well — you know, all that business with Veronica.'

'Well yes, but there was Gregory before that, and now . . . now there's Anthony. He's very sweet, actually. I'm sure you'd like him. Veronica was — well, not a *phase*, exactly, because that doesn't make it sound very important, and she *was* important, but . . . oh, I don't know. It's so hard —'

'But you *said*, Sarah, I remember you saying, that Veronica had changed everything for you. She introduced you to your nature: those were your exact words.'

'Well, obviously I didn't know myself very well when I said that. I mean, I was only young, Robert. We were both only young.'

'But what about — what about when you told me who your ideal partner would be? Do you remember that?'

'Vaguely . . .'

'You said it would be a female me. My twin sister. That's what you said.'

'I meant to ask you about that,' said Sarah. Cleo could hear her scraping the chair back and getting up. 'Did you ever go looking for her? Did you ever find her?'

'Hold on a minute,' said Cleo. 'I've just got to . . . I'm just going to take some rubbish out.'

She slipped out through the kitchen's back door, groped her way along an unlit passageway and eventually came upon another door, this one locked and bolted. It seemed to take forever to locate the key (it was in the keyhole) and to pull back the stiffly yielding bolts, after which Cleo found herself stepping out into the ragged kitchen garden, beneath a star-filled sky. She slammed the door behind her, doubled up almost immediately and vomited over the flagstones. She crouched on all-fours and continued to heave and retch until the convulsions were indistinguishable from sobs.

Scrambling to her feet, she felt in the pocket of her jeans. Thank God: the car keys were there.

She ran around to the front of the house. She could see Sarah's face in the kitchen window, lit from behind by the golden candlelight. Would Sarah be able to see her? Would she have spotted this absurd woman, out of breath, delirious with shock, her makeup smudged with tears, as she lunged towards the car and grappled with its door?

Cleo revved up the engine, reversed the car screechingly and sped off down the drive, just as Sarah realized what was happening and came running down the front steps.

She drove for many miles, with no awareness of the direction she was taking. She badly wanted to clean herself down, to wipe her eyes and face, but didn't dare to stop until she could be certain that she was not being followed.

At last she could wait no longer, and pulled the car over into a parking bay.

The ocean lay blue and somnolent beneath her, and there was no one else on the road; no sign of Sarah. The evening mists were rising now, and in all the broad expanse of tranquil light they showed, Cleo saw no shadow of another meeting with her.

Dr Dudden did not attend the second day of the conference. It had seemed so important, just twenty-four hours ago, but he could see now that the whole exercise was fundamentally pointless and trivial. There were far more urgent matters to consider. His career, his work, his reputation, the very continuation of his researches at the Dudden Clinic were all under threat. The forces massed against him — forces of ignorance, of jealousy, of reaction — were starting to mobilize. The conspiracy was gathering pace.

All this had become clear to Dr Dudden during the night, which he had spent energetically pacing the London streets. He had not slept a wink, and he felt better for it; in fact he was quite sure, this morning, that he would never want to sleep again. His lips curled in an involuntary sneer as he looked around the train carriage and saw how many of the passengers were already — so early in the day! — either dozing, or napping, or nodding off, or snoozing, or snatching forty winks, their mouths hanging stupidly open, their heads lolling, their eyelids drooping heavily. Did these people have no sense of dignity, no self-respect? Did they hate life so much that they had to shut themselves off from it at every opportunity? He sometimes wondered if such creatures were actually worth saving: but that wasn't the point any more. The idea that he was on some sort of mission to help mankind had been foolish, he realized. It was one of the delusions that had been holding him back, when the real issue — so plain, so suddenly obvious — could be summarized in a few words. Yes, the real issue was this: that Dr Dudden was right, and everybody else was wrong. *He* could see it, and they couldn't. It was down to a simple tussle, then, between good and evil. It was Dudden *versus* the rest of the world.

Now that he saw it in these terms, a hideous dissatisfaction with all his earlier mistakes, compromises and procrastinations began to overtake him. He had spent far too much time on futile interviews with half-witted patients; far too much time offering palliative treatment to malingerers, neurotics, hypochondriacs and weaklings. The first thing he would do when he arrived back at the clinic would be to discharge the patients. All of them. Phone for a fleet of taxis and clear them out: a clean, comprehensive purge. They were no more than a distraction, a grotesque obstacle to the business in hand. Everything that was important in that building took place below stairs, down in the basement: and even there, he had wasted too many of his energies. Those animal experiments should have been abandoned months ago: he had long since learned all that he would ever learn from the behaviour of rats, dogs and rabbits. From now on, he would work with human subjects. That was the only way forward. He should never have let that stupid accident deter him. It was shameful that he should have allowed himself to be frightened off by whispers, by malicious rumour, by ignorant gossip. That equipment, he knew, was perfectly safe, and he would prove it. He would prove it at once; openly, irrefutably, and by the only means possible. By using it himself.

As the pace of Dr Dudden's thoughts quickened, so the train taking him back towards Ashdown began to slow down, bringing him out in a sweat of frustration and impatience. Long, inexplicable stops were being made between stations. During the third or fourth of these, he stood up, tore off the headphones on which he had been listening to a favourite recording of the *Goldberg Variations*, and hurled his CD Walkman contemptuously out of the nearest window. Even his former tastes in music now revolted him. 'Pap!' he shouted, as he stormed back to his seat. 'Passionless pap! Soporific shite!' He ignored the anxious, sidelong glances of the other passengers. He cared nothing for the opinion of these drowsy fools. It no longer mattered what the world thought of him: they were all in league, anyway. All of them. Myers and Cole had hatched some sort of plot against him — he was certain of that — with Russell Watts as their willing stooge; and there was probably some spy, some mole at the clinic who was helping them out, gathering information on him, scheming away behind his back. Dr Madison, in all probability: that hateful old sow had always had it in for him. And what about Worth, the journalist? He wasn't to be trusted, either. It would be no surprise to learn that the two of them were in cahoots. He remembered, now, that on the very first night of his visit, Terry and Dr Madison had arranged a clandestine meeting out on the terrace; and the next morning Terry had taunted him with the information that they had become 'superficially' acquainted, and even had the nerve — yes, it was all coming back now, it was all making sense — the bastard even had the bare-faced *gall* to mention Sarah's name. So, they were in it together, without a doubt. Of course, since then (to the best of his knowledge) Terry and Dr Madison had barely seen or spoken to one another: but what was that if not a transparent ploy, providing further evidence — if any more were needed — of some sly, wordless understanding, some sinister alliance . . .?

And just at that precise moment, Dr Dudden's suspicions were confirmed in the most astonishing way. As his train sat marooned, stranded between stations, another, London-bound train crawled by in the other direction. He looked across and for a few seconds had an uninterrupted view of the passing vehicle and its occupants. And there they were: sitting together in a half-empty carriage, laughing, gesturing, and giving every appearance of enjoying a lively conversation. The two people at the very centre of his thoughts.

Terry Worth and Cleo Madison.

'Did you see that?' asked Cleo, craning back to look at the motionless train.

'See what?' said Terry.

'That was Dr Dudden. I'm sure of it. Sitting in that train.'

'I thought he was meant to be at a conference.'

'So did I.'

'Did he see us, do you think?'

Cleo shrugged. 'I'm not sure. What if he did?'

'Well, he mightn't be too happy,' said Terry, 'to know that his assistant has run off to London, and his favourite patient has discharged himself.'

Cleo watched the other train recede into the distance, then settled back in her seat. 'To be honest, I'm no longer very interested in what makes Dr Dudden happy, and what doesn't. I'm much more interested in *this*.' She picked up Terry's photograph from the table between them, staring at it in wonder. 'Are you seriously telling me it comes from a film that nobody — that *nobody* has ever seen?'

'Maybe two or three people. At the most,' said Terry. 'And even then, nothing's been documented.'

'Do you think anybody else has a copy of this picture?'

'I doubt it. I've certainly never seen it published anywhere.'

Cleo passed it back to him, her hands trembling. Even after more than twelve hours (during which time she had been far too excited to sleep), she was still trying to accustom herself to this new and incredible notion: to the possibility that this image, which had first visited her as a child and had haunted her ever since, might not have been the invention of her dreaming mind at all; that it might have another, independent existence. And to think that it should resurface now — just as Ruby Sharp had appeared at the clinic, only to vanish again, leaving behind her nothing but an extraordinary torrent of words in which the past and future secrets of Cleo's own life seemed to be magically inscribed. She was too confused and too agitated to know exactly what these events might signify, but had come to a rapid, strong decision all the same: she would have to abandon her work at the clinic that morning, with a hasty note to Lorna and a promise that she would return as soon as —

— as soon as what, though?

Terry continued to talk about the film as their train gathered speed and swept through the faceless countryside.

'I've got this theory,' he was saying, 'that I may have been looking in the wrong place. If a print exists anywhere, then perhaps it's not in Italy at all: perhaps it's in France.'

'Why France?'

'Because of this word.' He held up the photograph: behind the figure of the middle-aged woman in the nurse's uniform, pointing into the distance, there was a notice, partially hidden by her body. It seemed to consist of one word: *fermer*. 'That's French, isn't it? It means "close". So maybe the film was shot in a French version as well, and that's the one that's survived.'

Cleo examined the picture more closely. 'I don't think so,' she said. 'That wouldn't make any sense, because *fermer*'s an infinitive. Anyway, the image has been cropped, so you can't quite see the beginning of the word: and there might be more letters afterwards, where the woman's standing. So my suggestion would be —' she gave it one more look '— that it says *infermeria*.'

'*Infermeria?* What does that mean?'

'It's Italian: it means "infirmary", of course. That's what she's pointing towards — a hospital.'

A slow smile of recognition crossed Terry's face. 'Why didn't I think of that?'

'I'm not saying it's the *only* meaning,' Cleo added; but before Terry could take her up on this mysterious remark, she asked him: 'So, you're going to start looking for this film again, are you? That's going to be your life's work?'

'Actually, no.' Terry slid the photograph into a manila envelope and laid it on the table. 'I don't think that's the point any more. I'd rather just know that it's out there, somewhere . . .

maybe waiting for me — I don't know . . . In the meantime, anyway, I've got to think of something to do with myself: something worthwhile.'

'Journalism's worthwhile, isn't it? If you take it seriously enough.'

Terry shook his head. 'There've been times, recently — just in the last two weeks, I suppose — when I've thought about what I do, and it makes me . . . cringe, almost: really hate myself for it. Do you ever get that feeling? I don't suppose you do: not in a job like yours.'

'Oh, I know what you mean,' said Cleo. 'Working for Gregory Dudden — it doesn't guarantee that you feel good about yourself, I can assure you.'

'No, I suppose not. So why did you go there in the first place?'

'Well, it's unique, the Dudden Clinic. It's almost the only place which offers work to someone in my field.' She thought back to the day, more than two years ago, when Dr Dudden's advertisement had first appeared in the *British Journal of Clinical Psychology*: the rush of excitement when she had realized how perfectly the job suited her own skills, and then the disbelief, the trepidation when she found out where the clinic was located — the one place in the world she had resolved never to visit again.

'Working at Ashdown,' said Terry, 'that must feel very odd for you. All those memories . . .'

'Memories?' She was on her guard at once.

'Of Robert. Not that you knew him in those days, of course, but it must . . . bring him back to you.'

'Oh,' said Cleo. 'Yes. Yes, it does, sometimes.'

This was absurd, she told herself. Sooner or later she was going to have to tell Terry the truth: in fact she was astonished that it hadn't dawned on him already. Should she tell him on this train journey, perhaps? Or leave it until they had reached London, and take him for a drink at the station café? Or should she just get his address and phone number, and wait for a few days, wait until it was over, wait until she had followed Ruby's instructions and found her again . . . That was if she could ever summon up the courage . . .

'In any case,' she said, suppressing these thoughts hastily, 'your career and the future of the Dudden Clinic might not be entirely unconnected.'

'In what way?'

'Well, *did* you ever ask him?'

Terry frowned. 'Ask who, about what?'

'Dr Dudden, of course: about Stephen Webb.'

'Not in so many words, no: but I did . . .' He broke off, as the implication of her question became clear. 'So it was *you*, was it, who sent me that note, out on the terrace?'

'I thought a little hint might get you moving in the right direction, that's all.'

'Well, I suppose it did.' Terry shuddered, mentally revisiting a scene which for the last two days he had been doing his best to forget. 'One night — a couple of nights ago — he took me down to the basement, you see.'

'Where he experiments on the rats?'

He nodded. 'Have you been down there yourself?'

'Once or twice.'

'And did you ever see . . . the other equipment he uses?'

'What other equipment?'

Terry rubbed his eyes, trying to banish the thought of those whitewashed walls, the huge perspex cage . . . 'It's too big a story for me,' he said. 'I'm going to go into the office on Monday and tell the news desk about it. They'll be able to handle it properly.'

'But it's *your* story, Terry. You got there first.'

'I'm just . . . not that kind of journalist. That's all there is to it.'

'Yes, but you hate the kind of journalist you are. This is your opportunity to change.' She could sense that Terry wanted to hear this. He was on the point of believing her. 'I mean, you could make a real name for yourself with this story. Do you have any idea what happened down there — any idea what you might be dealing with?'

'All I know,' said Terry, 'is that Stephen Webb was a student at the university, and that he took part in a sleep deprivation experiment for Dr Dudden. I *presume* that as a consequence of this experiment, he was involved in — an accident of some kind? A fatal accident? — but nobody has yet made a direct link between his death and his time at the clinic.'

'It was a car crash,' said Cleo. 'The morning he finished the experiment Gregory had no beds available, nowhere for him to recover, so he was sent straight home. On his way back to the campus he walked out into the middle of the road and was knocked over. He died on the spot.' She reached into the overnight bag on the seat beside her, and pulled out two files. 'But as it happens, somebody *has* already made a direct link. There was another student taking part in that experiment — someone who survived it, and my guess is that Gregory paid her off, because she left the university and nobody's heard from her since. Except that *somebody* must have tipped off the Royal College of Psychiatrists, because a letter arrived from them this morning. Apparently they want to set up an enquiry.'

'What was this other student's name?'

'Bellamy. Karen Bellamy.' She handed Terry the two files. 'I found these in Gregory's office and made copies of them. Take them. They're yours. Do what you can with them.'

For the rest of the journey, Terry sat reading through the documents relating to these two unfortunate students. From Stephen Webb's file he was able to build up a fairly complete portrait of a popular, bright, academically gifted young man who was also a fiercely ambitious and talented actor. His involvement in Dr Dudden's experiment might have stemmed from financial need, intellectual curiosity, or a combination of both. The information on Karen Bellamy was sketchier, and she remained a more shadowy, altogether more problematic figure.

In her case, there did seem to be an obvious background of financial hardship. She had come from a poor area of London: her parents had lived in Denmark Hill, and it appeared that this was the last place anyone had seen her, more than six months ago. Terry made a mental note of this but found that his concentration was waning as he read further into Karen Bellamy's file. Vivid but sporadic images from last night's dream kept flashing through his mind, and he found himself clutching at them hopefully, only to watch them recede into spreading blankness, or feel them trickle through his fingers like sand. The sensation was maddening, and at the same time a source of inexplicable, immeasurable comfort. Once or twice, granted the sudden bounty of a vision slightly more concrete, slightly less ephemeral than the rest, he would seize his pen and scribble a few words down in the margins of whichever page he was reading: 'a meadow', he wrote at one point; 'a young girl, laughing; a woman's voice, humming beside me in the long grass; the knowledge that I can fly; cool water'. After recording these scattered impressions, he glanced up to find that Cleo was looking at him and smiling.

While Terry was occupied with the files, Cleo delved into her bag and took out the transcript Lorna had prepared for her: the record of Ruby Sharp's strange nocturnal monologue. She read it through for the fiftieth time, still finding it hard to believe that any of it was true, or that the miracles it promised would ever come to pass, and still baffled by its relationship — prophetic? coincidental? — to Terry's photograph, to that abiding image from her one well-remembered dream. Fumbling for rational explanations, she thought back over Ruby's behaviour: her failure to introduce herself, when they had met on the beach two weeks ago; her unexpected appearance at the clinic yesterday, and even more abrupt departure this morning — for she had slipped away without leaving any kind of message (or payment). Unless the transcript itself were to be regarded as a message, of sorts.

If so, could it be trusted?

Yes. Yes, of course it could. Cleo reached this conclusion just as the train had penetrated London's outer suburbs, and her reasoning was simple enough: for in the midst of all this confusion, all these unsettling convergences between past and present, at least one incontrovertible truth remained.

Nobody told lies in their sleep.

Terry was at a loose end. Half an hour after saying goodbye to Cleo, he could not decide what to do next. He felt restless, unsettled. The thought of returning to his flat depressed him. It was three o'clock in the afternoon, and he could not face the prospect of a whole evening alone, at home, with only his television and video recorder for company.

He bought a copy of *Time Out* and skimmed through the cinema listings, but somehow the titles meant nothing to him, and after a few minutes he tossed it aside, leaving it on a bench outside the station for the next passer-by.

He opened his suitcase and took out the manila envelope which contained his photograph, and the two files which Cleo had copied for him. Then he walked back to the station and deposited his case in the left-luggage office.

He took the tube across London to another mainline station, and from there he caught a connecting train to Denmark Hill.

Terry himself could not have explained this decision. He was merely obeying some instinct — probably formed after watching a good many films on the subject — that this was what journalists (or was it detectives?) did when they were starting to investigate a story. If they wanted to follow a trail, if they wanted to trace somebody's movements, then the first step consisted of empathizing with their quarry, getting inside that person's head. He had never been to Denmark Hill before, and felt obscurely that this put him at some sort of disadvantage in his new task, which was to locate Karen Bellamy and unearth the truth about Dr Dudden's sleep deprivation experiments. He was hoping that to visit the area in which she had grown up, and where she had last been seen, might yield something in the way of clues: a chance encounter with a friend, perhaps, or a conversation with a garrulous neighbour in the local pub.

Terry was forced to admit, after several hours' aimless wandering through the streets, bored loitering in cafés and solitary drinking of numerous pints of beer, that he still had a few things to learn about investigative journalism. He felt no closer to Karen Bellamy than when he had started; and he was also, by now, overwhelmingly tired. He was longing for bed, already, and nothing seemed more attractive at this point than the prospect of an early night — lights out by ten o'clock, say — followed by a solid twelve hours' sleep. Perhaps if he got enough sleep tonight he would be visited by more dreams, and there might be a chance that he would remember them in the morning.

He walked back to Denmark Hill station and ran down to the platform just as a train was pulling away. The disembarking passengers thinned out, plodded up the stairs to the ticket barrier, and left Terry with the platform to himself, apart from a solitary figure walking up and down past the snack machine. Terry had spotted this man before, while he was approaching the station from the road. Idly, he wondered why he hadn't got on to the train along with everyone else. What was he doing here, after all, if not waiting for a train to central London? He decided to walk to the other end of the platform, to give this bulky stranger a wide berth. He did seem to be behaving rather strangely. He was about six feet two inches tall, wearing black jeans and a green combat jacket. He was pacing backwards and forwards along the platform, muttering to himself and occasionally shouting. The blade of his knife glinted in the evening sunlight.

Earlier that afternoon, Lorna had finished her shopping in town, and then, walking back up the hill towards Ashdown, she

saw something most peculiar. Seven cars from the local taxi
service drove past her in the direction of the railway station:
five of them containing patients, it seemed, while the other two
contained members of the cooking and cleaning staff. She
stared after the taxis in bewilderment, and a sudden, nasty premonition visited her: she knew that something wrong, very
wrong was happening at the house. She quickened her pace up
the hill, and by the time she arrived outside the gates of Ashdown she was almost running.

She could tell, as soon as she entered the hallway, that the
house was now completely empty: it had a ghostly, abandoned
air, and the front door had been left to swing open and shut in
the wind. But although empty, it was far from quiet, because
somewhere beneath her — somewhere in the basement —
loud music was playing. Amazingly loud music: for not only
could Lorna hear it, she could even feel it, through her feet. The
whole floor was shaking with the force of this music. Lorna recognized it at once: nobody could have failed to recognize it, it
was one of the most famous arias in the world, sung by one of
the world's most famous tenors. As she dropped her bags of
shopping and stood in the hallway, fearful, undecided, the music came to an end but started again almost immediately. Somebody had loaded it on to a CD player, with the repeat function
engaged.

It took Lorna a few more minutes — during which time the
aria stopped, and started again — to summon the necessary
courage. At last, having looked into Dr Dudden's office, and
looked into the dining-room, and looked into the L-shaped
kitchen, she willed herself to open the door to the basement,
and slowly descended the stairs. Even when she had walked
only as far as the laundry, still ten yards from the half-open
door to the laboratory which she had never before been per-
mitted to enter, the music was quite overwhelming. She put her
fingers in her ears as she crept along the brightly lit corridor;

and then, after steadying herself against the wall, and taking a series of long, deep breaths, she gently pushed the door wide open and stepped inside.

Lorna could not have said how long she stood there, horrified, unable to move, struggling to make sense of the scene before her. Perhaps it was only for a few seconds. The room seemed to contain twelve tables, each supporting a glass tank. Some of the tanks had been upended, one or two had been shattered: four of them contained dead rats, and three contained dead dogs. In addition, there were a number of dogs, rats and rabbits scuttling dazedly about the room, showing every sign of malnutrition, mistreatment and exhaustion. Electric wires were strewn everywhere. Lorna drifted among the animals, regarding them warily, with a mixture of pity and revulsion, occasionally stooping down to take a closer look but unwilling to touch them.

Her priority, in any case, was to locate the source of the music and to turn it off. It appeared to be coming from a room at the far end of the laboratory, and she made her way hastily towards this, knowing that she would not be able to think clearly until silence was established.

The room she soon found herself in was large enough, but it contained no furniture except for one straight-backed, uncomfortable-looking chair, a television and sound system, and a variety of exercise equipment. Guessing herself to be in some sort of sleep deprivation centre, Lorna blocked her ears even more firmly and knelt down by the CD player, trying to see how it could be turned off. As she did so, a chill descended on her, and she froze in the act of reaching for the off button. She was aware, abruptly and very distinctly aware, of a human presence in the doorway behind her, just a few feet away.

She turned, saw Dr Dudden, and screamed at the top of her voice.

It was not the fact that he was almost naked — naked except for a pair of swimming trunks. Nor was it the crazy, hostile gleam in his eye, although that was frightening enough. What most terrified Lorna about Dr Dudden's appearance that afternoon was the condition of his hair. It seemed to have gone berserk, to have acquired a lunatic life of its own. He must have plastered it thickly with glue, for it stood up stiffly, in four or five spiky clumps, and he had stuck about a dozen electrodes at random all around his skull: some of them were wedged into his hair, one was even glued to his ear, and all were connected up to a network of thick, multicoloured wires which dangled along the floor behind him: yards and yards of them, trailing out of sight. He looked like a cross between Medusa and a deranged punk.

'Don't turn that off.' There was an icy control in his voice, even though he was shouting to make himself heard above the thunderous, endlessly repeating aria. 'Whatever you do, don't turn the music off.'

'But it's so loud . . .'

'What are you doing snooping around here, anyway?'

Lorna stood up, but came no closer to Dr Dudden. He was blocking the doorway to the laboratory, her only escape route.

'I wanted to know where the noise was coming from,' she shouted.

'Noise?' echoed Dr Dudden. 'You call this *noise*?'

'Well, it just sounded so different, from — from what you normally listen to . . .'

'What's the matter with you, woman? Are you scared of a bit of passion — a bit of emotion?'

'Dr Dudden . . . are you all right?' she asked now. 'Where is everybody? What's happened to all the patients?'

'Patients! Ha!' He snorted and, much to Lorna's relief, turned his back on her and walked away, the yards of wire slithering behind him. She followed him into the laboratory, straining to hear what he was saying but catching only a few words: 'patients . . . worthless . . . waste . . . cretins . . .' Then, quite without warning, he wheeled around and confronted her face to face. He had seized a loose length of wire from one of the tables, and was now stretching it between his hands, winding it around his fingers, tugging it viciously taut. Lorna took a few steps away, until her back was to the wall.

'Look, doctor . . . don't you think you'd be more comfortable with some — with some clothes on?'

He ignored this suggestion, and hissed: 'Who's Ruby Sharp, then?' The aria faded away, and promptly started again, seeming louder than ever. 'I found an EEG in my office relating to someone called Ruby Sharp. I've never heard of her.'

'She . . . she was a patient,' Lorna said, her eyes not leaving the wire, and his restless hands. 'She came here last night.'

'You admitted a patient, without a referral? Without my permission?'

'She was — Dr Madison seemed to know her. She said that she talked in her sleep.'

'And did she? Did she talk in her sleep?'

'She . . . she talked, yes. I transcribed it this morning. But —'

'But what?'

Lorna hesitated, constrained by her own incomprehension now, as much as by fear. This incident had been worrying her all day: she did not understand the secrets, the private history shared by Ruby and Cleo, who so clearly knew each other from some bygone period in their lives. Nor did she understand what Ruby had been trying to tell her former friend — or former lover, whatever she was — by pouring out the unbroken, incantatory stream of words which had been captured on tape during the early hours of the morning. But she did know one thing: Ruby had not been asleep at the time. Lorna had not mentioned this to Dr Madison, but she was certain of it. The polysomnograph readings had proved it.

'Well — she talked, but she wasn't asleep,' she explained, stammering. 'I think she was faking it, for some reason.'

Dr Dudden looked at her for a moment, then started to laugh. It was a shrill, mirthless laugh, with an audible undertone of mania.

'I see,' he said. 'I see: they've started already, have they? They're already sending their spies down here. Sneaking into the clinic, posing as patients. Snooping around in the middle of the night. Planting cameras and microphones, I wouldn't be surprised. Oh yes, it's started, all right. But they won't smuggle any more people in here — and do you know why? Because from now on, there are going to be no patients at all. From now on, Lorna —' he advanced towards her, raising the wire towards the level of her throat '— it's going to be just you and me.' They stood like that, inches apart, their eyes locked together, until he lowered the wire, took hold of her wrist in a pincer-like grip, and said: 'Come with me.'

He pulled her in the direction of the second door at the back of the laboratory: the door behind which his long trail of wires seemed to disappear. He tugged it open with his free hand, and for the second time Lorna screamed, as soon as she saw the enormous perspex cage, with its giant turntable and its blue pool of water.

'Let go of me!' she shouted. 'Where are you taking me?'

'Pull yourself together, woman, for Christ's sake. You've nothing to be afraid of. You're looking at one of the most remarkable pieces of scientific apparatus ever designed. You should feel privileged.'

'Let *go* of me,' Lorna repeated. 'Let go!'

'I need your help,' said Dr Dudden. 'That's all. I need your help with a little experiment. There must be two of us, Lorna: otherwise there's no point. It takes two to tango. Remember that.'

Lorna glared at him: more angry, now, than afraid. 'I have no intention of *tangoing* with you, doctor. Now or at any other time. Nor do I have any intention of getting into *that* —' she indicated the cage, with a toss of her head '— in the company of someone who is quite clearly mad.'

Dr Dudden winced visibly at this last word, as if at a sharp pinprick. Then, slowly, miraculously, Lorna felt the grip on her wrist begin to relax. The burning fury in his eyes died down, faded, until it was no more than a feeble glow, superseded by something colder and blanker: a hard sheen of disdain, mixed with bitter resignation. He let go of her wrist altogether, and backed away.

'Of course,' he said. 'That was silly of me. Why should you be any different from the rest, after all? Why should you be any more enlightened?'

Standing slightly ajar in the perspex wall was an almost invisible door, through which the wires attached to Dr Dudden's skull had been fed, lying flat across the turntable and leading all the way up to the hole at the top of the wooden partition dividing the cage in two. Now he gathered up the loose wires in his arms, opened the door even further, and stepped on to the turntable itself.

'No, I should have remembered that I'm alone,' he continued, turning to address Lorna. 'Quite alone. Nobody could understand, nobody could even begin to understand. I'm so far ahead . . . It will take you all years, *years* to realize what I was trying to do.' His smile was rueful, ironic. 'Very well, Lorna: you can run along now. I shall be quite all right down here. They'll come and find me in a few days, anyway. They'll be here soon enough.'

'*Who* will be here?' she asked, in a kind of despair. 'What are you talking about?'

He shook his head, and closed the perspex door.

'Dr Dudden —'

But Lorna realized that he could no longer hear her, and she could only watch helplessly as he sat down on the turntable, crossing his legs, folding his arms, as if he were preparing himself for meditation. Then he began to speak, but to himself, not to her. The words were difficult to make out at first. Lorna was already on the point of leaving, of running upstairs to phone for the ambulance service, when she realized what they were.

'None shall sleep,' he was saying. 'None shall sleep': over and over, like a mantra, as the CD continued to play in the next room, at full volume, and Pavarotti's celebrated rendition of 'Nessun Dorma' swelled to yet another deafening climax.

Cleo lay on the bed in her hotel room, listening to the traffic noise from Russell Square, the multilingual babble of voices drifting up through her open window, and thought to herself that, no matter what came of this evening, her life would never be quite the same again. There could be no going back.

Later, as she applied her makeup, changed her skirt, prepared herself for a fortifying drink in the hotel bar, she realized that there was too much fatalism, too much melodrama in that idea. She had managed without Sarah for twelve years now. Just recently, she had been managing rather well. There was no reason why this sudden resurrection of hope should change everything, no reason why she couldn't go back to the clinic tomorrow, no reason why she shouldn't continue to live without Sarah, just as she had resolved to do on that terrible night at Ashdown, the last time she had seen her, the last time she had heard her voice. Since then, Cleo had lived the life of a single woman, and could continue to do so.

If only to prove this very point, she lingered in the bar for more than an hour, drinking two gin and tonics and pointedly ignoring the overtures of the several lone men who attempted to catch her eye. She went on to an Italian restaurant, where she had a small carafe of red wine and an excellent vegetable lasagne, and declined an invitation to join the gentleman sitting at the window table for coffee and liqueurs. After that she began to walk, not in any great haste, towards the tube station, brushing shoulders with the tourists and the young people hurrying past her on their way to a Friday night out in the West End.

For once, on the train, she took no notice of the advertisements, declined to read the back pages of other people's newspapers, and instead looked closely, for the first time, at the faces of her fellow passengers. She saw happy couples, and unhappy couples; couples who had nothing to say to one another, and couples who could not keep their hands to themselves; couples who had just met, and couples who seemed to be on the verge of splitting up. She saw married men on their way home to their wives, and she saw single men on their way home to their videos and their microwave dinners. She saw women on their own, women in pairs, and women in groups, and she thought to herself: Yes, I can take my place with these people. Whatever else has gone wrong, whatever other mistakes I may have made, I know who I am, now. I know who I am, and it suits me.

Darkness was falling as she emerged, twenty minutes later, into the evening air. Cleo had bought an *A – Z* that afternoon, and committed the route to memory; as for the final stretch, Ruby's directions, although minimal, proved perfectly adequate. She left the main road behind, and after walking for perhaps half a mile, found herself turning into what surely had to be the quietest street in the whole of London. There was no music, no party noise, no voices coming from any of the gardens. Not even a television turned up loud. Cleo's footsteps seemed to be making the only sound in the world.

She stopped outside Sarah's house. Although it was still not quite dark, the curtains were fully drawn, with just a chink of light gleaming at the edges. Cleo pushed open the little wrought-iron gate, which squeaked plangently, and walked up to the front door. She paused, smoothed down her skirt, and adjusted her handbag, shifting its weight on her shoulder. Then she lifted the door knocker, and knocked twice.

A light came on in the hallway. Seconds later the door was opened, and there she was: alone, older, looking a little tired, a little sleepy; a little apprehensive, perhaps, to be opening the door to a stranger at this hour. She was wearing jeans and a T-shirt, and her hair was now completely and wonderfully grey, and the moment she saw her, Cleo knew that she had been lying to herself; knew that she could not do without this woman at all. It wasn't possible, and never had been.

'Sarah?'

It was all she could manage to say, at first. Sarah stared back at her, not recognizing, not yet guessing.

'Do I know you?'

'Of course you do,' she said. 'It's me: Robert.'

APPENDIX 1: Poem

Somniloquy

Your gravity, your grace have turned a tide
In me, no lunar power can reverse;
But in your narcoleptic eyes I spied
A sightlessness tonight: or something worse,
A disregard that made me feel unmanned.
Meanwhile, insomniac, I catch my breath
To think I saw my future traced in sand
One afternoon 'as still, as carved, as death',
And pray for an oblivion so deep
It ends in transformation. Only dawn
Can save me, flood this haunted house of sleep
With light, and drown the ghosts that nightly warn:
Another lifetime is the least you'll need, to trace
The guarded secrets of her gravity, her grace.

APPENDIX 2: Letter

FROM: Pamela Worth
TO: Professor Marcus Cole, FRC Psych.

Dear Professor Cole,

Just a short letter, I'm afraid, to thank you for taking the trouble to write to us last week.

Your kind words were very much appreciated. In a situation like this, the sympathy of friends and well-wishers starts to mean everything. It's all that we have, in a way. And you can rest assured that, as far as we're concerned, no blame attaches to you in this matter. Over the last few weeks we have often found ourselves looking for people to blame — individuals, the government, the 'system', whatever — but really there is no one. That's what's so unbearable about it.

We visit Terry every day. There is, as you say, no improvement, and no real prospect of improvement, it seems. But we shall be patient. He looks very peaceful, and rested. You probably don't know this (why should you?), but my son has had a lot of trouble sleeping over the last few years. Of course I never said anything to him about it, but it did worry me, and when I see him now, I sometimes try to tell myself that he is just catching up on his sleep. The doctors tell me I'm imagining it, but once or twice I've thought that I can see a tiny smile on his face, and then I wonder if perhaps he is having pleasant dreams.

You will probably think that these are just silly fantasies: but we all have to find our way of coping, somehow, and I am doing my best.

Yours very sincerely,
Pamela Worth

APPENDIX 3: Transcript

PATIENT: Ruby Sharp
DATE: 28.6.96
TIME: 02.36–02.40
TECHNICIAN: Lorna

never quiet   never quiet this house   I remember that   years ago   always the waves   never quiet   sitting upstairs   with her   sitting with you   I remember   I was listening   remember it all the beach   the day at the beach   the things you said   no limits you said no limits   do anything   anything to earn her   and the scars   I remember the scars   on your legs   two scars like like French quotation marks   then I saw   last week I saw   on the beach   another beach   another beach the same person   another person the same body   on your ankles   the two scars I know you   who you are   but listen   listen   know her too London now   where she lives   what she does   alone all alone   you must go   must find her   I know   have known always   since the beach   together be together   I felt it happy so happy that day   remember it all   never so happy always wanted   always somehow   repay you both   sandman what I called you   sandman you made   castle   beautiful castle   away   swept away   not lost   not lost yet nothing lost yet   not if you find her   go now she is waiting   London easy to find   empty house   cold house   she lives alone North London   quiet streets   you turn in   turn in from station   first house   first you see   don't wait   hurry go now find the road   remember   remember the name   Fermer Road Fermer   she does want you   find her please go to her now